FEAR NO EVIL

FICTION

By
Q

Chitlin' Circuit Media
USA
ccmedia.pub

Q

Chitlin' Circuit Media
ccmedia.pub
USA

Publisher's Note: This is a work of fiction and product of the author's imagination. Locales and public names are sometimes used for atmospheric purposes. Any resemblance to actual people, living or dead, or to businesses, companies, events, institutions, or locales is completely coincidental.

FEAR NO EVIL
Fiction by Q. – 2nd ed.
ISBN 978-0-692-51981-3

FOREWORD

FEAR NO EVIL is influenced by music, as is my life; it's in my blood. Throughout, the text references music, primarily jazz, and rhythm and blues music. In particular, *This Is My Beloved,* lyrics and music, by Arthur Prysock, Mort Garson, Walter Benton.

The Night We Called It a Day, music by Matt Dennis, lyrics by Tom Adair.

Axis, Bold As Love, music and lyrics by Jimi Hendrix.

O Amor Em Paz, music and lyrics by Antonio Carlos Jobim.

Props to rabble-rousing writer Ishmael Reed for the phrase, 'writing's fighting.'

Hopefully *FEAR NO EVIL* possesses a musicality, with a mood and movement, tonality and tempo of its own. Fiction that packs a punch, touches the reader, and lingers. I'd probably have become be a musician, like my father, had I not become a writer; it's in my blood.

I use a pen name to preserve my anonymity, and in order to continue observing unnoticed life unfolding. Observing others talk and hurt, laugh and love, and freely intuiting the world around me. It's the only way I know how to live and write, and I wish to continue doing so as freely as ever. My identity is irrelevant. Writing isn't performance art. Nothing is more solitary. I'm a writer; that's it. 'The story's the star.'

FEAR NO EVIL is a work of fiction based in part on real events and actual persons, and otherwise completely inspired by the madness around and within us.

Ay!

Q

Q

DEDICATION

FEAR NO EVIL is a love story telling many love stories. Love of family, and love of friends. Love of country, and love of craft. The magic of romantic love, and tantric spell of erotic love. The redemption of love, and love of life itself.

FEAR NO EVIL is dedicated to my first love, Ada.

For your gifts of life and love.

Your loving son,
    'Dal Fa'

MENU

Q

Q

CHAPTER ONE

MISTERIOSO

*"A wise parson once said,
That where mystery begins,
Religion ends.
Cannot I say, as truly at least
Of human laws, that where
Mystery begins, justice ends?"*
Edmund Burke

Here on Death Row is constant gloam. Dim and dank, bone cold radiates from the cobblestone floor and walls, worsening the fear and chilling feel of death. The only source of light and ventilation is a hole in the cell's ceiling, more like a cave located somewhere in the bowels of this Caribbean prison.

Quarters are close and bare except for, off in a dark corner, a flea-ridden, malodorous, burlap blanket atop a roach-infested cot, useless items against those scattering rats and roaches. My furniture, a toxic cot and one diseased rag of a blanket. My pets, those rats, the roaches and vermin. My window to the world, a hole in the ceiling. The playlist of my life, the sound of constant running water coming from that filthy commode, situated in the middle of the cell. That's the sum of it. My life has been reduced to this.

What's happening outside is the reason why. Even in this distant, dingy dungeon, the sounds of artillery fire and pungent smell of munitions seeping from the ceiling's aperture. The buzzing sounds of low flying aircrafts, strafing fire at nearby targets. These sounds of fury, the smell and more. They're unmistakable signs of full-scale war.

Off in a dark corner, curled in a fetal position trembling with fear and cold, in shock I lay. How long have I been on Death Row? I don't know. I've lost all sense of time. My best guess? Based on my beard growth, a week; maybe? A week of those goon guards beating me without rhyme or reason. With such abandon, I can't take anymore. I've been passing blood lately. I'm going down slow. It's just a matter of time. Death is but days away.

Broken body and spirit, I'm long ready to roll over, flip. Snitch, rat, dime; whatever. Just tell me what to say and where to sign. But no matter how many times I tell them, they won't believe me. They don't want to believe me. They don't just want to beat and break me. No, they want to kill me. And at the rate they're going they're almost there. I'm a dead man walking – barely - at that. I might as well kill myself.

I've been thinking a lot about suicide lately; a whole lot. I even have a plan. Tonight, I'm going to wait up for them and once I hear the goons coming into my cell, I'm going to start banging my head against the wall or floor and keep on banging it until I crack my skull and kill myself. That's how desperate I am. I really want to die. I'm not going to let them drag this out. No way. Any quick death is better than what I'm being put through. Kicked, beaten, broken on Death Row in some banana republic. I sure ain't going out like this. I'll kill myself first. Damn right, suicide. *Felo-de-se*. Tonight!

Depression and despair long ago set in, got the better and eventually defeat me. I feel anxious, paranoid, fear, helplessness and hopelessness. I know I'm dying. At times overcome by a sense of lightness of being, my mind and soul seem transported elsewhere, as if out of body experiences. Scenes of my life from childhood on flash across my mind's eye. Here in the gloam I'm haunted by visions and conversations with my parents and brother. At wits' end, depressed to the point of suicide, I haven't just lost my will to live. I'm non-stop, free form psychosis hallucinating and going crazier by the hour.

So, what happened? W*hy* am I on Death Row in the middle of some Caribbean *coup d'état*? I don't know; I'm in shock. My memory's fragmented, I only have bit recall. That's it. All I remember is words, like 'capital crimes.' 'Crimes against the State.' 'Espionage.' 'Possession of classified State secrets.' 'Enemy of the State?' 'Death penalty crimes' in a part of the world where being an American doesn't help. Where justice isn't for all, and the pursuit of the truth considered empty talk and waste of time.

Tomorrow I'm to be dragged in front of a 'tribunal.' Some tricky-quickie military kangaroo court with a foregone sentence. Sentenced in absentia. Sentenced, not in the absence of my person, but in the absence of justice. Convicted and sentenced to speedy execution. In testate and stripped of all identity, my anonymous and unconsecrated corpse then dumped in the shark infested Styx beneath the

Room of Doom. Between my ill health and dire straits, death's near and clear.

'Espionage?' 'Enemy of the State?' 'Possession of classified State secrets?' 'Treason?' 'Capital Crimes?' That's somebody's bad idea of a joke. I don't have that kind of nerve. I mean, come on. Nothing's that important to me. Me, a spy? That doesn't make sense. Why me?

I'm being 'profiled.' That's why. And what is my 'profile?' Am I a political prisoner? No way, I hate politics. A prisoner of conscience, like King or the Mahatma? Not me. Whatever I am; I sure ain't no saint.

What I really am is a victim and prisoner of circumstance. I keep telling them that I was in the wrong place at the wrong time with the wrong people. That this is a mistake. A big misunderstanding. A coincidence. An accident. An anomaly. Some random variable. A cosmic event, or act of nature that can't be explained; like an eclipse or Pi.

I've become a 'person of interest' due to 'circumstantial evidence,' very incriminating 'circumstantial evidence,' and no longer presumed innocent. My crime? In the eyes of the authorities, I'm 'guilty of association.' I know 'certain people.' These 'certain people,' the Mentis family; particularly my friendship with Ayrton. That's why I'm being 'profiled.' That's why I'm a 'person of interest' and 'guilty of association.' That's why.

But in this hell hole, they don't care about justice, King or Gandhi, random variables or anomalies, eclipses or Pi, and they sure enough don't believe me.

The *truth?* Long story short, I'm a high school teacher, English and physical education, Harlem City. At least I was. Until recently, that is. Presently I'm on 'assignment,' invited by a former classmate to work on a 'project' in his country.

"*Oh, Amada! Amada mia!* Guiding star to all!' Those are the words of our national anthem. *Amada mia!* Crown jewel of the Caribbean. Q, I'm telling you. The women. The food. The music. Q. I promise. You'll love it. Amada! You'll not want to leave. You'll see. *Por mi, por favor?* I'm a proud man, Q. Don't make me beg too long or too loud." Ayrton said.

Amada was everything promised and then some, with skies and sea almost identical shades of aquamarine. No surprise there, his word was and always has been good. After all, we're longtime friends. By the same token, Ayrton also trusts me. No matter how long we haven't seen each other, we know we can always depend on one another. So much so, our families became good friends; including his sister, Didi.

Although my memory is fuzzy, I recall her screaming my name, fear echoing in her voice, the terror on her face, the morning we were arrested and forcibly separated. I'd promised Ayrton I'd look after her, and now I'm feeling worse about what's happened to her than about what is happening to me. If only by half, at least I'm still alive. But what about Didi? What about Ayri? He must be worried crazy about what's happened to us. That is, if they're still alive.

Everything. It's so out of the blue. All of us, Ayrton, his family, and I, arrested and charged with 'treason and espionage.' Declared 'enemies of the State' and charged with 'capital crimes against the nation's sovereignty.' This, within weeks after my arrival. None of this makes any sense. Especially since Ayrton and his father are part of the Amadan government... or used to be?

True, Ayri is my friend and I've always trusted him. But now, here on Death Row, with my mind playing these kinds of tricks on me, I'm not so sure anymore. Maybe Ayri values our friendship differently? Too late, I'm beginning to realize that Ayrton has been less than truthful with me, on occasions misrepresenting the truth, even lying to me by concealing critical information and minimizing my concerns. Did he, knowingly or unwittingly, maybe betray me? If so, why? Or am I hallucinating again? None of it, nothing makes any sense anymore.

This much, though, I do know: Amadan citizens charged with treason are even worse off, with the Mentis family in more trouble than I am. Making matters worse, though, is the not knowing. Worrying and wondering about what has happened to them.

What'll I do? I can't just suddenly tell them the whole truth now. That I'm not just a schoolteacher. You see, the thing is... okay, it's like this: I'm really a journalist on assignment working for Ayrton. But they've confiscated my laptops and belongings, so they probably know all that by now. Still, confessing will only make bad matters worse with, given my poor health, deadly consequences. Best if I just keep shutting up and try buying myself a little more time. That, and continue praying for a miracle.

With this bleak-to-grim prognosis, and little more than half of a half-life left, suddenly the goon squad bum-rush me screaming, hollering, "What are you doing? Stop! Stop banging your head!"

They restrain me from killing myself and bandage my bleeding skull. Next, they handcuff and shackle me, then pushing and jabbing me with their rifle butts and nightsticks in the kidneys and stomach, they drag me out of solitary confinement and into the prison corridor.

Here a stench, much like the hot breath of death, abides. Rodents scatter in the filth under foot. In the corridors, military personnel in hushed conversations with other uniformed and plain clothed officials are indifferent to the moans of suffering from the battered and bandaged, the injured and dying prisoners propped against the hall walls. Many of the prisoners, me included, are in shock. From here, Hell's foyer, cries grow ever louder as we approach my destination, the Room of Doom. The interrogation unit located behind the *Door of No Return*. Once there, my voice will be added to that captive choir of the condemned reverberating all around.

Until now, I always considered Ayrton my friend. But now? I'm no longer sure he didn't set me up. At the same time, he's also my last and only remaining hope. The very person directly responsible for my being here is also the only one able to save me. Or soon I'll be rendered a ghost in the army of the dead.

The *Door of No Return* is bolted shut. Darkness descends upon the Room of Doom. Someone removes my shirt. I'm blindfolded and strapped to a chair. I cry out but someone's hand smothers my mouth. Panicked, my mind kick-starts into overdrive. Blinded and suffocating, I start hyperventilating. Unable to breathe, in violent vain I struggle for air and trying to free myself. Gravely ill, suicidal and losing my mind, my sensorium starts fluctuating. I'm having chest pain. My duress so severe I think I'm having a heart attack. The room starts spinning. I feel my body and spirit splitting... twinning, separating... slowly drifting, fading away. I'm goin' down fast.

Then someone enters, and the dark falls quiet. A presence, an immediacy suddenly fills the room. Is this - say nay – the Reaper? Have mercy. Thanatos done come for me.

Then he says, "Tilt... A little more. Tilt. Back. Right...there!" The chair leans back. I feel the pressure easing off my face somewhat and I can breathe again. But not long. Suddenly the chair flips backward, my feet now above my head. Someone grabs hold of my chin, pours water in my nose and mouth and keeps saying: "Where is it? Where is it?"

Choking, gagging, my eyes bulge. I hold my breath and seize. Someone pinches my nose and forces my mouth open, my throat, my nose overflowing. I can't breathe. I'm drowning Stop! Help! Then they yank me upright, repeating, "Where is it?" But before I can answer, they tilt me backward again and continue waterboarding me until I pass out; or am I dead?

CHAPTER TWO

MAIDEN VOYAGE

"See the sky - let's explore
Its blue! Tide is high - time
For your debut. Like a ship,
You must leave the bay.
On this trip...the time has
Come to take the dare.
Maiden voyage - first affair."
Maiden Voyage
Music: Herbie Hancock
Lyrics: Jon Lucien

Ayrton, Didi, and I attended university together and fast became good friends. He was an MBA student, Didi an anthropology undergraduate student; I studied journalism and creative writing. After graduation, though, except for sporadic contact and news from classmates and acquaintances, eventually we lost touch.

Born into a distinguished Caribbean family, Ayrton was destined for achievement. An economist by training, he was well-traveled with far-flung tastes and interests, and whose politics were pragmatic and progressive. Someone who believed foremost in consensus and in the greater common good. No surprise, following graduation Ayrton returned home and began working for the Amadan government.

Smart as a whip and ambitious to a fault, despite his background, it never went to his head. Humble, self-effacing, at times even somewhat embarrassed by his privilege, he was good sport and plain easy going, fun company and good people. Someone who fit comfortably in any setting, and chose his friends based on his sense of *simpatico*.

Every bit a ladies' man and all-around gadabout with an ever-ready killer smile and winning ways, the consensus, unanimous. 'Ayrton? Ayri's best-ever,' women gushed. Men called him '*Mr. Lucky*.' Ayri had it all.

So imagine my surprise when, some five years later, there was a knock on my classroom door. Quietly as not to interrupt motioning silence to the class, out of the blue Ayrton entered my *Harlem High School* class room.

"*Ay, chihuahua! Q! Mi hermano! Harlem High,* if you only knew. Your teacher? Best teacher you'll ever have. The man's a genius. He understands. It's all one love. Oh, pearls before swine. Author! Author! Give me a hug, *Q!*" He said, flashing that signature smile.

"Look out, Harlem! Ayri's back in town! If it ain't *Mr. Lucky* himself. What are you doing here? I'll be good and..." So surprised to see him, I almost cursed in front of my students before calling the class to order.

"Attention, class. Wake up, potato heads! We have an important visitor from the world of politrix; I mean politics. It's with pride and pleasure that I introduce to you my good, old friend... I'm sorry, Ayri. What's your current position?"

"Under-Secretary of Economics and Foreign Affairs of Amada." Ayri said.

"That sounds mighty VIP to me. So, pray-tell, how do we little people properly address the Secretary of Economics and Foreign Affairs?" I said.

"Not Secretary; not yet. Just Under-Secretary; for the time being. And normally the correct diplomatic protocol and appellation is Your Excellency." He said.

I laughed. "Say what? '*Your Excellency?*' 'Protocol?' 'Appellation?' Is that what you just said to me? Is that what other people really call you; '*Your Excellency?*' And you expect me to call you '*Your Excellency?*' Stop playing, Ayri. There're countless two-word combinations I can think of calling you; although not in front of my class. But those two words, '*Your Excellency,*' directed to you, will never cross my lips. I think I'll just stick with *Mr. Lucky.*"

"Never need for protocol or appellation with you, Q. Especially in front of your class. *Porque por ti, yo soy siempre tu amigo. Tu Ayri.* After all, we're family. *Mi hermano, Q. Ay!*" He said, then we embraced.

"*Harlem High.* Listen up! Stop texting and act like you know. Class, please give our distinguished guest, *His Excellency*, the Honorable *Don* Ayrton Villareal Mentis of Amada, a loud and proud *Harlem High* welcome!" I said. No surprise, *Harlem High* responded with chorus of loud and proud boos and hisses.

"And by the way, *Harlem High*, I'm not a politician. I'm really a diplomat. There's a big difference. But that's your lesson for another day from... good Professor Q here." Ayri said, no sooner than *Harlem High* booed even louder and longer.

Surprised by his sudden appearance, I made hasty arrangements for another teacher to cover my classroom. To a cascade of classroom booing, Ayri and I then headed to the staff lounge.

"My man! *Mr. Lucky*. I can't believe my eyes. What a surprise. Welcome back. Good seeing you, Ayri." I said.

"You too, Q. Is every day like this at *Harlem High*? The kids? It's like in the movies." He says.

"Every hour, all day long. Tomorrow's leaders." I said.

"The future's bleak." Ayri said.

So, you're a diplomat now?", I said.

"That's right." Ayri said.

"The problem is I know you too well. You'd never win a general election because you'd only get the women's vote for being *suave* and *debonair*. That means you had to get yourself appointed to high office. In my book that makes you the ultimate politician." I said.

"Everyone's a skeptic, none worse than writers. And, speaking of *your* book. Congratulations! In fact, I remember when you first got the idea. At the bookstore, I was boasting to the sales clerk how we were students together. My compliments. So, tell me; what are you doing still teaching? Why aren't you writing full time?" Ayri said.

"Weak sales. And if they don't pick up like soon, it'll be remaindered. Off the shelves and forever out of print, as if I never wrote it. And since I no longer own the copyright, I might as well not have. Medical bennies, pension, 401-K. IRA, IRS. Your normal, working-class anxiety blues. Things you don't know anything about. That's why I still teach. Unlike you, I wasn't born with a silver spoon lodged in my jaw. Look at you. A power worshiper playing with your country's tax money. Woe unto Amada! So, Ayri, I'm curious. Do you have diplomatic immunity? Safe conduct and all that? You know what I mean? One of those 'get-out-of-jail-free-cards?' How's that work? Have you ever had to use it? What's that like?" I said.

"Look what I have! Please, do me the honor." Ayri said and, in a flattering gesture that caught me off guard, he produced a copy of my novel and requested my autograph. As I pondered over the inscription, Ayrton said, "This. This is what you really should be doing."

"What? Signing books? Yeah, right. From your lips to God's ears. I wish." I said.

"You know what I mean, Q. I mean writing. Fighting. That's what you really should be doing, writing full time, not 'suffer the children unto me.' You're much too talented for this." Ayri said.

"Don't blaspheme, Ayri, terrible things could happen. Besides, talent has nothing to do with getting published, marketing and distribution. And, I'll have you know, teaching is an honorable, a noble profession. It beats being a politician." I said.

"I'm not blaspheming and I'm not superstitious either. You know I'm right. You, it's you who blasphemes by wasting your talent and time. Always remember, and never forget. He who looks back with regret dies of remorse. Look, all I'm saying is, do what you love and love what you do." Ayri said.

"'Always remember...?' 'He who looks back...?' 'Do what you love...?' 'Make it do what it do...?' You just said that too; didn't you? 'Make it do what it do?' That's good stuff. Did you just make that up? I never knew you had those kinds of literary riffs in you. Not bad. Sounds like the writer in you is screaming to get out. You know, I might what to use one of those sayings one day. Are they copyrighted? I mean, I don't want to use them and then you turn around and sue me for plagiarism. I'm not too sure about that 'make it do what it do,' though. I think I've heard that one before." I said.

"Make fun all you want. But in your heart, you know I'm right. Given the choice, you'd rather be writing than teaching. Doing what you love to do rather than doing what you need to. That's all I'm saying." Ayri said.

"Man of principal, at least you're consistent and practice what you preach, I give you that. A player at heart who's a politician in life. And nowadays, politics, with politicians selling access, pretty much resembles prostitution. A marriage of multiple conveniences. Thanks for buying my book, though. Don't worry. I said nice things about you in the inscription." I said, returning his autographed book. "So, to what do I owe the honor? What brings you back to Harlem City?"

"How soon can you arrange a sabbatical? An extended vacation?" Ayri said.

"What are you talking about?" I said.

"I knew you were the right person once I started reading *Homeboy*. I knew it right away." Said Ayrton.

"What do you mean? 'The right person' for what?" I said.

"I'm making you a serious offer. An important writing assignment. Interested?" Ayri said.

"That depends on what kind of writing. Where's the hook, Ayri? There's got to be a hook. I mean, with all due respect, you're a politician. So, there's got to be a *quid pro quo* hidden in there somewhere. So, what's the real? What are you cooking, Ayri?" I said.

"Please, *Q*. I keep telling you; I'm a diplomat. There's a big difference." Ayri said.

"What? You want me to write some high-falutin speech? Some political propaganda. Is that it? You know how much I despise politrix; I mean politics. 'The art of tricking people.' Or, knowing you, you probably want me to ghost write some porn. Am I right?" I said.

"How about a biography?" Ayri said.

"What? A porn biography? You're nasty. Call it, *I, Booty Man* by *Mr. Lucky?* That about sums you up. You know, you've got a lotta nerve showing up after all these years wanting me to write your Rudy Ray Moore, *Dolomite,* I, *Booty Man,* urban lit, porn bio. Hell no. I'm not committing career suicide. Not me. Kid's a serious journalist and novelist. Straight up. Me no write no urban lit porn. I really should be offended. There's just no shame anywhere in your game. Besides, you're too young for a biography." I said.

"Not my biography, *studpido! Papi!* We want you to write *Papi's* memoirs!" Ayri said.

Considering his background, I was stunned, humbled even by the offer. At present, his father was Foreign Minister of Amada.

"How is your dad and the rest of the family?" I said.

"Oh, *Papi's* doing great. Still strong like bull. Everyone else is fine too. Thank you very much. They all send their love. *Papi* just thinks it's time. He just wants to tell his story while he's still able to. That's all." Ayri said.

"Thanks, Ayri. I'm flattered. I really am. But your father is an accomplished man. I'm sure he could write his autobiography better than I could do justice to his life's story. Or what about you? I mean, the way that you steady riff bromides like, 'Always remember...' 'He who looks back...' 'Do what you love...' 'Make it do what it do.' Free flow riffin' like that? You don't need me. You could just as easily write your dad's biography. I'm sure there are a lot of good Amadan writers who know more about your country and Amada's history. So, with all due respect; why me?" I said.

"Because you're a real writer, *Q*; not some boring professor. You have style, a distinct voice. Plus, you have a clear advantage and insight into what you're writing about. You already know us. Besides in terms of background, you and me, we're a lot alike. We really are. Go ahead. Laugh and roll your eyes all you want." Ayri said.

Q

"Yep, *Mr. Lucky*. That's me. Let's see? I'm rich, handsome. I'm a player at heart who's a politician in real life. I'm regularly featured as one of the '*Most Eligible Bachelors*.' 'The people's economist.' Nativist art collector. Every woman's dream, and every man's envy. So heavy the burden of expectations, having to live up to being *Mr. Lucky*. Heavier yet, being *Mr. Lucky* and *Your Excellency* at the same time. And a more apt name, besides *Your Excellency*, there'll never be than *Mr. Lucky*. If only people knew how difficult it is, being *Mr. Lucky*." I said.

"Come on, *Q*. You're perfect for this assignment. You know my family, you're practically part of our tribe. Plus, your background, you lived abroad, you speak different languages. You've got that cultural, social filter. You know how to make things clear. You talk to the reader. You're a natural, born writer, *Q*." Ayri said leafing through my novel.

"I mean, take *Homeboy's* opening scene, the eulogy. What kind of a writer – other than a genius – begins a novel with a eulogy? It gives you goose bumps. No lie. I swear." Ayri stopped in mid-sentence, still leafing through the book.

"I know what! How about a *Reading by the Author?* This paragraph, where from the pulpit the preacher denounces the deceased as scoundrel, and the parents as 'unfit to raise a pet or a plant let alone a child.' Please, please read it. Besides, I couldn't read it with a straight face." Ayri said, handing me his copy of my novel.

"With all due respect, *your not so Excellency*. I'd rather go back upstairs and keep suffering *Harlem High* unto me than read to *Mr. Lucky*, of all people." I said, shoving aside the recently inscribed book, opened to that passage.

"I mean, come on! Opening scenes don't get any better than that. You nailed it. That's just great stuff. The whole book. You got a style, a voice. You know how to tell a story. You're very good. You really are." Ayri said.

"That's very flattering. Really. Thank you very much." I said.

"Oh, don't be so modest. We want you. You're a perfect fit for the assignment! At any rate, once it came out in Spanish and Portuguese - it's called *Jibaro* - and *Papi* read it, he agreed right away." Ayri said.

"Your dad read my book?" I said.

"Sure. The whole family read it. We remember you fondly. We watched you on *Oprah's Book Club*. Didi went berserk. We all agree. You're perfect for this assignment. You can't say no." Ayrton said.

Then he began outlining a startling proposal. Unfettered archival access, as well as to Dr. Mentis and family. Six months of initial research and interviewing followed by another contractual six months' term of writing and editing. Twelve months, one full year, in Amada.

"'*Oh Amada! Amada mia!* Guiding star to all!' Those are the words of our national anthem. Crown jewel of the Caribbean. The women. The food. The music. Come on, *Q*! The two of us, working together again. Like back in the day, when we did that seminar, 'Press and Politics,' when they first called us 'the journalist and the politician.' We killed it. Remember? That was our dress rehearsal. You'll love it. You'll see. Amada! You'll not want to leave. I'm a proud man, *Q*. Don't make me beg too long or too loud." Ayrton said.

But I was skeptical for any number of reasons. "Well, that was then; this is now. You're crazy if you really expect me to just up and leave on a whim for a year. Just 'cause Ayri's back in town again? I don't think so. I'll tell you what: how about next time email, text, Zoom or Skype a brother first; why don't you? Come on, man. Think about it. It would take me months to wrap up things here. Besides, I write fiction and journalism. I don't know anything about biography writing. Seriously, let's just start out by email. I can send email drafts. Tempting as it is, I just can't up and quit my job for a year. How am I supposed to pick up the pieces after the assignment?" I said.

"What pieces? By then you'll be a rock star writer." Ayri said.

"Think of me as a jazz writer instead. The song, the story is the star." I said.

Ayri's deal was sweet. Double my current teacher's salary, plus full expenses. A car and travel allowance of two round-trip air tickets back to the United States for personal and family time. Also, if all went well there was the possibility of a documentary project sometime down the line. Plus, the project was bonded, insured. No matter what happened - I would be paid. Guaranteed money.

Critical acclaim notwithstanding, considering *Homeboy's* likely remaindering, this assignment was a once-in-a-lifetime opportunity - never mind its tropical paradise location - just too good to be true to even think about refusing. Truth told, I'd been wanting out of loud and proud *Harlem High* for a long time. So much so, between Ayri's persuasiveness and my personal circumstances I probably gave in too hastily.

We simply shook hands in agreement. No contract needed. After all, we were '*hermanos*'; brothers.

"Now, about your accommodations. Of course, while in Amada you will be our guest at one of our government's seaside villa. And understand: you are on the family's payroll. The family is renting the villa. You will have a jeep and moped at your disposal. A secretary and housekeeper. And, if you wish, I will personally arrange for you a hostess for the duration of your stay in Amada." Ayri said.

"'A hostess?'" I said.

"Why yes, a hostess. You Americans, you call them 'interns.' For those occasions when you need entertainment and companionship. You know. A hostess, for stress." Ayri said.

"'An entertainment and companionship hostess;' for 'stress?' What? More 'hoe,' less 'stress?' Sounds like an escort service to me." I said.

"Oh, stop pretending you're shocked. You know what I mean. It's a discreet practice. A professional courtesy for officials engaged in lengthy overseas assignments. I mean, how else is a man supposed to think? But don't worry. I can take care of that; for you. You can trust my taste in women. Think about it. Or, of course, you can always bring someone with you. You think about it." He said.

"You really are running an escort service down there; aren't you? What? Women just volunteer to 'intern' their time and hospitalities in order to hostess?? I'll tell you what you can do for me, *Mr. Lucky*. How about Didi for hostess? Huh? Make *that* hostess theme happen; why don't you? You know; for me." I said.

"You think you're funny? Hear me clear, Q. I know you have a thing for Didi. You always did. Everyone knows; Didi too. And Re-Re is only twenty-one years old? Think about it, so much as even think about it, and trust me, I'll know if you think about it; and I'll put you in traction. My saintly sisters - both of them are off limits to you and everyone else. No one is good enough for them. Understand, Egghead?" Ayri said.

"Yeah, I get it, alright. You're the one who doesn't. I mean, you've got this primitive, Latin *machismo* thing about women who aren't related to you. To you, women are prey. 'Volunteer hostesses' for occasions of 'stress,' 'entertainment' and 'companionship.' Except for your sisters. Then you become a normal, decent human being. If you ever have daughters - that you know about - you'd better hope they don't meet someone like you." I said.

"I'm already married. I don't have time for another family. Amada is my bride. She's selfish. She won't share me with anyone else. *'Oh, Amada! Amada mia!* Guiding star to all!' My one and only! My true love!" Ayri said.

"Yeah, right. I've heard something like that my whole life. One of my Dad's favorite expressions is, 'Music is my mistress.' My Mom's response is, 'Heaven help her.' To paraphrase my mother, 'Heaven help Amada!'" I said.

"Heaven help us all. All we can do is our best, each in our own way, to make sure the music never stops. Without a song? Without a dream? Without love? Life's just a pale creation, an imitation. So, you see, in different ways we're both right. How often do I have to keep telling you? The two of us, we're alike. That's why, Heaven help us all, *Q.* Heaven help us all." Ayri said, with what would be deadly prescience. Instead, heaven would keep us waiting, indeed hanging on for dear life; and barely at that.

"Now, how soon can you leave?" Ayri said.

After school, we discussed details and then some. Over dinner at *Red Rooster,* and during drinks catching jazz sets at *Minton's.* Well into the night and until early next morning. No doubt, this was a serious offer and a viable project.

With the benefit of Death Row hindsight, it now seems that Ayrton had played me. Appealing to my conceit as a writer by asking for an autographed copy of my book and praising my work. By invoking our friendship and recounting his family's fondness of me. In doing so, Ayri had seduced me against my better judgment and basically bribed me into accepting this assignment.

Actually, he bought me the same way lobbyists buy politicians, willing to sell their influence and be manipulated. He was always good at that. After all, he was a politician, and a very skilled one. So, I should have known better; and I did. I knew Ayri was a politician, but I still trusted *mi hermano.* Instead, like some quick trick, I sold myself.

But there were other reasons why I agreed. There was something different, something new about Ayrton. Always charismatic, there was a depth and maturity about him. Focused and persuasive, Ayri was in his prime and at the top of his game. An impressive person, his presentation conveyed conviction and passion, an appetite for life and belief in his cause and himself with such enthusiasm hard to resist; or at least for me. Plus, I desperately wanted out, not just of *Harlem High* but teaching. So, for reasons more than one, I agreed.

What I didn't know at the time though was that, for whatever reasons, Ayrton did not fully inform me about the gravity of the political realities on the ground in Amada. Or maybe he didn't even know the extent and scope of the situation. Either way, neither one of us, nor anyone else for that matter, could ever have anticipated the dizzying, out-of-control, spiral descent into experiential madness just beyond the horizon's bend.

One month later, I departed Harlem City for port Amada. *En route,* I began ruminating. Was I really a skilled enough writer; or in over my head? I knew little next to nothing about biography writing. What if I became ill? What if there was an accident? What if I had a family emergency while I was abroad? In the end, though, the project was bonded. I had two round-trip tickets. On this maiden voyage, more a headlong rush into perils unbeknownst, during the eight hours' flight these and other second thoughts remained nagging concerns. I kept wondering; what could possibly go wrong? The answer, in a word, was e-v-e-r-y-t-h-i-n-g.

To my surprise, upon arriving a chauffeur carrying a sign bearing my name greeted me at the airport and drove us some twenty miles to Ayrton's office at the Palace of Government in Salamar, Amada's capital.

Ayrton had blocked out time that morning and much of the afternoon and, promising an extended island tour later, within minutes we were on our way to the island's eastern shore and arrived at a picturesque villa. Typical of Ayri's forethought were a jeep, a moped and a bicycle. What he called 'perks.' And there was more, in addition to a spacious, three bedrooms, two bathrooms, satellite-ready beachfront villa. For, carrying my wishes too far, no sooner was I greeted by Clotilde.

"Sorry. No themes, no interns, no *motif* hostess available. And you'd better not mention my sister again either. But I think I found your theme. I told you; you can trust my taste. I know you. Cougar Man, you prefer mature, experienced women. Trust me, *Q.* Clotilde's your kind of woman, settled, serious. You two are soulmates destined to be together." Ayri said introducing me to a toothless, old woman.

"She's the family's nanny. She raised me and my sisters. I trust her with my life and my family's lives. So can you, *mi hermano.* You'll see. Now, shake off the road dust. Unpack, settle in. You and Clotilde, relax. Get to know each other. Then, this evening you will be my family's honored dinner guest. In the meantime, you two have fun. Take a shower.

"Maybe a massage afterwards? You know, bond and mate. *Ay!*" Ayrton said the whole time laughing while helping me with my luggage as we entered the premises, his laughter later trailing him on his back to work.

His laughter still echoed later that evening when he, along with his parents and his two sisters, Diandre, and Deidre, warmly welcomed me at the Foreign Minister's official residence. The dining room, its table and extensive buffets appointed with the finest china, cutlery and crystal, foods and beverages, was resplendent, the atmosphere expansive and well-crackling with conversation, and the only unacceptable opinion was not having had one at all. Presiding over it all was their *paterfamilias*. Dr. Rodrigo Mentis, truly His Excellency.

What was to have been an initial working dinner discussing the biography assignment instead turned out to have been an elegant dinner party, with no mention of the project. A privileged opportunity to observe and appreciate this truly remarkable clan with its tradition of public service, the shaping influences of Ayrton's life.

Each sibling was skilled and accomplished with high standards and expectations for themselves and each other, at once competitive with while also supporting, complimenting and challenging each other's ideas. There was Deidre, Re-Re, the youngest. Twenty-one years old, she was fascinated by popular American culture and with dreams of moving to L.A. and becoming an actress or singer, although her family had something else in mind for her future.

"I keep telling you; jumping up and down babbling non-sense. Glorifying negative appearances and perpetuating dangerous perceptions, that isn't talent. Rap and hip-hop isn't art. Whatever happened to music, *Q*? You're a writer, explain *that*." Ayri continued.

"Want to express yourself? Become a painter, Re-Re. Try sculpting? Pottery. You like fashion. Take up photography. The visual and plastic arts. That's where the money is. I know these things. I'm an economist and collector/investor looking for the next Basquiat. I don't want you becoming some rapper's booty dancer. What a bunch of clowns. *Q*, you're American. Those rappers, what are their names again, *Q*? *B-Daffy*? *Y-Me*? That sound right? No? Diddy and Jay-Z? Whoever they are. Too many sharks on land. Can't trust those show business types. I'd end up having to kill some rapper. And believe me; I'd get away with, too. Remember, I do enjoy diplomatic immunity." Ayri said.

"*Basta!* You are being uncouth. It is unbefitting. Especially in front of our guest of honor. *Ay!*" *Donna* Dolores chided Ayri.

"*Mi hermano* here? He's no guest, he's family. My brother from another mother. I'm telling you. After this project, *Q's* next assignment will be *'Cultural Wasteland: Rap-Hop's Social Psychopathology and Toxicity.'* And I'll personally commission the assignment." Ayri said.

And then there was Diandre; Didi. Two years younger than Ayri, I met Didi when she was an undergraduate. I always had a thing about Didi and, no secret, she liked me too. We just clicked. There was something about her. Something smoldering, a spice, that made her stand out. At present an Amadan museum curator, her real interests lay elsewhere. What those interests were, though, she wasn't sure.

"Right now, I'm thinking about going back to the States next year to study. I'm not sure what. Maybe architecture? I'll contact you once I do. Maybe you can help me look for a place? So much has happened. I'm glad you're here. There's so much to talk about." Didi said.

"No worries. I'll start looking once I get back. Harlem's changed. You'll see. Let me know when, and I'll pick you up from the airport. We'll work things out. Time becomes you. It's good seeing you again, D." I said.

"No need to trouble our American friend here. We can make those arrangements for you, as the family always has in the past." Ayri said.

"I can speak for myself, and so can Q. You just heard him say 'no worries,' he will pick me up. So, no worries then." Didi said.

"Remember what I told you, Egghead." He said.

"Never mind, Q. We'll talk later, *entre nous*." Didi said.

"Oh, stop all this code flirting in French and playing footsies under the table. *Mami* just said I was uncouth; but Didi isn't? Especially in front of Baby Re-Re? As the older sister, you are setting an unbefitting example. You're being uncouth." Ayri said with evil eye.

"Stop calling me a baby, you bully. No one takes me seriously. I'm moving to L.A." Re-Re said.

"Oh, no you're not!" The entire family said in unison.

"This is so unfair. Q, you're a writer. You know how to say what I mean. You tell them. Didi says you... Never mind. This is so unbefitting... You're all so... uncouth! Not you, Q." Re-Re said, storming out the room.

In this setting, seated among the finest of china, cutlery and crystal, the leisurely evening and rich conversation left me spellbound as the family recalled Dr. Mentis' rich personal history. So much so, by the end of the dinner party I felt embarrassed for having doubted Ayri's sincerity or questioned the assignment. Dr. Mentis' accomplishments were remarkable and more than worthy of biographical profile. Honored by the family's trust for such a prestigious assignment, by now I had come to view Ayri and our friendship in an entirely new light. I felt as if in a writer's dream world, seduced by the assignment's setting and sophisticated tapestry amidst fine china, cutlery and crystal.

But I also knew Ayri. He was always up to something. This time, supposedly more concerned than I was about my 'need' for so-called 'hostess entertainment and companionship' during my stay in Amada, Ayri invited two dinner companions. 'Hostess candidates,' and urged me to choose one; or both. In case, in Ayri's words, I want 'to rotate.' "How do you say? Keep things funky fresh? I know I would." A cunning move, likely intended to keep Didi away from me.

When I declined his offer, Ayri wrapped his arm around my shoulder and reverted to Latin *machismo* chauvinist type. "I know you're an intellectual. You think things about things. So, I'm sure you'll understand me. Me? I'm a man of action. I do those things you keep thinking things about. I know you, Q. You've been here what; six hours? And already I see you thirsting for Didi." Ayrton said.

"That's not true. We just haven't seen each other in such a long time. That's all." I said.

"Oh, stop it. You don't just look at her. No, you leer, ogle. Your nostrils flair. The lust, it's all in your eyes. You do everything but lick your lips and grunt. It is disrespectful. *Ay!* What? You think now that she's divorced..." Ayri said.

"Divorced? I didn't even know she had been married. So, how long has she been divorced? Do tell more." I said.

"*Basta!* Right now, she's furious at me. Why? Because of you. I can't remember the last time I saw her this angry. Not as an adult. Why? Because of you." He said.

"What did I do? I just got here." I said.

"It's all your fault. Why? Because I brought along two dinner dates for us. That's why. Now she's saying I disrespected her. She says she has 'things' she 'needs' to talk about with you. How can that be? You two haven't seen each other in years. I don't understand? What all 'things' can there be she 'needs' to talk to you about '*entre nous*' and without your date? Don't bother denying it. Re-Re all but said so." Ayri said.

"She ain't my date. I ain't brung her and I ain't leaving with her either. Besides, you just heard Didi. I'm sure it's all small talk about relocating. Harlem. School. Old times. Anyway, what does Re-Re know?" I said.

"Re-Re knows because they're sisters, and sisters talk. That's all sisters do; they talk. And apparently they've been talking about you, *Q. Ay!* Don't congratulate yourself on your good timing. She's very vulnerable right now. I'm warning you. Mess with my saintly sisters. If any harm comes to them through you. Don't make me become a man of action. Understand this, Egghead." Ayri said, jovial and serious at once, then kissed my forehead.

"So, what this? You're welcoming me to the family now, brother-in-law?" I said.

"Think more like *The Godfather.*" Aryi said, referring to the movie's kiss of death scene between two brothers.

"Remember what I told you, *Q.*" Such was the riddle of the Sphinx of Ayri.

The assignment began in earnest. First off, by gaining a basic understanding of Amada, its history, its cultural and political landscape, its economy and natural resource. Its geographic location, geomorphology, its shaping influences, and Amada's present-day problems.

The *Golden Quadrant,* located in the Lesser Antilles Caribbean Ocean south of Trinidad off the sea coasts of Venezuela and Brazil, Amada once was Portugal's sole colonial Caribbean possession until it achieved independence at the same time as Brazil. With a population total of about one million, nearly one half million people live in Amada's capital, Salamar. The island's principal commodities, other than charcoal and coffee, sugarcane and fruit, are modest amounts of aluminum and bauxite, plentifully sunshine and white beaches. That, and the Amadan people and their native hospitality. In a word; tourism.

Along with this and other background information, I became better acquainted with Amada, its history, culture, and geography. The biography project was greatly aided by ideal working conditions and the perks provided by Ayrton. Particularly the jeep and the travel guides to Dr. Mentis' birthplace and the rest of the island during field research's photography and videography, interviewing principals, colleagues and relatives. Everyone was most gracious and generous with their time, interrupting their busy schedules and itineraries in contribution to the biography.

During my field research, I first came across certain pamphlets, propaganda and other inflammatory material intended to incite public passions, destabilize the government and antagonize the body politic.

Propaganda questioning the integrity of certain government officials and whether officials are beholden to foreign influences and making unsubstantiated allegations of corruption and charges of 'massive kleptocracy.' The pamphlets also questioned whether Dr. Mentis had struck personal deals and, in the process, unjustly enriched himself and his family. Whether Amada is independent or, in a clear reference to Ayrton, 'ruled by primogeniture?' Every pamphlet always ended with the same exhortation, 'People of Amada! Stay woke! Follow the *Guiding Star!*'

"So, what's up with all these pamphlets about *Guiding Star?* Who are they? What's going on? 'Stay woke?' How deep is this?" I asked Ayrton about the leaflets.

"*Guiding Star* is a recent reactionary, populist movement currently active in Amada and elsewhere in the *Golden Quadrant*. They take their name from our national anthem.

"We don't know that much about them; yet. It's a grass roots propaganda campaign distributing these pamphlets. It's disinformation that falsely accuses the government of corruption and inefficiency without any offer of proof other than rumors and lies. They pretend to have simple answers to complex problems and age-old questions by sowing seeds of suspicion or undermining popular support for the government." Ayri said.

"How wide spread is their support?" I said.

"None. None whatsoever. Zero. We don't know yet for sure who's behind this. We have reason to believe they may be based in a neighboring island. Because they're anonymous, generally people don't take them too seriously. But conditions are very much under control and we don't foresee things changing. Still, whoever these troublemakers are we're not taking these pamphlets too seriously, though." Aryton said.

"A foreign country misappropriating your national anthem; that's sick. How long has this been going on?" I said.

"About six months. But believe me, none of this will impact your assignment. We're on top of the situation and will continue to monitor the situation and remain vigilant and prepared." He said.

"Stop it. Just stop! You make me crazy when you do this." I said.

"What are you talking about? What did I do?" Ayri said.

"'Troublemakers.' 'Conditions are very much under control.' 'We're on top of the situation...' ... 'monitor the situation...' 'remain vigilant and prepared.' Stop talking in sound bites. You sound like the politician you are." I said.

"How many times must I tell you? I'm a diplomat." He said.

"That's a difference of degree, not kind. A distinction so fine, there is none." I said. The 'situation,' though, was more complicated. After all, Ayri was a politician, and I a journalist. And this journalist was rightly suspicious of his 'diplomatic' explanations.

In conversations with Amadans there was popular support of the government. People afforded the government goodwill in terms of education and infrastructure. Roads and construction, health care and agricultural reforms. But the government's response to *Guiding Star* allegations was puzzling and poorly handled, lending credence to some of *Guiding Star's* claims. Citing health and family reasons, some Amadan cabinet ministers and other officials suddenly resigned, and certain capital improvement projects were suddenly canceled without explanation. Although these and other incidents cited by *Guiding Star* appeared incriminating, there wasn't necessarily a pattern and, despite those and other *Guiding Star* charges, most people supported the government. People knew the government wasn't pillar-to-post corrupt. At worst, the government came across as inept. By and large, most Amadans agreed that *Guiding Star* offered no evidence or solutions to the island's problems and instead was trying to score political points.

As for *Guiding Star*, no one knew that much about it. Most people didn't trust them and were somewhat dismissive. Some compared the pamphlets to the mark of *Zorro,* suddenly appearing and striking no sooner than vanishing back into nowhere. For the most part though, *Guiding Star* activities were limited to these propaganda pamphlets and occasional graffiti on government and public buildings. Once and awhile their supporters drove through Salamar blaring over bullhorns, but never more than that. In all, *Guiding Star* activities seemed to be having a marginal effect upon daily Amadan life.

To this journalist though, there was something suspicious about the pamphlets. In terms of the language, grammar and syntax, composition and style, whoever wrote this stuff was no backwoods hick. Its ubiquity was also telling, suggesting a sophisticated system of reproduction and organized distribution. The resources necessary for that kind of planning, production and distribution were limited bar one; the military.

The assignment was going smoothly, even better than expected with, thanks to unfettered access, no obstacles encountered. Thanks, in great measure to the new woman in my life, good old Clotilde. Her good and healthy cooking, primarily seafood and poultry, fresh fruits and vegetables, smoothies and salads, as well as spotless housekeeping, helped make daily living and writing easy and worry-free. Thanks also to Iveliese, the translator and secretary, a married mother of four who spoke English and who kept me on-schedule. Mornings I edited the previous day's work for transcription before writing and interviewing later in the day. I also established a personal workout routine and schedule, swimming and running on the beach twice daily to counter the toll writing has taken on my lower back and posture over the years.

Early one morning, much to my surprise Ayri arrived with, to my even greater surprise, Didi. "Clotilde told us you swim every day. And here I thought eggheads float. You know, the laws of physics. You see who tagged along, as if I don't know why. Ever since you got here, all Didi does is hound me about helping you with this assignment. All I hear now is, 'He's my *Papi*, too.' That's all I hear. 'He's my *Papi*, too.' 'He's my *Papi*, too.' So, when Didi here took the call that Iveliese called out sick, ever since that's all I hear. 'He's my *Papi*, too.' 'He's my *Papi*, too.' If I hear, 'he's my *Papi*, too' one more time, I'll get sick." Ayri said.

"Oh, stop it, Ayri. He's my *Papi*, too. All I said was that I want to contribute. You're not monopolizing this project. He's my *Papi*, too." Didi said.

"I know whose *Papi* he is." Ayri said. Then he turned to me. "Take good care of her. Promise with your life, Egghead." Ayri said.

"Okay, I promise." I said.

"No. Not, 'okay, I promise.' With your life." Ayri said.

"You two sound like children. And stop whispering and talking about me, like I'm not here. You two are so opposite. Why are you even friends? *Q*, the elective mute, never talks. He just looks and stares and stays in his 'zone.' No one knows what he thinks. All he does is scribble notes no one else can read and stuffs them in his pockets. And you, Ayri. You love to hear yourself talk so much you never stop talking. You run your mouth like it's the Olympics. *Ay, basta*, the both of you! I don't need you or *Q* or anyone else to protect me. I can take

Q

care of myself. No one makes decisions about and for me, but me. *Ay!*" Didi said.

"Hear Didi roar." Said Ayri. Then he said, "Promise with your life. Your life. Promise."

"Okay. With my life; I promise. Alright?" I said.

"*Ay!* That's better." Ayri said.

"Enough already, will you? Just go, Ayri. Go to work." Didi said.

Then Ayri pulled me to the side. "You can stop procrastinating and get dressed now, *Q*. Don't you think I know what you're doing; walking around here half naked? What, can't wait for me to go to work? Don't think for one second that you're going to have eye opening morning sex on the beach once I leave. There'll be no *entre nous* going on here. How many times do I have to keep telling you?"

"How was I supposed to know you and Didi were coming over this morning? I swim every morning. What am I supposed to do? Swim fully clothed just in case you and Didi might stop by? You're delusional." I said.

"No, you're delusional. Clotilde has strict instructions not to leave you two alone, *Q*. Didi is not a perk in our agreement. *Comprende?*" Ayri said, then took a seat at the veranda table and ordered breakfast for all of us and then lingered for hours before finally heading to work.

Contrary to Ayri's suspicions, Didi and I did not have 'eye opening morning sex on the beach' once he left. Instead, not much later we began loading our gear onto the jeep for that day's scheduled events. Then there was this sudden, rumbling groundswell sound pronouncing hell was about to bust loose. Two armored cars rapidly approached from both ends of the beach road, with a third one racing down the hill road towards the villa.

Holding hands, Didi and I ran; but it was already too late. Trapped in no man's land, between the villa and the jeep, too far from either one and with no escape or safety in sight, our path was blocked by the jeeps and advancing masked men. We scurried towards the ravine off the dirt hill road. Gunfire erupted and the jeep's tires were shot flat. Next three vehicles pinned the jeep in, obstructing our path. Then nine armed masked men alighted, rushing towards us. We tried fleeing, but neither long nor far. Things occurred at a break neck pace. Other moments seemed blurred, elongated and fragmented, some memories as if frozen in time. I heard Didi screaming and shots ringing out. I see Clotilde running for cover. I recalled my solemn oath to protect Didi with my life.

A masked man jumped me from behind and tackled me. I judo-flipped him. He counter-judo hurled me onto my back and then violently presses his knee into my chest and a semi-automatic pistol under my eye. "You move you die, you spy." He said.

Masked troops ransacked the villa and confiscated my laptops, other hardware and software, my notes and passport. Things kept getting ever scarier. I remember Clotilde's wailing and Didi crying out my name. I remember screaming her name before the three of us were blindfolded, gagged, rolled onto our stomachs and hogtied. In shock and afraid like never, I began losing track of rapidly disintegrating events, especially once we were separated and taken to different vehicles. Hoisted into the rear of an armored vehicle, the last thing I remembered about this violent ordeal before losing consciousness was this bumpy ride along the road to perdition.

Q

CHAPTER THREE

THE SMOKING GUN

"I'm standing here bewildered,
I can't remember just what
I've just done...I know that
I should be running, my heart's
beating just like a drum.
Now they've knock me down and
taken it, that still-hot, smoking gun."
The Smoking Gun
Performed by
Robert Cray

These then were the circumstances prior to my arrival and recent arrest in Amada. Here on Death Row I now await a tricky-quickie military kangaroo court trial without benefit of an attorney or American government assistance. Charged with espionage, my conviction and speedy execution certain. Beaten, drowned, broken, I'm goin' down slow. Delusional and wholly psychotic, by now I'm ready to kill myself before they can kill me. *Felo-de-se.* Damn right. Suicide; tonight. Or am I already dead?

Once I regain consciousness, I'm terrified by clanging noises in the room. Suddenly my gag and blindfold are removed and my vision begins adjusting to the gloom and things start coming into somewhat sharper focus. Suddenly blinding bright strobe lights are shined in my eyes. Then, after thirty seconds or so, just as quickly the light torture abruptly stops. Even with my eyes open or closed, bright dots bounce about my field of vision and off the insides of my eyelids. A cubist's fractured horror vision set to strobe light. Once my sight clears reveal in bits, shapes, vague, opaque silhouettes. What look like ghosts and odd facial features illuminated by cigarettes' ember glow suggest themselves briefly before slipping back to darkness.

Between the whispering voices, footsteps and other noises, perhaps four to six other people are in the torture chamber. And then there is that sound. That sound I know all too well and come to dread so much. That awful sound responsible for my sleepless nights on Death Row. That sharp, rhythmic sound, at first slowly and then increasingly rapid. That smacking sound they always make at night, making sure I'm fully awake. Pretending to be asleep only makes matters worse. But no matter, awake or asleep, before beating me first they always make that same scary, slapstick sound. Slapping their nightsticks and getting ready. Yep. The goon squad is here, psyched up and ready to crush my bones again.

The strobe light torture starts over, then they 'tenderize' me again. 'Tenderizing' is what they call the beat down to the back, legs and torso, kidney area. Those soft body parts. Then they throw water on me, trying to revive me. Suddenly the lights, the abuse, everything stops. Then someone says, "Give him a cigarette. Do you want a cigarette? Someone, give him a cigarette."

"I can't smoke. My lips are swollen... I can't even feel them. Besides, I'm trying to stop. Smoking's not good for you. Look, this is all a big mistake. I'm not a spy. I swear. Please! Look, all you..." I say.

"*Calma, amigo.* No worries about cancer. We will kill you long before smoking does. Now *tranquilo.* Here, on the Row, we have a ritual. A tradition we call... the Last Cigarette. It is when the dying man can smoke one last cigarette and is given a chance to confess his crimes. A humanitarian gesture. Maybe we show him mercy? Maybe? Maybe not? It all depends on you. Un-cuff one of his hands." The goon guard says and then produces a blue pack of *Gitanes* cigarettes.

"Time to smoke... Time to smoke your Last Cigarette. Here, you smoke. I tell you what: I'm going to smoke one, too, while you smoke your Last Cigarette. This won't be my last cigarette, though. I will still smoke many cigarettes long after you smoke your... Last Cigarette. Now we smoke together while you confess. This way, while I'm smoking I will decide if you are telling the truth – and if you live or die. Now, you listen carefully, foreign agent. It takes approximately five to seven minutes to smoke a cigarette. That's all the time you have left. I will ask you questions. You will answer my questions. If you lie, then you die sooner. But before we make you die, for each time that you lie they will hold you down, then I will burn you with the cigarettes. First, I will start with the back of your hands, then your wrists, right at the arteries. I swear I will burn you all over." He says.

"Tell me; what do you think happens when a cigarette is extinguished in the human eye? It is not a pretty sight. That's when all of us will probably have to hold you down and keep your head still. Your eye, it will liquefy and run down your face, like egg yolk. It will leave an ugly hole. The pain will be much worse than the final blow of death. You will really want to bang your head then. You will beg for a quick death. You will curse your parents for having spawned you. These things and more, I will do to you. I swear. Now, no more lies." He says, then slowly lights two cigarettes and deeply inhales on both before he shoves a cigarette in my mouth.

"Now why? Why will I do these things to you? After all, I was raised Catholic. True, I'm not a practicing Catholic. Still, but I once was one. I'm no sadist. So, tell me; why am I going to do these things to you? Why? I'll tell you why. Because we have proof. Proof of your guilt. That's right. You know what you are; and we know what you aren't. No. You're not a teacher. You're a spy. This we know. Foreign agent. Spy. That's what you really are. Enough talk. Time's come. Time to smoke... your Last Cigarette. You have five minutes, seven if you smoke it down to the nub. That's all you have left. Do you understand? Now smoke." The goon says.

"Look. Just call the U.S. Embassy. Call. They'll confirm my identity. I'm not a spy. Please!" I say.

"I said smoke. Spies are no position to demand anything. Spies don't have rights. Spies are enemies of the State. Death to spies. Death to all enemy of the State. You're not smoking. I told you to smoke. Now smoke." He says.

"I'm not a spy. I'm not an enemy of the State. I'm no foreign agent. So help me God." I cry out.

"In here there is no god. In here, god would be afraid. In here, we are god! Know this; I believe in what I know. And I know you're a secret agent. That, I know. And I also know that we have ways of making spies talk." He says.

I shake my head. But he blows cigarette smoke in my face and says, "Don't make me burn you, spy! Now, smoke; your time is ticking. You have four minutes left - and counting. State your full name and then spell it. The same with your *nom de guerre*. Do it now. Now what is your *nom de guerre?* Who is your control and contact?" He says.

I state and spell my name, but the soldier becomes more agitated and starts the interrogation all over again. "State and spell your full name. *Nom de guerre*? Spell them. You know what we want. Where did you hide it? We searched the villa and the Mentis family homes. Where is it? What is your mission? Who is your contact and control? Who sent you here? What is your mission? Now confess. For whom do you work? Where is it? State and spell your full name. *Nom de guerre*? Spell them, foreign agent."

"I'm a high school teacher. Harlem City, USA." I say.

The goon slaps my face. "Stop lying! We know the truth. We have your laptops, your hard drives. Video, audio. We reviewed your manuscript. We know everything. Everything; except for where it is. So, where is it? I'm warning you. For the last time; where is it? What is your mission? Who is your contact and control? Who sent you here? Where did you have the surgery? When? Search him again for any scars." He says.

"Surgery? What surgery? What scars? I've never had surgery in my life. What are you talking about? And that other stuff; that's nothing. That's just... just... travelogues. You know. People, places and things. I'm a freelance travel writer." I say.

"Oh, really? It just so happens you travel in privileged company, like the Mentis family, with letters of introductions and safe conduct. Letters, it just so happens, all issued by the respective Mentis ministries? You lie. Look what you did. Didn't I tell you what I will do if you lie? I told you not to make me give you the pain. I warned you. Hold him down, so he can't move." The three goon guards leap into action with evil intentions.

"No! No yet. I'm not done smoking the Last Cigarette. See? I'll tell you everything." I say.

"Too late. Hold his arms and legs. I warned you I will burn you." They restrain me and he begins burning the backs of both my hands with the glowing cigarette.

Long since stripped of all dignity and crazed by the smell and sight of my own burning flesh, in searing pain I scream, reduced to the mortally wounded, chance living creature I've become. I feel my spirit separating, twinning... drifting, my life slowly slipping away. Death seems imminent.

Then someone enters the Room of Doom, the *Door of No Return* door is quickly bolted again, and everyone falls silent. I hear footsteps somewhere in the dark, and hushed silence seizes the room. A presence, an immediacy, suddenly fills the room.

Tortured, burned and beaten and on the verge of losing my mind, the room seems slowly closing in, crowding me. Even though I'm goin' down slow I can tell someone important has arrived on the dungeon scene. The newcomer whispers with others and at times their voices rise. I can't understand everything they say but I do hear some of them are calling for my execution. Although the newbie is partially shrouded in darkness, I can see him holding something shiny as he approaches me. I freeze. Gig's up. I feel it. It's Reaper. The Angel of Death is near. Thanatos done come for me.

"Does he have any recent wounds? Any scars or sutures?" He says.

"No. Not yet, *Comandante*." Someone says.

"Look at me." He says full voice leaning into my face. "I said; look at me. Don't you look down when I talk to you. You look me in the face. Look at me. There, that's better. You look afraid; you should be. Now, tell me; what did you do with it? Where is it? Is it still local?" He says.

"What?" I say.

"Don't act dumb with me. You know exactly what I mean. Where is it? Is it local or wiki?" He says staring me.

His questions about surgery, sutures. This 'is it local or wiki' babbling nonsense is creepy enough. But there is something else about him. It's his accent. It's not Caribbean nor English, not Spanish nor Portuguese, usually heard in these parts. I've heard it before but in the anxiety of the moment I can't identify it. Still, his accent is significant because it bespeaks something telling. This *Comandante,* the ranking officer on the scene. Even though I can't fully see him, based on his accent, dude is white.

"Where is it? Which way? Wiki way or local?" He says *sotto voce.*

"I'm not a spy. I don't speak wiki-talk." I say.

"You're afraid. I can tell. And you should be. You see, fear, the fear of death, it's a good thing. Understand, you're never more alive than when you fear for your life. Fear of death means living in the moment with every fiber of your being. The feel of death, when you're at the precipice, the razor's edge. When at any moment your next breath may be your last. With no place to run and time has run out. When death is near. When panic sets in, and time starts counting down. Such fear, you can't breathe or speak. When you're paralyzed, and that adrenaline rush and fight reflex kick in." He adds.

"How much longer do you have? A little longer or a lot longer? It all depends on you. On how afraid are you? How much do you want to live? After all, we all want to live. So, you see, fear is good. What will you do to live? Will you tell me? You have proprietary information. What did you do with it? Surgical chip implant, maybe? Or is it wiki? What did you do with it?" He says.

"Chip implant? What chip implant? What surgery? I don't have any information or implants. I'm not a spy. Look. I keep telling you over and again. I don't know what you're talking about! I don't know who 'wiki-wiki' is or what it means? I'm not a spy. This is a big mistake. Really. Just call the embassy." I say.

"Tell me; do you want to live?" He says.

"I don't want to die. Please. I want to live. I want to live. Please!" I say.

"A little longer, or a lot longer?" He says.

"A lot longer." I say.

"Remember, the tribunal is tomorrow. They will sentence you to death. The only question is; when will you die? Will I kill you today if you continue to lie? Or tomorrow? Or do I keep you alive for further interrogation? A little longer or a lot longer? Today, or tomorrow? Which one do you want? Which one? Look at me. Don't you look down. You look at me! When do you want to die? Today or tomorrow? Do you want to die today or tomorrow? I have the power to decide if you will live past today to see tomorrow. Choose." He says.

"No! I don't want to die at all." I say.

"You're not answering my question. That's not what I asked you. What did I tell you? What did I tell you when I walked in? What did I just tell you? I said look at me. Look at me when I talk to you. You look at me. That's better. Now answer my question. Do you want to die today, or tomorrow? Here and now? Sooner, or later? Which one?" He says.

"Later. Later!" I say.

"Then this time, tell me the truth. Otherwise, there is no later. The only thing you have left is now." He says.

"I'll tell you the whole truth and nothing but the truth. I promise." I say.

"We'll soon find out." He says.

"Okay. Just don't hurt me. My hands hurt. I can't take any more. I'll tell you everything you want to know. My hands. I'm a writer. My hands!" I say.

"You have it or you know where it is. Where is it? Did you open it? Has anyone else seen it? Did you make copies? How many? Who has them? I think you're a spy. Remember: you lie, you die, spy." He keeps talking in riddles.

"This is crazy. How can I disprove a negative? I'm not a spy. I'm a teacher. That's the truth." I say.

"You can start by stop lying. We've been watching you. We know you're connected with the Mentis family, and they are traitors. This we know for sure. So, don't make things worse for yourself. We have your writings and recordings." He says.

"Nothing in them says I'm a spy. That's just travelogue. Impressions. There's no 'proprietary information.'" I said.

"They are political; very political writings. They are propaganda." He says.

"No, they're not. They are work product. Rough drafts, research. Thoughts and outlines. Little more than scribbling in the margins." I say.

"And then, there is your handwriting." He says.

"What about it?" I say.

"It's illegible." He says.

"I know. I think too fast and can't get it all down on paper quickly enough. Teachers refused to grade me unless I printed." I say.

"No, this is something else. I've seen it before; very rare. I think it's deliberate. This is code writing. How long did it take you to learn to write this way? Spontaneous code writing, so no one understands but you? Maybe I'll ask you to read your notes out loud so we can transcribe them and find out where it is? But moving forward. You say you are a schoolteacher? So? What do you teach; political science? And then, of course, there is your name. Very peculiar. People, they call you Q, like the letter in the alphabet. Very peculiar. Sounds like a codename. Code writing, codename. Who are you? Where is it?" He says as he paces about the dungeon.

"And here's something else that's so confusing. It's your passport. It's American. What kind of spy uses an American passport? Foreign agents won't use American passports because they're afraid of ending up in Gitmo. Who wants that? U.S. spies had been using Canadian passports; even though Canada says it has put an end to that. Or Australian, British, Irish or New Zealand passports. But yours is American. Why risk Guantanamo using an American passport? Any way, you have my property. Where is it? Who sent you here?" He says.

"I keep telling you; I'm not a spy. I'm too afraid to be a spy. Look, I'm a high school teacher. Honest. English and Phys. Ed., Harlem City. That's all I am. See, what had happened was, is... So, it's like this. Ayrton Mentis and I, we go *way* back. We went to school together. He invited me here; I accepted. Okay? That's all! I swear on all that's holy to life. The notes are work product for articles I was going to write once I got back home... Although it doesn't look like I'll be writing anything anytime soon now. Look at my hands! I'm not a spy. I don't know anything about your property or any secrets. Honest." I say.

"End of story?" He says.

"No! Not 'end of story.' End of truth. End of truth. I'm not a spy. My hands! They hurt!" I say.

"You look nervous. Why? Tell me; are you afraid?" He says.

"By the second." I say.

"Good. Then just tell me the truth. You know where it is; don't you? That's why you were banging your head. Forgot your spy manual? Forgot to pack your cyanide capsules? Rather kill yourself than have us kill you? Want to spoil everyone's fun? Take your ball and go home? No. I don't think so. First, we'll make you talk. Then, we kill you. Maybe today? Maybe tomorrow? It all depends on you. Do you want to live a little longer or a lot longer? Now, tell me; where is it? Implant? Local? Wiki?" He says.

"Stop 'wiki-wiki' stuttering. I keep telling you I don't know what you're talking about. I don't have anything to hide worth this! Look at what you've done to me. You broke my face. I look like Quasimodo! You nearly drowned me. My hands. You burned my hands! I can't write! For what? Because you think I'm a spy? This isn't even my country. Why would I jeopardize my life for some third world banana republic I've never been to before? I wouldn't suffer this much for my own country. I would have confessed by now. I'm not political. I hate politics and politicians." I say.

"Or, maybe you are a spy masquerading as a journalist? Maybe you're using teacher as a cover for espionage? I think you went wiki rouge." He says.

"I'm a teacher. I'm not a spy. I'm not masquerading. I'm not 'wiki rouge,' whatever that means. I'm no secret agent. I don't know or have any secrets. I can't make copies of something I don't have. Stop digging in my head!" I say.

The interrogator lights a cigarette, offers me one, and continues pacing around the dungeon. "Well, let's forget your writings, for the moment. Your papers - they appear in order. You seem to be an American. But your name... something about your name bothers me. I think it's a cover name." He says.

"It's no cover name. It's not a codename. It's my name. It's my childhood nickname. I'm an American. My papers don't *appear* to be in order; they *are* in order. I don't *seem* to be an American; I *am* an American. And that's a *fact,* Jack!" I say.

"Spoken like a true American, Jack. Now Jack, on the other hand – now that would be a good cover name, a good codename. Just like colors are good codenames. Why? Because they're so common. *Q,* on the other hand? Not so much. But time will tell, *Q.* That is, if you have any left. But right now, I'm more interested in something else. And remember; the longer you talk, the longer you live." He says.

Then he stops circling me and, full of evil intent, again he leans in my face. "What did I tell you? Didn't I tell you to look at me when I talk to you? I said look at me when I talk to you! Look at me. Why are you so nervous? Is it, maybe, because you're lying and hiding it? You say you're innocent. Time will soon tell. Like I said, right now I'm more interested in something else. Your clothing, a certain garment. I think you know what I mean; don't you?" He says.

"See? Here you go with another riddle-me-this. No, I don't know what you're talking about. I really don't. What I'm talking about is that I'm not a spy. I'm innocent. That's what I'm talking about." I say.

"I think you know exactly what I'm talking about. I'm talking about your clothing. Do you recognize this? You know whose it is; don't you? You know. That's because it's yours; isn't it? We have pictures of you wearing it. Look at me. You heard what I said; look at me when I talk to you. Good. That's better. Now I can see your fear. And remember; fear is good. Fear can keep you alive. Now, answer my question. It's yours; isn't it?" Next, he throws that shiny object which, until then I thought was a gun, in my lap.

"Oh, that? Yeah. Sure, it's mine. I never denied it." I say.

"So, what? Suddenly, when confronted, now you confess it's yours. Well, if you admit it's yours, then you know what it is?" He says.

"Yeah? It's my shirt. That's what it is. It's my shirt. That's no big secret. So, what? I don't get it? My shirt makes me a spy? That doesn't compute. What are you getting at? What's your point?" I say.

"No. It's not *just* a shirt. It's very unusual, a unique garment. So much so, it has its own name. It's more than a shirt. It's a brand. Do you know what kind of shirt this is?" He says.

"I don't know what you're talking about. I really don't. It's a shirt. A shirt. That's all it is. A shirt by any other name is still a shirt; just like a rose. I don't know any other name for a shirt. For this or any other kind of shirt. What are you talking about? What does my shirt have to do with being a spy?" I say.

"It's called 'special issue.'" The interrogator says.

"'Special issue?' To me it's just a khaki shirt. That's all." I say.

"'That's all'? 'Just some khaki shirt?' No, I don't think so. It's a very special kind of khaki shirt. You're lucky. This shirt, more than anything else, will determine if you live. This shirt, it can save your life. So, think hard and tell the truth." He says.

"It's khaki, not the *Shroud of Turin*. Believe me, there's nothing 'special' about it. It's a khaki shirt. That's all it is. The only 'special issue' going on up in here is that I'm innocent. That's the really 'special issue.'" I say.

"Yes, it's khaki. But it's called 'special issue' because it's given only to a limited few. 'The select.' The military elite. This shirt must be earned. There's nothing select or elite about you. This shirt you could never earn; that's for sure. But the shirt, it's genuine. One look tells me so. I know this. The silver buttons and shoulder epaulettes. The zippers, the compass and pen pockets on the sleeves. The collar. It's one of a kind. 'Special issue' given to 'the select.' Which, I repeat, you're not." He goes on.

"The others here, they've never seen anything like it before. The moment they saw it they were convinced you're a spy. To them, only a spy would wear such a unique military shirt. To them, it's all the proof they need of your guilt. They don't believe you're a journalist. They don't want to wait for your tribunal tomorrow. They want to kill you right here and now." The interrogator riddles, again pacing about the room and smoking.

"Well, you're the one in charge in here. You can stop them." I say.

"True. But I can't stop the tribunal. With all the evidence against you, I'm talking to a dead man. But I can keep you alive to interrogate you. A little longer or a lot longer? It all depends on you. What do you have to tell me to make me want to keep you alive? Will I believe you? How much will I have to make you suffer before you tell me where it is?

"But right now, I want to know about the shirt. I know what kind of shirt it is. The question is; do you? So, I'll ask you again. How did you get this shirt?" He riddles.

"I keep telling you; I don't know what you're talking about. This is crazy." I say.

"Where did you get this shirt?" The fiend waves the shirt and leans in my face, his nose nearly touching mine.

"I picked it up in an Army/Navy surplus store in Harlem. The sign didn't say 'elite,' 'select' or 'special issue.' It said; 'Close-out.' 'Size XL.' It's a great looking shirt. Unique; I agree. So, I brought the last two in my size. I don't know anything about 'special issue,' 'the elite,' 'the select.' But if they're selling them off an outdoor Army/Navy store closeout rack in Harlem City, it can't be all that special." I say.

"Where's the other shirt?" He says.

"It's back home." I say.

"Where's that?" He says.

"I tld you; Harlem." I say.

He backs down somewhat, no longer all in my face, his tone not as hostile. "I understand. Relax. For the same reason that the others here think you're a spy, your shirt; I don't. No. I don't think you're a spy. You're clumsy and far too obvious to be a spy. No spy would be as open as you were. In public always driving around and asking questions and taking pictures and notes. Always with a government guide and or a translator. You don't even speak Portuguese. There never was anything clandestine about your activities. No. Spies, we cultivate and corrupt. So, no, I don't think you're a spy. But I don't believe you're a school teacher either." He says.

"Oh no? How about I give you a spot literature assignment to prove I am? 'The question; what all does this encounter have in common Kafka? List all the ways; and why? Must be written in the first person, present tense.'" I say.

"Yes, Kafka. Yes, I remember reading him. Interesting. Poor Kafka. True, you may have been a teacher at one point. But, like with Kafka, you're helpless too. So, the question is academic. No, what you are... I think you're a journalist. That would explain your depth of knowledge. Your writing style, your language skills. Either way, spy or journalist, you possess classified information. Or, you know where it is. The others here, though, they think you're a spy. They want to kill you based solely on your shirt. For me to convince them, first you must convince me. So, what kind of shirt it is? Answer me." He says.

"Those same folks that give us those cool pocket knives, Rolex watches, Tobler chocolates, and Wilhelm Tell. Where the drug dealers, dictators and fat cats stash their cash. Dudes who guard the Pope. The Swiss army. It's a Swiss army shirt. They make these cool shirts. Switzerland, it's a neutral country, just like me. See? I'm neutral, too. No one sent me. I'm no spy. I'm a tourist." I say.

"That's right. It's a Swiss army shirt. Ask me; how do I know it's genuine? How? Look at the label. Just like your safari jacket we confiscated. I bet you bought the jacket at the same time; same place?" He says.

"That's right. How'd you know?" I say.

"On a closeout rack?" He says.

"That's right." I say.

"In Harlem?" He says.

"That's right. An Army/Navy closeout rack in Harlem City. What's so strange about that?" I say.

"Unbelievable." The interrogator says with an air of exasperation.

"The label? What's the shirt label read?" He says.

"I don't know. I never paid attention." I said.

"Here; read it." He says.

"It's dark. I can't see. Besides, you took my glasses." I say.

"It says *Willis & Geiger*." He says without looking at the label.

"So?" I say.

"So? So now I really know you're not a spy. You don't even know what you're wearing. *Willis & Geiger* is the premier military tailor in the world. Any military warrior knows that." He says.

"See? There you go. Why would I know? Like you just said; I'm not a 'military warrior.' I'm not a spy, either. *Willis & Geiger*, best tailor in the world; really? Never heard of them. I paid two hundred dollars for all three off a closeout rack in Harlem. Not bad, huh?" I say.

"Two hundred dollars? Not bad at all." He says.

"Two hundred dollars – for all three." I say.

"Best tailors in the world; and the whole time you had no idea." He says.

"Why would I know them? But I could tell from the tailoring and the material that they were quality items. That's why I bought them. How much retail?" I say.

"Tailored, like these? Close to one thousand dollars - minimum just for the jacket. The shirts, two hundred to three hundred dollars - per. Look at you. You still don't even know how valuable they are. Funny. We almost killed you, and here you're not even a spy." Says mystery man. Then he retreats somewhat, explains to the others in the room what just happened, and together they burst out laughing. Then he takes a stance, crosses his arms in front of his chest and stands before me. "Listen carefully; I'm going to make you an offer. More like an ultimatum. So, consider carefully. I already have your safari jacket. Now I want your shirt in return for your life. Not that I need to ask, mind you." He says.

"Say what?" I say.

"You heard me. The shirt and jacket for your life. Your move. So, what's it going to be?" He says.

"Hey, man. This is your world. You rule in here. I told you; I ain't looking for smoke. You want it, you got it. Take all my gear. No problem. None what-so-ever. Anything you want.

"Whatever it is, help yourself. Like you said, my life depends on it. I may be stupid, but I ain't dumb." What's so important about *Willis & Geiger* gear?

"There, then. The deal's done. Don't worry. You did the right thing. After all, you can always get another jacket and shirt. But another life? Now that would be a real miracle in Harlem. Now all you need to do is tell me where it is. Is it local or is it wiki-wiki?

"It must be you. I know it's you. No one else makes any sense. It must be. All I need to do is read your writings. They tell me you're are a journalist. That tells me everything I need to know. That you have guilty knowledge. That you're holding the *Smoking Gun*. I can smell it on you. There are other people with guilty knowledge still out there. We know this. What we don't know – yet – is if you're chief among them. Nothing says so, so I don't think so; for now. Right now, the only thing keeping you alive is your passport. We didn't expect any Americans. Otherwise, I'd have killed you already. But for now, I need to keep you alive to get my property back. We'll soon find out, though. Most of you are already in custody now. We will continue our investigation. We will shake down any information and probe the extent of your guilty knowledge." Then he continues.

"And if we discover anything suspicious. If you're holding the *Smoking Gun*; if you know anything about it or its whereabouts; if you are in any way connected. Then the next time you see me will be the last time you ever see anything. It will be curtains, lights out for you. But that's academic. The tribunal is going to convict you guilty, and sentence you to death tomorrow anyway. But for now...." Then he says.

"There. See how easy that was? You just earned yourself a few extra hours. You still have time left. Maybe a day or two, even? Now, *calma. Tranquilo*. We're done - for now. But remember what I just told you. You don't want to see me again." He says, almost smiling. Then he backs off somewhat, his tone no longer as hostile. But the guards continue laughing and taunting me for wanting 'a little bit more time.'

"This is so full-time wrong. Why do you keep drilling all up in my head like this? I'm not a spy. I'm innocent. We're all innocent. Hello? Do you hear me? I keep telling you. I swear I don't know you're talking about. What property? What's 'wiki' local? I'm no threat to you. Listen to me? I'm not a spy. I'm a teacher. That's the truth. Somebody help me." I plead.

"You're making a big mistake. Would you want to die like this? Accused and killed for something that's not true and you didn't do? This is all so wrong. You keep talking that 'riddle-me-this,' wiki-wiki stuff. That only makes sense to you. I keep telling you I'm not a spy. I don't have your property. I don't even know what property you keep talking about." I say.

I've felt, seen, and smelled my flesh burning, tasted my own blood, and licked my own wounds. My mind, body and spirit, beaten down, broken, I'm goin' down slow. It's only a matter of time before soon death finally ends my suffering. Oddly though, as much as I want to die, I still cling to life.

"Don't do it. What's your name? How can I talk to you if I don't even know your name? Come on, man. What's your name? Talk to me. What? You're not big on names? That's cool. Whoever you are, I'm telling you; this is all a big mistake. I'm not a spy. I'm innocent. The Mentis family, my friends, they're innocent. We're all innocent. This is straight out of *Midnight Express*. Don't do it." I plead with him.

Then he stands in front of me and says. "And no. They - the Mentis' - they're not innocent. The Mentis family, they're guilty..." He says.

"How can a foreigner say what natives in their country are guilty of? Guilty of what?" I say.

"Guilty of interfering with the fulfillment of contractual obligations. Guilty of impeding the flow of commerce. Guilty of geo-political interference. That's what they did. That and more. They're traitors. Spies. Enemies of the State. All of them. That's what they are. And for that they'll be punished. All of them." He continues.

"With you, though, it is different, unique. You may be an innocent who happened to come into possession of, at minimum, guilty knowledge. But you do have guilty knowledge. You know more than you're saying. You know secrets. I know you know. It's written all over your face. And now that you know that I know, we both know what that means. It means that how much time you have left depends on how long it remains missing. I don't have time to waste, and that means you don't have much life left. I smell the *Smoking Gun* on or near you and I'm going to find it. And once I do, your usefulness will expire."

Then he steps behind me, pulls out his pistol, releases the safety, and I hear him cock the hammer, taunting me.

"Funny, human nature. Like why do people always flinch before they get shot? As if anybody could survive at this close range. Just take a deep breath and... surrender. This is what it will be like. Like this!" He says, then suddenly pulls the trigger on an empty chamber. "Like that." He says.

I flinch.

He laughs, then holsters his weapon and paces the dungeon, all the while staring at me. "No. Not right now. But that's what it will be like; and now you know. But for the time being at least, you're more important to me alive than dead. I'm going to keep you alive; alive and afraid. If you know what's good for you, if you don't want to see me again, then you'd better tell me. Where is it? What did you do with it? Or, maybe you've had a chip implant? Maybe I'll order exploratory surgery on you; I think I will. That way, I'll find out for sure. Surgery will make you tell me everything I want to know. Know that." He says.

His silhouette blends into the dark dungeon, but he is still in earshot when I overhear him berating the others in the cell.

"What the hell happened to his head? What do you mean; 'He was banging his head against the wall, trying to kill himself?' Are you crazy? Look at what you did to him. You almost killed him. Look at how swollen he is. That's why he tried killing himself. Don't touch him again. Take him to the infirmary - right now! Tell the doctor to stitch him up and put him on suicide watch. Tell the doctor to examine him for any fresh surgical scars. I'm going to schedule an MRI and exploratory surgery on our off-shore hospital ship once he recovers." Fully furious, he says.

"Your zest has set back this investigation. Make sure he can't bang his head again. And don't touch him again. And if he dies... I'll made the three of you kill each other. And I'll kill the last one of you standing. Do you understand me?" He threatens them.

"*Si, Comandante.*" The goons say and then un-cuff me from the chair.

"Keep him in the infirmary until I need him again. Make sure he doesn't have any writing material. Hand me everything he has written. I'll take the laptops. And give him back his eyeglasses. Just what I don't need. An American, a journalist - dead or alive - gumming up the works. They were supposed to take care of that. Well, not on my watch."

To the sound of his footsteps, I hear the dungeon door close behind him. The goon guards un-cuff and carry me off to the infirmary; and none too soon. Aside from my broken state of mind, my injuries are severe, including blood in my urine, indicating kidney damage. I respond well to treatment, though, and my condition eventually stabilizes.

For reasons never explained, the tribunal is 'postponed indefinitely pending further discovery and interrogation.' Here in the prison infirmary, for the first time since my arrest I'm able to reflect on the past month.

Much has changed about me. My injuries have damaged my health. I've lost weight and become fatigued. I'm gaunt and haggard, my appearance etched by stress and ill health. By now my hair has grown into an unruly mop and, for the first time in my life, I have a full beard. And while I'm thankful for being alive 'a little longer' and hoping to stay alive 'a lot longer,' I keep worrying. Worrying about myself and frightened about the pending exploratory surgery. Exploratory surgery for a chip implant? This can't be happening. Will I even survive surgery? Playing Russian roulette? What else is going to happen to me? How much more abuse can I take?

I'm curious about what is going on outside of prison, with running gunfire battles raging in the not too distance. I'm curious about *Guiding Star* and I'm curious about my interrogator. Who is he? What kind of accent is that? Why is a white man involved in Amada's politics? As important, what's the 'secret?' What's with this 'wiki wiki rogue' babbling? What is everyone looking for? How am I going to get out of here?

Most of all, I'm curious about what happened to Ayri, Didi and the Mentis family. But no matter how often I inquire, there's no news. My thoughts and prayers, they always return to Ayri and Didi; and to my health. What's so important they would perform exploratory surgery or play Russian roulette looking for it? Maybe my chances with the tribunal would be better? Worrying and wondering, hoping and praying that somehow Heaven will somehow help us all. But all I'm left is hanging.

Instead, my situation only worsens once a new set of events unexpectedly come into play. A prisoner now almost a month, I'm no longer shackled while I'm in the infirmary. My diet improves. Normally the highlight of my day consists of playing chess with the doctor and the regular guards. As the only patient, security is lax in the medical unit. The night prior to my scheduled transfer to an off-shore hospital ship for next day exploratory surgery to locate any chip implant, the doctors and I play chess until the guard completes his rounds. The doctor leaves for the night, the guard locks up and then stations him outside of my door. Terrified by the thought of

Q

exploratory surgery and the goons' past beatings, I sleep very little and light that night.

Round about midnight, I hear the infirmary door opening. Two dark figures carrying a large bundle enter, then quietly lock the door. Then one of them begins unfurling something. But these aren't the usual hospital guards. I've never seen these two before. *Guiding Star* has come to assassinate me in my sleep.

My ninth life's about to run out. I know I sure ain't going out like this. Hell no! I know what to do. I almost succeeded the last time. Trapped with no place to hide, I leap from my cot and start banging my head against the wall while reciting the 23rd Psalm:

> "'The Lord is my Shepard; I shall
> Not want. He maketh me to lie
> Down in green pastures: He...'"

> Then, when I get to that part:
> "'Yea, though I walk through the
> Valley of the shadow of death,
> I shall fear no evil...'"

The guards restrain me and, motioning silence, then one of them drops the news I've been praying for.

The entire Mentis family is alive and under house arrest ever since our arrest. They are scheduled to be sent into exile in Brazil the next day. Everyone except Ayri. He refuses to cooperate. Not only that. The guard tells me that Ayri is being held in the same cell block, literally only a matter of feet away from where we're standing! And what's more, the guard says that Ayri even arranged for us to meet. Right now!

The plan is for me to switch clothing and places with the other guard and then be secreted away to an undisclosed location to meet Ayri, who's waiting. This, according to one of the guards, who explains in hushed tones and urges me to hurry.

The news is startling, the plan plain daring. But no matter how desperate I am for news about Ayri and Didi and their family, I don't trust anyone. I'm not about to walk blindly into a death trap or some set-up. Shot in the back in these dingy dungeon prison corridors during what later would be called an 'escape attempt.'

No, I don't think so. It's just too risky. I'm going to need something. Proof of life. A note with his signature, some mutual knowledge, an old address. Something only Ayri and I know, something that confirms he's alive and nearby. No surprise here, the guards have no proof of life.

But the lead guard is insistent, explaining that we don't have time. "Please. Soon it will be daylight. We're already in danger."

Any meeting, the lead guard explains, can occur only between the guards' hourly rounds. "Hurry! Before it's too late." He says.

"Nope. At this point, only a selfie or a video chat session is the kind of proof of life that will convince me." I say.

"Ayrton, he said you would do this. He says that sometimes you can be... what did he call it? An 'anal retentive German.' 'Anal retentive?' He wouldn't tell me what it means. Ayri said, 'ask Q.' It doesn't sound good. Like you're sick. I'm sorry if you are ill. Everyone says you're American; but you're German?" He says, while the other guard keeps pointing towards his watch and begins tugging him towards the door.

"Hold on. What did you just say? What did you say Ayri called me?" I say.

"His exact words were: 'Sometimes Q can be a real anal-retentive German; and tell him I said so.' It is a disease? No?" He says.

"Yeah, that sounds just like something wack Ayri would say. No, I'm not sick. Ayri's sick; sick in the head." I say.

"But if you are German, then why do people think you're American?" He says.

"No, that's just Ayri talking stupid. I'm American. If what you say Ayri said is true, well since I'm so 'anal retentive,' the 'German' wants proof of life. And 'tell him I said so.' When was the last time you saw him?" I say.

"Five minutes ago, right before we came for you. He is just three cells down the corridor. Señor, this is the only chance before you go onboard the hospital ship in the morning. Ayri heard what they want to do to you there. No one knows how long you will be there, if you return here or will be transferred somewhere else? You could die onboard? I've never heard of such a thing, slicing someone open to find something. Would you rather die than try to escape? He is determined to stop this from happening to you. This is the only chance. We must hurry. Otherwise, there'll be no tomorrow for both of you." He says.

"What do you mean?" I say.

"Just like for you, if you board that ship, so for Ayri there will be no tomorrow." The guard says.

"Say what?" I say.

"You must hurry. At midnight next, Ayri will see the face of God above the firing squad." The guard says.

"What?" I say.

"*Es verdad, señor.* I'm sorry. He is my friend, too. We grew up together. His mother even taught my parents how to read. We all played together. But it is true. You must believe me. *Rapido, por favor.*" He says.

"But why?" I say.

True to self, Ayri refuses to cooperate or compromise. As the leader of the resistance, he won't go with his family into exile. In the words of the lead guard, Ayri 'spit in their eye.' Moreover, *Guiding Star* is about to launch a major military offensive and rightly regard Ayri as a threat. Now, and further down the line.

"But he hasn't done anything. He's innocent. We're all innocent. The only thing he's guilty of is patriotism. He loves Amada! He thinks Amada is his 'wife!' Well, then get a quickie, no fault divorce. It doesn't matter if he doesn't want to go into exile. Put him in a psychiatric hospital. Give him an injection and put him on a plane to I-don't-know-I-don't-care-where, and when he wakes up, he's in Tibet. Governments do it all the time. They don't have to kill him. This place is full time crazy." I say.

His solemn expression tells me it's true. "Shh! Shh! You must control yourself, or we'll all be killed. Look, I'm not an educated man. I'm a peasant, a prison guard. But this much I know; it's political. There is no government. There is only *Guiding Star*. Right now, they are the government, the military, and the courts. Democracy is dead. *Guiding Star* is in control. Other than that, no one knows exactly who they are or who's in charge.

"Now, *señor.* Please! They don't know that I know Ayri. He trusts me. I promised him. If they find out... my whole family will suffer. Then we too will see the face of God above the firing squad. And you will too. We all will. You must hurry. *Rapido, señor!*" He pleads with me.

"Does he know about midnight?" I say.

"No, I don't think so. Not based on the way he's acting. He doesn't know. No one knows except for on a need-to-know basis, and I know because I was on duty the night they decided. And now you know. The order came down thirty-six hours ago. We now have under twenty hours left; and counting." He goes on.

"What's the matter, you? What more do you want? You're not the only one who cares about Ayri. Others here in the resistance have known him much longer than you. That doesn't mean any of us cares any less or any more. Everyone loves him. It simply means we all love the same person in different ways. None's love is greater. It's all one love. We who love him, we must do our best to save him, each in our own way." Next he says.

"Who knows what will happen in twenty hours? Maybe a miracle? There's still time left. But you're not helping. We have put our lives at great risk coming here tonight and working behind the scenes for someone we don't know. Now you must make the same choice in front of you. So. What will you do?" The guard says.

"He doesn't know? His family; they don't know?" I say.

"How many times must I tell you? No." Guillermo says.

"He doesn't know; but I do? How can't I look him in the eye knowing what I know. No. I can't do that. One look and he'll know something is wrong. I'm not going to lie to him. What am I supposed to say if he asks me what's wrong? Then what? Then I'd have to tell him. I'm not going to lie to him. There's no way I'm doing that. I can't." I say.

"If you don't go, then for sure he will know that something is wrong. He has been very worried about what has happened to you and what is about to happen to when you board that ship. You would rather get on that ship like a sheep than see your friend who risks everything trying to save you? He wants to help you more than he is worried about himself. He feels guilty about what happened and will happen if you get on that ship.

"There is only one thing you can do to help him now. We must go. Now stop thinking about yourself, or I leave. I won't die for you. For Ayri? Yes, I die. But for you? No. Not for you. I told you; I'm not educated, like you and Ayri. The journalist and the politician. But I think Ayri is right. I'm beginning to understand what 'anal retentive' means. And it's not a good thing. My name is Guillermo, and Guillermo is tired of arguing with you. Make up your mind. Follow me; or get on that ship." He says.

Guillermo is right. Forced choice means no choice. I switch into uniform and trade places with the other prison guard, then we steal our way along the dark and dank winding prison corridors, my heart pounding with every breath, my mind racing with every step along the way concerned for my own personal safety. Trapped in a moral dilemma, what *is* the right thing? I'm ambivalent, afraid that sooner or later my body language and affect will betray me. That Ayri will sense something wrong. No one ought to be blindsided like that. Doesn't he deserve to know? Shouldn't I tell him the truth and give him a heads up? At least he can try to escape. Knowing Ayri, would he want to know? Would I want to know? I doubt it. Can I, should I, lie to him? What's the right thing?

Weighty questions with no easy answers to any of them, they soon recede once we arrive at our destination. Guillermo signals silence, again surveys the vicinity, then he ushers me into a dark cell. There he retreats to a corner, mumbles something in Portuguese and then exits the cell, leaving me alone. Or so I think. For once my sight adjusts to the gloom, there in the middle of the cell stands Ayri in his trademark pose as ever I'll remember him, flashing that signature smile with arms outstretched as he approaches me.

"*Ay, chihuahua!* There he is! *Q*! *Mi hermano*! Author, author! Now you really have something to write about. The pacifist in uniform. I wish we could take a selfie so you could see yourself. You've even grown a beard. *Hombre*, you really do look like one of us islanders. It's so good to see you. I have so much to say.

"I don't know where to begin and we don't have a lot of time. I'm so sorry. Give me a hug, *Q*!" Ayri says.

Instead, I recoil from his awaiting embrace, angry and uncertain how I'm going to play my part.

"From the look of you, I can tell you're not happy too to see me; and I understand that. I'm gutted with guilt, *Q*. I really am. I can't begin to imagine what you've been through because of me. I'm so sorry. Let me look at you. What? Why are you staring me down with this *loco* look in your eyes? Like I said, I know you've been through a lot. Just listen, *Q*..." Ayri says.

"Don't '*Ay, chihuahua*' me, Ayri. What's wrong with you? Going around telling complete strangers I'm 'anal retentive.' What's up with the dumb stuff? Saying something like that to people who don't even know me or what 'anal retentive' means. What's up saying something that stupid? I mean; suppose I write a book, and dude says, 'Oh, I know him. Let me tell you; he's really 'anal retentive.' Dude doesn't know me or what it means - and I'm not sure you do either - and he's telling me I'm 'anal retentive.' Next thing you know, he's going to start calling other people 'anal retentive.' You just started an 'anal retentive' daisy chain. And stop telling people I'm German. *Ay, chihuahua!*" I say.

"Sorry. Did I blow your cover? I thought your journalism cover identity was 'ethnic musicologist; this time.'" Ayri says.

"Oh, shut up. What? That's funny to you? Calling me an 'anal retentive,' musicological German makes you laugh? Oh, really? Yeah, what? A couple of laughs and jokes and then we're all 'mi hermano' good again? Do you see me laughing? I don't think so, either. There's nothing funny about this. Don't glad-hand me, *Mr. Lucky*! You can cut all that 'mi hermano,' 'player-to-player, brother-in-law crap. I know your routine by heart. I'm not feeling you right about now, Ayrton." Then I say.

"I'm telling you straight up. I think you set me up. You lied to me the whole time. You looked me dead in the eye and lied. From the very beginning, you lied to me. The beaches. The food. The women. Amada! Crown jewel of the Caribbean!' But this one I like most, 'Amada! You'll won't want to leave!' What I should have been writing is tourism slogans. 'Amada! It's like Hell on Earth.' 'Amada! The Smell of Death's in the Air.' 'Amada! Once is Too Much!' Or simply, 'Amada? You Crazy?'

"So; what? You just 'forgot' to tell me about the revolution? You know you lied. You *lured* me into this hell-hole. What; am I lying? You set me up. Yeah. look at yourself. How would you know I have a crazy look on my face? You can't even look me in the eye. People have been wailing on me for over a month. So, now I'm about to go get real retro-primitive on you." I say and then try to go after Ayri before the guards together with Ayri they restrain me.

"Shh! Not so loud. Now listen. I can explain everything. Listen to me. The worst is behind us." Ayri says.

"Listening to you is what got me in this mess in the first place! So, no. I don't think I'm going to be listening to you again anytime soon. 'The worst is behind us.' Listen to yourself. Nothing but one *cliché* after another. You're such a politician."   I say.

"Chill, Q, before you get us killed. I listened to you, now you listen. Will you listen? I feel awful about what happened to you in my country and because of me. I am responsible for everything that's happened to you. I won't let you get on that ship and let them slice you open. I feel sick about all of this." He says, grabbing my wrists.

"And I'm sick of your political mumbo-jumbo double talk. You got me into this mess. The only thing you can do for me is to get me out of this hellhole banana republic you call a country. I don't understand you? Who are you? You've become a stranger." I say.

"Just hear me out; will you? You're safe; for now. There won't be a tribunal. Initially they thought you're Amadan because you look like one of us. But now, they know you're an American journalist we hired to write *Papi's* memoirs. They know the truth. They don't want that kind of scrutiny and being seen holding an American citizen prisoner. That's why the tribunal was canceled. But on that ship, all bets are off. I won't let you board that ship." Ayri says.

By now, it's obvious. Anyone that brimming life's energy, that full of optimism and enthusiasm; Ayrton really has no idea about midnight's deadline. Ashamed that I really do possess 'proprietary' knowledge,' not knowing what else to do all I can do is listen to him.

"Here's the plan, Q." After our meeting, instead of boarding the hospital ship for exploratory for the non-existent chip implant, Guillermo is to take me to a safe house at a deserted air strip where my passport will be returned. Ayri then explains details.

"From there, at first light you'll then take flight to safety in St. Lucia. Everything has been arranged. Don't look so surprised. Unfortunately, *Papi's* memoirs are on hold. Have heart. The worst is behind you. In less than four hours you'll be in St. Lucia. I told you; they don't want to appear to be holding an American journalist prisoner. What's going on right now is a purely domestic, homegrown matter. It concerns only Amadans." Ayri says.

"I wouldn't be too sure about that, Ayri." I say.

"What do you mean?" Ayri says.

"Don't play me, Ayri. Stop pretending. We all know you're a good politrixian. I'm sorry; I mean politician. Oops, that right. I forgot, you're a diplomat; that changes everything." I say.

"Just get to the point, Egghead." Ayri says.

"Stop lying. How come I'm only here a little over a month and already I know this isn't something domestic/home-grown that's just going to 'blow over?' How about, maybe, blow up?" I say.

"I'm not lying. This is a strictly internal, domestic political phenomenon." Ayri says.

"Oh yeah? Really? 'A strictly internal phenomenon' that's all just going to 'blow over?' Strange. When I was doing research for your dad's biography, in traveling around, other than tourists, I never noticed any white native Amadans." I say.

"That's because there are only few white native Amadans. So? What's your point?" Ari says.

"Well, if this so 'internal,' domestic,' then how come the last time I was interrogated was by a white guy? And for some reason I don't think he was one of your few white, native Amadan cousins." I say.

"Look, Q, I can't begin to understand the ordeal you've been put through. The stress, the shock, the trauma. It's beyond my imagination. But Q, we're in Amada, the Caribbean. Remember? And you're saying... Listen to yourself. You're saying... you see white people. Maybe it's the stress? Maybe you have amnesia? Are you okay?" Ayrton says.

"Hell-to-the-no, I'm not 'okay.' I'm in prison. On Death Row. Talking to the person responsible I'm on the Row. The Row. That's what we, the condemned, call Death Row; the Row. I guess it gives me real street cred with my students now. Dead teacher's still walkin', talkin'. Before that I was in the Room of Doom, right behind the *Door of no Return.* Did you know that? No? Better don't ask me, 'you okay?' 'Am I okay'? No, I ain't 'okay.' How could I be 'okay?' What a stupid question. And no, I don't have amnesia. I ain't trippin', either. I know this ain't Wisconsin. I know I'm in the Caribbean. Right about now though, Wisconsin is looking mighty good. For real, anywhere other than here works good for me. I know exactly where I am and I know exactly what I saw and what happened to me. I know exactly what I'm talking about." I say.

"You were interrogated by a white man? Here, in Amada? You're mistaken, Q. That's impossible. No, no." Ayrton says.

"That's right; dude was white. Even though they kept flashing this strobe light in my eyes, I could tell from his accent. That wasn't some Caribbean lilt. Whatever it was, English wasn't his mother tongue, but he spoke fluent English. Dude was white." I say.

Ayri is stunned, speechless.

"I'm telling you what I saw. I could see his outline. He was the ranking officer on the scene. He's blond, blue eyes. Around our height and weight. There was something strange about his eyes – real creepy. I couldn't make it out. I know what I saw. Dude was white. I know what I'm talking about. More than you seem to." I say.

"Maybe all the pressure you've been under. Plus, you've always been a little OCD. I mean, listen to yourself. Saying you see white people. Maybe you had a mental break? Maybe your mind's playing tricks on you?" Ayrton says.

"So, now I'm OCD? Trick or Treat? Isn't that your game? You're the one who tricked me into coming here. You're the

Q

one who kept on lying to me once I got here. What's real?
What isn't? Who's real? Who's fake? Who's my friend? Who
isn't? Who's got my back? Who's stabbing me in the back? I'm
still waiting for my treat. They're a lot of people all in my head
at times. Why shouldn't I be hallucinating? Right now, the
voices are telling me to go 'oops upside your head.'" Then I
say.

"Yeah, look at yourself, Ayri. Right about now, Mr. Big
Mouth, you don't know what to say; do you? You just look at
me real stupid, like I'm speaking German. Like you don't
understand a word I'm saying. I may be crazy but I'm not so
crazy that I don't know the difference between being crazy
and being driven crazy. Even though I'm being driven crazy
my mind's not playing those kinds of tricks on me. I know
what I know. I know what I know because of the way I came
to know it. I'm not hallucinating. I know what I saw. No, Ayri.
Don't tell me what you think I saw or where you think I think
I am. You listen. I know I'm not in Iceland. I know I'm in the
Caribbean. I know who you are although I don't know or like
you anymore. I know today's date. I ain't trippin'." I continue.

"I didn't say 'I see white people.' I didn't say anything
about seeing pods of self-replicating 'white people' wading out
of the ocean. I didn't say anything about seeing 'white
people.' All I said was that I was interrogated by a white
dude; singular. That's all I said. That's what I said, because
that's what happened. Just like I know that you know more
than you're admitting.

"Don't play me, Ayri. This is bigger than I imagined. Is it
bigger than you imagined? Nah! I bet you knew all along;
didn't you? That's why you weren't just straight-up-front with
me from jump. Why can't you tell me now? What's happened
to you? Who have you become? How you can live with what
you are now? At what price, Ayri? Your soul? Who are you
anymore? What happened to the you I once knew? All I know
is you owe me an explanation. You owe me. Big time. I don't
want to die not knowing why. Start talking, Ayri." I say.

"First, you have to tell me everything that happened the
last time you were interrogated. Everything." Ayrton says with
urgency.

"I ain't telling you jack, Ayri. Right about now I don't really
like you very much. I'll never trust you again. You're no
longer my friend. You're just someone I used to know." I say.

"You insult my country. You insult me. You say I set you
up. You call me a liar. You ugly American, repeatedly you
belittle Amada. You say I 'lured' you here under false

pretenses. You call me a backstabber. And then, on top of all that, you have the nerve to thirst openly for Didi. Oh, I see how you lust after her. Everyone does, even Re-Re. You don't even bother looking her in the eyes. You scan and size her up and down and stare at her *tatas*. When she walks away, you linger admiring her *bobo*. And then, Re-Re has gall enough to say, 'I wish a man looked at me like that.'

"I have told you before, Didi is not a perk in our agreement. You're not here on sex vacation with my sister and make women's blood boil. You show me no respect. *Ninguna! Nada! Ay!*" Ayri says, now beside himself.

"I'm not discussing Didi's anatomy with you. Want to know what I want? I'll tell you what I want. I want out. All the way out of this banana republic. That's what I want – now." I say.

"There; see? You just insulted Amada again. *Q*, will you just tell me what happened? Then, no matter what you think of me, then I'll tell you everything. But if you want out of here, I need to know everything you know. That's the only way I can help you. *Fale comigo, Q!* (Talk to me, Q!)" Lusophone, Ayri says in Portuguese.

Ayrton listens in stone silence as I tell him about the interrogation, all the 'is it local or is it wiki' babbling and surgery questions in search of the interrogator's 'property.' "What do you know about *Willis & Geiger*?" I say.

"Only that they're the finest military tailor in the world." Ayrton says.

"That's what he said, too." I say.

"He took your jacket and shirt? I don't get it? None of this makes sense. Unless... I'm beginning to get a bad feeling, *Q*." Ayri says.

"What's wrong?" I say.

"Listen to me. Certain classified national security intelligence information I'm not allowed to share, they report a high-ranking terrorist, nationality unknown. Other than prison ID, no known photographs, only descriptions, just like yours. Multiple aliases: Prime Evil, *Captain Blood*, *Nosferatu*, *Shiva*, *Crazy Horse*, among others. Real name, unknown. Occupation: Private contractor, security consultant, weapons broker. Mercenary for the highest bidder. Specialties: Assassination. Economic sabotage. *Agent provocateur.* Primary employers: Corporate, military, political. Said to have a body count. Little else is known about him. Supposedly he lives at sea on board his custom boat." Ayri says.

Q

"The others called him *Comandante.* He was straight out of some horror movie. This doesn't sound too homegrown to me. If it is him, what does that tell you?" I say.

"It confirms what I've long suspected. That outsiders, foreign interests, our arch enemy is behind *Guiding Star*. They must know. They found out." Ayrton says.

"They found out what? What is it they know? What? Is that why he was interrogating me? Dude kept sweating me, 'is it local or is it wiki?' He's the one who ordered exploratory surgery. What is he talking about?" I say.

"Don't worry, Q. I told you; I'm not letting you get gutted on that ship. It's a flash drive. A memory stick that contains decryption software. It is read-only and can't be opened without the decryption codes on that drive. Most importantly, it also contains patent applications Amada must register them by a deadline. If they're not filed by a date-certain in Washington, D.C. our proprietary rights will expire. They're betting against us filing on time.

"This is our only window of opportunity. This is a race against time. It also contains other, classified information. Explosive stuff, evidence of corruption, chapter and verse, which is why it was smuggled to us. That's all I can say; for now. But you'll soon find out." Ayri says.

"And these are patent applications for what?" I say.

"Amada has huge energy reserves. Natural gas. Oil. On and offshore oil. Energy reserves were discovered, maybe seven years ago. The patent applications concern our drilling and production plans and must be filed in Washington, D.C. The deadline is fast upon us. The problem is, the deposits are not only within our territory but extend into international waters. This is a big problem for us. A mixed blessing and double-edged sword and gift from the devil. On the one hand, the benefits are enormous. Health care, education. Capital investment, infrastructure renewal, wealth creation. At the same time, we received credible reports of disturbing information about certain offshore problems, problems we had no control over. It turns out that for some time shipping vessels from a neighboring island have been secretly dumping refinery waste and other toxic materials in international waters. This, we know, is intentional because of the currents. They know this will spill into our ecosystem and wash up on Amada's beaches." Ayri paints a grim picture.

"We know this for two reasons. First, there were sightings and independent confirmation from private and commercial fishing and other boats and aircrafts of recent offshore exploration and pollution. Some of those vessels were even fired upon by the violators. Second, we soon noticed some very alarming ecological phenomena. Increasingly and at different places in Amada, parts of beaches began bubbling with toxic flotsam. In the words of Marvin Gaye's *The Ecology*, 'Poison is the wind,'... 'oil wasted on the ocean and upon our seas, fish full of mercury. Animals and birds who live nearby...' began washing on shore. There were signs of beachfront erosion. Testing revealed PCP and other chemical contamination, threatening well water and food chain poisoning. This is especially disturbing since seafood is a major part of our diet and primary export. This offshore dumping and oil exploration were completely beyond the resources of our government or our political control. In effect, this is a declaration of war." Ayrton continues.

"The *Golden Quadrant*. Golden in more ways than one. With more blessings, it seems, than we could handle at once. So, the question became, at what price progress? Ecological disfigurement and exploitation, with rigs and drill platforms on the horizon, like skyscrapers? It would have been an environmental disaster of the highest magnitude. An invasion and increase of heavily capitalized influence and all that would have meant. Hotels and casinos. Pizza, burger and chicken franchises." Ayri pauses, deep in thought before continuing his disturbing narrative.

"It would have amounted to a total distortion and eventual loss of our cultural and national heritage and control of our destiny. After the discovery of those energy reserves in the *Golden Quadrant* we particularly studied what happened in Venezuela and Trinidad/Tobago. We became very concerned. Their sudden wealth exceeded their ability to manage it. So, they licensed their wealth away to the energy corporations.

"We did not want that same mistake for Amada. After numerous feasibility studies and years of research, our Dial decided Amada would follow a model of prudent economic growth. Resource and capital preservation and moderate energy production without exceeding our plant capability and managerial capacities. We wanted a business model without licensing agreements so we could prosper slowly and prudently develop our infrastructure, production, distribution and management.

"Somehow our research and planning fell into their hands. We're all but certain it's Amada's arch enemy neighbor. Spañada is responsible for all this. Talk about a banana republic. Their Prime Minister is one of those crazy Caribbean dictators, like the Duvaliers, the Trujillos and Samozas. Mobuto and Geary." Ayri says.

Listen. There. It just happened again. Moments earlier I heard it but paid it no mind. But it just happened twice more. Three times. Birds in the prison yard begin chirping. First light and midnight's deadline fast approach. My dread worsens.

"That was the turning point. That's when *Guiding Star* graffiti and soon thereafter other propaganda began appearing. Then things started happening that never happened before in Amada; at least in modern history.

"Car bombs going off in downtown Salamar, arson in public buildings, sabotage. Our radio, television, internet and phone services were disrupted, cell phone signals jammed. There were financial manipulations and runs on our currency. Counterfeit currency was dumped into circulation. The police monitored suspects but we never had enough to make an arrest or acquire more information." Ayri then says.

"That's why we decided on *Papi's* memoirs. To tell the family story of what was going on in our country. We knew things were changing, but we never imagined this. I swear. I hope you know. You must believe me; we never would have intentionally put you through any of this." He says.

"I know, I know. But this is big, Ayri. Oil, natural gas. Drilling, toxic dumping, sabotage. Real estate and currency destabilization. Terrorism. A crazy dictator. This is high stakes stuff. It doesn't get any bigger. We're not safe. Not now, not for the time being, not in the future. We've got to get out of here; together. Otherwise, they'll kill us. We've got to get out of here before it's too late. Don't be a martyr, Ayri." I say.

"I can't; even if I wanted to. I can't. I won't. Not now, with outside influences in Amada. It's a question of duty. I refuse to desert Amada, so stop asking me. If you know me even a little bit, then you must know this about me. My place is here, with my people. But you, your place is out there." Then he says full of urgency.

"Listen to me, *Q*. Forget about the memoirs. I need your help like never. We'll still be working together but on something much more important and time from different places. You're the only eyewitnesses and lone survivor. That's why you must escape. To do your part." He then explains.

"From now on, this is your assignment. You must tell the world everything that happened here in Amada. You must write the record so we can 'right' the record. Write about what happened to you, to my people, to my country. About everything you saw and experienced here. Write about how freedom and democracy are being strangled by outside forces trying to steal Amada's resources. Use the flash drive. Use it to tell my country's story. Go back to Harlem and write. Write like you've never written before. Write like you'll never write again. Write with all your might. Write, Q. Fight." Ayrton says.

"What are you talking about? How can I use it? I don't have it. I'm glad I don't. They thought I had it implanted. No way; I don't know where it is and I don't want to know either. I don't want to be anywhere near it." I say.

"Listen, Q. It's too late. You already have it." Ayri says.

The birdsongs; my 'proprietary' knowledge about midnight. My forebodings steadily worsen.

"No, no. Stop. Listen. I don't want to know. Whatever you do, don't tell me; don't. I don't want to know. I can't afford to know. If they're willing to do exploratory surgery on someone, count me out. I've got to be able to say, 'I don't know anything about diddley.' That's the only way for me to survive. It's not knowing anything. If I know something, and they torture me – again - then I'm as good as dead. So, just shut up, Ayri." I say.

It's too late, Q. " He says.

"I told you; stop it. I'm serious." I say, covering my ears.

"I'm so sorry, Q. I really am. I didn't mean to get you any deeper into this. But you're the only one. I didn't know what else to do." Ayri says.

Unease, disquiet, nausea, overcome me. "What did you do now, Ayri? What the hell did you do this time? What?"

"I told you. The flash drive; you have it." Ayri says.

"Stop it. I told you. I don't want to have anything to do with it! I'm out. Done. That's all dude kept sweating me about. He kept calling it the *Smoking Gun*. He kept tripping, on and on, about that so-called *Smoking Gun*. Don't you start, too." I say.

"You have it." Ayrton says.

"Stop playing, Ayri." I say.

"No. You stop. Listen, Q. Tag; you're it. You have what everyone wants. Listen to me. This is a race against time in every sense of the word. Go to the *Banc de Paris* in Fort de France. That's where the decryption software and flash drive is deposited along with your salary package in your name. It contains everything you need to know. The applications, send them to your brother the first thing after you leave the bank. He's an attorney, he can file them for us in Washington. Once he has them, he'll know what to do. We can beat that deadline and it will be registered in Amada's name and not some off-shore corporation. Once they find out it will be too late for them to do anything. That's the first leg of the race against time. Filing those papers." Ayri explains further.

"The other information contains names of corrupt energy, hospitality and transportation companies' executives. The Prime Minister's and associates' banking account information. The country's history of dirty tricks in the Caribbean. People in high places, politicians and officials on the take. Their cooked black books. Hydrocarbon, hospitality and travel industries' black payments to crooked, self-dealing politicians. Dates, bank account numbers. Chapter and verse. Everything.

"It's a bombshell. They don't want it seeing the light of day. That's why he kept asking you if it's local or wiki. They're desperate. They don't want it falling into the hands of online media where there's no filter. That's what 'wiki' means. Unexpurgated, that stuff will break the internet. That's why they'll do exploratory surgery on you. They'll do anything to anyone to stop publication." He continues.

"Just press a button. Six seconds; that's all it takes. Six seconds to upload, six seconds to download. Six seconds to send, six seconds to delete. That's all it takes. Six seconds. Once it's out there, it stays there. Once it's deleted, it stays gone. That's all the time there is. Six seconds. Who owns those six seconds? Right now, you do. You do, because you have it. Seeing it to safety, that's the second leg in your race against time." Ayri says.

"Why do you keep doing this? Dragging me deeper and deeper into this? Is this some new parlor game you sick politicians play? 'Kill the Journalist?' You keep trying to get me killed. What? If at first you don't succeed, try again until I finally die? I'm not a party in these proceedings. I'm a writer, I communicate information and opinions about events of the day. That's all. You're destroying my credibility as a journalist and writer and as an honest broker of information. No way I'm trafficking classified information or state secrets." I say.

"Amada is under lockdown. No one else can leave or get into Amada. You're the last man out. Only you can get the information to safety. I can't emphasize how vital those applications are to the fate and future of Amada. You must take it to freedom. Once you're back in New York, once you read it, it will all but write itself. You'll see. Use it to write, *Q*. Write about Amada and about us. Guillermo will see you to safety." Ayri says.

"This is a nightmare. Why do you want me dead? Why do you hate me this much? What did I ever do to you? Oh, I get it. It's because of me and Didi; isn't it? That's why. This is payback. Just come out and say it. That's why you hate me. That's why you want me dead. Because of me and Didi. This is you playing big brother." I say.

"What do you mean; 'me and Didi?' What about you and Didi? Are you saying you and Didi...? Ayri says.

"I'm saying this; why do you keep trying to get me killed?" I say, my hands covering my face and peering at him through my fingers.

"I'm trying to stop you from getting on that ship. That's where you'll die for sure. I'm trying to help you escape so you can write. That's what I'm doing. You're the only witness. That's why you must leave. That's why I must remain behind and do my part. My work, my fate is here. Your work, your fate it's out there. Promise me, *Q!*" He says.

"No. You promise me we'll leave together. That's what *we* need to do. This is bad. If there's enough room for one there's room for both of us on that plane." I say.

"What? And leave my family behind? They'd kill Guillermo. You know me better than that. That won't happen. I told you: my place is here. We don't have much time left. Remember when I offered you the assignment in New York? I told you; the project is bonded. Well, that bond has been redeemed. Your whole salary plus bonus and expense account have been deposited in an offshore account in your name in two separate safe deposit boxes at the *Banc de Paris* in Fort de France. One of them contains the flash drive. They went out per courier with the last diplomatic pouch. It's vital that you take it to safety." He goes on to say.

"Consider the money well spent payment in advance. You've more than earned it. This way, you can say good bye to loud and proud *Harlem High.* No more 'suffer the children unto me.' From now, you are free to work on a new, much more important assignment. The money is the least I can do. I'm responsible for what happened to you here. If something worse happens to you on that ship... That would kill me. There's nothing more dishonorable than having to die more than once, when the first time is out of guilt. Fate, it seems, has chosen you. You have no choice; you must. There's no one else. Once you open the flash drive, we can begin to 'right' the record. Write about what is happening here and let the world know." Then Ayri says.

"You're our last, best, our only hope. I trust you. That's why you must leave. And that's why I... must stay. Besides, some of the most beautiful women in the world are in Martinique. It's absotively breathtaking. It's impossible not to fall in love there. You'll see. Mark my word." Ayri says.

"I'm not shopping for love right now, Ayri. The hell with the money. It's blood money. Listen to me. Go underground, please. Just work in the resistance from abroad. Stop being so hard-headed. There's still time and room for both on that plane. We'll leave together. Staying is suicidal." I say.

"The stakes, they're high. It's that moment of truth for both of us. We must be equal to that moment. It's called courage. Leadership means meeting challenges head on. Leaving family and friends behind to save my own skin doesn't meet that moment. Look, for better or for worse, it's too late. I've got skin in the game. I've been a player for a long time. I can't help it. It's in my blood." Ayrton says.

"Life's not a game. Life's a gift, Ayri. Don't..." I say.

"Life and love, they're the same thing. They're the gift of time, that miracle from which everything else flows. I know this. That doesn't change my responsibility, though. I know your low opinion of politics although I keep telling you I'm a diplomat. You call it 'politrix.' At their best, politics is the art of the possible, and diplomacy the art of persuasion. It is demonstrating humility in victory and equanimity in defeat. Well, for better or worse I am who I am. All those dinner table discussions with *Papi* and growing up in that environment.

"You're no different. You grew up in the arts. Writing, music they're in your genes. We can't help ourselves. We're hardwired that way. Even if I wanted, I can't change what I am. Contrary to what you think and even though you keep calling it 'politrix,' honor and duty, conscience and integrity. Loyalty and principle, dedication and perseverance. These values are important to me. You're no different, Q. They mean something to you, too. You always laugh at me when I say that we're a lot alike. But what I admired most about you when we first met and to this day is your determination, it's your will. You let nothing stop you from writing. You paid a heavy price, too. It even cost you a relationship. But you stuck with your passion, your dream, writing. Well, I'm no different." Ayrton says.

"You keep comparing the two of us when we're nothing alike. I'm as much a politician as you're a writer. I want to get out of here. You want to stay. You have a death wish; I don't. Like you always say, I'm an egghead writer. I think things about things. You're a man of action. You do those things I think things about. We're friends because we're different. Not because we're alike, Ayri." I say.

"Would you turn tail and run when your family, your country, your people need you most? I don't think so either. That would be high treason. We both know what you would do. You would have no choice. You would stay and fight. Any decent, right-minded person would. So, what makes you think I'm any different, even if the ugly American in you thinks Amada is just some banana republic? Otherwise, how could I ever respect myself? I don't want to be remembered that way. That would kill me a thousand times. So, don't ask me to leave again. You're the one who must leave to write about our fight. As you always say, 'writing's fighting'. When done right, the two become the same. You've shown that." He then says.

"Go home and write, Q. I'll stay and fight. The writing and the fighting, once they become one then, with God's help, every little thing will be alright. It's all one love. The journalist and the politician. It must be fate, Q. If so, then surely, we will see each other again. Who knows? God willing, maybe even soon in Martinique? If not in this, then surely in the next lifetime. Until then, *mi hermano*."

"Ayri. I can't go home and leave you behind and abandon you just like that. I'm who won't be able to live with myself. It's not right. Friends don't do that. There's still time. Come on." I say.

"Listen to me, Q. Just like I can't leave my family, you're not leaving me behind. This is my home. This is my country. These are my people. I know every inch, every tree, and every rock of every village. It's in my blood. I'm Amadan. This is *my* fight. I can't guarantee your safety any longer. You must leave. Now, while there's still time. Go home and write, Q. By now, after everything we've been through, we're brothers. I love you like a brother and trust you like the brother you've become. I know I can count on you to carry on from afar for me while I fight from here. You're my best friend, *mi hermano*, Q. My bro, as you say. And what I'm asking of you only a brother could. You're the only one in the world right for this mission. Fate, it seems, has turned you into a man of action. So, welcome to the game, player. Welcome, and play on. That means you must leave, Q. Don't worry about me. I'll be fine. You stay strong. G-Mo will get you out of here. As soon as I can I'll contact you; but only through the *International Red Cross* and IRC only." Then he cautions me.

"And remember; your lead is six seconds. Six seconds to the good. That's your head start. You must guard and grow your lead. Put distance between yourself and danger. Take it to safety. And *Q;* when you walk out of here, whatever you do, don't look back. Don't turn around. Look straight forward. Don't look back until you're safe. Use that flash drive to write. 'Right' the record. Tell the world what happened here. First, though, go to the bank in Fort de France. Then go home. Go back to Harlem City and write. I'll be watching and cheering you on from afar. *Ay!*" We reach the cell door and then embrace. "*Via con Dios, mi hermano.*" He says.

"*Dominus vobiscum* and God's speed, Ayri... Now and always. But don't leave it all up to Him. You take good care of yourself, too. For all of us. Like you said, 'It's all one love.'" I say.

At the dungeon door, Ayri cautions me to remain inconspicuous and never anxious, with collar high and cap brim lowered, before giving Guillermo last instructions. Then, after a final heartfelt hug and best wishes, words of friendship and encouragement, all too soon this unforgettable encounter with this most amazing man, my friend, *mi hermano*, it comes to its end. Crestfallen, I look in his direction as I walk away.

"Don't look back..." Those the last words I hear Ayrton say.

With Guillermo occasionally whispering instructions along the way, we steal through the dark prison corridors. Once outdoors, we proceed unnoticed by jeep to a safe house where, as promised, my passport is returned, along with twenty-five hundred dollars in cash that Ayri enclosed. We then drive along dirt back roads to a remote airstrip, where I board a waiting crop duster propeller plane.

Once airborne and out of harm's way, I feel no joy over my freedom. Instead, I experience flashbacks, in my mind reliving recent events and anxious about the clock ticking toward midnight. At safe altitude, I ask the pilot repeatedly to radio back for any news. But to no end. I'm told that, since no flight plan was filed for this unscheduled flight, for security reasons radio silence, even beyond Amadan territorial waters and skies is crucial until we reach our destination. Desperate with worry about Ayri, in such shock I completely forget about the mysteries of the safe deposit boxes in Fort de France. Three hours later, at dawn we touch down in Castries, St. Lucia's capital. After everything I've been through and dreading what Guillermo predicted will happen at midnight, I can't hold it together any longer. I let go, break down, and cry.

CHAPTER FOUR

DON'T LET THE SUN CATCH YOU CRYING

"You can cry, cry, cry, yes, baby,
You can wail. Beat your head
On the pavement 'til the man
Comes and throws you in jail."
Don't Let the Sun Catch You Crying
Performed by
Ray Charles

Looking back, I somehow managed to survive my ordeal, although barely. Once out of harm's way, in St. Lucia my condition suddenly worsens. So much, hours after arriving I admit myself into Castries University Hospital. Tests confirm elevated protein and creatinine levels secondary to renal lacerations and bleeding. Diagnosis: nephritis. Treatment: dialysis. Prognosis: full recovery.

Not so good, however, my mental health. Psychiatric observation and evaluation confirm multiple axis I diagnoses: PTSD. Depression. Anxiety and adjustment disorder secondary to grief. Rule out current suicidal ideation (self-reported history of recent multiple head banging). Rule out thought disorder. Cranial and burn wounds treatment. No traumatic brain injury. Symptoms include ruminations. Fear and panic attacks. Sleep disruption, night terrors, dysphoria, melancholy. Noise association, crying spells, fits of rage.

But by far, worst are the nightmares. Chronic nightmares, always the same ones. About the goon squad and passing blood. About Ayri and I being blindfolded and executed. Visions of Didi calling out for help. Of our families grieving over our gravesites. Nightmares of the beatings. Feeling those rats and roaches crawling all over me again before I awaken in a cold sweat. In a *maelstrom* of depression, for no outward reason I'm gripped by sudden tremors and fits of crying spells. Nights I shiver curled in a fetal position in search and in need of comfort.

One week later, after discharge from the hospital, although I'm physically much improved, particularly my skull injuries, my frame of mind remains raw. By now, I have contacted my family and alerted my brother about important application papers that will require his immediate attention. News about Amada is sketchy other than accounts of political turmoil, high casualties and human rights violations.

Trapped twixt depression and despair, I'm in a sunken place. Free from the near-deadly past but unable to enjoy the fruits of freedom. Making matters worse, I isolate myself in my hotel room, brooding, haunted by forebodings.

Deep down I have a bad feeling. Although his family is now in exile in Brazil, notwithstanding Ayri's courage and charisma the guard's chilling words have come to pass. At midnight past, just hours ago *Mr. Lucky* beheld the face of God above the firing squad. As much as I don't want to admit it, I know Ayri's gone. There's no reason other than hope to believe otherwise, and hope alone is insufficient.

This new assignment honoring his dying request poses some tough questions and introspection. Questions about my abilities and limitations as well as about this part of the world. A place which on the one hand fosters a spirit as noble as Ayrton, yet on the other hand brutally executes such a rare person's shining life in his prime. How can I understand or reconcile, never mind explain these and other contradictions? There are other hard questions. Who is my interrogator? What is *Guiding Star*? What is their agenda? Who is the Sinister Prime Minister? Even if I hadn't sworn to honor Ayri's dying request, as a journalist I'm duty bound to write about these events. As Ayri said, I've become a player with skin in the game with my own game plan and tactics.

Honoring Ayrton's memory raises other questions, beginning with a personal inventory. What's my mettle? What kind of man I am? I know the kind of man Ayri was. But what is my stuffing? What am I made of? Who am I and what do I hope to become? How near or far along am I? Am I up to the task of honoring my commitment to his legacy?

Any judgment about the kind of man I am and hope to become must remain a suspended work-in-progress. There's no uncertainty, though, about the kind of man Ayrton was or his legacy. He was a hero who twice paid the ultimate price. First, for his country, his 'wife.' And then, when he saved my life. Without Ayrton or Guillermo, I'd never have survived Amada or the Row. His death, particularly the way he died, makes Ayri transcendent. A man of conscience, principle and idealism, ennobled by his supreme sacrifice for his country. In death valiantly smiling into the face of God. Right there, just above the firing squad.

Remembering and commemorating Ayrton humbles me.
Humbled that he placed my life above his own, sacrificing
himself so that I can write his story. He could have left me to
die and saved his own life. Instead, he saved me from that
ship.

A true hero, in life and in death who will always remain my
friend. By far a much better man than I am, but he still
considered me not only his friend but *su hermano*; his
brother. That someone that special, a hero, entrusted me with
such an important assignment touches my core.

To the bitter end, a prince among men felled in the prime
of life, his premature hero's death crowns him king of his
kind. That and indescribably more, that's Ayrton to me.
Thanks to him, I'm still alive, grateful for my life and for his
friendship, I rededicate myself to my commitment to honor
his legacy.

Far from being at peace about everything that went down
in Amada, in order to survive, to heal and write, first I must
face the bitter truth. And the truth means that Ayri – Ayrton is
dead. That he beheld the face of God above the firing squad.
And so, before departing St. Lucia. Before heading to
Martinique. Before writing about recent events. Before
anything. First, I must bid farewell to my best friend, *mi
hermano.*

Early morning, I enter a downtown Castries Catholic church
and, even though I'm not Catholic, I kneel in prayer.

> "Farewell, Ayri. Farewell, good
> And faithful friend, fearless and
> Peerless, exemplar and prince,
> Loyal to the end. That, and so
> Much more, is what you are,
> Your memory forever now
> part of me.
> Farewell and God's speed
> On your soul's journey.
> May Light Perpetual forever
> Illuminate your afterlife's path,
> And peaceful rest be yours.
> May His Mercy comfort us.
> Until our spirits again
> Meet at all days' end.
> Your spirit now free,
> May God commend you,

Q

To His highest rank.
Farewell and peace unto you.
"*Via con Dios, mi hermano,*
Ayrton Villareal Mentis."
"Amen."

CHAPTER FIVE

LITTLE MAN

"Summertime, and the livin is easy'
Fish is jumpin'... There ain't nothin'
Can harm you, so hush, little baby,
Don't you cry."
Summertime
Heyward/Gershwin

Martinique's constant trade winds and evanescent relief
from heat and humidity aren't the only differences
between Amada and nearby St. Lucia. Indeed, as all the
archipelago's islands are distinct from another. Lusophone,
Amada's official language is Portuguese. In St. Lucia, it's
English. In Martinique, a French colony, French is the official
language and Creole the native dialect.

Beyond Martinique's official language, cuisine and currency,
geographically the island's coastline is a near-identical Riviera
replica. Architecturally, Martinique's capital, Fort de France,
resembles Nice or Cannes, St. Tropez or Marseilles, Monte
Carlo, or any other *Cote d'Azur* municipality/principality.

There's something unique, not only in terms architecture,
geography, language and culture, about Martinique. More
different, in fact, than any place I've ever been. There's this
spell, something special, arresting. Something pacific and
peaceful much like the Polynesian Islands, an utter abundance
of natural beauty. That spellbinding, it's impossible to
overlook or not to be seduced by this botanical garden's lush
scenery and eye-popping colors.

In a word, Eden. A menagerie of paradisiacal livestock, its
climate conducive to stocks of exotic fauna, colorful, oversized
butterflies and iridescent lizards. Snow white cockatoos, multi-
colored macaws, parrots and hummingbird choirs, with
crickets sounding like castanets accompanied by tree frog
choirs. The oceans' fruit of the sea bountiful and where every
conceivable variety of florae abound. Wild orchids, mimosa,
and redolent hibiscus bushes exhaling intoxicating fragrances.
Banana trees and pineapple groves. Sweet potatoes and
mangos, guava and papaya fruits. At the island's heart,
nature's tropical, is a rain forest. Towering above it all, the

now dormant volcano that at the turn of the 19th century nearly destroyed Martinique, angry Mt. Pelle.

A tropical arcadia encased by skies and ocean blue alike, Fort de France's bustles cosmopolitanism. Commerce and prosperity flourish here, making Martinique one of the most beautiful places anywhere.

There is an abundance of what I need most. A sanctuary safely ensconced in a perfect nature cocoon, much like Gilead far removed from harm's way, in Martinique my shell-shocked soul soon finds balm. My wounds, physical and mental they begin to sooth and past anxieties gradually recede.

The night I arrive from St. Lucia, a taxi driver takes me to *Hotel Bamboo,* apparently everyone's favorite hotel in southern Martinique. Once we arrive, I hear loud music and party noises in the background. The registration desk is deserted, except an unleashed Doberman sitting on top of it. I send the cab driver to find someone to check me in. He returns to explain that the hotel staff is too busy catering to a large party, and that I should return the next day. We leave in search of another hotel and I finally check in elsewhere shortly thereafter.

In the next morning's light of day, I soon spot that same distinct, lopsided exterior weather worn sign I had seen the previous night. Even from a distance, the scene is enticing. The beach stretch is immense. Tourists and natives mingle. There is plenty of shaded area, with pleasure boats and yachts floating atop, along and dotting the wavy periphery. There are multiple beach soccer games. A picture-perfect scene.

Not much later, I find an isolated stretch of beach and eventually camp out. Later that afternoon, an attractive young woman, accompanied by three small children, arrive on the scene and settle in not too far to me. Medium height and, like most Martinican women, with a deep bronze complexion. Eerily, the woman, she resembles... Didi. Or, is my head just playing PTSD tricks again?

From under my straw hat and behind sunglasses, I observe them as she tends to the children, cautioning them before they run into the water and from the beach, she continues keeping a watchful eye on them. A short time later, she summons the children and, after drying them off and feeding them a snack, then they run off playing again. She makes herself comfortable reading, relaxing, but never letting the children out of sight for too long.

Her attire and accessories, her interactions with the children and their reactions, suggest certain things. But her relationship with the children is puzzling.

While the children appear to be siblings their relationship with her, though playful and loving, is ambiguous. It's unlikely she's their mother; she seems too young, although they do resemble each other. Also, the children appear to address her as a relative. A cousin, a babysitter, or family friend, perhaps?

The oldest child, a boy, appears to be ten years old. The middle child a girl seems around eight years old. The youngest boy appears no older than four or five years old.

From my location, I watch as they spend an enjoyable day at the beach. Melancholy, I recall what happened the last time I was at a beach and her uncanny resemblance to Didi. No sooner, ruminations and recurring depression begin darkening my mood, much like gathering clouds shrouding and darkening the volcano's summit. With thunder roaring, the clouds suddenly burst and sheets of rain send everyone scurrying for cover until the sun gradually breaks through. While gathering my belongings to leave the beach I notice something amiss.

The woman is standing on her tiptoes nervously scanning the scene, worry etched in her face. And for good reason; only two children are with her. In the thick of this sudden, heavy down pour, one of the children - the youngest and the most playful one - he who laughed loudest and longest and splashed the most – he's nowhere in sight. The beach spans over two miles. Between the thinning crowd and sudden cloudburst, he should have been spotted or have heard people calling his name. If nothing else, the rain should have flushed him out. But there's neither hide nor hair of him. Puff! Be gone! Little Man's vanished.

Eventually the cloud burst passes over, and a few of us resume searching for Little Man, fanning out across the beach. The woman paces the beach stretch, then starts running and scampering around the scene on a frantic lookout. Anxious and struggling for composure, quietly weeping she clutches the two remaining children. Then they start all over, running, searching and desperately calling out his name, "Gaetano! Gaetano! Gaetano!"

Once the rain stops and the temperature cools off, no sooner biting sand flies invade the beach and send us rushing for cover again. I jump in the water until the insect swarm passes over. But worse than the insects, it's getting dark. What then?

Q

We continue searching for Little Man, the woman and children by now well ahead of others but, by now exhausted from the weight of the wet sand, their pace soon slows to a heavy-legged stagger. Gnawing at her lips and wringing her hands in anguish, at times she closes her eyes and quietly moves her lips as if praying and repeatedly glances over her shoulder, hoping and praying that Gaetano will appear suddenly out of nowhere.

Up until, we haven't spoken one word. This time, we don't speak either. She doesn't have to. Her worried expression says it all. With her head, she motions to the ocean. Non-verbally she's asking me; is he out there? Did he drown? A water accident? It can't be ruled it out; we are at the ocean. But any drowning on a crowded beach would not go unnoticed and have sparked some outcry. Her fears are justified, though.

By now, what else can she think? Kidnapping? Sharks? Nothing is in our favor, and time running out. Who would have thought he would stay missing this long – by now well over an hour? Calling the police, now? It will be dark before they get here. That would be giving up hope and admitting our worst fears. Fears worsening with the dwindling light and imminent ebb and tide about to ruin any chance of finding Gaetano.

Obviously, what we've been doing, repeatedly combing and scouting the same beach stretch back and forth end to end; running around in circles; covering old ground and bumping into one another. It's just not working. What else is clear is that we need to do something different, and soon before nightfall. Time isn't on our side.

By now, the woman is a wreck completely beside herself as she drops to her knees and angrily pounds the surf with her fists, crying bitterly. Even though I don't know them I'm feeling helpless and deeply affected by their plight and deteriorating state.

While I'm in the water it dawns on me. Based on instinct, abandoning tried orthodoxy, instead I improvise, swimming some fifty yards out to sea, and then parallel the coast line. When the woman sees me swimming in deep waters she assumes the worst, that I spotted or recovered the missing child, and then runs into the ocean screaming. I wave her off, though, and instead she continues running along the beach parallel with my progress in the water.

In fact, the ocean offers a different perspective and better panorama of the beach. A view with a lower horizon, in scale not unlike a child's point of view. Swimming due west eventually I reach the far end of the beach and the vegetation line gradually shifts to coastal rocks and seashells. To one side is a small tackle shop, on the other side two rowboats are tied to a small pier.

There I spot the first clues. Beach toys. A plastic shovel and pail! I race out of the water and onto the rocky beach towards the boats while the advancing tide is about to reach them. I yank aside the boat's drop-cloth covering, but that lifeboat is empty.

But here in the second boat, here he is fast asleep. Awakened from his slumber, once I lift him to safety Little Man lets loose a scream. That sound, like a newborn. The sound of life, music at its best.

By now, the young woman is nearby and when she hears his voice she cries out over and again. "Gaetano? Oh, Gaetano!", her voice trembling with joy and relief. Once on the scene, she collects him in her arms and showers him with hugs, kisses and tears.

Witnessing this touching reunion scene from aside - having been of assistance – is intensely gratifying. A healing experience even. For the first time since my arrest, I feel useful and good about myself again. A cathartic experience and pivotal encounter. A portal moment. Not just a sign of healing and beginning of my recovery. But my re-engagement with life. An initiation and the beginning of Ayrton's new assignment. No longer a prisoner, I feel free. Off the bench and into the game. In Ayri's words, I'm 'a player.'

In many ways, I identify with Little Man. Somehow, we both survived our respective ordeals and, for that as well as for Gaetano and his loved ones, I'm grateful. These reunion scenes and feelings of self-worth suffuse me with inner calm. This time, at least for now, death has been cheated and life triumphs.

Eventually the woman remembers my presence and interrupts her tearful reunion and approaches me and thanks me, repeatedly shaking my hand. We head back to our original beach location, she animated and ever watchful not to let the children out of her sight again, lest lightning strikes twice.

She reminds me of Didi. She isn't wearing a wedding band nor engagement ring, and probably I could have invited her to dinner. But considering the circumstances, it would have been wrong. Lonely for female company and tempted though I am, taking advantage of her misfortune just doesn't feel right.

Instead, after her many thanks and my 'your welcomes,' by then it is almost completely dark, I collect my gear and about to leave, she approaches me again, shakes my hands again and kisses both my cheeks and says, *"Vous êtez un bon homme, monsieur."* (You're a good person, sir.')

We say our goodbyes, particularly to Little Man, before head our separate ways. As I wave goodbye she says. *"Merci et bon chances, monsieur! Au revoir!"* I wave farewell to the woman, whose name I never learned, and then head on my way, full well knowing I'm going to need much good luck along the way. I also know that, contrary to her farewell, I would never again see the woman and children.

***

From then on, nearly every day I return to *Bamboo Beach*. In fact, I almost stayed at *Hotel Bamboo* except for a hearty party going on the night of my arrival in Martinique. At the time, then late in the morning once I finally arrived at my new hotel, I didn't pay much attention to its appearance or detail except for a red-carpet runner leading into the hotel foyer and lobby and spacious registration desk. I just checked in. That night, all I wanted was a hot shower and a good night's sleep.

But twelve hours later? And man, what a visual delight seen in the day's light. *Hotel Madinina,* its *ambience* and accommodations far exceed my expectations, particularly after life on the Row. A Caribbean portrait, this five-story dream hotel with twenty-eight rooms and two rooftop suites is nestled out of sight in Pointe Le Bout's picturesque marina, with its vista of pleasure boats and yachts docked and moored all along the piers and wharves.

Two outdoor cafes and a spacious restaurant flank the boardwalk. Leading to the restaurant are two entrances, one from the street leading also to the hotel lobby, the other entrance from the beach. Both provide brisk beach, boardwalk, street and hotel business. The main dining room's exquisite exterior *al fresco* design offers spectacular views of the marina and of Fort de France. That view. The menu, seafood, French and Creole cuisines. And it's *ambience,* particularly the flying fish. Five-star gastronomy is on offer at *Madinina Sur La Mer.*

The eponymous establishment is owned and operated by a middle-aged Creole widow and her three daughters, who were all business and no play. Throughout the four of them remained aloof, if not outright rude. In all fairness though, the entire hotel staff is equally haughty towards everyone.

Off-peak season and with only half of the hotel rooms booked, when I arrive there are vacancies on all floors, including both fifth floor suites. I'm particularly interested in the suite facing south, towards the marina with its spectacular view of Fort de France in the distance. *Madame* Madinina finally agrees but only on the condition that my hotel bill always be paid in U.S. currency. Back and forth it goes until we reach agreement. In the end, I lucked out more than imaginable.

In contrast and in other ways, *Hotel Bamboo* is different than Martinique's luxury hotels and particularly compared to *Hotel Madinina*. In fact, no place on the island, or anywhere else for that matter, is nearly as unique as *Hotel Bamboo.*

Hotel Bamboo houses a tropical *motif* compound with thatched roofed, bamboo bungalows and cottages scattered along a naturalistic beach stretch, with artificial mini-waterfalls, orchid groves, and banana and coconut trees. Even though its neglected facade and lop-sided, weather worn sign implied a certain lack of social status, *Hotel Bamboo* still oozed a hip identity and casual charm with a laid-back *ambience* all its own.

The hotel's spacious veranda houses a restaurant and bar with good and reasonably priced food and affordable lodgings. With its expansive beach stretch and oceanic panorama, *Hotel Bamboo* is something of a natural meeting ground. According to some guests, while its housekeeping and room service is prompt and friendly, the food and drink, the hotel's mainstay, while reasonably priced, could have been better, especially when compared to *Hotel Madinina.*

But no matter *Hotel Madinina*'s five-star hospitalities and gastronomy, there is this vibrancy about *Hotel Bamboo* and *Bamboo Beach,* as there is about the island itself. *Laissez faire* and heterodox, its landmark bar scene headquarters a vast beach expanse and social check point that draws me back daily during my stay in Martinique.

Seafaring vessels, local fishing boats, catamarans, motor boats, cruise ships, leisure boats and yachts sporting colorful, billowing sails and flags, bob atop the sparkling ocean surface set against a verdant hillside landscape. An aquamarine seascape splashed in sunset crimson suspended between azure skies and turquoise water. Dwarfing it all like Rio de Janeiro's famed Sugarloaf, Martinique's dormant volcano, Mt. Pelle.

Propped up against a lifeboat, thanks to Ayri still alive, instead of nightmares now daydreaming, I feel reinvigorated by my newfound freedom and second chance at life. No longer the stench of jail rot and hot breath of death, instead trade winds wash over me, fresh sea breeze air now fills my lungs.

Sceneries and aromas stimulate to revive my shell-shocked senses. I sit there for hours, lost in reverie and hypnotized between the ocean surf's bobbing mantra and beautiful women passing by. I resume my old regimen, sort of writer's boot camp. Daily swimming, running the beach and regular scrimmages with those amazing Rastafarian soccer players. Thanks to plentiful good food and daily exercise, my hearty appetite soon returns and slowly I feel myself, body and mind binding, gradually mending and healing. In respite from the past, my weight and previous good health, physical and mental strengths return, nearly back to my old self again in preparation for the editorial project ahead.

As *motif*, *Hotel Bamboo* is rich in color, perhaps more so than anyplace else in Martinique. Raunchy and ridiculously funky, host and home of many fond memories. Microcosm and metaphor, symbolic and pregnant with meaning. A microcosm and metaphor meaning not just beautiful crossroads soon to be the site of imminent confrontation with a ghost from the recent past. When, cloaked in the vestments of familiarity, unexpectedly danger will strike. Drawn daily to this spot, I will remain unawares that one of the most dangerous chapters yet of these Caribbean chronicles is about to be written here at *Hotel Bamboo*. Unawares until it's too late, and hell suddenly breaks loose.

Unforgettable for more reasons than one. That's the one, the only, cool *Hotel Bamboo*.

***

On my second evening in Martinique, a rainbow overarches the marina vista and Mt. Pelle, with Fort de France twinkling beyond as I board the ferry. The view recedes in scale as we approach the capital city's Riviera replica in sight ahead, the rainbow gradually dissolved by the fading light.

Adjacent to the Fort de France harbor is the city's botanical garden featuring a statute of Martinique's most famous daughter, Empress Josephine, beloved of Bonaparte. Beyond bustles busy metropolitan life, businesses and offices, banks and department stores, movie theaters and eateries. Also located in the heart of the city are the municipal offices, national ministries and palaces, the university campus and hospital complex.

Perhaps a half a mile beyond that, at *Avenue Charles de Gaulle*, is the line of demarcation where *Centre Ville* Fort de

France ends, with different territory ahead. West on *Avenue Charles de Gaulle*, perhaps a mile down the road, nestled out of sight is an area not as frequented by tourists. The hill region, home to an open-air market, known as *African Market*. A Yoruba portrait, offering every variety of foods, clothing and fabrics, trinkets, potions and powders. Iconography, livestock, *bijou* and *bric-a-brac*.

Beyond *African Market,* way up those steep hills, the poor section of town is located. The hill-side shantytowns where, in addition to cock fights and gambling, local customs and rituals take place. Secret *voodun* ceremonies and rites practiced in *Santeria* temples and *Macumba* dens venerating *Shango*, *Obatala,* and other *voodun orisha* deities and adorations.

Where *patrons* and shaman wield magic and potion spells and enjoy social rank. Elsewhere, political and social graffiti about Bob Marley, about Rastafarians and demands for independence for Martinique and anti-French slogans proliferate throughout the shantytown.

Arguably, one of Martinique's most notable citizen was the renowned poet/essayist/politician, Aimé Césaire. Cabinet Minister and advisor. Literary exponent of *negritude*, the embrace of African aesthetics and imagery in literature, and after whom Martinique's international airport is named.

Clearly though, Martinique's favorite son was Césaire's *protégé,* Frantz Fanon, in whose honor schools, streets, an amphitheater and countless other commemorations are dedicated. Denied school admission despite posting the highest test scores in the country's history, Césaire singlehandedly championed Fanon's cause. Fanon was granted full academic scholarship admission to Fort de France's most exclusive private school, as well as all Martinican children were granted equal education. Once again posting the best grade point average in history, following graduation he attended *Paris Sorbonne* medical school and again graduated top of his class.

Physician and psychiatrist, his anti-colonialism and political activism rooted in his childhood experiences, Fanon's activities abroad were that controversial, as his politics that radical, advocating armed resistance ('For violence, like Achilles' lance, can heal the wounds it has inflicted.'), in certain circles Fanon was perceived as a threat to society. The relationship between Césaire and Fanon, like many other mentor/*protégé* relationships, eventually deteriorated due to philosophical differences.

Q

So much so, his active role in the Algerian Revolution during the 1960's and his activities elsewhere in Africa likely cost him his life. Like Malcolm X and Paul Robeson, Fanon was also poisoned in an assassination attempt. Adding mystique to the Fanon legend, like Patrice Lumumba and Malcolm X, his death was marked by considerable controversy.

Thirty-six years old, he was treated at the U.S. government Walter Reade Hospital near Washington, D.C., at the time usually reserved for ranking U.S. military and government officials and foreign dignitaries. Frantz Fanon died there under mysterious circumstances. Likely at the invisible hands of interested intelligence agencies and their illegible fingerprints. MK-Ultra again? Perhaps.

His activities and mysterious death as well as his published writings, most notably *The Wretched of the Earth,* elevated Fanon, together with Fidel, Che, Malcolm X and King, to mythical stature in Martinique and around the world.

Whatever their differences, crucially both Aimé Césaire and Frantz Fanon were defined by Martinique's natural beauty and their common love for their people, which shaped their respective outlooks and voices.

Eventually I settle in at an *al fresco* Creole restaurant. The food, while excellent, is small-portioned. After months of prison grub, illness and significant weight loss, the big boy in me is still hungry for big boy food portions. To the waitress' astonishment who's already begun placing new settings at the table, I order two more entrees served on one plate and a bottle of *Bernkasteler Doctor.*

Over dinner, I can't help ruminating. Only recently and reluctantly am I coming to grips with Ayri's death. Without him I'd be dead too. So, in that sense I feel his blood on my hands and weighing heavy on my conscience. He saved my life, sacrificing his. That makes him a hero. But if that makes Ayri a hero, then events mark me little more than a coward.

Deep down, I know that's not true. Ayri was uncompromising. He refused to go into exile, even in the face of death. Instead, perhaps foolishly, he stood his ground. It's his country, though, his fight. But his death has now become my fight to carry on in his behalf. More than ever, I'm determined to write about the man I knew, the kind of man I know I'll never become. That, and nothing less, is my solemn duty as his friend, as *su hermano,* his brother. As the trustee of his memory and executor of his Last Will and Testament. As a witness, a victim and survivor of Amada. As a man and writer. Now more than ever, writing means fighting.

The tasks ahead, my responsibilities, my purpose, they're crystal clear. My mind free of doubt and at peace, I vow the justice for Ayri, the justice denied to him in life. Anything short spells failure. A failure of talent and lack of resolve on my part and betrayal of his memory. A permanent stain of shame and coward's living death. Having to die twice, something Ayri abhorred and refused.

En route to *Hotel Madinina,* two things suddenly occur. First, I experience this intense surge, a full-bore adrenaline sensory rush. A metabolic desire like hunger or thirst, so strong. I'm back in that place, reanimated, locked in and ready to do what I'm best at and love most.

Second, I reach a decision. Just like Ayri didn't leave Amada, I'm not leaving Martinique. Hell no. I'm standing pat and staying put. I'm ready to write, and raring for a fight.

Q

CHAPTER SIX

CREOLE CATALINA

"I saw in her face... in her gestures
And attitude the distinct signs of
Independence and pride, which are
So characteristic of her race...
Their soul... is not revealed
Immediately. It requires
Patience and study to obtain
A grasp of it.
At the moment you believe
You have seized it, it is far away,
Inaccessible, incommunicable,
Enveloped in laughter and variability.
Then of its own free will it re-approaches,
Only to slip away again as soon as you betray
The slightest sign of certitude.
And when confused by its externals
You seek its innermost truth, it looks
At you with tranquil assurance out of
The depths of its never-ending smile and
Its easy lightheartedness."
Paul Gauguin

Time has come.

Three days after arriving in Martinique, that Monday morning I finally go to the Fort de France *Banc de Paris* offices to collect the 'blood money.' *Mi hermano's* final act of foresight, friendship and generosity.

In no time I turn melancholy again, in a good way, though. Once again, Ayri was right. Just as he had predicted, exiting the ferry into the Fort de France morning rush hour I see some of the most beautiful women anywhere on earth, one more attractive than the other.

It's obvious why Paul Gauguin spent the early part of his post-impressionist career here, immortalizing the island's landscapes and its women's beauty. Who married a Martiniquaise woman, and whose paintings are on permanent display in Martinique's *Paul Gauguin Museum* in Anse Turin. Or, why war-mongering Napoleon lost his heart, mind and empire over *Martiniquaise* Josephine. They have allure.

But there's more to Martinique and Fort de France than gorgeous women. Tourism bustles and accounts for most of Martinique's prosperity, making Fort de France, with its congested, narrow cobblestone streets, one of the Caribbean's largest capitals. These spices added to the mix account for Fort de France's Mediterranean veneer and Creole flavor.

That busy sightseeing, I lose track of time and arrive at the bank just before lunch. A bank customer service representative escorts me to an office to sign authorization documents. Due to the amount of money and circumstances involved, the branch manager, a jaw dropping beauty, must personally review and approve the transaction. She inspects my passport, social security number verification and other personal information before releasing the funds. Afterwards, she retrieves two keys and then leads me to the bank's safe deposit section where she leaves me in privacy.

Inside the safe deposit box is a *Banc de Paris* cashier's check, double my teacher's salary plus expense account and bonus. Dumbfounded by this sudden inheritance and overwhelmed by Ayri's generosity, his death is just too heartbreaking to find any joy in the money. Instead, I just sit there, shivering at the thought of profiting from his death. I'd give everything for his return. Blood money - Ayri's blood – that's all it is. Disgusted by the thought of it, returning the money is impossible though. Besides, I swore to honor his dying request.

No, bloody that it is, the money's mine now. Mine to cleanse by putting it to good use. First and foremost, by rededicating myself to honoring his memory and writing. Pride aside, as a practical matter I don't have any other choice. The travel money Ayri provided is all but spent and, with little more than the clothes on my back, I'm broke.

Dejected I sit there while the bank official finalizes the necessary paper work. Shortly thereafter she says, "The depositor also enclosed this for you, *monsieur.*" Then she hands me another key and escorts me to another safe deposit box and again tactfully leaves me alone. There is an envelope, addressed to 'Q,' and a small jewelry box containing a metal flash drive, accompanied by another, smaller envelope, addressed to 'Q.'

Opening the letter, there's no bout a doubt it. None. The handwriting; it's his. A letter from Ayri. First the money, and now this. Alive at the time. One last time, this time from his grave, Ayrton speaks to me.

The enclosure reads:

"Mi Hermano, Q!

"On behalf of my family and myself, our deepest thanks for your dedication to our father's biography. More convinced now than ever of your talent and of the biography's success, as well as for other reasons, I have taken the liberty of advancing your salary package to an offshore account at the *Banc de Paris* in Fort de France, Martinique. After everything you've been through already you more than earned it. Besides, this way you can't let your false pride try and talk me out of it. Also enclosed is an item of utmost importance. Once you read it you'll understand its value.

"Much, about which I can't talk, duties of state and such, has kept me busy these days and prevented my greater attentiveness, which is why we haven't seen much of each other lately and for which I apologize. After all, you are my guest and I am responsible for your well-being.

"At any rate, also enclosed are pictures taken at the dinner on the day of your arrival in Salamar. Remember? One of them is of the two of us. A very handsome portrait, if I say so myself. Then, of course, remember, Didi just insisted on having her picture taken with you. Look at the two of you! When you get your picture taken, you're supposed to look at the camera. So why are the two of you looking at each other instead? Hello! And I don't like the way she's looking at you, either. What's going on between you two? I told you; I don't trust you two. That's why I don't like this picture. I'm sure you will, though.

"By far, though, my favorite picture is the one with my parents, my sisters, you and me. I'm telling you, this picture, I love. The tribe. A family portrait. Now you are officially part of the family. You are *mi hermano* – the brother I always wanted. And I wish upon you all the blessings of life as I do for the rest of my family.

"And now, on to the enclosures in the safe deposit boxes. You must take every measure to safeguard it and ensure that its content sees the light of day. It explains itself. Go home and use it to write the truth as it happened. Tell your brother to file the patent applications in Washington. Without them, without you, without your brother, we are doomed. I have every faith in you.

"And so, although we may be apart as this letter reaches its conclusion, our friendship knows no end. Pray for us as I shall continue to pray for you and your safety until, God willing, hopefully someday soon we shall see each other again.

"Until then, stay strong and above all, love life. Which, once you're in Martinique, won't be difficult. It is impossible not to fall in love there. You'll see. Always stay as you are! Only the best for the best - that's what you are!

"Remember; we're always only a thought apart! This time and until the next time, I shall remain, with every best wish, as ever, *tu hermano!* (But never your Brother-in-Law!)"

"*Ay!*"

Signed,

"*Siempre,*

"Ayri"

The jewelry box containing the flash drive's decryption software codes. The money, the letter. The pictures, the USB drive. Events in Amada, everything in between and since. Our history together, Ayri's death; and now this undated letter. Everything. It's all too much at once. I ain't no more good. I slump backwards, feeling ill, dizzy and nauseous. I begin hyperventilating, in the grip of another post-traumatic stress attack.

Upon her return, the branch manager notices my distress.

"Are you alright, *monsieur*? A glass of water, perhaps?" She says.

"*One Scotch, One Bourbon, One Beer* would do me a world of good right about now." I say, quoting a blues song.

"*Monsieur.* We are a bank, not a *bodega*. Whatever is troubling you though, hopefully the money will act like medicine and make you feel better. Now, this is a very large sum, *monsieur*. Do you know how you would you like your funds managed? Perhaps you would you like to open an account with us? How may we be of service to you?" She says.

Eventually I collect my wits enough to discuss options and then make some basic choices. Two thirds of the money I transfer in my teacher's 401-K, my IRA and mutual fund account, as well as replenishing my stateside personal checking and savings accounts.

The remainder, earmarked for living, business and entertainment expenses, I deposit into *Banc de Paris* business and personal accounts. Credit cards are issued, and I make a large cash withdrawal for immediate expenses.

Flush with what politicians' call 'walking around money,' the flash drive back in the safe deposit box, I exit the bank into a bright Fort de France afternoon. With little more than the clothing on my back and my hotel bill due – in dollars - those two things require immediate attention. After shopping, with so many bags I return to the hotel by taxi.

My physical transformation seems to soften *Madame* Madinina's attitude towards me. Although still haughty, her reserve eases somewhat once I pay my bill in dollars, as she

Q

demands. That's why she also agrees to my new proposal; for more dollars.

In return for three months' rent in advance, I want separate internet and satellite TV connections. She agrees but also increases my rent by ten dollars daily; with meals included, twenty dollars daily extra. Still a sweat steal of a deal for what inarguably is the best food I've ever savored.

The money also affords other necessities. Most importantly, the tools of my trade. In addition to my new assignment, I remain dedicated to Dr. Mentis' original biography project and decide to merge them, parallel and intersecting storylines. Two men, father and son, at the frontline of their country's history. I owe them and myself my bests efforts. That begins with replacing the hardware confiscated in Amada and reading the flash drive.

"Do you have a cash discount policy?" I ask the manager of Fort de France's only computer electronics store.

"That depends on how much cash; and what kind of cash. No rupees." The owner, from India, says.

"Oh, no worries. No rupees, no pesos. No monopoly money. I'm talking American dollar bills. I have all the presidents with me." I say.

With a change of expression, suddenly serious he says. "That depends on what kind and how many dollars. You do mean U.S. dollars? The one on the hundred-dollar bill. Next to Obama, him is me favorite president. You have him with you?" He says.

"Oh, yeah. But Poor Richard, he wasn't a president though." I say.

"I knew it. You're not American. Real Americans spend the Benjamins, after President Benjamin, not Poor Richard. I knew it. Get out, Jamaican man, trickster fraud." He says.

"No, Poor Richard was his pen name. He was an inventor, among other things. He played with electricity and kites." I say.

"Ah! See! Him wasn't Poor Richard, him was Prometheus. I knew it. Get out of my store, Jamaica Man trickster." He says.

"Not Prometheus. He played with fire and got burned. Poor Richard flew a kite. Invented the lightning rod, wrote an almanac. Founded a university. He was an ambassador. Stuff like that. He wasn't a president, though. Google him." I say.

"No worries. Me have a special. A one-day-one-hour-only, special cash discount sale for anything over five hundred American Benjamins. A Presidents' Day sale. Me miss Obama.

"Me wish him was still President. Him should be on the money."

"The world misses Obama. Franklin wasn't a President, though. But I'm feeling the spirit of your idea. Let's go shopping." I say.

"Tell me what you want?" The storeowner says.

"It'll be easier if I just show you. Come with me." I say.

He just stands there incredulous, watching me, like a child in a toy store, run amok in his store searching for the tools of my trade. Convinced this must be a hoax, the owner says, "What are you doing?"

I pile items after another onto the sales counters. Two laptops, software suites, all-in-one printers. Two cell phones (one an emergency burner phone), digital cameras, routers. iPod, iPad. Headphones, microphones. Cables and peripherals. The gear I need to set up shop and lock back into writing again.

"You just hit the lottery. Ring it up." I tell the store owner.

"You can't be serious? What are you doing?" He says.

"Today's your lucky day. Go ahead; ring it up." I say but drive a hard bargain. "Everything at thirty percent discount. No taxes. Delivery and installation included. How you cook your books is on you. Take it, or leave it." I say. Who wants what more? He, my Poor Richards; or I, his stuff?

Mouth agape, he stares at me and then says. "You have this much money? Cash? On you? U.S. Dollars? In your pockets?"

"Yep." I say, all the while inspecting the merchandise spread out on the counter. "Yo, I'll tell you what. Throw in those two camcorders and that DVD player. Oh, and tripods; let me get two tripods. That should do it. On second thought, let me get that there telescope. And check bid; give me those binoculars, too. That's it. I'm done. Ring it up." I say.

"No credit cards? No gift cards? No bitcoin funny money? No 'I have to go to the bank first, and then I'll be right back?' Then I end up having to put everything back on the shelves. Cash money. You have that many hard U.S. dollars on you? What? Who walks around with that much money? You know what you want, you see what I have. Now, you show me what you have. You show me Poor Richard. Show me the Benjamins and the other presidents. Then, we can do business. Otherwise, we are wasting our time." He says.

Once he sees the rogues' gallery in hand he says, "No worries.", and we complete the sale.

Laundering the blood money, making bad money good by spending it on this editorial project, is having a medicinal, quickening effect upon me, much like the bank manager said.

Tired of being ripped off by high taxi fares, frustrated by infrequent ferry service (none past ten o'clock at night), and wanting to see more of the island I indulge in a few creature comforts. I rent a jeep a *Vespa,* creature for sightseeing and local runs.

Next, I return to the computer store. Eager to get back to writing, instead of waiting for next day delivery and installation I load the hardware into the jeep. For an additional few Poor Richards, I persuade the storeowner to close shop for the day, and we drive back to my hotel.

That much equipment, we make three trips back and forth through the busy hotel lobby. There, on guard and noting my every move, *Dragon Lady* watches, her displeasure visible. During the second trip through the hotel lobby, my arms full of electronics, *Dragon Lady* suddenly steps into my path, all but tripping me.

"What do you think you're doing? This is a respectable establishment with a reputation to maintain. All these boxes and traffic through the lobby, it's unacceptable. From now on, use the delivery entrance. And another thing; I see you have video cameras and computer equipment. What are you doing? I'm warning you. No boom-boom movies at *Hotel Madinina*! Shame on you.

"I'm beginning to have second thoughts about our agreement. There's something about you. *Vous pensez que je suis stupide?* Yes, I checked your passport. *Mais oui et certes!* You've been many places. Particularly the last stamped entry, Amada. With all that's going on down there? And now suddenly, you show up here?

"Well, whatever you're up to. Whatever's going on upstairs, I don't know; yet. But already, I don't like it. From now on, I will be watching you even more closely. I'm warning you. And remember! No boom-boom movies at *Hotel Madinina*! *Alors, allez! Plus vite!* Before I change my mind. And stay away from my daughters! *Je suis sérieux. Sacré bleu!" Dragon Lady* says.

Not about to use the delivery entrance, no matter her indignation, we continue using the lobby. Again, *Madame Fu Manchu* intercepts us. "I thought I told you two..." She says.

"With all due respect, *Madame* Madinina. What other guests use the service entrance when they take merchandize to their rooms? Who else pays their bill in U.S. dollars? I don't pay my hotel bill in dollars to use the rear service entrance. That smells like apartheid. And no, *Madame*. I'm not a boom-boom movie man. I'm a travel writer on assignment in Martinique for a major American travel magazine found in every airport and travel agency in the world.

"We're supposed to remain anonymous so we can appear objective. Of course, confidentiality agreements prevent me from revealing which magazine or which establishment I'm writing about. I'm sure you understand. It's intended to discourage gratuities and bribes. You can't imagine what a good review does for business. It well could be *Hotel Madinina*, but I'm not at liberty to disclose that. You may draw your own conclusions why I'm staying here. What I can tell you is that I review and recommend and critique hotels, restaurants. Their bed and board, fare and service. How helpful they are in accommodating their guests' special requests. Things like that. "We use a scale, a star system. A hospitality rating that measures intangibles such as promptness of services and courtesy. Admittedly, our star scale has bias, but we all do. That's human nature. On balance though, our reviews and recommendations try to take everything into consideration.

"And by the way, *Madame*. *Sur La Mer*, the food, the flying fish. It's simply superlative. It's received our highest rating. But I've said more than I should. I'm sure you understand.

"And while we're talking, two more small favors, if I might. First, we'll take room service lunch for my associate and me. I also rented a jeep. So, I'm going to need a garage parking space. Oh, and one more thing I almost forgot. I also rented moped. I'll need parking for that, too. Just add it to my bill. As you can see, we have our hands full. So, please excuse us, and thank you in advance." I say.

Volte-face, hard-hearted *Madame Fu Manchu* turns *Madame Butterfly*. "*Alors*, a travel writer? You say you need parking? Late lunch? *Pas problems*. Whatever your needs, *monsieurs*. Of course, we'll take your purchases to your suite. And rest assured, parking arrangements for your vehicles are available; No extra charge. And please do let us know if there's any other way we may be of service to you. After all, hosting you is *our* privilege." She says, then busies the staff, who relieve us of the boxes and take them upstairs.

"And what you said about your little girls, *Madame*. Frankly, I take great..." I say.

"You mean my granddaughters?" She says.

"Granddaughters? The three young ladies, your sisters. No? You mean? *Jamais*. You look so young, *Madame*." I say.

"*Très charmant, bien sûr. Merci beaucoup, monsieur.* But they are my daughters. Those are my children's children." *Madame* says then, visibly flattered departs the lobby.

After lunch, with Mr. Guptar's help we complete setup within two hours.

First off, I forward Amada's patent applications to my brother for immediate filing. Then I lock into writing with vim, vigor and little sleep, and begin unpacking the flash drive's content.

It is voluminous, chronicling the economic and political intersections between hydrocarbon energy companies and the travel and hospitality industries. The nexus between the military and weapons contractors, suppliers and shady buyers.

Central to all this is a notorious, shadowy corporate security organization. Its Caribbean theaters of operations are centered in the Lesser Antilles and *Golden Quadrant*, near Amada. The island of Spañada under Geremi Quarrles, Prime Minister for the past twenty-five years, and his security apparatus. Initially *Mongoose Squad,* and lately known as *Guiding Star*.

Even to the non-forensic eye, the data is overwhelming and incriminating. There are records of financial payments for ghost goods and non-services rendered. Multiple fictitious third-party billing statements and duplicate bookkeeping totaling hundreds of millions of dollars.

Although dense with information, the decryption software's spreadsheets make overview easy. Details of international financial transactions and paramilitary security contractors' activities in the region. Account holder names, bank drafts and electronic fund transfers. Fake invoices, billing and fees for phantom services. Promissory notes and signature cards with different names in the same handwriting. Corporate balance statements and credit cards activities. Email correspondences, account holder deposits and withdrawal activities. Straw cashier checks purchase and disbursements. Irregular account activities and payments marked as 'services for cash.' Evidence of self-dealing. Everything, kit and caboodle. White collar crime as an art. As Ayri said, the story all but writes itself.

Next, I return to the computer store and buy every flash drive. Using the attached decoding software, I copy the content of the original flash drive onto five new flash drives.

On five other flash drives, I separate into categories of information for easier reference according to subject category.

The remaining flash drives I purchased I destroy so that no one else can make any copies of the information. I also take special precautions for Ayri's original flash drive by returning it as well as the ten flash drives to the bank safe deposit box, along with a separate set of written personal instructions, which I give to the bank branch manager for safekeeping. Insurance policies. A dead man's switch, in case something happens to me.

With these redundancies in place, once I finish working from one of the flash drives, I delete its content and upload my daily work product to a secure university server account.

This way, the entire flash drive's content is never on any laptop or flash drive at any one time, in the event I'm hacked or my laptops are stolen again.

In terms of composition, I decide to merge Dr. Mentis' biography with recent events in Amada, told from Ayri's perspectives. Three voices with overlapping storylines and intersecting experiences. Father and son, their struggle for Amada's future. Their experiences, including his untimely death, recounted by this journalist, beginning with my own experiences on the Row. Parallel narratives and overlapping storylines with interwoven plot elements, told in different voices and tenses. No small editorial ambition.

Other than backing up my daily work product, for this part of the assignment I take no extra personal safety precautions. No one here knows me, and I'm completely locked into writing. My social life on this a beautiful island consists of writer's boot camp on *Bamboo Beach* and occasional ferry rides into Fort de France for personal business and local shopping trips by moped or jeep.

One day shortly before noon, I summon the courage to do something I've been wanting to do since my arrival in Martinique. After some banking business, I invite the *Banc de Paris* branch manager to lunch. Pure fine, she also speaks fluent English, a benefit since my French isn't, and my Creole is non-existent.

Having set up my accounts, she knows a bit about my background but declines my invitation.

There's something about her, though. Knowing I shouldn't, I persist. But once again she refuses my invite.

"Why not? Come on." I say.

"You're American, *n'est pas?*" She says.

"Yeah. You know that. Why? I know Trump made us look bad, but I'm more like Obama. Come on." I say.

"You don't look like Obama. And that's not what I mean. It's just you Americans. You're so... what's the word? Pushy?" She says.

"Well, true, that we are. What else do you know about Americans?" I say.

"That Americans are pushy and refuse to take no for an answer. Everybody knows that." She says.

"Interesting. Anything else about Americans that everybody knows? Everybody, except me?" I say.

"Beyond that; I don't know? You're the only one I know. And you're still being pushy, even though I told you 'no;' twice. But my father and brother are pushy sometimes, too. So, you see, I think I know all about pushy." She says.

"Well, if Pops and your bro are also pushy then, according to you, that makes them Americans too. So, that means you're American too? But hey, it's all good. America is a big hemisphere." I say.

"Actually, America has two hemispheres. I'm from Martinique. In Martinique, we live in the southern hemisphere. But then, everyone knows only one country takes the name of both continents." She says.

"There you go again with 'everybody knows;' and thanks for that Americas geography lesson. Look, it's almost lunch time. What are you going to do on your break? Are you hungry? How about some ice cream or something to drink? Come on. You've been indoors all day. Let's take a walk, get some fresh air. Your lungs will thank me.

"I'll tell you what; just call it a business lunch. We can discuss my account management options and I can deduct the lunch as a business expense, if that makes you feel better." I say.

"That's funny." Her head still slightly atilt, one hand on her hip, she smiles. "*D'accord.* Let me finish up. Meet me in an hour." She says.

I leave, purchase a large bouquet of flowers and then return to the bank an hour later. Once she emerges, I offer her the bouquet.

"*Quelle surprise. Merci beaucoup.* They're beautiful." She says, smelling and admiring the flowers.

"Not as beautiful as you. Thanks for your company. Look. See what you just did?" I say.

"What? I didn't do anything." She says.

"Yes, you did. There, you just did it again. See? Wow! How do you do that? You make flowers smile. That's magic. Do it again." I say.

She blushes as we shake hands and I reintroduce myself. "Everyone calls me *Q*, though." I say.

"*Q*? You mean, like...?"

"Yeah... like in the alphabet. It's the initial of my first name." I say.

"*Q*? Cool name. I'm Catalina Canals." She says.

Being a tourist, I ask Catalina to choose a lunch spot. We leave the bank behind us and stroll along the ancient cobblestone streets amid midday pedestrian and motor traffic. Past vendors, through the botanical garden, down a side street, around a few corners, and into a trendy bistro; *Balcon.* Catalina has a few words with a waitress, who leads us up a flight of stairs. We're then seated at a balcony table with a splendid view of the lively street scene below.
"I love balconies." Catalina says.

Thanks to the Creole/French art of living life, for the next two hours we enjoy a leisurely lunch. Conversation with Catalina is easy. She is full of questions. About New York, Harlem City, life in the United States. About my impressions of Martinique. In no time, she proves to be comfortable company.

So much, that between her appearance and the balcony *ambience,* I feel myself becoming infatuated. Knowing I want to see her again, I mention some of Martinique's attractions. The rain forest and the remote northern part of the island, as well as the *Paul Gauguin Museum* and other places I want to visit. Then I invite her to accompany me sightseeing one day.

"That's interesting; very interesting." She says.

"Why? Because I want to see you again? Well, I guess I'm just a 'pushy' American gladly guilty in the name of love as charged." I say.

"No. The places you mentioned. Nature, art. You didn't say anything about the usual tourist destinations. The casinos, night clubs. *Bodega* hopping, the naked beaches. You receive diplomatic pouches with lots of money from war zones.

"And that letter you gave me; in case something happens to you. What do you do that makes you thinks something might happen to you? What do you do?" She says.

"That's what I'm trying to tell you. In the fullness of time, all mystery will reveal itself. The first step on our journey, though, is this: Go out with me, then I'll tell you what I do." I say.

"'Guilty in the name of love as charged?' 'In the fullness of time?' 'Our journey?' Who talks that way? You're funny." She says.

"You heard me; I want to see you again. That's what I said. I'm a proud man, Catalina. Don't make me beg too loud or too long." I echo Ayri's words.

"Actually, you chose a good time to visit Martinique." Catalina says, pointing to a prominent sign, *Le Ballet Martiniquais*, announcing a seaside arts and cultural festival.

"It is our biggest festival. All the biggest stars from Martinique, every year they come home from everywhere. From as far as Paris. People come from other islands. All *centre ville de Fort de France* becomes a pedestrian zone. No cars. It is our annual *carnaval*. We can go. You will see the best of my country." She says, to my surprise accepting my invite.

Le Ballet Martiniquais, that Saturday the national dance theater night puts on a rousing performance, its choreography is pastiche, unorthodox blends of classical ballet and colonial court elements and Creole rituals set to syncopated Latin-African polyrhythms. Distilled, the genius expression of Creole culture and customs.

Carnaval, a showcase produced by Martinique state television and broadcast live, in addition to *Le Ballet Martiniquais*, *carnaval* features multiple live music and theater performances with street magicians and clowns, jugglers and vendors. A festival atmosphere, flavorful aromas fill the air amid a colorful spectacle of crowd scenes. Steel drum music, Rastas and hippies, tourists and natives. Lovers and singles on the make. Young and old alike, they become a multitude. Here, if only briefly, the hoi poloi and Fanon's *Wretched of the Earth,* we rub elbows.

Ayri was right. Martinique is special. It's impossible not to fall in love here. So much so, between the occasion and *carnaval's* atmosphere and Catalina's beauty, combined they are having an arousing effect upon me, particularly after life on the Row. Following our fun date, we linger at a sidewalk *café* over food and drink.

"One day you show up at the bank looking like a beach bum and all beat up, your head bandaged. You looked like a mummy. But the next week? And *voila!* You are *suavecito*, well dressed. You stay at *Hotel Madinina* in the marina. You drive a jeep. You have lots of money. I'm not even talking about all the money you transferred to America. I asked you before, and you said, 'in the fullness of time,' and this 'journey' you're on." Catalina continues.

"Something doesn't feel right. Someone suddenly showing up with that much money, asking me out? I think; who is he? Who knows? Maybe you are cartel? Well, are you? Is that it? You are cartel? *Oui?* Tell me." Catalina winks at me.

"Am I 'cartel?' 'Cartel?' What does that mean? 'Cartel?'" I say.

Then, leaning over the *café* table, she whispers. "Maybe, all that money? Maybe it is cartel money? Maybe you launder cartel money at my bank? Maybe you think, if you flirt with the bank manager, she will keep laundering cartel money for you? So, tell me. You are cartel; *oui?* Is that why you wrote that letter in case something happens to you?" Catalina becomes animated.

"Don't lie. Never lie to the Creole. The saints and spirits of old, they will know, and I will never speak to you again. So, you are cartel; yes? You know? Narcotics. Because if you are, then I'll leave this second. Is that why you asked me out? To launder your cartel narco money?" She says.

"'Cartel narco money?' I'm not a narco dry cleaner..." I say.

"You're not what? Not a 'narco dry cleaner?' What's that? Why did you just use that expression; 'narco dry cleaner?' I didn't use those words; you did. Is that your cartel title? Is that what you call yourselves; 'Dry Cleaners?'" She says.

"What?"

"That much money? What else can I think? I will not lose my job because of a 'Dry Cleaner.' I've worked too hard. No. This; us going out. I think this is... It was a bad idea. So now, now, I think I must go home." Then she rises.

"Wow! This is beyond how dare you. You saw the checks. You cleared them. You know they came via diplomatic pouch. "The 'cartel' doesn't have number-controlled diplomatic pouches. You've seen my passport more than once. Maybe you're right? Maybe this, us going out, maybe it was a bad idea. But before you go, why don't you let me explain? If you still want to go home, I'll take you or get you a taxi." I say.

"I don't need anything from you. I only know what I see. That's a lot of money. Where did it come from? You have so much money at my bank. Why not an American bank? Why did you ask me out? Why?" She says and then sits down again.

"No. No cartel." I laugh her off. "I'd never do anything to jeopardize you or your job. I'm a writer here on assignment. That money is salary and expense account." I say.

"What kind of assignment?" Catalina says.

"I can't talk about that. It's confidential." I say.

"A cartel assignment?" She says.

"Stop. It has nothing to do with any 'cartel.' I'm not a 'Dry Cleaner' but I am under a confidentiality agreement and can't talk about what I'm working on." I say.

"Look, the cartel is everywhere, even Amada. So, what did you do in Amada? Were you in that revolution there? That's right, you can't talk about your work because of your 'agreement,' but it's not for the cartel. So, what? I guess that means you can't talk about your other confidentiality agreement then either?" Catalina says.

"What other confidentiality agreement?" I say.

"The other one. You know. Your wife and children. What do you do? Leave your wedding ring in your hotel room when you go out? What are your children's names? Do you have pictures of them with you? Maybe on your cell phone? Or in your hotel room with your wedding ring? Show me your phone." She says.

"You're a suspicious woman." I laugh.

She becomes angry. "I'm not joking. Just like I don't go out with Dry Cleaners? Let me tell you something else; I don't go out with married men. I will never steal another woman's man. That must hurt. The saints and spirits won't haunt my bed with that kind of pain. Never. The axis knows everything." She says.

"No wife, no children; honest. Look. See? No ring, no tan line on that finger. And while we're at it; with whom do you spoon?" I say.

"I don't know what that means?" She says.

"It means; who's sleeping in your bed?" I say.

"You don't know me to ask that kind of question." She says, aloof, near incommunicable, as if the question had offended her pride and soul.

"Oh, but you can ask me? I think you're right. This really was a bad idea." I say.

"That's because you're a man, and men lie to women like it's a sport. But I don't need to lie. You need to know my rules, though. Just like I don't see drug dealers and married men? Well, I don't go out with tourists either. Those are my rules. But thank you for doing business at my bank." She says, remote and nearly unapproachable.

"Wow, you really are an angry bird. Who hurt you? This is a bad idea getting worse. Look, you're the only person I know here. I just thought... Never mind; that's alright." I say.

Her mood now variable, suddenly full of easy lightheartedness at my bewildered expression, she says, "You should see your face."

"That's because I don't get it. I really don't. I mean, okay, I get it about not going out with drug dealers and married men. But tourists? Since when is being from another country a crime? 'Don't date tourists' isn't one of the Commandments. When we had lunch together a few days ago and nothing bad happened, even though I'm a tourist. We just attended the arts festival together, and there was no natural disaster; even though I'm a tourist. Whenever I come to the bank…" I say.

"You come to the bank every day. Recently, it's twice a day." She says.

"And what do you think is the real reason I come to the bank every chance I can think of? Do you really think I like writing in a vault? I don't think so, either. Look, it's not my fault you make flowers smile. You make me smile. You're pure fine, that's why. Come on, Catalina. That's right. Finally! You're smiling. After all this cartel, wife, baby mamma, tourism drama. Finally, you smile happy." I continue.

"Please don't go. What's with you? You're hard to figure. The moment I think I'm getting to know you, suddenly you pull back and slip away, only to pop back up again with your smile. No one's ever kept me off balance like this. What are you doing to me?

"Listen to me. Nothing bad is going to happen. You're safe with me. I'm not 'cartel.' I'm not married. Don't think of me as a tourist or a 'pushy' American. It's not my fault, I can't help where I'm from. Just think of me as a person. Think of me for who and what I am; a writer. But don't hold being a tourist, being an American, things I can't help, against me. That's not fair. It's already rough enough out here as it is." I say.

"I didn't say that. What I'm saying is, it must hurt if you meet someone, if you fall in love, and then the day comes, and he must leave. I don't want that. That's why, just so you know, so there's no misunderstanding. You are a nice man, but I don't go out with tourists. I'm not one of those women, some tourist's *puta* vacation fling. Those are my rules." She says, distinct pride and independence mirrored in her gestures and attitude.

"You don't look like a fling to me. You look like I'm crushing on you the more I'm around you. All I want is for you to like me back. And I think you do; don't you?" I say.

"You're very sure of yourself; aren't you? It's true. You Americans are really aggressive." She says.

"I'm just keeping it real. That's all. I know I like you. And you haven't said you don't like me. Well, that's keeping it real, too." I say.

"I know I'm not being fair. It's just something I've always believed. I'm not sitting around waiting if my tourist will return next year. So many women do that, but I refuse. I will stay by myself first. But I don't want to talk about that anymore. You have been very kind to me. I had a good time tonight. And for the flowers, again thank you very much." Catalina says.

"Well, I'm going to do my best to make you break your rules and make it hard for you not to like me. So, how about we go to the beach next weekend? Or I'll start coming to the bank three times a day every week. Look, I had a good time. You just said you did, too. I'm glad you did. I want to see you again. That's all. Come on." I say.

"You refuse to take 'no' for an answer; don't you? But you're right. I had a good time tonight; and at lunch. But especially tonight. I wouldn't have gone by myself. I would have stayed home and watched this on television. But it's not the same thing. So, thank you for escorting me, Q. Besides, a woman doesn't have to say words. Otherwise, I wouldn't go out with you. But you know this." Catalina says, then adds.

"Now that I think about it; I can't remember the last time I was at the beach. It was forever ago."

"How can you live in paradise and not go to the beach?" I say.

"I'm not a tourist, I must work. Besides, there're too many tourists at the beach. I don't want people thinking I'm another tourist *puta*." She says.

"You're serious about that 'tourist' *'puta'* thing. Besides, you'll be with me." I say.

"*Alors*, that's what many women do. For some, it's a way of life, an industry. On the beaches, at the casinos, in the clubs. At the hotel bars and *bodegas*. I won't let people think that about me.

"You're right, though. Being with someone is different. Just imagine; being able to relax by the ocean. That'd be like a vacation. I'd become the tourist. That does sound like a nice idea. I'd like that. Maybe we can have dinner where you stay? They say *Madinina* has the best food." Catalina says, smiling with easy light-heartedness.

"The best food anywhere on planet Earth." I say, adding. "On one condition."

"Oh, oh. What's that?" She says.

"The weekend." I say.

"The weekend?" She says.

"The weekend. The whole weekend." I say.

"Yes? And? What about 'the whole weekend?'" She says.

"You heard me. We spend the weekend together, the entire weekend. Friday night, Saturday and Sunday. Breakfast, lunch, and dinner at *Madinina's*. Every day, every night. We get to know each other. Pack a suitcase. Better yet; clothing optional. We'll take room service." I say.

"What?" Catalina says.

"What didn't you understand? 'Pack a suitcase?' 'Clothing optional?' Or 'room service?'" I say.

"You're unbelievable. You really are." She says.

"Well, yeah; I'm American." I say.

"In your words, 'in the fullness of time' you will know. So, please stop pushing. I'm getting tired now. Please take me home, Q." She says.

After dropping her off, between thinking about her and driving on pitch black roads back to my hotel I end up completely lost. Driving on the beach though gives me time to reflect.

Other than Ayri and family, Catalina is the only acquaintance I've made since arriving in the region, and I haven't felt this alive even before I got here. Such a rush, I can't wait until next weekend. Throughout the drive back to the hotel, with yet another gift from Ayri, I feel myself falling in love with Martinique, and with Catalina.

So much so, for the first time since my arrest and escape from Amada, not only do I sleep soundly for more than eight hours; and without flashback nightmares.

Except for daily boot camp, that week I'm completely locked in writing and editing. That Friday morning, Catalina calls to let me know to pick her up on Saturday morning.

After five days of non-stop writing, the wait for the weekend is more than worthwhile. Ten o'clock that Saturday morning, I pick her up from her job. To my surprise, Catalina brings a suitcase. We purchase food and beverage and then head to *Bamboo Beach* and soon settle in a shaded and sparsely populated beach area.

Whatever the setting, in the past at work, this morning, she's dressed casually with little jewelry or make-up. A baseball cap and a white T-shirt featuring a brightly colored macaw, khaki shorts, espadrille sandals, with a large straw beach bag hanging from her shoulder.

From under my straw hat and behind sunglasses I observe her as she removes her baseball cap, loosens her hair and then begins disrobing. Simply stunning, she's bioluminescent and cinnamon all over, clad only in an emerald green bikini, with both cups spilling over and more beautiful than I ever imagined. Unpretentious and at ease with herself, there's something about her. In the words of Paul Gauguin, 'a...smile of tranquil assurance and easy light-heartedness.' Sensing my stolen glances, she blushes slight embarrassment, smiles, then offers me something to drink.

The next hours we spend at the beach before enjoying a late lunch and afterwards taking in a movie. Later that evening, we attend a cruise ship dinner party hosted by relatives of Catalina.

The occasion celebrates the return of her cousin, a recent medical school graduate in France who's about to hang his shingle in Martinique. Plentiful spicy good foods, choice beverages amid flowing conversations are on generous offer, the hospitalities set to pulsating Afro/Latin polyrhythms. In all, a primer in Creole and Caribbean customs.

Thankfully many guests speak English. A good dancer, Catalina is at ease performing these intricate dance steps. And although I am envious of her occasional dance partners, who are far better dancers than I am, at the same time I'm able to admire her from afar and congratulate myself, proud that she is my date. She's that stunning.

Most of the evening we spend talking or sway dancing to tropical melodies until all too soon the cruise ship docks in the marina. By now past midnight, we cross the catwalk and adjacent boardwalks leading to *Hotel Madinina*, closing the white metal marina gate, leaving behind us a busy day's events.

Closing the marina gate turns symbolic, with a new set of new discoveries ahead of us.

The hotel suite's double doors open to a long hallway. Master bedroom with wrap around balcony, adjoined by a large bathroom with sauna and steam room areas, are to the one side. A wardrobe walk-in closet/dressing room and storage area, with another bedroom and full-sized bathroom, are located on the other side of the hallway. At the end of the hall are spacious living and dining areas that I've converted into office space.

Open sliding glass doors in the bedrooms, living and dining areas circulate the trade wind's constant salt air breeze, naturally cooling the interior. A wraparound, half roof balcony deck offers a panoramic view of the marina below and Fort de France in the star-bright beyond.

Catalina kicks off her shoes and rushes to the deck. Facing the vista, the trade winds' sea breeze caressing her figure, she revels and absorbs the scene.

"What a view of my city, my country. It is huge. Half the roof. Brick grill and hammock. Bedding with the mosquito net. Table and lounge chairs by the master bedroom. Cameras, a telescope. *Mon Dieu!* You sleep out here; don't you?" Catalina says.

"Except when it rains." I say.

"You live well. This is an office. You really are a writer. I owe you a big apology about the narco cartel. I was wrong. I'm so very sorry. I didn't mean to insult you." She says.

"No blood, no foul. No narco cartel, no apology needed." I say.

"Still, I was... "She says.

"No worries; really. I'm easy like that." I say.

"Why the cameras and telescope?" She says.

"The telescope is for the heavens. That bright, you can count every star. The camcorders? I don't know yet. Maybe a documentary? It's more like a feeling. I'm just learning how to use them. Filming the harbor, the sunset. Stuff like that. They could come in handy one day. You never know." I say.

"May I read something?" Catalina says.

I'm ambivalent about her request, always uncomfortable whenever others read my work, particularly unedited work product, never mind in my presence. Denying her, though, would be rude and only dampen our new friendship. Besides, she deserves to. She's become important to me. So much so, I even started writing about her.

I open the laptop to the work-in-progress, the chronology and description of events in Amada, and then take a walk along the beach.

Not much later, I return upstairs. Wafting steam and perfume co-mingling hint of a recent shower. I find Catalina on the balcony, still reading. I also shower.

Once I emerge, the living room area is deserted. The laptop sits closed on the desk. The sliding doors to the balcony are wide open. Somewhere through the dark laments a nightingale in keys minor. Up high in the night sky, a cloud drifts across the moon's full face.

Q

On the balcony, suspended between the twinkling firmament above and the reflecting pool below, stands Catalina facing me, a satin bedsheet wrapped around her *pareos* fashion, her arms casually extended leaning against the balcony railing, her expression wide-eyed and aglow. The yacht-dotted marina and catwalk below in frame, the balcony the scene, the full moon as if her halo, her portrait is sublime.

For the longest I stand there, spellbound by life's supreme morpheme before me.

"It's true?" Catalina says.

"You're so beautiful... I can't even talk. Is what true? That I'm crazy about you? In the words of Bootsy: 'The answer to the question is very yes. Very yes' indeed." I say.

"No, seriously, *Q. Gaetano? C'est vrai?*" She says.

"Little Man? Yeah, it's true." I say.

"And that in Amada you were accused of being a spy and were on Death Row? Drowned, tortured, burned? That why your face was so swollen, your head bandaged? The Last Cigarette? And the interrogator? The exploratory surgery and fake execution? But somehow you escaped? All these things really happened to you? It's true?" She says.

"Yeah. I was 'the last man out,' as Ayrton called it. With help. That, and lots of luck. But yes; it's true." I say.

"I looked at the pictures, too. Your friend, Ayrton, he was a very handsome. How did you meet?" She says.

"We were university students together." I say.

"It's a nice picture, the two of you and his family. You two, you look like brothers. And the woman? The one who was arrested with you. The one in the picture together with you. She's beautiful. She is your friend's sister?" She says.

"Yeah. That's right." I say.

"She is your woman; yes?" Catalina says.

"A long time ago; yes." I say.

"Did you really... bang your head... trying to...?"

I don't answer.

"Also, you write that you don't have more than six seconds. What does that mean?" She says.

"I can't... I just can't talk about that. That's part of what's confidential." I say.

"Well, if all you have is six seconds... Six seconds? That's no time at all. You can't do anything in six seconds. Blink your eyes maybe? I don't understand. But whatever it means, I hope you gain more time. You will.

"Anyway. So, your friend... you were writing his father's biography. Then, before you escaped you promised your friend you would write about Amada? He's the one who deposited the money along with the computer stick. Is that it? Am I right?" Catalina says.

"That's right. All that and then some. I just haven't gotten to the 'and then some' part; yet. But I will. I will." I say.

"Do you still have nightmares every night?" Catalina says.

"Just about. Until recently, that is, when I met you." I say.

"But there's something I don't understand. You have the money. Why haven't you returned to New York? Why are you still here?" She says.

"Because I'm not running away. Ayri didn't run, and I won't either. This is where all this went down, in the Caribbean. Why leave the region and then write about it? That doesn't make sense when I can stay here and write about what happened. I promised myself I'm not leaving until I've have a finished manuscript in Ayri's name. And I'm not cutting my hair until I do, either." I continue.

"Plus, your part of my decision, too. I already told you; I'm crushing on you. I'm crushing hard, Baby Girl." I say.

For the longest, wide eyed she just stares at me. *"Mon Dieu!* It's very good. You've been busy. Almost three hundred pages. It's sad and scary. Sometimes it's even funny. The way you describe your friend and the guards and the names they called you, I didn't want to stop. It makes me want to know what happens next and how it will end. But why did your friend keep calling you German if you're an American? That's something else I don't understand. The German cartel, maybe?" She says.

"That's another long story. I'll tell you one day. But no. No German cartel." I say.

"Thank you for letting me read your writing. It's very good. Now I understand." Catalina says.

"Thanks. But what is it you understand?" I say.

"You. Why you are so quiet, so serious. Why you always seem so sad. You never talk about yourself, unless I ask. Sometimes you just stare into space. It's because of what happened to you. You almost died. You are haunted. Grieving, healing. Reading this helps me understand you much better. Thank you for allowing me to read your work. I also read what you wrote about me. I didn't know. Thank you." She says.

"Well, now you know." I say.

"What you wrote about me, the way you write. It's from the heart. You speak like a child. Honest, touching, very easy to understand. Writing, it's your way of talking." Says Catalina.

"I wrote about everyone important to me since I've been here. And, other than Ayri, no one's been more important than you." I say.

"Thank you. But when I read what you wrote; you keep blaming yourself for what happened to your friend. Why?" She says.

"I can't help it. I should have done more to save him. I could have stayed longer instead of running the first chance I got." I say.

"But then you would be dead too. Don't think that. It's not your fault. It's not your country. It's not your fight. Time heals. Time tells, too. Who knows? Maybe, your friend, with His Grace, is still alive? Never give up hope." Catalina says.

"I'm not. But there isn't much hope left. It still hurts. It's getting better, though. Thanks to you, I'm feeling better. It's funny. You know; the last time I saw him he told me that I'd fall in love in Martinique. He said the same thing again in the letter he deposited at the bank that you gave me. He made all this happen. He could have deposited the money elsewhere. As usual, Ayri was right. I met you. That's why thinking about Ayri, talking about him, it hurts all the time. It just won't go away." I say.

"Well, if your friend, Ayrton, was right, then you must continue to keep faith, like he had faith in you. You'll see. Give yourself credit too, though. No matter what your friend predicted, what he liked in you, I see those same things." Catalina says.

"What's that?" I say.

"That you are a good man. When you said not to think of you as a tourist but for what and who you are, a writer. That you can't help where you're from or what you are. It makes sense. I don't want people looking at me or *Martiniquaise* women as tourist *putas*. When I look at it that way, I get it. It's the same thing. All I see is the person is good. When I read what you wrote, all I read is a good writer. The story about how you saved Gaetano..."

"I didn't save Little Man..." I say.

"Yes, you did. You found him. You got there before the tide took the boat out. You saved him. You did. Ask him or the woman with him, and they'd say the same thing. *You* saved Gaetano. When I read that. What you did for someone you didn't know." Catalina goes on.

"And then, what you wrote about me. That's so... When you did that. That; that was it. I realized I was making excuses not to trust you, not to like you. That you're a tourist and that you will leave one day soon. That someone like you must have a woman; maybe many women?" She continues.

"You and your friends; you live in a world I will never know. The woman in the picture with you, the way you two look at each other. It's the look of love; it shows. Seeing the picture, it makes me sad because I might never know that kind of love. Because I want to love and be loved that way too. It hurts to think my love may never happen. I become afraid. Afraid I will like someone for the wrong reason. Because I am lonely. Afraid you will hurt me. Afraid of that day, that day when you must leave.

"You look *Martiniquais*, like one of us, but you're not. The way you behave, the way you treat people, you aren't like the men here. You don't chase the tourists for their money and for sex. You're not impressed by them. You don't have to be. You're American. You're rich." She says.

"I'm American, but far from rich. And money doesn't mean much to me." I say.

"Compared to us, yes, you're rich. You look like us but you don't act like us. You don't act like a tourist either. You have money but you aren't arrogant and demanding like some tourists. Believe me, I know these things." Catalina says.

"'You 'know these things?'" I say.

"That's right, *Q*. I know certain things. I work with the public and for an institution and I observe. So, I think I know how to judge people." She says.

"So, what's your take on me?" I say.

"One look says something happened to you. You're in shock. It's in your face, your body language. There's this sadness. It's in your eyes. You're wounded. It's the first thing I noticed; I told you." She says.

"What else?" I say.

"Your friend, Ayri. The same things he saw; I see in you too. You're complicated. Like I said, you don't talk much. You're reserved, private. Polite, observant. Always serious, like you're thinking about something. You have background, education; it shows. It makes sense now that you're a writer.

"I watch you, *Q*. You don't go to night clubs. You don't get drunk. You don't run to the casinos. Whenever we go out, you don't stare at female tourists. Some walk around naked on the beaches in front of our children. Some tourists, they think they can buy us and treat us like we are objects; and some of my people sell themselves and their dignity.

"You're different. You know who you are and look for other things. You're curious. You see people. You ask questions, you take time to learn, not buy us. You show people respect and treat others with dignity, not contempt. You are generous. The way you tip in restaurants. These things, they say something about you. It tells me about the kind of man you are. I don't mind if you look. I see you. It's alright. Men can't help looking at women, not just the naked tourists. But you see us too. *Martiniquaise* women are world famous for beauty. You could go out with any woman here just because of your lifestyle." She says.

"You know how I feel about you." I say.

"Why should I keep fighting my feelings, or the facts? Especially after the things you wrote about me. I don't want to anymore. You make me feel special, and the person who makes me feel special... Well, now you have become special to me. At the beach today, I saw you under your *Bardolino* and sunglasses." She says.

"Well, you know what that means; don't you?" I say.

"What's that?" She says.

"It means you were digging on me while I was digging on you making your body call my name." I say.

"And you were cool like an igloo. You didn't make a move. You just kept... staring... undressing me... Touching me with your eyes... Like now. When you look at me... Your eyes... Like that... It makes me feel... all naked." Catalina says.

"You don't have to imagine me touching you." I say caressing her cheek.

"You didn't just make it hard for me not to like you. You made it impossible. Plus, your name. *Q. C'est très sexy*. Just like that name you call me. Say it again." Catalina says.

"What? Baby Girl?" I say.

"I like that, the way it sounds. Your voice, when you say... Baby Girl. It makes me feel... warm. Say it again." She says with tranquil assurance and easy lightheartedness.

"Baby Girl." I say.

"Don't stop calling me that. Say it again, *Q*..." Then Catalina lets fall the satin bed sheet, and naked she steps into my arms.

"You make me crazy. I want to taste you. Kiss me." I say.

She removes the towel from around my waist and naked we stand there. Then she stands tip toe and cradles my face in her hands.

"So long, I prayed to the saints and the spirits that one day... And you were led to me. One day, you will know, *cher Q.* "You were led to me... You will know." She says with innermost earnest, then soul kisses me.

"Come here." I draw her closer. "You taste sweet... Your body jiggles good... You're so soft... so warm... You're all juicy. I want you." I say.

"*Ne me quite pas...*" She says.

"Never that. I got you. Lay down." I say, the whole-time licking, tasting her all over.

"*Aime-moi, Q. Aime-moi...*"

"Give it to me, Baby Girl. That's right." I say.

"Love heals; even the past. Love heals everything." Says Catalina, then begins to heal me, intimately so.

"Yeah... That's it... Right there. Right like that there. You got it. Ah... Do it, Baby Girl..." That's all I can say before Catlina takes my breath away.

At this point, discretion dictates fade to black. Anything else would be unseemly, kiss-and-tell. No, there isn't a thing left to say about the night we called it a day. There, under the stars, on our beloved balcony.

Q

CHAPTER SEVEN

MESSAGE IN A BOTTLE

"Just a castaway, an island
Lost at sea. Another lonely
Day, with no one here but me...
More loneliness than any man
Can bear. Rescue me before
I fall into despair. I'll send
Out an S.O.S. to the world.
I hope that someone will find
My message in a bottle."
Message in a Bottle
Performed by
The Police

By now, I've been in the Caribbean over three months. One month in Amada before all hell broke loose, followed by that nightmare month on the Row. Initially, I'd planned on returning to Harlem City. But between magical Martinique and Creole Catalina, combined I'm seduced into extending my stay and writing in Martinique.

On the mend and almost fully recovered, I'm locked back in. My world soon follows a familiar routine. Up at six o'clock, always browsing the internet keenly interested about the latest news from Amada, followed by swimming before breakfast. At seven o'clock, once Catalina drives to work I resume writing, editing, research. From noon until three o'clock is personal time, usually beach boot camp followed by lunch. From three o'clock I resume writing until Catalina returns to the hotel by six o'clock. Afterwards, we dine, shop, entertainment and sightseeing. From ten o'clock until midnight, I review and outline the next editorial phase.

All's going well. But no matter how productive this last month, I'm far from finished. Determined not to leave Martinique without a completed manuscript, thanks to Ayri I'm able to extend my stay and continue writing in Martinique. Also, for the first time since my escape from Amada, in Catalina I have someone I can confide in about Amada and about Ayri.

Well into my second month in Martinique, one morning the *conciergerie* leaves word that the American Consulate called with an urgent message for me to visit their Fort de France offices the next morning.

The Consulate? Why? My passport is in order. It can't be my family. We regularly Skype and they know my phone number and e-mail address. I have no idea why the Consulate wants to see me. Not only that? How did Uncle Sam even know where to find me?

The next morning at the Consulate, after reviewing my passport the U.S *Chargé d'affaires* begins questioning me. So, I see you were recently in Amada. Tell me about that."

Why I was in Amada? What was the nature of my business there? How long was I in Amada? Did I witness any of the *coup d'état*? Was I personally affected by events? Did I notice any foreign, outside influences? How 'massive were military applications?' What about casualties? Just how extensive were my observations? What were my impressions? Did I video-record anything? More like a military debriefing, I'm begin feeling uncomfortable.

"How did you know I was in Martinique and where to find me? How did I come to your attention?" I say.

Glancing at folder papers and scrutinizing my passport, then he says. "Sir, do you know the dates of your itinerary?" He seems to be on to something. But what? What does he want?

With more firsthand knowledge than I am willing to admit, I hedge. "No, not off-hand. I don't know those dates. Anyway, what does that have to do with anything? Why am I here? What do you want?" I say.

"Sir, you don't know your departure date from Salamar, Amada? Or your arrival date in St. Lucia? Why aren't they reflected in your passport? How can you just exit one country and enter another without going through customs?" The *Chargé d'afaires* says.

"No. I don't know those dates. I didn't know my passport wasn't stamped until you just pointed it out. May I see for myself?" I say, then he hands me my passport. "No. I don't know why? Anyway, is that why I'm here?" I say.

"I'm not done with your passport, sir. Sir, your customs stamp indicates you arrived in Salamar, Amada, approximately one month *before* the outbreak of the civil war. That's your last customs time stamp. But you appear to have arrived in Martinique well over two months *after* the beginning of the war.

"Not only that. There is no official Amadan exit stamp in your passport, or St. Lucia entry stamp. I don't understand that? That's standard international customs procedure. Your passport doesn't show any recent time stamps. I repeat; I don't understand that." The government official says, adding.

"That means, obviously, you were still there. So, sir, my questions to you are these. Where were you during that second month in Amada? I'm curious. What were you doing during the *coup d'état* while the civil war was going on? Where were you? And why wasn't your passport stamped at your exit? You just can't drop in from country to country the way you seem to have. How did you escape Amada?" He says.

He's caught me dead-to-rights in more ways than one. That's the month I spent on Death Row, something I can't admit without prompting more questions.

Then there are other problems. My handshake agreement as a U.S. citizen to work for a foreign government official, Ayri. Bank checks issued to me in Amada were drawn from the Mentis family Amadan trust accounts, as was Ayri's final bond payment to me was from the Mentis family's trust account, without having registered with the Department of State as an U.S. agent working for a foreign government. Additionally, no taxes were deducted. There could be troubling repercussions from the I.R.S.

Instead, I adopt a less-is-more, minimally cooperative approach in dealing with his stacked, leading and loaded questions about my itinerary while never mentioning my Mentis family connection, Death Row, or being a writer.

I continue parsing and shading the truth and again identify myself as a teacher on vacation in the wrong place at the wrong time. That month in question during the *coup d'état,* I was in the countryside doing 'academic music folklore research' for the next school year when hostilities first broke out. There was less turmoil in the countryside than in the capital, so I went to ground there until I managed to arrange safe passage out of Amada on a commercial fishing vessel to St. Lucia a month later. That's why there is no custom's exit stamp in my passport, I say.

"You were recently in St. Lucia; weren't you?" The *Chargé d'affaires* says.

"That's right. You just said so." I say.

"So, walk me through this. You arrived in St. Lucia, illegally; right? And then, first thing; what? You checked yourself into the hospital for more than a week? You seem to have recovered, though. Once you were discharged you left St. Lucia for Martinique. So, why were you in hospital? Did you have surgery in St. Lucia; or what? Are you okay?" He says.

I can't believe my ears. He knows more than I ever thought.

But now I want some answers. "I'm touched by your concern for my wellbeing. But that's really none of your business, though. HIPPA laws, and all that. I don't have to answer that and, if I did, I refuse. Why don't we just cut to the chase? You still haven't told me why I'm here? What do you want? What's my itinerary and customs stamps have to do with anything? Bottom line; what? What's the real? Why did you call me in here?" I say.

"Actually, there are any number of good reasons we invited you in." He says.

"'Invited?' How did you even know where to find me?" I say.

"Easy. You cashed a large international check worth well more than ten thousand dollars. That automatically triggers an inquiry. Once we had the bank information, we started calling the hotels. When we got to the Letter-M, there you were. That's how.

"By the way, *Madinina Sur La Mer;* I've dined there many times. Some of the best food this side of paradise. And then, the view and the aquarium waterworks. Quite impressive. I'm sure you agree." He says.

"I know you didn't ask me to come here to sit and chit and chat about the view, the chew, the flying fish, or anything else. What do you really want?" I say.

"We recently received a *Message in a Bottle.*" The *Chargé* says, steady eyeballing me.

"What are you talking about?" I say.

"*A Message in a Bottle.* Addressed to the U.S. Consulate, Martinique. Care of the *International Red Cross.* But no return address." He says, scrutinizing my reaction.

"A *Message in a Bottle*? What's that? What's that have to do with me?" I say.

"*Message in a Bottle.* It's intel-jargon... Government-speak for unusual correspondence through unconventional channels. Situational stuff. Emergency and next of kin contacts. In this case, the *Message in a Bottle* is addressed to you, sir, courtesy of our good offices. The IRC delivered your *Bottle* two days ago.

"Just as we agree about the food and the flying fish, wouldn't you agree that someone trying to contact you that way is very strange. Don't you agree? Who would want to contact you this way? Never mind who; ask why?" He says, non-stop staring at me.

Slack-jawed dumbfounded, I'm getting scared. I'm not as anonymous as I thought. "Why did you feel it necessary to track me in the first place? I'm sure you don't track everyone who deposits a large check. That would 'trigger' a lot of government 'inquiries.' So, why me? What's for real here?" I say.

"Only rarely does an American raise a red flag here in paradise. Sometimes kids getting popped for rowdy behavior, drugs, driving without a license. Here and there, petty, nickel and dime stuff. But multiple red flags? Three red flags within a month? Back-to-back-to-back? That means you've been on our radar three times. For check, for *Bottle*, and then, of course, for your mystery hospitalization in St. Lucia.

"In sports, that's a three-peat. Trifecta. Triple Crown. Hall of Fame stuff. Never in all my experience. Only, in our business, we don't believe in happenstance. Someone with multiple red flags we consider radioactive, that means dangerous. We eliminate danger. That's our creed, that's what we do. Do you fully understand what I'm telling you?" He says, all-but threatened me.

"I'll have my *Bottle* now." I say, outwardly composed, my heart is pounding, my mind racing.

A Message in a Bottle, sent via the *International Red Cross*? True, I was a pest at the *IRC* offices both in St. Lucia and in Martinique. True, I visit their web sites daily, always for information about Amada and about the fate of the Mentis family.

But hold on! I clearly recall our last conversation. Ayrton and I then agreed to use the *IRC* as our only safe source of contact. No one else knows. That means... It must be... Ayri!

Is he alive after all? Was I wrong? Did I give up on him, on hope, too soon? Is Catalina right after all? Ayri's... alive? Is this proof of life? What about Didi and the rest of the Mentis family? Is there more information he is withholding? Is this news credible?

"I'll take my *Bottle* now." I say again.

"Of course. Just a few more questions. Sir; do you have any idea why, within minutes after the sender delivered your *Message in a Bottle* at the *IRC* offices in St. Lucia, agents of the so-called New Amadan Republic then appeared asking questions about a flash drive? Why agents of the so-called New Amadan Republic began chasing the sender, while other agents at the *IRC* were intimidating people, demanding to know to whom the *Bottle* was addressed and asking for the return address. Was there other correspondence? They kept asking about a flash drive and demanding that the *IRC* hand over the *Message in a Bottle* to agents of the so-called New Amadan Republic?

"These so-called New Amadan Republic agents were so menacing, the *IRC* called the police. Then the agents ran away. Very unusual; don't you think? Who would go to such lengths? Considering it's addressed to you, what are your thoughts about all of this? I don't understand. Why would anyone try to contact you this way? It sounds prearranged. And why are agents of a government only two months old after you and trying to intercept correspondence addressed to you? That's strike four, and you're still in the game, let alone alive." Like a dog with a bone, he won't let go.

The *Chargé d'affaires* scrutinizes my papers and stares at me, then says. "Who are you? What were you really doing in Amada? Why were you hospitalized in St. Lucia? Did you have surgery there? Did you have any microchips implanted or removed? What do you know about a missing flash drive? Are there any copies of it? Do you know its contents or whereabouts? Are you in trouble, sir? Radioactive man on the run? Is that who you are?

"Perhaps our good offices can be of some assistance and bring you in? But you need to let us know what's going on. That's the only way we can help you. You need to tell us everything. So, if there anything you'd like to share with us, sir I strongly encourage you to do so now. Otherwise, we will draw the appropriate professional conclusions and assume that worst, that you're radioactive. Then by creed, we're duty-bound." The *Chargé* says.

I've gone from the frying pan to the fire. In Amada, I was interrogated by a mercenary and now in Martinique I'm being interrogated by a CIA agent, who thinks I'm 'radioactive.'

He's laid out a scary scenario, and his curiosity is valid. But how does he know about the flash drive and my hospitalization? What else does he know about me that I don't know?

My unease increases. *Message in a Bottle*? Amadan agents following someone - whoever it was - to the *IRC* offices in St. Lucia and then chasing that person? Those same agents even asking questions about me and the whereabouts of the flash drive and demanding my *Bottle*? Only Ayri knows about the flash drive. That is, Ayri, my interrogator, and now a CIA agent. This is some sure enough scary cloak-and-dagger stuff.

Particularly considering that I almost died at the hands of agents of the New Amadan Republic, better known as *Guiding Star.* Maybe I'm really in trouble again and don't even know it; yet?

What if the *Chargé's* suspicions are legitimate? Maybe I really do need protection. But from the CIA? Frying pan, fire, or radioactive elimination? Pick a poison.

Once again, forced choice is no choice. I continue trusting no one and disavow all knowledge with very good reason. Whoever sent that *Bottle* - it can only be Ayrton - is in greater danger than I am and only steps ahead of his pursuers - if they haven't already caught up with him.

But if they haven't found him, if he's still alive somewhere out there, then that means that as recently as two days ago Ayri was in St. Lucia. If that's true, then we're only hours apart and with good luck soon reunited. It means I must go to St. Lucia; right away. Seeing Ayri again tops everything else; even risking my life doing so.

Mindful of these and other risks involved and rightly suspicious of the motives of all parties concerned, I continue stonewalling. Finally, the *Chargé* relents.

To my surprise, but then not, considering how many people have been after my *Message in a Bottle*. It's been opened!

The crumpled paper reads:
> "*Auxilio, por favor!*
> I'm in Great danger!
> Please help me,
> As I once helped you.
> *Guiding Star* are after me.
> I'm afraid. Can't hold out
> Much longer. No money!
> No food for my children!
> Time is running out!
> You are our last hope.
> Plus, information about
> Aryton and family.
> I'm in St. Lucia.
> Help! *Rapido!*
> *Por favor, señor!*
> Guillermo"

CHAPTER EIGHT

THE SINISTER PRIME MINISTER

"Hey now, baby, get into
My big, black car, I want to
Just show you, what my
Politics are. I'm a political man...
I support the left, though I'm
Leaning, leaning to the right.
But I'm just not there when
It comes to a fight."
Politician
Performed by
Cream

Guillermo?
That *Bottle* triggers another tsunami of post traumatic flashback attacks about everything that went down in Amada and since. Disappointed it's not from Ayri, at the same time I'm eager for any new information about Ayri and what happened to the Mentis family.

From the *Message's* tone, G-Mo's in bad shape and needs urgent help. My duty is clear, no question. He once risked his life saving mine.

Thanks to Ayri, helping Guillermo is possible and I'll finally finding out what really happened after my escape. Did Ayri survive after all? What about Didi and the other Mentis family members? Since *Guiding Star* agents were searching for the flash drive in St. Lucia only a few days ago they aren't that far off my trail anymore either.

Not only that. If Uncle Sam can track me down, so can others. Most troubling, whoever opened my *Bottle* knows I'm headed to St. Lucia. Other than Ayri, no one knows I am holding the flash drive. Trouble is only a few islands and matter of miles, hours, if even minutes, or only moments away.

Questions multiply. How did Guillermo know to contact me? Ayri must have told him. Who else knows about our *IRC* arrangement, other than CIA? *Guiding Star* and, obviously, everyone in the game.

Just as disturbing is the *Message's* tone. Clearly, G-Mo's desperate. What if he has been captured by now? What if, to save himself he is being forced to set me up? What if Guillermo is no longer alive? And what if, not knowing I travel to St. Lucia? What happens if I'm flushed out, trapped and triangulated by *Guiding Star* death squads? What then? Then I'm dead; that's what happens then.

Can I overcome my fears enough to go to St. Lucia? What if G-Mo is alive, safe or otherwise, but I decide not to go to St. Lucia? Will I look back with regret and be wracked by guilt? The coward's way and stigma of shame. What will happen if I do go but, between the time that the undated *Message in a Bottle* was sent and the time I finally received it, is it already too late? Is Guillermo even still alive? At the same time, with *Guiding Star* death squads hot on his trail, delaying my departure only increases G-Mo's risk of exposure and detection.

Returning to St. Lucia, scene of my hospitalization and worst post-traumatic stress attacks, it's risky and against my better judgement. But, after everything he did for me, saving my life by risking his, even if I'm walking into a trap, I'm duty-bound. I must help Guillermo and hopefully find out what happened to Ayri and the Mentis family. Especially if Ayri is still alive. Forced choice soon becomes no choice.

The next morning, I board a commuter flight to St. Lucia. Perhaps an hour into the three-hour flight, in the Caribbean Sea below I see an armada, perhaps eight unmarked warships, including an aircraft carrier and a hospital ship identified by a hospital ship flag. Military maneuvers, I assume.

Turns out, I'm right and wrong. True, it's the military but these aren't military maneuvers. Based on the scope and scale this is something else. This is a military operation. One, I will soon learn, that is directly connected to events in Amada. To my *Message in a Bottle*, to *Guiding Star*. To the flash drive, to *Comandante;* and to me.

As soon as I lay eyes on Guillermo, his expression funereal, absent of any joy or relief at our reunion, unable even to look me in the eye, his affect, mood and demeanor flat. Then and there, I know right away.

"You are late by many weeks. I gave up hope. So... can you... help us? Please." Guillermo speaks first.

"Ayrton... he's dead; isn't he?" I say, barely able to speak the words.

"Si, señor." He says.

"How do you know for sure?" I say.

"I know." Guillermo says.

"Who told you? How do you know?" I say.

"I know. I know because I was there." There is this sadness, such gravity about him, in his voice and posture. I know he is telling the truth.

"What do you mean, 'you were there?' What happened to Ayri? What about the rest of the family? What happened to Didi? Yo, G-Mo. What happened? What did you see?" I say.

"I didn't see what happened. Still, I know. I was there." He says again.

"If you were there then you had to see something. Just tell me what you know." I say.

"I was there. Outside the door. I heard everything." He says.

"You're not telling me anything, Guillermo. What happened? What did you hear? When was this? Was it right after you helped me escape? What happened?" I say.

"This was many days after you escaped. That night I was on duty when the leader of *Guiding Star*, *Comandante*, he..." Guillermo says.

"*Comandante*? He's the leader of *Guiding Star*?" I say.

"*Si, señor. El gringo. El terrorista en jefe!* That's the one. That night, he rounded up the Mentis family in a cell and demanded that they agree to exile. All of them. If one refused, they all died.

"*Señor*, you know Ayri. You can imagine his reaction. The two of them, they were loud. I was stationed outside of the door. I heard Dr. Mentis' voice. I heard his mother and sisters crying. *El loco*, he threatened to kill Ayri on the spot. Now the whole family is screaming and crying.

"What happened next is unclear. It was so loud. They say that, even though he was shackled Ayri apparently lunged at *el loco* or spat at him. I don't believe that. Ayri wouldn't endanger his family by spitting. Ayri doesn't need to spit, Ayri know words. All I remember is that seconds later two shots rang out and then the screaming and crying, it got worse." Guillermo says with sadness.

"Ayri. Ayrton." I cringe and close my eyes, cradling and rocking myself back and forth, sickened by the details of his death.

"That is when *Comandante* called for *Body Bag Brigade*, his personal detail. Whenever they show up, people die. But this time, something very strange happened. This time, *el loco* wouldn't let them in. Very strange. Instead he blocked the door, took a body bag and then he said something odd. Very mean. Cold blooded." Guillermo says.

"This is a nightmare. Go on, Guillermo." I say.

"I'll never forget it. He opened the cell door grinning, took a body bag and then he said, 'This one, I'm bagging personally.'
Full of pride, like Ayri was some big game trophy he just shot. Minutes later, he called *Body Bag Brigade,* and they carried Ayri's body out." Guillermo says.

"And you saw all of this? You saw them carrying the body bag out?" I say.

"*Si, señor.* I saw blood dripping from one end of the body bag. The family flanked his body as he was being carried out. They were crying. No, it was worse than crying. It was howling, howling like wounded animals.

"Oh, *señor.* It was heartbreaking. Then *el gringo* ordered them to board a waiting boat and sent them into exile in Brazil." Guillermo says.

"Do you remember anything else? Anything? Even if you don't think it's important? Think." I say.

"No. Nothing else. I'm sorry to tell you this. I saw the ship cast off with my own eyes. It was bound for Pernambuco. That was the last I heard or saw of them. That's all I know." Guillermo says.

For months now, almost from the beginning, in my heart and head I've known that Ayri is dead. But still. The gory details. *Body Bag Brigade...* 'This one, I'm bagging personally.' Executed like that, in front of his family. It's beyond sickening. After everything he did – that Russian roulette - the exploratory surgery he wanted to do. Now this. *Comandante* really is psycho. I want revenge. So much, I lose sight of the situation.

Guillermo's in a bad way, his wife and two small children, huddled in this St. Lucia shanty. "*Por favor,* can you help us, *señor*?" Guillermo says.

"No worries. I got your back. But what happened? Why did you leave Amada?" I say.

"At the pier, when they put the family and Ayri's body on the boat, I was there too. Not just because that was my assignment. I wanted to pay my respects. The family knows me. Ayri and I went to basic school together. They knew they couldn't acknowledge me without putting me in danger. But I wanted them to see me, to know I stood together with them. I couldn't help myself; I cried too. I'm not ashamed to admit it. He was my oldest friend." Guillermo recalls tearfully.

"What they did to him - to all of them. The way he died. Foreigners coming and killing our best people. What they are doing to my country, it is wrong and I don't like it. Yes, I cried. Ayri was Amada's best. Some in *Guiding Star,* they saw me crying and then reported me. The next day, the warden called me in and asked why I had been crying. I told him the same thing. About foreigner killing our people. That as an Amadan, I don't like it. I didn't tell them that I knew the Mentis family, though. Then warden, he warned me, maybe because he agreed with me. He told me to leave Amada at once. He didn't want to know my plans. From that moment on, he considered me AWOL. He gave me ten hours before reporting my absence. Two hours later, we were on my brother's fishing boat for the closest port of call. Eventually, we arrived here at my cousin's." Guillermo says.

"How long ago was this?" I say.

"A little over six weeks ago. At first, I felt safe. Maybe one month ago, I followed Ayri's advice to contact you through the *International Red Cross*.

"A month ago?" I say.

"*Si*. When I got to the *IRC,* three men approached me screaming, 'It's him! The one in the picture. Stop that man!' They had a picture of my work identification and called out my name. 'Stop that man!' I ran in the opposite direction from my cousin's house. Two of them followed me for maybe two or three miles but I managed to outrun them. I ran for miles afterwards and I kept running, even when I knew they had stopped following me. That was at ten o'clock in the morning. I did not go back to my cousin's until after dark that night.

"That was almost a month ago. Since then, I have not set foot outside. I'm too afraid. Now I must send my wife and children out. *Guiding Star* does not know them. My cousin says I have brought danger to his door and that we must leave. We have no place to go, no money for food for the children or money to leave. We have waited weeks for you. I gave up on you. What took you so long?" Guillermo says.

"A month? I got it yesterday. I think the Consulate was deliberately sitting on it. Once I got it, it had been opened." I say.

"Oh, no. Now they for sure know who I am. If you've been followed, then they know where we are. Help us, axis!" He says.

"Listen, G-Mo. Pack only what you need. Get your family. We need to get rolling. *Rapido!*" I say.

Like most Amadans, the Semperteguie family has roots in Brazil, Sao Paulo, Bahia. But, instead of vanishing in Brazil's largest city, Guillermo insists otherwise. Brave man he is, based on what he overheard, and motivated by his loyalty to the Mentis family and patriotism, on a hunch Guillermo insists on going to Pernambuco; a thousand miles north of Sao Paulo.

But, without passports, how? Travel by sea would be slow and leave them exposed to *Guiding Star* death squads already on his trail, with his picture circulating the docks. By plane would be the best solution. But without passports, how?

Well, thanks to a 'diagnosis from one newly-minted doctor, Catalina's cousin. Using my journalism credentials, I contact the *IRC* in St. Lucia about a 'human interest story' I'm working on and inquire about their refugee, political asylum and medical emergency policies.

The *IRC* refers me to a local doctor. In exchange for a 'generous gratuity,' a bribe, the local good doctor confirms the original diagnosis and, due to the youngest child's 'acute pulmonary distress disorder,' makes the necessary arrangements for the family's next day 'emergency medical air evacuation for chronic obstructed respiratory treatment' via *IRC* to Brazil.

During our farewell dinner at a seaside restaurant, I hand Guillermo an envelope for their relocation expenses to Brazil. *"Con permiso, señor Q. Pero, por que?"* Camilla asks me.

"Why do I do what?" I say.

"Why do you put yourself in danger? Why do you help us? The doctor's arrangements? The plane tickets? The hotel? This dinner? And now; *los dineros*? *Por que, señor*? You don't even know us." Camilla says.

"Do you know how I met your husband?" I say.

"He says you are a friend of his friend, *Don* Ayrton. Ayri. The one who was murdered. God rest his soul." Camilla says.

"True that. Ayri and your Guillermo, they grew up together. I wish I knew Ayrton that long. I've only knew him maybe ten years before he... It's still hard to believe he's gone. But there's more. I think Guillermo left out a few things." I say.

Camilla is stunned at the extent of Guillermo's involvement in my escape, then berates and slaps at him before showering him with kisses.

"When your man risked his life to save mine, he didn't know me either, Camilla. All I'm doing is giving you money. That doesn't compare with what Guillermo and Ayri did. That was bravery. They're heroes, real heroes. You should be very proud of him." I say, adding.

"Besides, this isn't my money. It was a gift from Ayri to me. I wouldn't be here without Guillermo. I'm just paying it forward. It's the least I can do. It's what Ayri would expect me to do; especially for Guillermo." I say.

Guillermo rises, lifts his glass and offers a toast. "God bless Ayri!" Following suit, we all rise and gather around the restaurant table and join in a joyous toast to the memory of our slain friend.

The next morning, we taxi to the hospital, exchange best wishes and, promising to stay in touch, the Semperteguie family then boards a waiting the medical transport aircraft to Brazil.

After their safe departure, I learn there are no more flights to Martinique until the next day. Instead, I book ship passage to Martinique for later that evening. Such pleasant weather, I decide to spend the return journey in a comfortable deckchair under the stars. A few hours *en route*, the ship's captain announces a six-hour detour to Martinique.

The delay suits me. I don't sleep much that night, instead ruminating about Ayri's death. All the horrific details, his final moments in front of his family, his executioner my interrogator. *Comandante* then personally disposing of Ayrton's body. *Body Bag Squad* and *Guiding Star* loading the body on a ship and sending the family to Brazil in exile. Considering what happened to Ayri, I'm lucky. Between Guillermo's escape and with death squads on both our trails, it's a wonder I'm not dead. I know I'm going to need time to process recent events and plot my survival.

Soon I will learn the actual reason behind the detour. It's that military armada I saw on my way to St. Lucia. Military forces poised for imminent military action in the region. Actions related to *Comandante's* mission, and to my return to St. Lucia.

There's something bedeviling about the archipelago and human nature. For concealed behind the tropical masks of friendly natives and pristine beaches, *gourmet* food and island music, lurking beneath this Caribbean *façade* which, when peeled away, bit by bit reveals a world of mysticism and history rife with violence and corruption.

For generations, the Caribbean Basin and Central America have been little more than a political and economic grab bag, spawning an often-bizarre cast of shady characters and crooked leaders.

In Hispaniola, it was the Dominican Republic's dictatorship and repression under the Trujillo family and their playboy/ambassador/spy and real-life James Bond, the notorious Porfirio Rubirosa.

On the dysfunctional island's other side, Haiti's serial plunder by France and by the Duvaliers, Papa and Baby Doc, their terror *voodun* politics enforced by their official boogeymen, *Ton Ton Macoutes*.

In Cuba, it was the poet Jose Marti's fight against Spain. Later on, Batista twice, pawn of U.S. crime and business cartels before being toppled by the Marx Brothers, Fidel and Raul Castro in defiance of U.S. policy in pursuit of their own agenda.

The Samosas in Nicaragua. Grenada's Sir Eric Geary.

United Fruit Company and Guatemalan death squads. Salvadoran death squads and Honduran death squads. Nicaraguan contra death squads.

Jamaica's prophet, his hypno-rhythms and message music championing one love, Bob 'Rasta' Marley.

In Martinique, diametrically opposite giants, Aimé Césaire and Frantz Fanon.

In St. Lucia, its two Nobel laureates. Sir Arthur Lewis, for his economic abstractions and his thoughtful political considerations, and Sir Derek Walcott, awarded for his evocative imagery and his verse's poetic essence.

Toussaint L'Overture, Henri Christophe, Simon Bolivar, Romulo Betancourt. Fidel and Raul Castro Ruz, Ernesto 'Che' Guevara. Jacobo Arbenz, Juan Bosch. Rodrigo and Ayrton Mentis. The list is long.

All of them and others, for better and for worse, their patriotism was shaped by their love of their countries' respective histories and dynamics. Nearly all, though, were determined to break free from the yoke of the Lord of the North, the United States of America. It's always been thus.

At best, the emergence of political leadership is a nebulous process and an inexact science and, once ideology is added to the mix, the temporal brew more closely resembles alchemy or witchcraft than any actual states craft.

Small wonder then, that political center stage has been routinely occupied, almost farcically so, by a succession of charlatans and dilettantes, 'madmen and generals.' In the words of a once popular song, '...Clowns to the left... jokers to the right... Stuck in the middle with...' those who came to power without democracy's ultimate touchstone test of true leadership; free and fair elections.

They and others in a long list of unpopular dynasties and bizarre cults of personalities acting as willing pawns in a geo-

political, economic and ideological war game, collectively they
came to dominate the region for generations. One nasty,
tough, winner-take-all, free-for-all game of greed and power
with so-called free trade zones and spheres of
influences. Special interests and rights of imminent domain. A
game with high stakes and for keeps. A game played
exclusively by ruthless, high roller, players-only-nation-states,
along the way attracting some dangerous players.

Based on what Ayri told me, and based on information
gleaned from the flash drive, particularly one player is
responsible for the *Golden Quadrant*'s current upheaval. This
profile is of one of the Caribbean's more notorious characters,
his rise to power and shocking decline of the island of
Spañada under his bizarre cult of personality leadership.

Originally a Spanish colony also known as the Spice Island
after its principal exports, following the Anglo-Iberian War
Spañada retained its Spanish name but became an English
colony.

Enter Geremi Quarrles. His rise in Spañadan politics
coincided at a crucial time in the nation's history when things
were rapidly going from bad to worse. Regardless his
questionable rise to power, Geremi Quarrles' early personal
history and remarkable escape from a family background of
abject poverty is inspirational.

A sharecropper's son, he lived with his family on the
outskirts of the jungle thicket where they scrounged for wood
chips and charcoal. A precocious child full of verbal energy,
his gifts were apparent. Bright though he was, the family of
six could not afford the loss of Geremi's share cropping labor
to the luxury of an education.

For years, he begged his parents to let him go to school. To
Geremi, education was a metabolic desire to do the same
things, the same way, in the same place and at the same time
with all the many happy children he saw every day on their
way to and from school. He wanted so much to join in, to be
one of them. He promised his parents he would do extra work
after school, on weekends and holidays, anything. But his
father always refused.

So intelligent, one Sunday the parish parson took the
father aside and admonished him that a child as bright as
Geremi belonged in basic school, not just Sunday School, and
not in the fields. The clergyman warned Geremi's father that
Sunday next he would shame him from the pulpit with a fire
and brimstone sermon about 'the sins of usufruct, and the

wickedness of parasite parents living off child labor at the expense their children's education.'

The next day, Monday morning the parish parson personally enrolled Geremi in school.

An apt pupil, Geremi soon blossomed into the kind of student teachers dream about. Bright and obedient, he began skipping grades. At age fourteen, Geremi tested for and was admitted to *Georgetown School for Boys* in Spañada's capital, a prestigious private English secondary school for children of the wealthy, foreign diplomats and senior government officials. A rare privilege and honor, not only for a backwoods black boy but also for his family, the parson and his community. That, as well as it was a lot of pressure on bright, young Geremi.

Again, Geremi outshone his peers and quickly outgrew *Georgetown School.* At age sixteen, he made a crucial decision opting for a military career. Again, accompanied by glowing references and top grades, at age eighteen Geremi was awarded a full scholarship. This time, to England's prestigious *Sandhurst Military Academy.*

Sandhurst proved formative, although for all the wrong reasons, approximately dating certain changes in his values and personality. Initially, were it not for the ignominy of failure and having to return to the charcoal fields, otherwise Geremi would have left soon after he arrived at *Sandhurst.*

England proved lonely. It was cold, he was homesick and, exposed to the British Empire's caste system and none too subtle racism among the empire's select scions, he was made to feel ashamed of his background of poverty.

The work now much harder, his star no longer shone as brightly. Ambitious and bright, so was everyone else at *Sandhurst.* No longer the smartest student in the room, work was harder and took longer to understand. Self-confidence gave way to self-doubt.

Or perhaps it was all in Geremi himself. Perhaps his future wasn't that promising unless he prodded and plotted even more. No longer driven by the past, Geremi became future-focused, and reverted to type. Just like getting out of the charcoal fields, getting out of *Sandhurst* became his obsession.

Five years prior to Spañada's independence, he was graduated from *Sandhurst* one year early, commissioned with distinction but still with a lower rank than usual. *Sandhurst* graduates usually commissioned as captain, but Geremi instead was commissioned as a lieutenant in the Spañadan

Army, something he attributed to his ambition to escape the ostracism he experienced and insisting on early graduation.

The slight in rank, though, was well worth getting out of *Sandhurst* early.

Geremi never believed in the British agenda. He knew too well that, although he was someone schooled at one of their premier institutions, they regarded him as a *savage savant,* trained to advance British imperial interests. Someone almost, but not quite, like them.

To Spañadans however, Lt. Geremi Quarrles was one of them. A hero, a brilliant military officer and dashing figure in his prime and at the beginning of a bright future, a role model and worthy of emulation.

His values, though, weren't rooted in Spañadan nationalism, anti-colonialism, or civic mindedness. Instead, his interests were selfish and inner-directed. Interests limited by a traditional military career, at odds with British imperial policies, and in direct conflict with his personal and career ambitions.

Easily Geremi Quarrles' most controversial contribution to Spañadan life and history was a clandestine military intelligence gathering operation established early on in his career. Initially a small unit that spied on politicians and shared intelligence at the military command level and with top government officials, often for the purposes of blackmail. An operation so successful, he quickly bypassed ranks Captain and Major and bumped to the rank of colonel.

Even before his meteoric rise and long thereafter, their operations expanded to include so-called 'special functions.' A unit whose 'special functions' quickly became the political life's blood of Colonel Quarrles' stronghold on power and without which he never would have acquired or remained in power for so long. In its ranks were a *cadre* and network of finks, goons and gangsters. Spies, double and triple agents, moles and plants all over the island. An army of low-lifers, much like *Ton Ton Macoutes.* A notorious unit only few knew who was in charge and that terrorized all walks of Spañadan life for years. *Mongoose Squad.*

Thirty-four years old and by now the first Brigadier General in Spañadan history, with not much more room for military advancement, a terrible condition for someone ambitious, eighteen months after independence from Britain General Quarrles decided to embark upon a career change.

A profession offering more opportunities and few, if any, restraints or restrictions. With Spañada's problems mounting,

Lt. Quarrles' began focusing his attention and energies on that horn of plenty attractive to scoundrels and short-cut artists alike, particularly lawyers and the military.

It was his *métier*. Something he came to regard his as his calling. He was a natural, if not original. Geremi Quarrles entered politics. But instead of standing for election which he would have won, Geremi Quarrles entered politics the conventional, *Sandhurst* old school way. Or, in the lyric of a *Beatles* song, 'he came in through the bathroom window.' In other words, a military *putsch*.

Along with a few trusted *Mongoose Squad* conspirators Geremi Quarrles seized power. During a television and radio address to the nation he dismissed the government due to incompetence and loss of popular support and nationalized all media. He dissolved all political parties and declared himself Prime Minister and foreign and defense secretaries of Spañada. For all practical purposes, a military dictatorship.

In his proclamation, in addition to sweeping control over the media, private ownership of printing or publishing hardware were criminalized. He moved swiftly against the opposition and neutered his enemies, real and imagined, including former military brass. Political parties' leadership past and present were imprisoned, exiled, placed under house arrest. That; or killed.

Other than work, church, funerals, soccer and cricket matches, all public or private gathering of more than fifty adults were outlawed. Demonstrations required a permit. The waiting period for a demonstration permit was now one year. Public discussion of politics was prohibited and criminalized. Advocating the change of the government was declared a capital crime. Enforcement and oversight of these and other matters resided in the black khaki clad *Mongoose Squad,* who infiltrated and intimidated every segment of Spañadan society.

Despite these measures, some policies such as land and education reform initially enjoyed wide spread support and always the Prime Minister's core support. Everyone was impressed by his obvious smarts and command, his youth and urbane manner, always ram rod straight and natty dread dapper in his crisp uniforms. That 'Sandhurst polish,' the people once called it. For the first time in decades, Spañadans dared to hope for a brighter future. A hope that resided in the Prime Minister's brilliance and easy manner, regardless his questionable rise to power.

If grudgingly, even critics acknowledged his achievements. He had inherited a stagnant economy and empty treasury after Spañada's independence and still managed to initiate several successful recovery measures few thought possible. Given his popularity, some even thought that there wasn't all that much wrong with a little 'stern rule' and 'firm authoritarian guidance.'

What the people did not know, at least not at first, were the secret treaties and deals that aligned Spañada with certain intelligence services. Deals in the form of security arrangement agreements. Weapons' purchases and training for Spañadan military and *Mongoose Squad* officers at *SOA*, the U.S. Army's *School of the Americas*.

These and other things, the influence peddling and the beginning corruption, the subversion of the bureaucracy and civil service, *Mongoose Squad's* increasingly heavy-handed tactics. These and other things the people didn't know or didn't want to know; at least not at first.

To avoid any appearances of conflicts of interests as a head of state, for his loyalty Geremi Quarrles was richly rewarded, quietly appointed to various boards-of-directorates of major corporations. He also held silent partnership shares in several Caribbean hotels and casinos in return for greasing their skids. So that by age forty-six, close to twelve years in office and halfway into his administration, the Prime Minister had amassed immoderate wealth, with other large sums paid to subordinates.

With an eye on his legacy, Prime Minister Quarrles planned on building major tourist and casino attractions, residential and commercial real estate development in partnership with airline and hospitality interests, crowned by the completion of a world class airport complex. The profit potential was dizzying. But for reasons beyond the Prime Minister's control, construction and material cost increases came into play. The project soon exceeded budget and the deal completely stalled.

Driven by greed and delusions of grandeur, the Prime Minister entered back-channel negotiations with the Sixth Estate. Not with any foreign country or government, or the Church. Neither the court, military nor the press. In an affront to the rule of law, the Prime Minister's interlocutors were shocking to the conscience and in disregard of civil society.

In return for project completion, the Prime Minister of Spañada entered a sweetheart deal. In exchange of disco and alcohol receipts, food and beverage vending, dry cleaning concessions and user privileges, board memberships and stock options, Geremi Quarrles granted unprecedented concessions to the Sixth Estate. Variously known, *Mafia, Friends of Friends, La Cosa Nostra*.

Crime cartels were granted unheard of privileges in perpetuity, including unlimited cultivation of narcotics, cocaine, marijuana, heroin. Protection of all narcotics laboratories, unfettered air and sea access, contraband distribution and money laundering through Spañadan banks and official government accounts.

Not surprisingly, the once stalled project soon advanced under the watchful eyes of *Friends of Friends* and the heavy-handed *Mongoose Squad*.

To the extent that the Spañadan people were unaware of the Prime Minister's wheeling and dealing and official corruption, those rumors notwithstanding, most still supported the Prime Minister. So, what if he was pocketing money? Everyone knew the Prime Minister's salary was low paying and the ceremonial requirements of his office could not have been met on a low budget. Moreover, the reasoning went, he was 'an activist Prime Minister' who traveled a lot. True, *Mongoose Squad* was repressive, but then so were CIA, FBI, MI-5 and KGB. So was China. Everyone does it. That's big boy politics.

One thing the people knew, though. No one thought Quarrles would ever betray them. Not 'the People's Prime Minister' who held the popular Constituency Meetings and personally heard petitions. Who championed education and health reform and paved the roads. Who in his crisp uniforms had always cut such a dashing figure. Not Geremi Quarrles. After all, he was one of them, straight out of the charcoal fields.

There always was whispered talk and speculation about his personal life and why he never married? Some Spañadans believed that life in the barracks had limited his contact with women. No doubt, that was somewhat true.

There were also other rumors about lifestyle, about the private jets, luxury automobiles and yachts. Government expenditures he defended as 'legitimate necessities for government hospitality purposes.' Yachts rumored to house the hospitalities services and favors of rotating 'entertainment and companionship hostesses' onboard the Prime Minister's flotilla. Yachts in international waters hosting corporate fat cats and celebrities, purportedly video-recorded *flagrante delicto* in compromising *bunga bunga* positions.

Gossip coursed about his silent partnerships in various casinos and hotels interests. Concerns were also voiced about the Prime Minister's frequent sightings at the hotel casino gaming tables where he was said to have wagered huge sums - perhaps even tax payers' money - fueling talk of his gambling addiction.

After twenty years of whispering, people began connecting the dots, rumblings that soon grew louder. About how Spañada's character somehow had changed for the worse. About the influx of foreigners in construction and tourism while natives couldn't get hired. About the shady characters and dubious narco-money laundering schemes and crooked land deals. How once-spice plantations had been expropriated and transformed into narcotic fields and underground laboratories, hidden landing strips and constant uncharted air traffic to and from Spañada. How jobs were vanishing and unemployment was skyrocketing even though Spañada was awash in narco-dollars. About how Spañada was going from bad to worse.

Little did they guess how much worse.

But even *Mongoose Squad*'s strong-arm tactics could not overshadow other larger realities forever. Realities which, gradually and eventually permanently tainted the Prime Minister's once popularity. And for the first time, serious doubts about his further fitness for office were raised. Mounting evidence suggested that his lifestyle had begun affecting his faculties and impairing the performance of his public duties, sullying the nation's reputation. Leading the way, his deteriorating personal appearance and his increasingly erratic official behaviors.

There were always suspicions about the Prime Minister's cocaine addiction, citing the Prime Minister's frequent medical trips to Switzerland and the United States. Following one such medical trip, Geremi Quarrles returned having purchased what people called 'a new nose.' Reportedly the Prime Minister underwent rhinoplasty surgery because, according to the rumor mill, continued cocaine abuse had destroyed his nasal membranes and sinuses.

There were other signs. Once fastidious and physically fit, he became a gaunt ghost of his former self, emaciated and with sunken cheeks, the full extent of dissipation and lethargy concealed behind dark sun glasses he now wore on all occasions.

Gone his once proper English, correct appearance and dignified bearing, now marked by slurred speech, incomplete, halting sentences and involuntary lapses into *patois* and pigeon English and exhibiting cognitive impairment symptoms.

Q

Struggling to understand the written word, digital tremens and impaired concentration. Repetitive thinking and perseverative speech. Short term memory loss, forgetfulness and mood swings. His baseline cognitive and intellectual functions showed marking decline.

His once razor-sharp mind gone, increasingly he demonstrated poor judgment and insight and increasing impoverished thinking, his handwriting reduced to an illegible scrawl. Loss of appetite and weight loss, disturbed and self-medicated sleep habits. His work habits, once self-disciplined, were now disorganized and he became forgetful. Staying up and pacing all night obsessing and ruminating, then sleeping late into the afternoon.

Hung-over and depressed, he frequently forgot the day or date. Hung over and depressed, that is, until re-fueling his daily prodigious drug consumption. Then he'd go without sleep for days on end, embarking on disorganized work binges, waking everyone else and demanding they match his mania. He spent time obsessing about bacteria, suspicious and irritable without provocation, convinced that others lay in wait conspiring against him.

He became preoccupied with extraterrestrials and alien visitations, UFO sightings and extraterrestrial abduction. Delusional, he experienced auditory hallucinations claiming spiritual and political advice, religious revelations and visitations from the Holy Ghost and from on High, 'the upper chamber,' as he called it. He conducted *séance* sessions and *voodun* ceremonies. In all, clear signs of a vegetative mind.

Scheduled dignitaries and other state business were kept waiting without explanation or apology. Some appointments or meetings, no matter their importance or the sacrifices of others in attendance, were canceled often at the last minute or abruptly terminated in midstream without explanation. More and more, he delegated responsibilities to deputies and confidantes, something he had carefully avoided his entire career. On other occasions, he was out of the country, often months on end. 'Medical treatments' in New York and Los Angeles, Zurich and Geneva, actually plastic surgery trips and shopping sprees, and frequently occasions when he deposited money into his embezzlement accounts. That and, according to *People* Magazine, secret drug detox treatment at *Betty Ford Clinic*.

Towards the end of what Spañadans came to refer to as his 'Insane Reign,' the Prime Minister suddenly announced the complete renovation of the executive mansion, although already in good repair. He abruptly vacated the residence and, much to Spañada's chagrin, Quarrles moved into his favorite hotel casino's penthouse. No longer dressed in military epaulette uniform or crisp khaki fatigues instead, since as Prime Minister he had wanted to 'set a good example,' citing the casino hotel's dress code he now wore a white dinner jacket, white shirt, black bow tie, white cummerbund, black tuxedo trousers, cowboy boots, and a ten gallon Stetson cowboy hat. As ever his craven, crazed expression hidden behind thick black sunglasses. Most government business and cabinet meetings were now conducted at the casino Black Jack or Baccarat tables, one of his many addictions.

But no matter how drug addled or alcohol hung-over, no matter how psychotic his frame of mind on any given day, one thing never changed during his twenty-five years' control of Spañada, except when he was out of the country. The one meeting he never canceled or missed was the Constituency Petition Meeting, once and always the bedrock of Geremi Quarrles' support. Kind of a dictator's town hall meeting, when he personally heard and often granted petitions and settled disputes. Although never canceled this meeting changed, too. Not just the location, now also at the casino, but other changes as well. Changes that undermined his support and resulting in his loss of popular confidence, marking the beginning of his end in power.

In one such change, Constituency Petition Meetings no longer were free or open to the public. Instead, people now waited their turn until the Prime Minister or, new now, one of his staff then met alone with each petitioner.

The Prime Minister's staff now levied an 'administrative fee,' a bribe, in return for the 'Prime Minister's valuable time in select assistance.'

The descent of Spañada's national life, initially imperceptible, reached critical mass. More impoverished than ever despite the now open presence of wealthy dummy corporations and shady banks, dubious charter airline companies and narcotics cultivation on former spice plantations. Despite the flow of goods, services and money, unemployment was pandemic. The only jobs advertised were for women, ages sixteen to forty. No experience required with 'on the job training' in the 'hospitality industry.' Too late, people realized that Spañada had become an undisguised drug haven. A narco-cartel money laundering nexus and ATM for the drug and gambling, the hospitality and travel industries, their respective controlling stake holders and their *Friends of Friends*.

What once was dismissed as 'benign dictatorship,' that '*Sandhurst* polish' couldn't conceal the obvious. For the first time in recent history, indeed since independence from the British Empire, Spañadans, no longer afraid of *Mongoose Squad* reprisal, defied the government and began protesting and picketing.

A political vacuum and dangerous vortex soon developed, swirling with virulent anti-British and anti-American rhetoric and pie-in-the-sky politics. The consensus was unanimous, though. The Prime Minister had to be removed from office and prosecuted. From this cauldron emerged a hitherto unknown fiery student leader, Milton Travisent who with the slogan, 'To hell with our Quarrles,' rode the crest of popular unrest.

Twenty-five years after his own coup the Sinister Prime Minister himself was ousted from power, finally ending his insane, corrupt reign.

In Spañada, there was 'Great Debate' and outrage over the mysterious circumstances surrounding Geremi Quarrles' escape from Spañadan justice and punishment. An escape, according to the popular Spañadan version of events, made possible by a large cast of shady characters. By anonymous Swiss and American bankers, by the *Friends of Friends,* by CIA and MI-6. Those *Mongoose Squad* unable to escape were met with mob retaliation and violence, beaten, tortured, and even killed.

There was also 'Great Debate' and outrage among the *solons* in Washington and in Langley. About who had lost Spañada? About why and how?

Fearful of another populist independence movement in the hemisphere, State Department spin doctors began concocting clandestine contingency action planning. Despite overwhelming evidence of corruption and embezzlement, murder, corruption, and direct responsibility for other high crimes committed by the Sinister Prime Minister and *Mongoose Squad* during his insane reign, the new Spañadan government repeatedly failed in their extradition efforts.

Washington D.C., citing their misgivings about a show trial and concerns about due process and human rights violations, recommended the 'constructive engagement of all parties' and refused his extradition. Instead like other dictators, *junta* henchmen and strong men once at the end of the line, Geremi Quarrles was also granted political and humanitarian asylum in the United States where he remained a free man. No sooner D.C. experts and *solons,* their spooks and spies and *Friends of Friends* together began plotting the Sinister Prime Minister's return to power.

A scheme not long in the making. Couched in the vocabulary of concern to mask its true intentions, Washington voiced unfounded allegations about the treatment of U.S. citizens in Spañada and concerns about certain 'vital business and strategic interests and objectives in the region' (the new airport and hospitality complex). Concerns also about an 'axis of evil' alliance, according to 'reliable classified intelligence.' Officially on the record, off the record Washington, citing the Monroe Doctrine, began setting the political stage for eventual military action in the region.

Less than a year later, Spañada's popularly elected socialist government was ousted in a military *coup,* and its new Prime Minister, Milton Travisent, assassinated.

With the laws now retroactively re-written granting immunity for prior crimes and bad acts, once safe from prosecution and punishment the Sinister Prime Minister was restored to power and re-installed in the geo-political orbit of Washington and under the protection of an assortment of other underworld *Friends of Friends.* Still crazy but this time without the disbanded *Mongoose Squad,* thereafter the Sinister Prime Minister instituted another, subtler organization with farther regional reach and with a more powerful list of clients, hydrocarbon companies, travel and hospitality industries; *Guiding Star.*

This time his 'Insane Reign,' while less overt remained pervasive and still at the direct expense of the Spañadan people. This time, though, with a reach beyond Spañada's borders. Still unchecked and unchallenged, his powers absolute, during his second administration and into the present day, the Sinister Prime Minister destabilized not only Spañada but the region as well, sponsoring political mischief, sabotage and subversion in neighboring Amada with an eye on its arch energy resources on behalf of his powerful friends with their friends of friends.

It is during this detour to Martinique that the nature, scope and timing of events fully dawn on me. That the Sinister Prime Minister's restoration to power and preceding *coup* in Amada are one and the same military operation and part of a larger nefarious plot.

And here I am smack dab in the middle, trapped between the devil and the deep blue sea on a slow boat to Martinique.

Q

Journalist on the run with information that everyone is after it and are willing to do anything to get their hands on.

A phrase heard in Bob Marley's music assumes new meaning. A metaphor and proverb, harbinger of evil and confusion, dread and imminent doom. That phrase, it resonates over and yet again in my mind's ear. Steady whispering, 'Babylon, Babylon... Babylon, Babylon... Babylon, Babylon...'

HEART OF DARKNESS

"Mr. Kurtz, he dead."
Heart of Darkness
Joseph Conrad

Returning from St. Lucia, late that afternoon, I head to *Bamboo Bar* for a few well-deserved cold beers to quench my thirst and chill my anxieties.

After everything I learned from Guillermo. Grieving for Ayri and worried about my personal safety from *Guiding Star* death squads roaming the Caribbean looking for me and the flash drive. Suddenly, from somewhere across the veranda I hear a group of Germans in conversation.

Ayri wasn't altogether joking when he kept referring to me as German. I was born in Harlem City. My father is an expatriate pianist who, for career reasons, relocated our family to Munich, Germany when I was two years old, and we lived there for the next twenty-two years.

My mother wanted me to attend the local private American school along with my older brother but my parents couldn't afford tuition, so the enrolled me in the German school system, which was free and provided an excellent education. That's what Ayri kept referring top.

During my second year at *Ludwig Maximillian University of Munich* (LMU), my family returned to New York City, and I transferred to *Columbia,* where I met Ayri and Didi.

Pleasantly surprised and nostalgic at hearing German voices, from across the veranda one of the men at the table of German speakers rises, approaches the bar, stands next to me, and then places his order, cloaked in the vestments of familiarity.

Nausea replaces my nostalgia. In spite of the heat and humidity, I'm overcome by chills and shakes. Light-headed, dizzy, my senses fluctuating, I'm physically and mentally overloaded, in the grip of another high anxiety, post-trauma shock and panic attack, haunted and flooded again by flashbacks and memories of Ayri and Didi and Amada.

Dude standing next to me, as soon as he rises and makes his way across the veranda and approaches the bar, right away I recognize him. I don't just recognize him, I know him. I don't know his face, but I remember him. Not only do I recognize him; I know him. I know who he is, and what he did.

No question, it's dude with that strange accent, my interrogator in Amada. The one who had me transferred from the Row to the prison hospital and who ordered exploratory surgery. The one Ayri said lives on a high-powered armed yacht.

Even though standing shoulder to shoulder next to me, he doesn't say a word, still, I know it's him. The one mentioned repeatedly on the flash drive and who's been looking for the *Smoking Gun* ever since.

The ranking *Guiding Star* terrorist and security contractor. *Comandante,* among other aliases. The one Guillermo says oversaw *Guiding Star*'s death squad, *Body Bag Brigade.* Even though I never really saw his face. Even though he doesn't speak to me at the bar, he doesn't have to. It's him. No question; none.

Now I recognize his accent. It isn't German or Austrian; I would have recognized that straight away. His dialect, it's *Schwyzerdütsch;* Swiss-German. He's Swiss. That's why he took my gear. And, adding insult to injury, dude is sporting my stolen *Willis & Geiger* Swiss Army shirt and safari jacket all up in my face. That's why I recognize him. It's Ayri's killer, wearing my gear! Ain't no bout a doubt it.

I'm nauseous, dizzy and light-headed; my knees buckle. My pulse becomes arrhythmic, skipping beats. I can't breathe. It's feels like I'm about to have a seizure or a stroke. But he doesn't notice my distress, unawares we once met. Instead, he places his order, pays, and then returns to his table.

I stumble blindly out the bar and puke. Minutes go by before I stop hyperventilating, and even more time passes before I can pull myself together.

Is there somehow a connection between my *Message in a Bottle* and *Comandante's* sudden appearance in Martinique? Did agents of the New Amadan Republic, aka *Guiding Star,* pick up my trail in St. Lucia? Did contacting Guillermo expose me to their death squads? Is a circle slowly closing around me? Am I being triangulated? Trapped in a kill zone? Am I dead man walking; again?

Obviously, I can't go to the Martinican authorities now and file a criminal complaint against someone whose face I never saw. My only evidence, an accent, a jacket and a shirt. After the *Message in a Bottle* and lying to a CIA agent about my activities I can't return with another story without incriminating myself.

I must do something, though; but what? How am I going to find out more? I can't stalk him, that's just too risky. Doing nothing, though, would be worse, that would be cowardly.

Even after calming myself somewhat, my choices are limited. I can't call him out *mano a mano.* Taking him on is out of the question and would defeat my larger purpose - staying alive.

There's something about dude, the way he carries himself. His walk, the way he talks. His body language, he ekes danger. If he's armed, he'll kill me. But he didn't recognize me at the bar. And why should he have?

In Amada my hair was short, my face lumped to pulp. But now? Three months later in Martinique, and I'm healed. I've gained weight and have a deep sun tan, a mop of hair and a full beard. Natives mistake me for being one of them. He must have interrogated so many people he can't recognize every one of his victims. There is no reason to think he will in the future. If I'm going to find out more then I must play a dangerous, deep game. Disguise my identity and go... *incognegro.*

Going *incognegro* is tricky, though. It means from now on I can only speak German. It's practically my mother tongue. But if I slip up - if *Comandante* somehow finds me out - then I'm dead. But my need-to-know clouds my judgment and overrides my common sense. I don't care. I must go... *incognegro.*

Increasingly confident in my plan and my ability to pull it off, I recompose myself and set out seeking revenge and reenter *Bamboo Bar.*

Sure enough, *Comandante* and the party of Germans is still on the scene. With Ayri all the while heavy on my mind, I put on my game face, take a deep breath, in silent prayer summoning courage as I approach their table.

With a tinge of Bavarian accent, I repeat a saying popular among Germans overseas. *"Gott hütte mich von Wetter und Wind, und von die Deutschen, die im Ausland sind."* (God, protect me from weather and wind, and from Germans abroad.), I say pulling up a chair, then adding. *"Also, Servus, Landsleute!"* (Well, hello countrymen!).

My concerns soon prove unfounded though, as one of the Germans is also from Munich, and after a few local and social references they are soon convinced.

The topics shift to soccer and *Bayern München,* when someone suggests a scrimmage the next day.

Conversation goes back and forth for nearly an hour. No longer afraid, in fact I'm at ease and even enjoying myself. So much so, I briefly lose sight of everything he did, oand having to remind myself that I'm sitting across from *mi hermano's* murderer, sporting my gear. But he pays me no mind and continues scanning the horizon with his binoculars.

I learn a lot and memorize details, including everyone's names at the table, which I write down as soon as the gathering ends. It seems that this Swiss has numerous aliases.

That day, though, he goes by the name Jürgen Naumann, possibly his real name. Others call him *Gulliver,* probably another code name for the sailor anchored off southern Martinique, not too far from *Hotel Bamboo.*

We linger over beers without his slightest inkling that I recognize him. Eventually, our gathering dissolves and we go our separate ways until the next day's *Fußball* game.

Once back at *Hotel Madinina,* abandoning all previous work on the Amada projects I compile a time line and dossier of events and people in Amada, Martinique and St. Lucia. Then, at one o'clock in the morning as the final order of a whirlwind day, I set up a dead man's switch, in the event of my sudden, violent death.

The sport I've played the longest, am best at and love most, that's the beautiful game, Pelé's *'juga bonita.'* The next day, despite little and only fitful sleep, my game sparkles. Between my game and language skills, from now on I'm always welcomed by this group of boat owners, including *Gulliver.*

Once deep *incognegro,* I entrench myself by becoming something of a regular beach fixture, always on the lookout for a soccer game and for the 'boat people.' Particularly for *Gulliver,* whenever possible making sure our paths often cross, sometimes more than once a day and always on purpose. No matter during the day on the beach, whether at night at different restaurants and bars.

How? With my own binoculars and telescope, tracking his boat and stalking his every movement from my hotel suite's deck. Wherever he goes, soon I 'happen to appear.' Our conversations are always pleasant and cordial if superficial, and over time I no longer feel threatened. Some of the 'boat people' invite me onboard their vessels, which I always accept.

A few days later, as hoped *Gulliver* also invites to his ship, *Canton*. A few days later, I do just that and swim the roughly half mile to the off-shore *Canton,* climb the anchor and board his ship. He isn't there, though.

Beyond the basics, I don't know too much about boats. This ship, though, it's clearly one of a kind, state-of-the-art. A teak-paneled, high powered small cruise ship and armed luxury yacht with extensive electronics. Off one side hangs an orange rubber outboard motorboat. The interior is just as impressive. Such a sight, I stand on deck admiring the luxury vessel, much the way Ayri had described it.

It is a golden opportunity. I can search his ship for my shirt and my jacket, my laptops or any other incriminating evidence in support of criminal charges. Better yet, I can take my revenge and vandalize his boat. But that would only raise suspicions. Instead, with nothing gained I swim back to shore.

And it's a good thing I did. Even though he isn't onboard, still he had eyes there. For no sooner than I'm back on shore, we cross paths. He is in the company of fellow boat owners and wearing his signature binoculars around his neck.

We greet, and I mention that I just returned from *Canton.*

"I know; I saw you. You're a good swimmer." He says. He's monitoring his boat; maybe not just with his binoculars. An alarm system? And while he doesn't appear angry, he seems the kind of man who, if he suspected I were snooping or tampering with his boat, would have sprung into full force. But considering I wasn't there that long and did nothing untoward, he is nonchalant and re-invites me for another time.

From then on, knowing I'm pushing my luck and fearful of detection and reprisal, I back off and no longer seek him out. But I continue tracking his movements from my balcony and by cultivating contacts with the core group of boat owners.

One day, some of the 'boat people' decide to visit *Gulliver* onboard *Canton,* and I tag along. This time he's onboard and in the middle of repair work.

Glad to see us, he puts all hands-on deck to work, during which conversation is devoted mostly to nautical shoptalk about shared experiences, repair and supply problems, complaints about the inflated costs of ownership, docking, licensing and registration fees. That, and all sorts of embellishment and story-swapping. About the best ports of call and personal best and worst experiences.

That, and tall tales. Some patent sea lore and fish yarns, others' tales of lust and gore, murder and madness allegedly committed on the high seas. Some no doubt fact, other parts factitious fable, but all of which makes for spellbound listening. Particularly to me, the only non-boatman present.

When it is *Gulliver's* turn, he tells a gothic tale about events among four crewmembers, two females and two males, onboard a luxury clipper. Two young, attractive Belgian women met a wealthy, middle-aged Englishman in a bar in Cape Verde, who was looking to hire a crew for a fantasy voyage from the Canaries to the West Indies, ideally a crew of two men and two women, in return for a generous salary. Later that evening, he offered the two women the jobs, provided they were qualified. The fourth ship mate, who was not present, was said to be a well-to-do friend of the Englishman's.

The women were keenly interested and admitted lacking any seafaring experience, but tried allaying his concerns and offered to help with the ship's other duties.

But to the Englishman, no matter how attractive the women were, prudence counseled caution. An experienced sailor, he knew the demands of wind and sea during such a lengthy, expensive journey and decided to postpone any decision until discussing matters with his partner.

The two women were determined though, and insisted on an opportunity to prove themselves, then voiced their own concerns. After all, they knew what he wanted. Two women and two men on a fully stocked yacht, this was going to be a sex cruise. They appealed to his vanity, flattering him by telling him that he was an attractive man, a gentleman with good bearing who didn't appear to be a threat to the two women. They admitted being interested in the idea of a fantasy voyage.

At the same time though they voiced their own safety concerns. Two women sailing across the Atlantic with two strange men was asking a lot. Not many women would have been that open for such an intimate adventure. For all they knew, the fourth sailor could have been a rapist or murderer.

Then they made a bold pitch. That they should forego the second male sailor and instead settle for a shorter cruise, island hopping the Azores.

"Why don't we go to your yacht tonight and become better acquainted? If you're hungry, we can make a sandwich with you. A *ménage*. Two women, you in the middle? Front and

back? Side to side? Soft and warm all over. You can snack all
you want." One of them said.

But the Englishman wasn't that 'hungry.' A crew of four
sailors – four good sailors - was non-negotiable, he insisted
and again vouched for the other sailor's good reputation.
Eventually the three of them agreed to meet the second sailor
over lunch the next day.

The two women were introduced to Panos Yiftoproxinos.
Short, stocky and somewhat younger than the Englishman,
the Greek textile merchant was unassuming, mild-mannered,
and willing to co-finance a 'leisure cruise.' Over lunch they
came to an agreement to shorten the cruise through the
Azores and on the salary offered.

But the women continued to voice concerns during their
negotiations. This was all unexpected. They weren't quite
prepared. They needed certain things and demanded
a sweetener. A good faith cash advance to shop for essentials
for such an extended trip. Once reassured they could 'work'
with the Greek sailor, they reached agreement and received a
generous 'shopping' advance. Congratulating their all-around
good fortune and toasting to good times, during lunch they
began planning the cruise.

A week later, together they set sail on doomed voyage.
Only those involved knew for sure what really happened,
with sketchy and accounts and scant details, with varying
versions of conflicting events. Perhaps one or both men
became fixated upon one woman? Perhaps one or both
women had spurned one of the men? Perhaps, nce they
coupled off, then one of the women or men disliked the
arrangement or objected to the pairings, ruining things for
others? Another version painted a picture of two pot-
smoking, lazy viragos who refused to work and rejected the
men's sexual advances, ruining expectations. Whatever the
cause, sex seems to have been central to events triggered
onboard the yacht, with jealously the likely motive. But on
whose part?

Speculation and fascination persisted, but the only
certainties were ambiguity and confusion about what really
happened on aboard the ill-fated clipper. Even the official
Coast Guard investigation's version of events was deliberately
vague. So much so, in an unusual move quietly and quickly
the record was sealed; and for good reason.

Due to the sensational nature of the story, following
persistent press inquiries six months later a heavily redacted
inquest was released, offering few details not already in

circulation. Stating, among other things, that: 'Foreign nationals all... While there exists an abundance of forensic and physical and photographic evidence of the manner of death as well as two signed confessions and three eye witnesses' accounts and other corroboration, absent any prima facie proof to the contrary, apparently D.D.,L, as alleged by the female victims, repeatedly attempted imposing his carnal desires upon both women. The accounts of the alleged rape victims, B.H., and V.S. are mutually corroborative. Both females have entered judicial pleas of self-defense homicide.'

The incident was precipitated by what the inquest cited as 'an attempted rape,' reportedly followed by 'a free-for-all.' The truth became even more complicated, since both women confessed to the crime. During the struggle, one of the women, who is unclear, retrieved a spear gun and harpooned the Englishman to death, nailing him to the mast.

D.D., L., though, no peasant was he. Indeed, Peer of the Realm of the British Empire, Lord Douglas Dilworth was a retired member of the House of Lords, which was why the record had been sealed. Even more scandalously, the scene of the crime, the yacht *Peerage*, was property of the British Crown.

No less prominent was the Greek, although for opposite reasons. A routine finger prints and background check revealed he was no textile merchant. He was a thief and not just any thief. Panos Yiftoproxinos, wanted under the moniker *Centipede*, the Greek was a career criminal sought on multiple outstanding Europol warrants.

Called *Centipede,* he was a master thief with a history of burglarizing the ultra-wealthy in their backyard playgrounds under a variety of guises. Sailor, cook, gardener, groomsman, chauffeur, with a taste for snatch-and-run booty. Jewelry, cash, *objects d'arts*. Bearer bonds, credit cards, currencies and other negotiable valuables. This season his targets were wealthy boat owners in Cape Verde, and the Englishman operating the most expensive yacht was his prey.

The role, if any, *Centipede* played in the alleged rape as participant or a witness; his sexual relationships with the three others; and his role, if any, in the death of Lord Dilworth. All that remained unclear.

Complicating matters, both women signed murder confessions exculpating the Greek and each other. Although the women let *Centipede* live, their treatment of him after the Englishman's death wasn't exactly gentle.

According to the inquest, one of the women reloaded and aimed the murder weapon at *Centipede*, while the other woman hogtied, blindfolded and gagged him. Then they locked him in a small closet below deck denying him food, drink or toilet privileges for days. They openly discussing within his earshot the physical cruelties they were going inflict and frame him by planting his fingerprints and making it appears as if *Centipede* had killed the Englishman. They talked about cutting out his tongue and amputating his hands so he so he could never again talk or write; To kill him then, or kill him later? They had no choice. He knew too much. He had to go.

Disposal of the body was their foremost concern as they considered the best options. Weighting the corpse's legs and simply dumping it overboard and throwing *Centipede* overboard alive but would have attracted sharks. Besides, they needed his help sailing the ship. So that, for the time being at least, they kept *Centipede* alive even though he knew too much. Whatever they were going to do with him would have to wait. Unless he died first of starvation and dehydration. The inquest cited *Centipede's* testimony: 'Like hyenas, those two *putas* kept threatening me and laughing at me.'

They fine-tuned their alibis until they became second nature. Both would confess to the crime and not incriminate each other. Next, covering their tracks they vandalized the yacht to make it appear as if a struggle had occurred. Once they got wherever they were going, though, they were going to get rid of *Centipede* once his usefulness had expired. They had to kill him too.

Their only concern was their escape from justice. Eventually they settled on a plan. Once close to land they were going to torching the yacht with both Lord Dilworth's cadaver and Panos alive onboard, and then make their chances in one of the life boats.

Rumors about the events onboard *Peerage* became embellished and eventually distorted into sea lore beyond the facts of the case. What the Belgian women, identified in the official inquest only as B.H. and V.R., did not know or take into consideration was the dead man's identity or the yacht's rightful ownership.

Alarmed by his disappearance, D.D., L's family notified authorities, prompting an investigation. MI-6, other British intelligence agencies and Home Office, concerned about a

Q

terrorist act, quickly located the missing vessel and reclaimed ownership of *Peerage*.

Once British special operations commandos boarded the listing vessel, they encountered a stench of a decomposing corpse nailed to the ship's mast, and two sun-blistered but unflappable women without any signs of injury or remorse but with suspiciously identical alibis. Below deck was a whimpering hostage.

Tipped off about events on the government yacht, Fleet Street ran riot and published some of the dark details come to light. Given the story's sensational nature, both women's confessions to murdering a prominent victim accused of attempted rape and, with the only witness in a state of psychiatric shock and indefinitely unavailable, the case obviously sparked great debate.

To some, B.H. and V.S. were revered as feminist heroines; others regarded them as wanton villainesses. Adding to the controversy, 'in the absence of sufficient legal evidence to hold them over' the two women were released on their own recognizance. Not much later, under a storm of protests and outrage led by the British government and to the cheers of many, this bad girl duo, *Thelma and Louise of the Seas* were acquitted on the psychiatric grounds of *folie a deux,* a shared delusion. Lord Dilworth's demise was officially listed as 'death by misadventure.' Throughout and thereafter, *Centipede* remained in custody under intensive psychiatric treatment awaiting extradition.

Riveted that I am by these yarns, then someone says that the story has all the makings of a book or screenplay. Someone else then mentions that *Gulliver* had written about his experiences at sea, which has been published and serialized in various publications.

With that disclosure, I realize I've lost the plot. Lulled into a false sense of security, I've become lax and nearly forgot the reason why I had to go... *incognegro*. When one wrong move could prove fatal. But *Gulliver* being a writer piques my interest. Particularly, I'm interested in his most recent travels. Where was he prior to Martinique? When was the last time he was in Switzerland? What's the longest he ever stayed in any one place? What's his favorite place; I ask him.

His explanations are insightful. He hasn't been home, Switzerland, in a long time, not just because getting there by boat is difficult. A case of childhood rickets left him sensitive to cold weather. For that reason, he prefers the warm climates of the southern hemisphere, the South Pacific and the Caribbean, presently the *Golden Quadrant.* As far as the longest being in any one place was some three to three and half years, he says.

I imagine Brazil, Tahiti, maybe even Martinique, or some other exotic port of call. But three to three and a half years in one place for such an obviously died-in-the-wool salty dog? "That seems pretty long. So, where was this?" I say.

He pauses, then says, "Indonesia."

"Yeah? Bet you got your heart broken by one of those Indonesian beauties." I say.

"Yeah, I got my heart broken, alright." He takes a long swig of cold coffee and then says. "I was in jail - for murder."

He takes another gulp of cold coffee. "First person I ever killed." Then, comparing his story to the one he just told with his own situation, "But it my case, it really was self-defense." he says as if remembering to himself.

An otherwise light-hearted gathering, the moment turns awkward. Slack-jaw dumbfounded, as are some others present, I never expected such brutal honesty. Then he makes a thinly veiled comment, intended to discourage any further forays into his past. "Let's just say that." He says, steady sipping coffee. Then, with a piercing stare and menacing edge in his voice, he says. "Let's just say that... and let's leave it at that. *Alles klar?* (Am I clear?)" It isn't a warning; it's a threat. And that's the way I take it.

"*Ganz klar.* (Loud and clear.)" I say, then I drop it like it's hot; radioactive hot.

A tense atmosphere now hovers heavy onboard. A few, those who seem to know him the best (and refer to him as *Gulliver*), don't appear particularly surprised by his admission and soon resume conversation among themselves and with *Gulliver*. He doesn't register the slightest sense of embarrassment or remorse for confessing to multiple murders, one of whom my best friend. Instead, nonchalant, as if having admitted to nothing more than a traffic violation or income tax evasion, he pours us more cold coffee before resuming his chores.

After leaving *Canton*, I ask one of those who seems to know *Gulliver* somewhat about him and didn't appear surprised by *Gulliver's* revelations.

"He's someone who has seen and done it all; that's for sure. To think; he nearly entered the seminary. And now he's a veteran freelancer. Central and South America, Panama and the Gulf War. The Middle East. Works only for the highest bidder. Go figure." He says with a chuckle.

"Freelancing; must be nice. I remember someone said he's a writer." I say.

"No. That's not what I mean. I thought you knew. Everyone else does. He doesn't advertise it but he doesn't hide it either. No, he's a mercenary. A soldier for hire. He calls it 'private contractor' and 'security consultant.' He specializes in corporate contracts. He's somewhat ideological. Obviously, it's very lucrative. How else do you think he could afford that expensive, high-performance boat? Not from writing for that *Soldiers' Magazine* or from book royalties; that's for sure. That thing can outrun the damn Coast Guard. And it has on more than one occasion. Like I said, he gets ideological sometimes. Especially once he starts talking about *Novi Orbis*. But at heart he's really a nice guy. But you didn't hear this from me. *Alles klar*?" He says with a wink.

"*Ganz klar.*" I say, in Amada having seen firsthand his signature and ideology at work. *Alles klar,* indeed.

Back at the hotel, browsing the internet soon I locate *Soldiers' Magazine* and *Dog of War Magazine* web sites. In them, complete with his picture and code name, *Gulliver*, alongside his book cover and its sales advertisement, he also is listed on the masthead as a contributing editor. And prominently displayed on the magazines' web sites are links to his book's web site, featuring brief biographical information and his book, *Sails to the Wind,* penned under his pseudonym, *Gulliver*, available for hardcopy sale and download.

Carelessness overcomes me. Visiting his personal web site without using a proxy server or secure browser is the first in a series of serious mistakes.

The second serious mistake is ordering a copy of his book as well as back issues of *Soldiers' Magazine* and *Dog of War Magazine* through a university account.

Finally, I commit a third error. From that day on, particularly after receiving the book and magazines I continue visiting those and several related, ideological web sites and links. I never send e-mail inquiries, though.

These three mistakes, along with other missteps along the way, will come back to bite me.

Once in possession of that information, a previously shifting shape assumes gradual outline, and a distinct and disturbing profile emerges. Between what is on the flash drive and information gleaned from the circle of sailors who know him, admittedly a cursory biographical sketch, his profile reveals disturbing details.

In terms of background, none of which has been double-source confirmed, at least this much is known about him:
Born: Jürgen Naumann, age: circa 45
Alias(es): aka, Larry Talbot, Gunther Tell
Known code name(s)/Nom(s) de Guerre:
Gulliver, Prime Evil, *Comandante*,
Crazy Horse, *Shiva*, Captain Blood.
Nationality(ies): Born: Swiss,
Naturalized: Australian
Appearance: older than his age.
Muscular build, ca. 6'1," 190 lbs,
Features: blond hair, blue eyes,
Complexion: weather ruddy
Distinguishing Characteristic(s):
Fixed, dilated pupils
Marital Status: Single.
Residence: Ship *Canton*
Address: The Seven Seas
Occupation: Private corporate security,
agent provocateur, motivational speaker
Contractor expertise: economic destabilization,
Target triangulation/elimination, sabotage
Corporate/government Security Consultant.
Job description(s): mercenary, soldier of fortune,
dog of war, Cover Identity: Sailor, writer
Speciality(ies) Skill(s): merchant marine
Covert operations, Ordinance expertise;
Wet work contractor/Crime scene erasure;
Enhanced interrogation techniques, explosives
expertise
Previous Tour(s) of Duty(ies):
Asia, Middle East, Southern Africa,
Philippines, Central and South America
New Orleans, USA (Hurricane Katrina)
Clients: the highest bidder, C.I.A. Pentagon,
F*riends of Friends (Mafia),*
corporate, hydro-carbon and hospitality travel
industries, Dictators *du jour* Exception(s):
No communist contracts
Legal Status: Fugitive wanted on multiple
outstanding international warrants
Present Assignment: The *Golden Quadrant.*
Present Employer: Geremi Quarrles, Spañada,
a.k.a. the Sinister Prime Minister.
Present Rank: Commander, *Guiding Star*

Q

Born in Basel, Switzerland, middle child of three siblings, his father was a hardware storeowner, his mother worked as the store's bookkeeper. Prior to being diagnosed at age fourteen with severe rickets, he attended Jesuit school and once was regarded as a promising seminarian. During frequent and lengthy hospitalizations for his immunodeficiency disorder, Jürgen passed the time reading. Beginning with *Treasure Island* and with a fondness for *Robinson Crusoe* and Karl May novels. Characters like *Winnetou*, *Shatterhand*, and *Friday*. His eventual codename, moniker and *nom de guerre* he adopted from an early favorite novel, Jonathan Swift's title character, *Gulliver*.

Upon discharge from the hospital, he was sent to recuperate in what then was called a 'sanatorium' near Naples, Italy. That experience, the Neapolitan harbor scene at sunset, was life-changing. Naples Bay and later in Capri, in his mind those adventure novels came to life. He fell in love with the climate. He knew he couldn't return to the Alpine cold.

More than that, he felt disconnected from Swiss provincialism. Particularly once he discovered sailing. Due to his health and climate sensitivity, his parents enrolled him in a Neapolitan school hoping he would later fulfil their dream and enter the seminary. Instead, he decided he wanted to travel and joined the Swiss merchant marine academy for a two-year stint.

Due to his medical history, per his request he was assigned to Mediterranean ports. Moody Istanbul, buoyant Athens, Malta, Crete and all Sahara African ports in between. To Jürgen, the antiquities, Homer's *Iliad,* Ovid's *Aeneid,* the lost cities of Troy and Carthage, Phoenicia and Syracuse. He dreamed of a career in the merchant marine, the smell of sea air and promise of adventure opened his nostrils and imagination. He became hooked on the dream of seeing the world. Maybe one day even designing and building his own dreamboat.

Occasionally he socialized with shipmates but mostly he was something of a loner. Eventually he began doubting about attending seminary, something that had been his parents' dream who, for some reason, always wanted a priest in the family. But after hospitalizations over the years, he couldn't imagine a monastic, solitary life and quietly abandoned the idea of attending seminary. Particularly having tasted and developed a thirst for the outdoors, his imagination fueled by those ports of call and their promise of adventure.

But those dreams, indeed his whole life, came crashing to
halt on his first Naples/Macao/Naples tour of duty. While in
Macao bar hopping in the harbor's underbelly, green Jürgen
was instant, easy prey who was soon 'befriended' by two
locals, man and woman, who took him to various seedy
waterfront dives. Somewhere along the line, one of them
spiked his drink.

Eighteen hours later, he awoke in a seedy flop hotel.
Awakened only because the door was being kicked in and
raided by the police. By then, pimp and prostitute were long
gone, and so was everything else. His money, his passport,
his gun; and his ship. He had overslept and failed to return
from shore leave. He was AWOL. The only things left, a bottle
of *sake,* a pot of green tea and spent opium paraphernalia.

Turns out, it was an opium den. Everyone in the building
was arrested and charged with drug offenses. In his case,
possession of narcotics and contraband and with the intent of
distribution. Weeks passed before the Swiss merchant marine
confirmed his identity. Due to the nature of the case,
narcotics, the Swiss government declined any comment
pending the conclusion of Macao's legal proceedings. In other
words, they washed their hands of him.

Poor and white in Asia, his misfortunes multiplied.
Regardless if a native or a foreigner, local justice was harsh
with mandatory Draconian penalties for drug offenders,
including the death penalty for intent of distribution. In his
favor, those charges later were reduced to personal
possession and minimum ten years' incarceration. The cost of
official corruption, called 'administrative fees,' ran upwards of
fifty thousand dollars for white people. Whites were
considered wealthy; but he wasn't. All he had was ten
thousand dollars, savings earmarked for his boat. Ten
thousand dollars, to cover part of those 'administrative fees.'
In 'exchange' for those 'partial administrative fees,' Jürgen
was granted a sentence reduction; five years' imprisonment.

Thanks to his family in Switzerland who paid twenty-five
dollars, he was granted full 'exemption and commutation.'
That meant another two years' sentence reduction. In all,
including time off for good behavior, he served two and a half
years of an eight-year sentence in a Macao prison.

By now a dishonorably discharged merchant marine, any
maritime career or employment in civil society in general,
never mind his dreamboat, were impossible. Felon and
disgrace to himself and family, humiliated and too proud to

return home, with one thousand dollars to his name and still a sailor at heart, Jürgen left Macao.

Wayward seminarian booked passage on the first ship moving, whatever the destination. In his case, Sumatra. A month later, again he set sail from Medan hiring on a trawler. Destination, Java, where he disappeared into Djakarta's multitude.

His past and current circumstances, his new environment, they further corrupted him. Lying about his past and never filling out a job application, instead odd-jobbing as a hired mate, itinerant longshoreman and on junkets for day pay. Days he covered the water front work halls and longshoremen offices looking for work. A tough world inhabited by other tough and shady characters eking out an existence, with nights spent in a succession of nether world flop hotels and seedy bars staring into the bottom of liquor bottles.

Just how hardened he'd become he demonstrated one night in a seedy Djakarta water front bar. After buying an advance job listing, three strangers, two Indonesians and an Australian, approached Jürgen tried to bully him into 'sharing' the information with them. The listing was expensive enough without any more competition for already scarce work. When Jürgen refused to 'share,' they jumped him.

Big mistake. Jürgen snatched a bottle, smashed it by its neck, then disfigured one attacker. Another assailant he grabbed by the throat, smashed him face-first into the bar surface, then hurled him into the wall. Then there was an odd sound, and the man collapsed into a lifeless heap, dead of a broken neck.

This time, his situation was much worse even than in Macao. This time he had killed someone in a bar full of witnesses; even though self-defense. With the sound of approaching police sirens and, to his racing mind, with no other choice left Jürgen fled the scene.

Someone followed him, though. Two white men alighting from a car aimed guns at Jürgen and ordered him into the front seat. Once inside the car, a waiting gunman in the back seat levelled a gun at Jürgen's head, and then the four sped off.

Jürgen assumed they were friends of the Australian victim of the bar fight. He was convinced they were going to kill him. Once at a secluded location, the Indonesian gunman remained in the car while the two others, who were Americans, interrogated him. Then they issued an him ultimatum. Accept their terms or they would hand him over to the Indonesian authorities, who frowned on foreigners killing their citizens. This time, the death penalty was all but certain. Then they handed him what they called a 'get-out-of-jail-card'with an address and phone number of a lawyer. They promised him an alibi for the night's events and offered to testify in his behalf. At most, he faced three to five years in jail. They also promised him a job once he was released.

Whatever the sentence, in return for an alibi and lawyer's services Jürgen was to work for them for five years. The money was good, more money than he ever had, no questions asked. After five years, if he wanted, he could renew. With no choice, he agreed to their terms.

The three agents drove him to police headquarters where he surrendered. Events played out much as predicted. The agents and lawyer were more helpful than the Swiss government ever had been during his prison time in Macao. His surrender stood to his credit, and the agents testified on his behalf in their description of the bar fight. His sentence, manslaughter, was five years' imprisonment minus six months' pre-trial detention. In all four and a half years.

He never informed his family of his new ordeal, and it was only after his release that he learned his mother had died during his second jail stint. A stint, other than one visit by his lawyer, during which Jürgen had no contact with the outside world. With the only language he heard, 'that blathering Indonesian.'

During this hellish, second incarceration Jürgen resolved these three things. Caged for the last five plus years, his life seemingly cursed, Jürgen vowed he'd never go back to jail, that he would die first. Secondly, whatever the agents wanted after his release, even if illegal, he no longer cared. He would do anything. He wanted the money the agents kept promising him. His third vow was his renunciation of faith and renegade rejection of God. He could not conceive that God would allow his harsh fate spent in living hell.

Three and a half years later, Jürgen was met by the same two agents, who drove him from prison to a red-light district flop house hotel room and then presented him with an employment contract and its conditions.

Mr. Gray and Mr. Green were recruiters. They knew everything about him. His merchant marine background, about Macao. That as a Swiss citizen he was fluent in three languages as well as some Chinese and now Indonesian. What they were particularly interested in, though, was his maritime skills and knowledge of different kinds of sea faring vessels.

Specifically, they wanted him to employ him as a 'transporter' to pre-arranged destinations and use his 'language skills in the international market.' They offered no further details and refused to answer his questions. He was there to listen.

The salary package was too good to be true and only heightened his suspicions. With that much money, he would repay his family and even begin saving again towards his dreamboat. But that much money probably meant something illegal, whatever. That much good money, he didn't care what kind of cargo. All he wanted was a chance to sail again, even if it wasn't the ocean but sailing some wind still swamp river.

After a few trial runs, Jürgen was transferred to the Philippines' back waters as a transporter for the next year. Minimal work for which he was well compensated. As part of standard operating procedure, prior to each mission he was warned against inspecting the cargo.

A year later, Jürgen's new assignment was back in Indonesia. As part of a security arrangement, he was to locate and deliver a severed Silver Dollar to the bearer of the other missing coin half. If unable to locate the bearer of the coin half, he was to return to his hotel pending further instructions. Upon mission completion, he would be given new instructions. His instructions were to sail only at night and warned again not to inspect the cargo. Enclosed was a map with his destination, five thousand dollars' cash, and a new doubled salary package contract.

Not the least bit clear about the coin business or what to expect once he located the other coin half, the trek proceeded uneventfully. Once at his midnight rendezvous destination, someone on a bullhorn ordered Jürgen on shore. There, in what appeared to be nearby shrubbery, he noticed slight movement.

Shape-shifting out of environs' shadows, as if preternatural, emerged a war paint-camouflaged figure with a powerful torso, bald but otherwise notably hirsute with hands the size of catcher's mitts and fingers like sausages. Cheap sorcery which left Jürgen unimpressed, who simply displayed the severed coin. "I'm looking for this coin's missing match. If I'm right, I think I'm looking for you. If not, let's not waste each other's time and I'll find whom I'm looking for. But I think it's you. Anyone else wouldn't make much sense, now; wouldn't it?" He said.

"I'm Major Brown. Come with me." The officer said, then they headed to a nearby tent. "I believe this is what you're looking for." He said, then handed Jürgen the Silver Dollar's other-half, and congratulated Jürgen on a job well done.

Major Brown was another *Backwater* recruiter and trainer for the largest private army in the world, and this was the final phase of Jürgen's probation. *Backwater* was impressed not only by the way he handled himself during the bar fight but also by the way he had dealt with his jail stints by doing the 'stand-up right thing.' *Backwater* was equally impressed with his nautical skill, cunning and courage as a clandestine ordinance transport field operative.

Next, Major Brown proposed something extraordinary. Not continued clandestine ordinance transport; but school. Intelligence analysis as well as operations training and planning with a higher pay grade than his current pay scale. The choice was entirely Jürgen's.

He had not known a day's peace of mind since Macao. This whole part of the world, from Macao to Djakarta, and all points in between, it was an impenetrable world, eerie, opaque. Serially alien cultures, enveloped in secrecy, cast in superstition and ritualism, teeming with insects and populated with completely unknowable people and an unpalatable cuisine. A place with bad karma not only for him but too dangerous for any poor white man.

After years of a transient life in jails and flea bag hotels he had come to believe was permanent, apparently life was offering Jürgen a lifeline. School sounded just fine. The farther ways from Macao and Djakarta, from Asia, to his mind the better. So, what if *Backwater* school was in North Carolina?

Basically, school was boot camp. Heaven for someone who enjoyed the outdoors, especially after years in hospitals and jail.

The curriculum wasn't half bad, either. Sun Tzu, Hannibal Barca. Scipio Africanus, Alexander Magnus. Von Clausewitz, Machiavelli. Force and guile. Psychology, economic destabilization. Currency manipulation, counterfeit currency dumping. Guerilla warfare, covert operations. Ordinance expertise, agent provocateur activities. Wet work, crime scene cleaning and restoration. Martial arts and interrogation techniques. Torture methods and their limits. Vehicular sabotage, weapons training.

Above everything, psychological testing and training emphasized plausible deniability and doing 'the stand-up right thing,' especially if captured. That meant keeping one's mouth shut and disavowal of any knowledge of all *Backwater* existence and operations.

Backwater agents recruited among former military personnel and longshoremen with an eye and ear for certain traits. In him they correctly spotted the ideal recruit. Someone military caliber. Under ordinary circumstances, someone with a promising military career.

Someone with a command-and-control personality and capable of mission execution. Someone smart and bitter, broken and depressed. Given his recent background and lack of stability, someone with violent tendencies. In boot camp, he stood out among recruits and began attracting the attention of his superiors, who recognized his merchant marine pedigree. Word of him began spreading up the chain of command among the *Backwater* brass, and beyond. A *protégé,* someone with great future *Backwater* promise.

They were dead right on in their assessment of Jürgen. That midnight under a *Backwater* Bali riverbank tent marked a milestone. The failed priest's exact conversion date of his Faustian bargain and transformation into *Gulliver.* Master of the *métier*, the dark arts', one of his many codenames.

Six months after boot camp, *Gulliver's* first assignment was southern Central America and northern South America. The Canal Zone, Panama City and Belize City. Puerto Limon and Puerto Lempira. Islas del Maiz, Bocas de Toro and Colombia. *Backwater* mission operations included search and destroy of rebel operations and other enemy guerillas encampments - real and alleged. Drug interdiction and crop eradication throughout the region. Combat tours of duty usually lasted two months. Jungle combat duty was particularly tough, that sudden night combat, *mano a mano,* in the killing fields.

Starting with his hospitalizations, *Gulliver* kept a journal describing his illness and initial maritime impressions. Lengthier entries describe his judicial and prison hardships, his hardening of heart and his final renunciation of faith and rejection of God. The focus then shifts to the inner peace he finds in his passion, sailing. The last entries describe and defend his *Novi Orbis* beliefs. Writing under his synonym, *Gulliver,* he published excerpts in *Soldiers' Magazine* and *Dog of War Magazine*.

The response was enormous. So much so, both magazines jointly published his autobiography, *Sails to the Wind*. The book became a cult phenomenon among nationalist circles and made *Gulliver* an icon and spokesman as well as regular contributor and eventual editor in the pages of *SM* and *DWM*. Soon *Gulliver* was in great demand as a speaker under various aliases and *noms de guerre*. *Gulliver*, *Crazy Horse*, *Shiva*. Or, more recently simply his rank, *Comandante*.

In those pages and in other specialty journals, on the lecture circuit as a motivational speaker and other forum, his topics and targets were 'unregenerate welfare state socialism. 'Alien immigration.' 'Radical Islam.' 'The usurpation of Western values and way of life.' The 'gospel of capitalism.' All under their rallying banner: *'Novi Orbis*.' Claiming a religious experience, from rejection of God to revelation from God, in conversion *Gulliver* now saw himself and like-minded others as new Knights Templar, God's warriors and avengers in global holy crusade championing their creed's battle cry for a New World Order; so-called *Novi Orbis*.

In such demand, he was able to repay his family and began saving towards the construction of his boat design while climbing the ranks, and rising to regional commander and deputy director of *Backwater*'s intelligence network. So that between his salary, combat pay and income from *Sails to the Winds*, *Gulliver* became wealthy beyond his expectations, in demand as writer and lecturer, motivational speaker and movement icon.

He soon completed construction of his dreamboat, *Canton,* and lives onboard, traveling to the world's various *Backwater* hot stop and tours of duty, ever ready to service his diverse variety of clientele. Dictators and potentates, intelligence services and their *Friends of Friends*. Corporate security and weapons brokers.

Unspoken, his current paymaster and mission. But that much I already know that. The Caribbean front man for the hydrocarbon, hospitality and travel cartels. Geremi Quarrles; aka, the Sinister Prime Minister. His army, *Guiding Star*. Its leader, *Gulliver*, Ayri's murderer. A menace to the region directly responsible for the *coup d'état* in Amada and, together they are lording over the *Golden Quadrant,* with evil designs on the region's energy reserves.

I rightfully step-up safety precautions. First, Catalina and I stop sleeping on our hotel balcony. Second, I instruct the hotel not to disclose my name and switch my registration to an alias. Third, I stop writing in my suite. Instead, I back up my entire work product onto a separate flash drive and then store everything - all hardware, software and peripherals, in the bank safe.

Next, I re-deposit the original flash drive in the safe deposit box at the *Banc De Paris*. I go back to writing in the bank's safe deposit room. Then I compose a chronology of events and names. I have it notarized and, along with my notarized Will and instructions to trip that dead man's switch in the event of my sudden death or disappearance.

Lastly, I forward everything to my brother/agent/attorney. And while I continue monitoring *Gulliver's* activities from my hotel, I make sure our paths no longer cross as often.

One night, though, I run into him at *Hotel Bamboo* seaside restaurant and bar featuring fine food and chilled libation. That evening, he is in the company of a Canadian woman I had met on other occasions.

By the time I'm about to leave for my hotel to resume writing, on my way to the exit Gulliver waves me to his table. No longer in the company of other boat owners, the thought of being alone with him, considering everything that has happened between us, makes me nauseous, uncertain what to expect, how to act and react. Unsure I won't bust a gut and PTSD-spaz out on him.

Certain things about him are obvious. Not just that he's the only white man seated alone at a rear restaurant table. His race, his rugged appearance, his gruff manner and physical mien, they're overshadowed by something else and his most prominent feature.

Usually he wears sunglasses, not tonight though. It's clear why he does. It's his eyes. They're striking, and frighteningly so. Despite the late-night restaurant setting's dim lighting, his iris appears dilated, almost as large as his pupils, giving him a diabolical, hypnotic look. Those dilated pupils and his hot breath I recall from my prison interrogation in Amada.

By then, it's late. Although there is an assortment of bottles on the table, he doesn't appear drunk. Gone now any sign of reticence, he appears animated and expansive, as if looking for company and conversation. Not wanting to appear that I'm avoiding him, I have no choice and, against my better judgment and with Ayri heavy on my mind, reluctantly I join him.

Initially our conversation is small talk about mutual acquaintances. But that soon changes. I feel increasingly uncomfortable under his stare.

"You know; I just realized something. I see you all the time. You're everywhere. You always turn up but I don't know anything about you. I really don't. I don't even know your name. I'm serious. I'm not sure anyone else knows anything about you either, for that matter. You're an empty page. Why is that?" He says.

"Well, southern Martinique's a small slice of paradise. The same people keep bumping into each other." I say.

"Funny that you say that. That's my point. There's something about you, like I've seen you before. I can't put my finger on it, yet." *Gulliver* says with that cat's eye stare. Then suddenly labile, his mood becomes borderline hostile. "Who are you? Why are you following me? Who are you?" He says.

I knew it. As soon as I sat down; I knew I shouldn't be alone with him. I should have left Martinique and returned to Harlem, then I'd never be in this situation. But like the moth drawn to the flame, I can't help myself. I find myself in an empty seaside restaurant with the person responsible for everything that happened. Alone with Ayri's killer who will kill me too if he remembers my identity. I'm so out of my league. No, I'm out of my mind. In this case, the truth won't make me free. It will make me dead. He's already suspicious of me. Not all that long ago, *Gulliver* inspected my passport. He knows my real name. One false move may cost me my life. No longer am I so... *incognegro.*

But after everything he did, not so much what he did to me but to Ayri, to the Mentis family, my emotions override my common sense. I become reckless, blinded by revenge and in single-minded pursuit of a story. Reckless to the point of repeatedly putting everyone and everything at risk and violating my pledge to Ayri to write his story.

I can't help myself though. Not at the risk of my personal safety, not even at the expense of my promise to Ayri. If I want to keep living a little bit longer and try to get even, then my only choice is to keep playing charades. One false move though, or if he's figures me out, then I'm dead.

"Don't act like you didn't hear me. I asked you a question. Who are you?" Then easing off somewhat, this time more softly, much like in Amada, *Gulliver* says. "What's your name? Your *real* name?"

"Come on. You know my name. Are you really that drunk? Remember; we played *Fußball* and I was always open? You know the saying? 'Pass the ball to the open man.' Everyone kept saying, pass the ball to whom? Think! Even before then. *Denk doch, Mensch."* ("Think, man.") I say.

"Kai? Kai? That's right. I remember now." *Gulliver* recalls my alias and godson's name.

"That's right. Kai-Armand." I said.

"Kai." *Gulliver* repeats then, continuing in his interrogation. "So, what's your family name, Kai?"

"Richter." I use a friend's name. From then on, I'm in free association mode.

"Yes, Kai Richter. Yes, I remember. My apologies." He says, our gazes still locked, and then in a soft voice he continues interrogating me.

"So, tell me. Your mother. She's German; *ja*?" He says.

"*Ja.*" I lie.

"I see. But your father? What's his nationality? Turk? Kemal Ataturk was a great man. A very unusual man. Many vices in such a short life. So. What are you? No? No Turk? Maybe Roma?
You know, Sinti? Are you Arab? From your game, I'd say South American? You know; Brazilian? So? Your father? Where is he from?" He says.

"Almost; but not quite. Say U.S.A. My father is American." I say, aware that in Amada he didn't want an American journalist – dead or alive – 'gumming up the works on his watch.' And which is why he had me transferred me to the prison *lazaret* and ordered exploratory surgery looking for that *Smoking Gun*.

"So, you're a *Mischling* (Mixed race)? A taboo baby?" He turns pejorative, perhaps hoping to bait me.

"No, more like a music child." I say.

"Ah, ha. So, your father, he's a black American? A G.I? A G.I. musician? I bet he plays saxophone. Jazz. Am I right?" *Gulliver* said.

"Good guess." I lie.

"What city? Let me guess. He's from Harlem?" *Gulliver* says.

"You're pretty good at guessing. What's tomorrow's winning lottery number?" I say.

"I don't like jazz." He says. "So, I know you speak English. Have you ever been to New York?" He says.

"Sure." I say.

"I'm curious; tell me. You are a *Mischling*. But deep down, do you feel more German or American? Black or white? What are your loyalties?" He says.

"*Also halt deutsch.* (German.) That's what my passport says." I say.

"But your race? You are a *Mischling*. You're not one thing or the other. Sure, your passport says German. But you are also American. So, in your heart which one are you? American or German? White or black?" He says.

"Do I look white to you? I don't think so either. I am what I look like. I'm just another brown face in a brown world. In the end, it's not about that black or that white thing. It's all about that right and wrong thing." I say.

"Your passport? May I see it?" He says.

"It's in the hotel safe." I say.

"So, tell me; Kai. How long have you been here in Martinique?" He says.

"Almost two months." I say.

"That's a long vacation. And before Martinique; where were you?" He continues staring at me.

"Back home. *München*." I say.

"And what's your address in *München*?" He says.

"*Kurfürsten Strasse* 44." I say.

"*Also, Kai Richter aus München,* if that is your real name? What do you do for a living?" He says.

Avoiding any mention of being a teacher or writer, instead I stick to my alibi and cover story. "I'm a television producer. Children's programming. Game shows, academic contests, nature shows. You know; news for kids. Kids meeting celebrities and athletes. Stuff like that." I assume a friend's identity and occupation.

"Really? I never would have guessed that. Honestly, the first time I saw you play. Your first touch and ball control. The way you keep your head up. Your vision, the way you read the game. At first, I thought you might be Brazilian or South American, based on your game. But *Fußball's* a young man's game. You can still run but you're too old to be in one of the leagues.

"Then, when I watched you swim out to my boat and back, ocean swimming's hard. Then I thought; the shape you're in. Always checking things out. Elusive, mysterious. I have this habit. When people start watching things, I start watching them. I've been watching you. Like I said. The shape you're in. I wouldn't want to fair fight you. No... I'd have to shoot you. So, I thought you might be... You know... Intelligence services. A foreign agent. A spy. So, that means we are colleagues; am I right? Well, what's your branch? Military, political, or corporate? Or covert ops? Whose side are you on?" He says, his stare locked on me.

"Me? A foreign agent? A spy? That's crazy. I'm the biggest coward on earth. I'm afraid of the kids on my show. My knees are too weak for cloak and dagger stuff. Besides, I'm apolitical.
Politics, politicians, they stink. I'm not about to spy or die for one of them. The last thing I am is a spy." I say.

"You've been here two months; right?" He says.

"That's right." I say.

"How much longer will you be here?" He says.

"I don't know yet." I say.

"How can you afford it? A jeep? *Vespa? Hotel Madinina?"* He says.

"A promotion. I'm on sabbatical. Brainstorming, generating new show ideas. I don't know how much longer I'll be here. I hadn't planned on staying this long but I fell in love. Women can make you do things you don't want to but end up liking. You know how it is." I say.

"No; I don't know how it is." He says. Indeed, hard imagining anyone loving such an evil person. "I've seen you with her. The one from the bank. That's right; I know." He says. Then he breaks his stare, smiles, and he says. "You like playing games; don't you? Like now."

Not sure where he was coming from or heading, I say. "You mean like chess, backgammon, and blackjack? And well, after our game? The way I destroyed all of you? I played like a real *Weltmeister*. I know you can't mean the beautiful game."

"No. That's not what I mean." *Gulliver* says.

"You've lost me." I say.

"Like right now, you're playing games. That's what you're doing. You're a comedian? An actor? Funny man? What? This is some kind joke to you? You think you can play head games with me? Like I'm some toy? You think that you can outsmart me?" He says, an edge in his voice and posture.

"What?" I say.

"You want to play games - with *me*? You think you can play with me? Alrighty then. Let's play! We'll play *my* game. *My* head games. I ask you a question, you answer the question; truthfully. Then you get to ask a question, and I answer your question; truthfully." *Gulliver* says.

"'Truth or Dare?' What's the point? You've already asked me questions, and I've answered them." I say.

"I told you; it's a game. An exchange of information. It helps in getting to know a person. The ways questions are asked and answered, or not answered. Our responses, body linguistics. Tone of voice and rate of speech. Eye contact and involuntary movements, rapid respiration. Reading people, it's a skill." *Gulliver* says.

"We just played that game." I say.

"So, what? You can play games, but when someone else says, 'let's play a game', suddenly you don't want to? It's only a game. Come on. Unless you're hiding something? Are you

afraid? Afraid you'll let slip that you know where it is?"
Gulliver says.

"Alright. Okay." I say.

"Okay. Ready?" He says. "First question; your favorite
meal?" *Gulliver* says.

"*Sauerbraten und Semmelknödel mit Bohnensalat.*
(German pot roast, bread dumplings and green bean salad).
And yours?" I say.

"Pheasant-under-the-glass with *Spätzle.* What's your
favorite beverage?" He says.

"*Bernkasteler Doctor.* What's yours?" I say.

"*Sake.* What's your favorite place?" *Gulliver* continues his
so-called 'head games.'

"Barcelona. Yours?" I say.

"Melbourne. Your favorite musician?" He asks now
somewhat faster.

"My father." I say.

"Family doesn't count. Choose someone else." *Gulliver*
says.

"Keith Jarrett. Keith Jarrett makes me cry. You?" I say.

"Herbert Grönemeyer. Your favorite author and book?"
He says ever faster.

"Favorite writer, Hermann Hesse. *Magister Ludi - The Glass
Bead Game,* favorite book. And you?" I say.

"Favorite book, *Lord Jim.* Favorite writer, Joseph Conrad.
Your favorite movie and favorite actor?" His questions are now
staccato pace.

"Oh, that's easy. Rudy Ray Moore's body of work. Who
can't be affected by his fine, nuanced performances as
Dolomite. That's just pure classic stuff." I joke, trying to slow
the pace of questions and answers.

"Rudy Ray Moore? *Dolomite?* I've never heard of him.
Name another actor and movie." He says.

"Okay. Ben Kingsley in *Gandhi.* And you?" I say.

"That's hard. I have two favorites. The first one, that
master of fright and suspense in that classic horror motion
picture." *Gulliver* says.

Sensing something amiss although not knowing that we are
in the end game of his head game, I take the bait. "What's
that?"

"You'd never guess. That would be *Midnight Express.*
Right?" *Gulliver* says. Then he lights another cigarette, murder
in his eyes. For the longest studying my every reaction
through the thick cigarette smoke, then he says.

"But you already knew that; didn't you? Didn't you? Look at me. Don't you look down. You look me in the eyes. You heard me; I said look at me. You'd better look at me when I talk to you. There, that's better. You already knew that; didn't you? You knew because we already had this conversation; didn't we? Once before, in another time. Not too long ago, in another place. Didn't we? Didn't we? You look afraid. You have every reason to be afraid, and I'm going to keep you that way; very afraid." Then he says.

"Now, my property; I want it back. Tell me what I want to know. Where is it? At the bank? It's at the bank. That's where it is. It's at the bank; isn't it? The flash drive, it's at the bank so no one can get to it. Is that why you go there every day for hours? Is that's why you're so afraid? Afraid because now you know that I know you're hiding it. It's at the bank. That's where it is; isn't it? That means you know the secret. Who else knows? What side are you on? Did any copies go wiki? Where is it? It's at *Banc de Paris*. Where she works. Yes. I told you; I know. I know everything. Everything except; where is it?" He says.

I'm gob smacked. He knows. He really knows everything. If he doesn't know he suspects enough to monitor my movements. Where I'm staying, my itinerary. He knows about Catalina and where she works. It's just a matter of time before he fully connects the dots. My recklessness has placed Catalina in danger. "What? You're following me? What makes you think I'm a spy? What I'm afraid of is that this game doesn't make any sense." I say.

"I told you. The game tells us a lot about each other." *Gulliver* says.

"Yeah. superficial stuff. *Sake,* pheasant-under the-glass. Melbourne, *Lord Jim.* Tell me something important. Like how you became a sailor? Is that what you wrote about in your book? I'm sure you've had some interesting experiences. You tell me yours, I'll tell you mine. The way real people normally talk." I say.

But *Gulliver* zooms in. "That's a feeble attempt at changing the subject. Tell me; where were you before you arrived in Martinique?"

"Already asked and answered. Remember?" I say.

"I'm asking again." He says.

"I already told you." I say.

"Then humor me; why don't you?" He says.

"At home in Munich." I say.

"Tell me; have you ever been to Amada?" He smirks, studying my every reaction.

"Where?" I say.

"You heard me. I said Amada." Slowly, softly, *Gulliver* says the island's name.

I have no choice. "Never even heard of it. Where's that?" I say.

"It's a small island in the *Golden Quadrant*. Maybe five hundred miles due south from here." *Gulliver* says.

"That's almost Brazil." I say.

"Just about. You remind of someone I met there." *Gulliver* says.

"Who's that?" By now I'm certain he's made me.

"An American. Said he was a teacher and writer from Harlem, New York City. Where you're from." He says.

"No. I'm from Munich." I say.

"That's right. Your father, he's the one from Harlem. Anyhow, this American, I only met him once. Somehow you resemble him. The same shifty body linguistics, just like you. Couldn't look a man in the eye.

See? Like now. You're being shifty again. That's what I mean. Just like him. What's wrong? Are you nervous? Why are you so fidgety? Relax. Here; have some more wine." *Gulliver* goes to refresh our drinks, but I shield my glass.

"What? Afraid I'll see your hands shake? What? Why are you so nervous; so shifty? You can't keep still. Why, spy?" He says with a wry smile.

"Is this what we're doing now? Playing *Spy Games?* I always thought spies have nerves of steel. Besides, what kind of spy admits being a spy? I say.

"Don't ask questions you already know the answers to; or ask questions whose answers you might not like. Answers you don't want to know, and questions you will regret having asked. And never you mind what I am. He's a spy." He says.

"Okay. Let me try this on for size and see how it fits. So, once upon a time you met someone from Harlem who looks different than I do. You say he was a spy. And since you think we're both shifty that makes me a spy or the same person? "Now, that's some stinking thinking. If you ask me, as near as I can see it seems to me to be a case of mistaken identity. Besides, they say everybody has a double." I say.

"He's a spy. I know it." *Gulliver* insists.

"How would you know if you only met him once? What did I do to make you suspicious of me? Are you crazy?" I say.

"You don't know what you don't know. So, I'm going to tell you two things. Listen carefully. This is the third time you called me crazy. I don't like it when people call me crazy without calling me horse. You call me crazy, you'd better call me horse, as in *Crazy Horse*. Do you understand?

"Second, I know he was a spy. I know because it's my job to know these things. I work hard at my job. I'm very good at my job. That's how I know he was spy. He escaped; with help. And he also has something that belongs to me. I already took care of one Amadan traitor. The other one who helped the American escape, he got away; again. There's still a manhunt for them, the Amadan and that American.

"That American, he's holding the *Smoking Gun*. Sooner or later, I'll find him. Eventually, amateurs slip up; they always do. And when he does, I'm going to take care of him once and for all." He says.

"But why do you think we're the same person?" I say.

Suddenly his shoulders hunch as he leans across the table, now all but in my face. "There. See? You just did again; didn't you? I never said I thought you are the same person; did I? You did; didn't you? As a matter of fact, you slipped up and said it twice; didn't you?

"All I ever said was that you remind me of an American in Amada. That's all I ever said. That you remind me of someone in Amada. So? Why did you hear something I never said?"

"Unless, of course, it was a Freudian slip and you're really hiding something? Maybe your identity? Maybe the flash drive? Where is it? It's at the bank. That's where; isn't it? At the bank. Where Catalina works. I told you; I know. I know her name. I know everything. Except where it is. So? Where is it? It's at the bank? Isn't it?" He says.

"Keep her out of this. *Alles klar?* You just said I look like someone you're going taking care of. What? That's supposed me make me feel warm and fuzzy? You know me; all of you know me. I'm not a spy. What are you talking about? I think you need a career change. If you're not crazy, you must be drunk." I say.

"I'm as sober as a stone and I know what I know. And remember: don't ever call me crazy without calling me horse. "It's *Crazy Horse*. You remind me of him, that's all I said. If it's not you then, other than my apologies, then it's really none of your business, is it? But then again, the way you play the game, your Bavarian accent. Maybe I'm wrong. I haven't made up my mind about you yet. I can read people most of the time. That's what I do. With you, I'm not too sure. That tells me something." *Gulliver* says.

"Like what?" I say.

Suddenly he becomes edgy again. "Not to trust you. Not even a little bit. And here's why. Not too long ago, I saw you doing the same thing I do. I saw you on your balcony with your binoculars watching my boat from your hotel. I was watching you – not from my boat - while you were scanning for me. And it wasn't the first time I saw you doing that. One time, you pulled back once you saw me watching you. Remember? Yeah. Why pull back? Why not just... wave? Unless, of course, you don't want me to know you're tracking me. That would mean you have bad intentions. So, do you have bad intentions? That's right, I've been watching you. And I'm going to keep watching you." He says.

"This is so crazy." I say.

With a forearm shiver *Gulliver* wipes the bottles off the table top and leans in. "What did I just tell you? Didn't I warn you about calling me crazy? I said don't call me crazy unless you call me horse. It's *Crazy Horse*! *Crazy Horse* doesn't trust you, and neither do I. You ask too many questions. I've been watching you and I'm going keep watching you when I get back. Don't ask me where I'm going. It's none of your business. The *Smoking Gun,* it's at the bank. I know it. Smart move. Now you hear this. My client's property, he wants it back. That's what I was hired to do. I fix problems. I correct situations.

"I'm a facilitator. That's what I do. I don't care how you got it and, believe you me, I don't care how I get it back. I never make the same mistake twice. I'll fix my problem with you too. And you can take that to the bank, whoever you are. But I think we both know who you really are; don't we? Don't we? Now know this, and remember it well. You're only safe while it's at the bank. You can't stay here forever. And I'll be here when try to leave with it. But you won't leave with it. As a matter of fact, you won't leave Martinique. You will have reached your sell-by date and outlived your further usefulness. Just like your friend did. Don't bother denying it. Now you know. You've been warned. Get out of my way. Move!" He says.

Gulliver clears the table and chairs out of his path, then staggers out of the restaurant to the adjacent pier, boards his motorboat and returns to off-shore *Canton*.

Time stands still for I don't know how long as I sit alone at the table trying to process everything that just went down.

Stunned and wondering how I survived another deadly encounter with this mad man. Indeed, the only reason I survived this time is because we were in a public setting. Behind locked doors, in Ayri's case the outcome was deadly. But how he's on to me. I've put Catalina at risk. He knows where she works and he knows where she lives; and currently she's living with me. I've put both of us in danger.

Even without his involvement in Ayri's death, which he just admitted, he is flawed and corrupt beyond comprehension or redemption. From aspirant seminarian to avenging angel of death. His was a heart of darkness, murder in his snake eyes' death stare. Friend only unto himself, devoid of empathy or the human conscience. Instead bound only by his kind's creed - *Novi Orbis*.

The region now aflame, he and his pay master, the Sinister Prime Minister, are paving the way for the hydrocarbon, hospitality and travel cartels' ultimate gambit. I'm in greater danger than any other time; greater than Amada even. I have what everyone is looking for and will do anything to get. There's even a manhunt on for me.

It seems like forever before I can digest what just played out. While on my way back to *Hotel Madinina*, that metaphor echoes again, this time as a clarion warning call. Over and again trance-like whispering, 'Babylon, Babylon... Babylon, Babylon...'

CHAPTER TEN

BETWEEN THE DEVIL AND THE DEEP BLUE SEA

"...I'm in need of some restraint,
So if you meet me, have some courtesy;
Have some sympathy and some taste.
Use all your well learned politesse, or
I'll lay your soul to waste. Pleased to
Meet you. Hope you guess my name.
But what's puzzling you is the nature
Of my game."
Sympathy for the Devil
Performed by
Rolling Stones

I haven't seen *Gulliver* since our last encounter nearly one month ago; not that I want to. In fact, his ship isn't anchored anywhere off southern Martinique or elsewhere off shore the island. *Gulliver* and *Canton,* they're gone.

After nearly six months in the region and with the final draft of the biography project and *exposé* of the Amada *coup* finished, the time has come; time to leave Martinique.

A few days before my departure, perhaps not coincidentally the final chapter of these Caribbean chronicles begins writing itself unexpectedly in an unusual way. That is, as an object lesson and learning experience. When how we learn becomes as important, if not more so, than what we learn. When after a series of free associations and random re-combinations of ideas and symbols, all at the speed of thought, the mind yields answers to once long-vexing questions. That sweet moment of serendipity, when eureka occurs.

One Saturday morning, over breakfast banter Catalina comments about my appearance. Specifically, my hair and beard. "You know; you really should do something about it. How you can stand it in this heat and humidity?"

Following my escape from the Row and beginning the writing project, I promised myself I wouldn't shave or cut my hair until I completed the book and its publication. Something that could take forever. Six months later, and I have a mop of hair with a thick beard.

Q

"Don't turn up your headphones and ignore me. And why do jazz musicians' have these strange names? 'Bootsy.' 'Lockjaw.' 'Fathead.' 'Cannonball.' 'Trane?' 'Dizzy?' What's with that? You said that when you finished your book you will shave and cut your hair. You uploaded the book to your brother last week. I want to cut your hair and trim your beard. Trust me, it won't hurt. I promise. Just a little, *s'il vous plait?* That way, I can see more of you." Catalina says.

"Oh, no. Never that. I only cut my nails." I say.

"Please? It's just too much." Catalina says.

"Get back, Delilah!" I say.

"I'm serious, *Q*. I've never seen your face. I don't even know what you look like. When I met you, your head was wrapped like a mummy with a beard and long hair. Now it's even longer. After you swim you have dread locks. You look like a mad prophet. Right now, all that's left of your face is from your eyes to your nose. That and your cheeks. The rest is all hair. It's on your face and on your head. It's on your chest, your legs, your *derriere*. You have too much hair. It's everywhere.

"Please? Let me cut your hair. Just a little. A shape-up. For your Baby Girl. It won't hurt. I promise." Catalina says, then sits on my lap.

"You know you're wrong. Straddling me and giggling your ample goodness all in my face, talking that Baby Girl stuff. You put a spell on me. I can't think anymore." I say.

Against my better judgement we head to the balcony. There, like Delilah, Catalina shaves off my beard and crew cuts my hair, then laughs mischievously.

"What did you do? I look like I'm twelve years old. Why did you do that?" I say really upset.

"I couldn't help myself. The Creole in me got out. Wow! I'm glad I did. Look at you. Your cheekbones and chin. You look much younger. Mama, there's a new man in my life." She says.

By midday, the heat becomes unbearable. We drive to Fort de France for shopping and a movie, then return to the hotel early evening. We unpack, relax, make love and fall asleep.

Sweeter yet is the night. Cool is the air with skies clear, the trade winds fanning a constant ocean breeze. The southern hemisphere night is that bright as to count every star, their lights twinkle-dancing upon the Caribbean reflecting pool's bobbing tide. From the marina's magical field of vision, the firmament and the water line meld seamlessly at the horizon's bend, where in the dark beyond sparkles Fort de France.

But no matter how spangled star-bright a night, no element or panorama outshines Catalina. Clad in a silk *pareos,* a hibiscus blossom holds her hair in place. A night this starry, a woman this beautiful, separate and together they befit the commensurate setting - *Madinina Sur La Mer.*

Never mind the late hour. The veranda restaurant always bustles, and for many good reasons. The food, the view, and the show. With its spectacular marina view and of Fort de France's nightline and its classic French/Creole menu's sumptuous cuisine, surf and turf, desserts, beverages and spirits, gastronomy's best is on offer.

Al fresco by the sea, lantern-lit veranda dinner tables are situated atop and alongside an L-shaped, glass encased and illuminated marina aquarium, stocked daily with catch of the day. Countless colorful marine life. Sea turtles, sea horses, baby barracuda. Star fish, jelly fish, eel, shrimp, lobster, striped and Chilean bass and miniature sharks. The pool's bottom is strewn with seashells, coral, rocks, coins. Ear rings, bracelets, cuff links, and jewelry and other personal memorabilia. A large anchor, an open chest, and a throne chair are bolted to the aquarium floor, algae wafting slowly about.

The nightly highlight, the aquarium waterworks dinner show, begins with a warning. *Madame* Madinina cautions guests not to stand too close, then dramatically releases the aquarium cover. Next, restaurant wait staff start tossing food and bait into the water, stirring a literal foaming feeding frenzy of flying fish food fights all over the aquarium, with dinner guests eagerly participating and video-recording the spectacle.

Luxuriating in the setting, over desserts Catalina remarks. "No matter how often we dine here, seeing the flying fish; I marvel. Just like now, without all your hair and beard; I marvel. For the first time, I get to see your face, almost like a new person. It's something that I should have done a long time ago. Now I see why your friend's sister fell in love you when you were younger." Catalina says.

"Delilah! Cut my hair, took my powers. You put a spell on me." I say.

"That's right, and I'm glad I did. You must feel so much better; although you'd never admit it. Even though I admit casting my spell on you. And based on this afternoon, believe me, your powers are plenty good." Catalina says.

Q

"And now that I've been nutrified, I'm plenty strong like bull again. Let's go upstairs and love each other to sleep all over again." I say.

By now round about midnight, as I look to catch the waiter's attention much to my surprise I see *Gulliver,* sitting at the bar steady giving me the evil eye. Once he knows I've seen him, I watch him snatch my dinner bill from the waiter.

"I'll take that. Don't worry, I want to surprise him." Says *Gulliver* to the waiter and then heads towards our table.

"Listen, Catalina. I can't explain. Go upstairs and get my gear. You know what to do. You've seen me do it before. Hurry. No! Leave through the kitchen behind me. And tell *Madame* what you're doing. Go! You know what to do. I love you. You know what to do. Hurry!" I say, then Catalina rushes into the kitchen barely before *Gulliver* arrives at my table.

"May I? Not that I need your permission." *Gulliver* says and, before I can answer, he seats himself at the table. "Surprised to see me?"

In the past, we always spoke German. Not this time, though. For the first time since Amada, *Gulliver* speaks English. He is wearing the boat owners' usual dress code. Powder blue button-down shirt, navy blue blazer, white trousers, brown loafers, no socks. Once he unbuttons his jacket he intentionally reveals the handle of a pistol handle tucked under his blazer.

Knowing he's not about to shoot me in a crowded restaurant, I continue speaking German. "My bill; I'll take it." I say.

"She's a beautiful woman. The one from the bank." He says in English.

"I agree. So, I'm sure you understand why I can't stay." I say in German.

"I hope you enjoyed your Last Supper; both of you." He says.

Before I can process, never mind respond to his veiled threat, then he says, "I haven't seen you for over a month. I was away on business. You look different. You cut your hair and shaved your beard. That's it." *Gulliver* says and then orders a round of beers, although I decline. "I'm glad I ran it to you. I've been having trouble with my computer. So? Maybe you can help me with it?" He says.

"What's your problem?" I now speak English.

"See, I have these laptops. Remind me to tell you the story of how I got them. I took them from this loser. I took his shirt, and his jacket too. Coward wouldn't even fight back.

"A weakling, real soft character. But I don't think you're going to be around long enough to fully enjoy the story." He says.

"I told you I have someone waiting for me. Just give me the dummy version. You know; like when you're talking to yourself." I say.

"Anyway. I have a web site, and I'm also linked with other web sites. So, around two months ago I began noticing long, daily web site hits. Are you with me?" He says.

"You're rapidly losing my interest." I say.

"But my site was never hacked, virus-struck, or denial-of-service disabled. See what I mean? Well, I became curious. The site has a click-counter. That way, I always know how many hits there are. So, that's when I decided to have a forensic analysis done on the hard drive. They traced all traffic to an IP address. You know, like the computer's phone number. They then checked the server. It turns out, those hits were tracked to a proxy server. Those hits were routed to a server and an account with a very unusual user ID name and password. *Homeboy*. Very unusual; don't you think? I have no idea what it means. A boy from home? What's a *Homeboy*? What a stupid name. So, anyway. Once I knew the routing source... Well, you're a real techno geek. You tell me." He says all the while giving me the evil eye.

I haven't seen *Gulliver* since our *Hotel Bamboo* late night encounter a month earlier. After everything that's happened between us. After months of posing *incognegro* whenever in his company. Even though my appearance was different on the Row, my current appearance, clean-shaven, short haircut, trigger his ancient suspicions. He finally realizes that I'm the one who escaped from prison and exploratory surgery. Playing Russian roulette. Suspicious of me from go, especially after our last meeting at *Hotel Bamboo*, it finally adds up. I'm the one he been looking for these past months. My cover's blown. No longer am I so... *incognegro*.

His dilated pupils' crazed expression. Paranoid, always guarded, suspicious and scanning the horizon with his binoculars around his neck. Dude is plain creepy. No different tonight, oozing menace, a gun tucked in his waistband. Recalling our last encounter at *Bamboo Bar*, I admit tracking him with my own binoculars. Not with bad intentions, though. They only reasons I hung out with the 'boat people' was for nautical grist and context for this editorial project and an opportunity for speaking German.

There's still plenty time to leave the restaurant and avoid further confrontation. That is, if I wanted to. But I don't want

to. Considering our history, I won't run. I can't. In fact, I'm reveling in the danger zone, arrested by its violent potential and downright raring for a fight and moment of truth.
For the time being, I'm reasonably safe in the restaurant. That is, as safe as possible sitting across from a killer with a gun tucked under his shirt, murder in his eyes.

His appetite and tolerance for drink seem large but it's never clear just how intoxicated he is, if at all. Or maybe he's playing possum?

Gulliver drains both bottles of beers, one after another, each in one chug, then slams them on the table. He burps, and then says, "Ah! That's good!" Then he wipes his mouth with the back of his hand and continues. "Getting back to my story. Where was I? That's right. I tracked those hits. Well, we learned the destination account. But still; where did those hit originate? Well, guess what? They all came from where? Say no. That's right. Right here in Martinique. Now, what do you make of that?" He says.

"I'm not feeling this story." I say.

"Well, imagine my surprise when I discovered the IP address is an unlisted satellite connection. Right here." He says.

"What do you mean; where 'right here?' You mean like this here; right here. Here?" I say.

"That's right. Here where we sit and breathe. Your hotel. Right here. *Hotel Madinina*." He says.

"Get outta here. This is like that movie, *The Spook Who Sat by the Door*." I say.

"Only by now I'm not just angry. More and more, I'm getting curious. So, I do like you do. You know what I mean?" He says.

"You do like I do what?" I say.

"I do like you do; but without your *Bardolino*. I go undercover, investigative journalist mode. You know what I mean; pretending to be someone you're not. Nosing around and asking questions about things you shouldn't. Looking for trouble. Making a nuisance of yourself. Isn't that what you do? Trying to connect the dots.

"That's when instinct told me to reverse-connect the dots. So, I checked the computer stores in Fort de France. Turns out lucky, there's only one, which made things a lot easier. The manager, a friendly chap, he tells me he just returned with his family from vacation in *Disney World*. Apparently an American, some writer recently purchased a lot of hardware and software. Cash money. U.S. dollars, to be exact. He kept talking about somebody called Poor Richard. Enough dollars, it seems, for our good Mr. Guptar to afford a family vacation in Disney World. So, guess what I did?" He says with a knowing smirk.

"I can tell you can't wait to tell me; can't you?" I said.

"You're damn right, I can't wait to tell you. That American bought seven thousand five hundred Benjamins worth of equipment. I gave Mr. Guptar ten thousand dollars to tell me everything. With that money, I advised him to relocate to India. That way, he can't be called as a witness in your inquest. Mr. Guptar says he helped set up the equipment. Guess where? No. You'd never guess in a year. And you'll be lucky to live past tonight. Guess where he says he set up that equipment? The same place all that web site traffic came from." He continues.

"That's right. Right here, *Hotel Madinina*. Says the person has dreads and a beard. At first, he thought he was Jamaican or an islander. Says he rents a marina penthouse suite. Drives a jeep. The way he described him, it sounded just like you. Says that person came back and bought every flash drive in the store. In other words, every flash drive in Martinique. Now, what would that person do with all those flash drives? Why, make copies, of course. Make copies of... what? Well, we both know the answer to that. Now what do you think about all that? A coincidence?" *Gulliver* says plenty peeved.

"It must be. Either that, or cybercrime. A hacker, data breach or identity theft. Someone's digital fingerprint somewhere in criminal cyber dark web's world. You can't be too careful in Interweb world. That's what it sounds like to me." I say.

"So, tell me, Kai; do you like to read?" He says.

"Reading? Oh, no way. I don't want to know too much. Clutter. Takes up too much space. I keep my mind free and clear of things like ideas. Too much knowledge can be a dangerous thing. Sports and gossip. That's enough." I say.

"Me? I have culture. I read all the time. All kinds of books. Novels, non-fiction. History, biographies, essays. Of course, nowadays I do most of my reading on the computer. There's just so much information on the internet. You know. For research." He says.

"Well, like I said. I keep doing like you. By now, I'm in full investigative mode and began reverse-connecting more dots.

"So, I visited *Columbia University's* web site. And when I looked under alumni, well, what do you know? Behold! Under 'distinguished alumni,' first your friend, listed as 'Diplomat.'

"And not far from his picture is another biographical sketch. Lo! What see my eyes? A picture next to a book cover. The picture, it looks a lot like you. The book cover says, *Homeboy, Fiction by Q,* 'Author.' Now how could anyone forget names as bizarre as *Homeboy* and *Q*?" He says. Chain smoking, his dilated pupils' stare steady shooting death rays, he continues.

"The university is proud of the two of you. They devoted you with your own web page links and plenty of personal information. Lots of personal information." He says.

"It seems, you're really an American. Your bio says you grew up in Munich. That's why you speak German and play the game. Your parents, your mother isn't German. They're both American. Your father, he's not a jazz saxophonist. He's a classical pianist, very accomplished, and teaches master classes. Your mother owns a florist shop in Harlem. Your gift to her from your first royalty check. Flowers blooming in Harlem." He says, then suddenly bellows, "BOOM!"

Sociopath, psychopath, first he killed Ayri, then he threatened Catalina and me; and now he's threatening my parents' lives. My obsessions, my pursuit of a story and revenge for Ayri, they're putting everyone near and dear to me at risk; even my parents.

"I'm not trying to hear this conversation. How about let's not talk anymore? I have someone waiting for me." I say.

"She'll have to wait." He says then reads out loud from the dinner bill. "Let's see? What did you two have? Last Supper. It says, 'Champagne dinner for two. *Bouillabaisse.* Grilled striped bass. Mushroom *risotto* with asparagus *citron. Salade nicoise. Chateaubriand hollandaise avec pommes frites. Crème brûlée flambé*, fruit atop cognac vanilla ice cream. Champagne, *Taittinger,* of course; nothing but. Plus, coffee and bitters.'

"That's quite a meal. Total: none. Notation: 'Inclusive meal plan. Gratuity included.' Even though gratuity is included, you tipped thirty euro, 'for superb service.' Now, let's see? What's the room number on the bill? PS. PS? What's that stand for? Maybe, Penthouse South? Is that what it means? That means you have half of the entire top floor. That's where I saw you stalking me from your balcony with your binoculars. Now, what's the name on the restaurant tab?" He says, then reads out my name.

"That's your name; not Kai-Armand Richter. The same name I first saw in your passport in Amada.

"It's you; you're *Q*. Here I've been looking all over for you, and the whole while you've been hiding in plain sight. How ironic. Cunning even. You shouldn't have shaved or cut your hair. I knew I should have listened to myself sooner. The laptops, the jacket and shirt. I should have killed you a long time ago. But it looks like I have a chance now to correct that mistake." *Gulliver* says.

Although it's late, the restaurant's still busy. With recorded music playing in the background, our argument can't be heard all that clearly. His threats no longer are that worrying though, since Catalina is in the background carrying out my instructions, talking to *Madame.* I'm in safe space.

"Yeah, only this time is different; isn't it? This time I'm not tied down, burned, beaten and drowned. This time it's just the two of us. No *Body Bag Brigade*. And right about now - after everything you put me and mine through - right about now it's you who should be afraid of me for many good reasons. So, don't threaten me. If anything, you should be sucking up to me if you want what you think I have. Maybe I do? Maybe I don't? Maybe it's already wiki-wiki bye-bye viral too late? So, don't get tricky, or it will go wiki. Catch my drift?" I say.

"Better you be careful. Even though I enjoy it, violence isn't my initial impulse. It's a close second, though. I'm a practical man. So, before I skip an impulse and kill you, you should know that my client has authorized me to buy back his property. You'll be permitted to continue to live - and continue to live well. It's simple. Just give it to me, and you and yours live. That's all you need to do. Just give it to me. That way, no one gets hurt." He says.

"Property? What property? What client?" I say.

"The only thing worse than a liar is a coward. And you're both. I wish we'd have done that exploratory surgery on you - without anesthesia - just for the fun of hearing you squeal and watch you squirm like a pig." He says.

"Oh, that. You mean my property. My flash drive. The one with all the dirt on you and your client, Geremi Quarrles? Interesting reading. Especially that part laying the foundation for your cartels mischief maker, the Sinister Prime Minister, aka *Emperor Jones.* I'm sure you were at his coronation after his return from exile. You had to have been there. You probably made it happen. So, let me see if I get this right? You tell me. In Amada, you toppled a democracy. In Spañada, you reinstall a dictator. Am I right? See? That's the kind of sure enough must-read wiki viral stuff the world needs to know about. That's why you no likey wiki-wiki. And that's why it went viral." I say.

"You seem to fail to fully grasp the severity of your situation." *Gulliver* says.

With a watchful eye for any sudden movement for the gun tucked in his waistband, I edge closer to him. "Being called a liar or a coward by a killer, a murderer, now that's rich in irony. You're the one who fails to fully grasp the gravity of *your* situation once this stuff goes viral. I can't sell something I don't have. Tell your client some things, like the truth, aren't for sale, at any price. And even if I did have it, I sure wouldn't sell it to your client. Gig's about up. Things are about to get real tricky now that it went wiki. Soon you and your client will be wearing orange. Prison orange. Which is where you belong. Like back in Macao. Like in Indonesia. Back then. Remember?" I say.

"Again, my client is a very powerful man, very generous. Someone who values discretion and wishes to avoid publicity." He says.

"Yeah, right. So, he hires people like you..." I say.

"Because I'm professional. I'm a fixer. I initiate the necessary corrections. I make things happen. I get the job done." *Gulliver* says.

"At any cost..." I say.

"You're damn right, at any cost." He says.

"I know what you are. I know firsthand all about what you do. I don't care if you're packing. You didn't survive this long to think you can shoot me in a crowded restaurant, walk out and get away with it. No. You're not going to do anything to me in public. Maybe tomorrow? But not now." I say.

Then I shove my chair aside, climb atop it and, arms akimbo, I shout. "GUN! GUN! Dude's got a gun and says he's going to shoot me. He just said it again. Did you hear him? Look out! GUN! GUN!" I shout.

The veranda scene freezes.

Just as suddenly I resume my seat, then lean across the table. "There. See? You're not the only one who can make a scene in a crowded room. Now everybody knows you're walking with steel and threatening me. So, what're you going to do? Nothing." I say.

A day doesn't go by that I don't think about Ayri. True to his word, I fell in love in Martinique. His financial generosity made writing his story possible. Now sitting face to face and talking with Ayri's murderer, it's busting my gut. I want revenge. So much so, I feel subsumed, other, as if under some Caribbean *voodun* spell, no longer myself.

"Tell your client it's too late. It's already offshore and went wiki. Your worst fears are about to become your living nightmare. You had it right from the beginning in Amada.

"I'm not a spy. I'm a writer on assignment investigating your client, his activities, you and *Guiding Star.* Your other clients, the energy companies and energy service contractors. The hospitality and travel cartels. Weapons brokers, security contractors. Bank account numbers, signature cards, account activities. Self-dealing. It's a rigged game of contractors getting rich beyond imagination off public money. Talk about connecting the dots. The best dots are those that connect themselves. That's the Sinister Prime Minister and you." I continue.

"It's a bombshell. Once I read it, the first thing I did was drop it like it's hot. Quick and fast, like it's radioactive. I'd be stupid to walk around with that thing or a microchip implanted in me. You might be; I'm not. I didn't want that anywhere near or on me; let alone in me. I'm a marked man for long as I have it. So, the first thing I did was get that bull's eye off my back. I got rid of it as soon as I received it. Do you want to know you how I got rid of it? Right under your nose. The hotel and bank parcel shipped my belongings weeks ago. That's how. So, you see it's you who fails to fully grasp the severity of your situation. It's too late. It's gone. It's ether. Free, like all information and knowledge should be." I say.

"The damage you've done. You have no ideas. No ideas at all. None." *Gulliver* says.

"It is what it is. I've taken every precaution. You're damn right; I bought every flash drive in Martinique. That's how many copies there are. Chapter and verse. They're my dead man's switches. Insurance in case something 'happens' to me.

"Once I got rid of those flash drives, I had a complete physical and my clean bill of health notarized. Then I compiled a dossier on you, your web site, IP address and location, links. Your donors and subscribers. Your boat registration number. Everything on the flash drive, chapter and verse, beginning in Amada.

"The next thing I did was to email everything and my Last Will and Testament to the *International Consortium of Investigative Journalists* and *International Red Cross,* with instructions to flip that dead man's switch if I don't check in daily or if I suddenly die or disappear. I made these and other arrangements a long time ago. You spent ten thousand dollars and learned nothing you didn't already know in Amada; my name. I spent nothing and I know everything about you. Talk about return for investment. Well, there you go. Now you know. It looks to me like we have ourselves a Mexican standoff here in Martinique. You want your information? Get a

Q

search warrant for servers. Good luck with that. It's gone.
There's nothing you can do. So, don't do anything crazy." I
say with an ever-watchful eye for his gun.

"Didn't I warn you about calling me crazy? Look at me.
Don't you call me crazy without calling me horse. You don't
know *Crazy Horse.*" *Gulliver* says.

"And you know what you and the horse you rode in on can
do. I'm the one warning you; again. Stop threatening me, or I
will trip that dead man's switch. What? Oh. Your client won't
pay your recovery commission, your finder's fee, if you don't
return his property? Is that it?" I say.

"My instructions are to settle this simply, amicably and
quietly with limited exposure. He has authorized me to reward
the return of his property beyond the original offer." He says.

"Does your client have the powers to raise the dead? That's
my price. The return of my friend you killed and then exiled
his family. The Mentis family. Remember them? Just bring
them all back. Can your client do that - restore the status quo
ante - in return for his property? Do that, and we'll be even.
Go ahead. Do that." I say.

"You don't know what you're doing. You're an amateur.
This isn't a game." *Gulliver* says.

"What makes you think I'd ever do business with you after
everything you put us through? What I don't understand is
why you had to kill him? He was unarmed and posed no
threat. A civilian non-combatant. And still, you killed him
when you didn't have to. Like that, hog-tied in front of his
family. No one deserves to go out like that." I say.

"Your friend was a professional. He knew the drill. He knew
the consequences. He refused. Well, behaviors have
consequences, and consequences shape behaviors. Yes, I shot
him. But I didn't kill him. I punished him because of his
behaviors. From now on, his future behaviors will be shaped
by those consequences; if he survived. Maybe he died from
his injuries; maybe not? But I didn't kill him. He was alive
when he left. I said they could leave. I gave my word and I
kept it." He said.

"Yeah, sure. You're right. '*I Shot the Sheriff.* But me not
shoot no deputy. Not me.' Huh. Your word. What's your word
worth? Nothing. Hitman, assassin. Judas. That's who you are.
Pfui, Teufel!" I hear myself saying.

"Be careful. My patience's running out. Martinique is a long
way from Harlem. The Caribbean, this is my turf. This is my
game, my rules. I know how to hurt people and make them

talk. I made you talk. Your friends, I made them talk too.
Don't make me do it again." *Gulliver* says.

"Yeah. Your world, your game. Your rules, your gun. My
dead man's switch, though. I know you like to think of
yourself as this mysterious sailor. This modern Flying
Dutchman. A real Renaissance Man, you. International man of
mystery. Author/adventurer, with your binoculars and all.
Crazy Horse, Gulliver, Comandante, Shiva, Captain Blood,
Chief *Smoking Gun*. Whatever *your nom de guerre du jour*.
Crusader, Knights Templar. You and your *Novi Orbis*.

"There's nothing new about your old *Novi Orbis*. It's as old
as time. War, blowing up stuff, rip-off reconstruction costs,
inflation. Political and economic corruption and unjust
enrichment. *Novi Orbis,* it's the same tired world order
dressed up in new clothing with new names for failed policies.
And outdated philosophy that are incapable of addressing and
correcting modern social problems, or identifying future
political and economic realities. It's called stinking thinking."
Then I say.

"The point is, it's not just a new world order. It's a new
world. One that's completely by-passed your *Novi Orbis*.
Information is the biggest threat to your old-world order. The
management and prioritization of data. Information, data,
knowledge, they've become their own currency sweeping
aside your old-world order. That's what the flash drive
represents. That's its symbolic importance. That's your new
world order. Data evolving faster than our capacity to absorb
or understand or safely manage.

"Considering its importance and universal need for it and
its different platforms and storage technologies, the question
becomes; who really owns it? Is it proprietary and protected,
intended to benefit only people like your client and your other
clients' narrow self-interests? Or is it common wealth intended
to benefit the greater good? That's where we differ. As a
journalist and honest broker of information, I believe it's in
the public interest to know. That's why it's wiki-free. But then
again, these are moral and ethical considerations I wouldn't
expect you to grasp. We're done. I'm out, Judas." I then rise
from the table.

Gulliver also rises and blocks my path. "No. You're not
going anywhere. We're not done yet." He says.

"Oh yes, we are. We're gone and done. So are you. And so
is your client. So are his plans to corner the region's energy
resources. I'm tired of your threats. You and your gun need to
get out of my way." I say.

Gulliver crowds me and exposes the handle of his gun tucked in his waistband. "We're not done. Not while you're still breathing, which won't be much longer. We have unfinished business. Now start walking to the back door. And don't make any noise, no sudden moves. Walk it. Now!" *Gulliver* places his hand on the gun handle and steps in closer, trying to block my egress.

"I'm not going anywhere with you. Just like I didn't get on your ship for that exploratory surgery back then." I say.

"No, you're not getting away this time. This time, we're going back in time, and I'm going to correct the mistake I made, back when I took your shirt, your jacket and your laptops. Back in Amada, when I made a mistake by allowing you to live. I'm going to fix that mistake and finish the job this time." *Gulliver* says, his hand on his weapon.

"Or what? Or you're going to kill me in one of the most popular restaurants in all of the Caribbean? Get on your boat, and just sail off? I don't think so. I had the drop on you since day one. I made you the first time I saw you here in Martinique. A real spy would have killed you a long time ago. Who said it? 'Amateurs, they always slip up.' It's looking like your spy game is what's slipping. You're beginning to look like an amateur. It's amazing, when you think about it. You know, what we've been talking about. Technology and whatnot, the Interweb world and all; can't live without it. Strange things though, they happen at that intersection when technology meets human nature. You're a security contractor. You know all about the precautions you professionals take to protect your clients and their 'interests.' I'm sure you've seen things that make you shake your head. You know what I mean.

"Think about; privacy really is an illusion. There's no such thing. We live in a panopticon. Surveillance cameras are everywhere. So, why do people do dumb stuff even though they know they might get caught? Just because they're angry, or desperate? Stuff like criminals robbing stores even though security cameras are all over the place. What? Criminals just forget cameras are there? I don't understand it. I mean, you're doing the same thing right now; and you're the security expert." I say.

"Who cares about any of that? This time around, you're not going to buy any more time. I'm going to dispose of you this time.". He says.

"See, there you go again. Didn't I tell you about that dead man's switch? Turn around. Go ahead, turn around. Look. See what I mean?" I point behind *Gulliver* to the front of the restaurant.

Sur La Mer's veranda vista and aquarium are renowned beyond Martinique. Such an attraction, nearly everybody takes cell phone pictures and videos of the flying fish feeding frenzy. Including Catalina who, at my instruction has set up my gear, my tripod camcorders and, along with *Madame* Madinina's staff and other patrons, they are recording my encounter with *Gulliver*.

"Amada ran a background check on you. According to FBI and Europol databases, '… Other than prison ID, no known pictures in existence.' Well, now there are. Lots of them. Go ahead. Turn around. Don't look at me. Turn around. Look. See what I mean? See all those people? That's the hotel owner and staff, dinner guests and hotel patrons. Maybe twenty, thirty people. See what they're doing? You've been so busy threatening me you never noticed they've been recording us the whole time behind your back. They're recording everything. Video and audio." I explain.

"Look up. We're on closed circuit TV being simulcast and uploaded to a cloud server as we speak. All it takes is six seconds. Six seconds. That's my other dead man's switch. Go ahead. Wave to the camera and smile. Rewind to that part when I'm standing on the chair; why don't we? Don't want to see that part again? Or, how about the part when you scream 'BOOM?' No? I understand why. It's not a good look good.

"Know this: I gave instructions to record us and await my signal. When I do so, they'll call the police. And these pictures don't include pictures I paid natives and fishermen to take of you and your boat without your knowledge. I got you good. Now smile and wave to the people. Say hi to the *ICIJ*, the FBI and Europol. Now the world will know your face. Who said it? 'Amateurs, they always slip up?'" I say.

Gulliver eases off and conceals his weapon, his snake eyes shooting venom. "You have a big mouth, just like your friend. He had a big mouth, too. Look where it got him. He got what he deserved. Your friend, his sister; the same thing. She was mouthy mouth. I guess it runs in the family. I had to shut her up, too. She kept calling your name. '*Q*.' '*Q*'.

Now, that's one healthy woman. Full, firm jugs. I'd say, cup size a good 38-C; maybe double-C. Juicy. Tell me, *Q?* Do you know where her birthmark is? I do. I located it. You know; most women have one breast larger than the other. Well, when you lift her left breast - the bigger one - that's where her birthmark is. Shaped like a mango." He leers, saying.

"Did you know that, *Q*? I thought you would. It sits right on top of her heart's point of maximal impulse. When you lift and squeeze that breast you can see her heart muscle pulsate under her birthmark. She has passion. When I spanked that spot, she writhed. And she tasted good, too. Did you know that, *Q*? Juicy. You know what I mean? I had to shut her up too. Want to know how I shut her up?" *Gulliver* says.

"Yo! That's it. I'm shutting you down, man. *Madame!* Call the police." I say.

"Just joshing. No need for the police. I'll leave." He says.

"You don't get to decide what I do. No police? Why not? What's wrong? You have outstanding warrants; is that it? Can't handle doing time again? Having prison flashbacks? *Madame! Gendarme! Toute suite!*" I say.

"Look, no need to call the police. It's all a big misunderstanding. Locker room talk. That's all. I never touched her. Too much alcohol. I'm leaving. Really. See? I promise." He says.

"You threatened me. I'm pressing charges and having you arrested. The videos are enough to hold you over. Let's see what other charges stick once they process you." I say.

"What do you want?" He says.

"I want justice. I want justice for Ayrton." I say.

"Anything. No authorities, though." He says.

"Anything?" I say.

"Anything. Just no authorities. We can settle this. Forget about my client's property." He says.

I signal *Madame* Madinina to cancel the call.

"Gimme me your gun. That's the only way I'll feel safe." I say.

Gulliver hesitates and shakes his head.

"No? Okay. *Madame!* Make that call." I signal *Madame* to call the police. Then, in a convergence of moment and movement, in his moment of indecision I feel myself reaching across his body, and with a sudden movement snatch the gun from his waistband and disarm him.

One movement changes the moment, the table now turned. For the first time in my life, I'm aiming a weapon at someone and for the first time I feel like killing someone. Not anyone, just him; and for plenty good reasons. Given our history, after everything that happened to Ayrton and wanting to vivisect me. Playing Russian roulette looking for the *Smoking Gun*. With these recordings of him threatening me, I'd probably be acquitted in court. That, though, would make me the same as him.

Or am I any different? I remove the ammunition clip, tuck it in my pocket, double-check the weapon to make sure all chambers are empty, release the safety, press the weapon to his throat and cock the hammer.

"Human nature's funny, ain't it now? Like, why do people flinch when they know they're about to get shot, as if you could avoid it? When what you should do is just take a deep breath and... surrender. Like this! *Ay!*" I shout then, to everyone's dismay, I pull the trigger. "Like that!"

He flinches. Everyone gasps. A hush seizes the veranda.

"You're no different when a gun is put to your head. I just made you flinch." I say. Then I toss the ammunition clip into the open aquarium, tuck the nickel-plated .38 Glock pistol in my waistband, and say to him.

"Just like you took my laptops, my shirt and jacket? I just took your gun. It's mine now. I own it. It's my trophy. Another insurance policy. Or, we can keep on playing this game; you know what I mean? So, what's it going to be? Your gun, or your life? No, don't you look down. You look at me when I talk to you. That's right. Like that. Stop being so shifty. You seem nervous. Why are you so nervous? Maybe you're afraid of the police? So, do you want to be free a little longer, or a lot longer?" I parody, then turn serious.

"Now, listen here. It's round about midnight. By first light, you'd better be gone. Otherwise, I'll trip that dead man's switch. Your boat registration number, pictures, videos, the flash drives. They'll break the internet within six seconds. All it takes is six seconds." I go on saying.

"Leave Martinique; or everything will see the light of day. If I see your boat docked anywhere off Martinique. If I ever see you again, your face will be all over the place. All I've got to do is press this phone app. Or I 'forget' to check in, and the switch self-activates in... six seconds. No fail/safe. There are no redundancies, and there's nothing left to say. I think we understand each other. You know what time it is, and you know what to do. So choose wisely. Step off." I say.

"This is long from over. My client has friends. They have friends." He says.

"They'd better work at *ICIJ*. And the United Nations." I say.

"This is war." He says.

"It is what it is. We're done. *Madame*! *Gendarme*. Police." I signal her. This time she calls the police. "An emergency at *Sur La Mer?* The police will be here in less than five minutes. Five minutes. That's about how long it takes — oh, I don't know – say - to smoke... you know - the Last Cigarette. It looks like you've become – man on the run. Better run, running man. Run, before the police get here. Stay away from me." I say.

With his weapon tucked in my waistband, my trophy now in revenge for my gear he took, I keep a watchful eye out for sudden movement as he makes his wayout *Sur La Mer.* He then boards his motor boat, and heads for off-shore anchored *Canton.*

Hyper-vigilant on my way across the veranda through the adjoining hotel lobby and up to my suite, Catalina and I barricade ourselves inside. At my request, *Madame* increases security precautions in and around the hotel for the remainder of our stay. From then on and until my departure, our suite is guarded by none others than *Castor* and *Pollux* themselves.

Unable to sleep or rest and instead ruminating all night long, I recall something unusual about my confrontation with *Gulliver.* Something more than just the encounter itself. Something having to do with Ayri more than anything else.

As Ayrton was fond of saying, 'You? You are an Egghead, an intellectual. You think things about things. Me? I'm a man of action. I do the things you think things about.' And he was so right.

Some of the things I did. Standing on that chair, going toe to toe. Not backing down, not showing or knowing any fear. Snatching his gun, turning the table and playing Russian roulette with him. Saying *'Ay!'* like that. That was so out of character. That wasn't me. That was me channeling Ayri all the way life. I was simply a medium, a vessel.

Nor is this the first time I've felt his proximity since his death. His presence is never far nor confined to my encounters with *Gulliver.* In quiet moments as well as with Catalina. Or in a crowd. Sometimes like a passing breeze, other times like a touch on my shoulder. Sometimes I smile happy, sometimes it brings tears to my eyes. At times, it feels as if Ayri were dwelling within or passing though me. As if I could all but see him.

This occasion is different, though. Never this intense or this long. It's as if, not only were Ayri present but I had become his proxy, inhabiting and directing me actions me. There can be no other explanation.

Then, just as quickly as it began with *Gulliver's* arrival on the scene, just as suddenly the haunting, this channeling or transference experience, dissipated with *Gulliver's* departure, followed by intense feelings of relief, peace, and purpose.

Only briefly, though. That Caribbean chorus' metaphor began echoing in my inner ear again. Echoing once more, long after, and still.

'Babylon, Babylon... Babylon, Babylon...'

CHAPTER ELEVEN

O AMOR EM PAZ

*"Two things fill the mind with
Ever-new and increasing wonder
And awe, the more often and
The more seriously reflection
Concentrates upon them:
The starry heaven above me,
And the moral law within me."
Immanuel Kant*

There's a full moon over Martinique. Clear is the night, cool the air, and beneath, where Atlantic and Caribe meet, the reflecting pool's rhythmic ebb and tide nip at my feet.

Hovering above, palpably large-looming, as if an opaque, cosmic communion wafer, heaven's centerpiece and lunar glow is on full display. Starlight stardust give light to the dark night. The constellations form a candelabrum, an imponderable abstract inviting philosophic contemplation.

A dot-connected labyrinth weave, the heavenly bodies' shimmering outline's refractory play upon the reflecting pool's night waters deepen its mystery.

Off shore, on the not-too-distant dark horizon where Atlantic and Caribe meet, where the elements and firmament meld seamlessly into another, comet showers shoot across the night sky. A tropical planetarium, mine is a front row seat and privileged vantage point for nature's cosmic wattage magical light show to a celestial grand performance and complex composition. A writ large matrix design beyond mortal comprehension, proof positive of the omniverse's Devine design.

That night, Mother Nature, Her phantasmagoria in full regalia, sure enough struts Her stuff. Poised ever so slightly off-center, as if Nature were imperfect, tangibly near hangs the large, full August moon. Blue lunar light spreads out, imparting an eerie neon glow and altogether otherworldly, surreal aspect upon beach environs. So that everything surrounding and within this planetarium, the moon's delicate balancing act above Mt. Pelle. The star bright cosmic tapestry's refractory reflection upon the Caribbean waters.

The sum of these stellar parts constitutes a supernatural wonder portrait and majestic *memento mori*. Its moral, that Nature is eternal, and time all too fleeting.

The night, already mesmerizing, is made *ne plus ultra* by life's universal language, music issuing from *Hotel Madinina's* veranda. As ever, the last song of the night, composed by Antonio Carlos Jobim, *O Amor Em Paz.*

How fitting, that last song, Once *I Loved.* After six months in the region, this is my last walk along this beach stretch, where I spent many hours healing, thinking and writing. My last night in Martinique before returning home the next morning.

During this sabbatical season, acceptance and an inner peace, as if grace, seem to have washed over me. Grateful to be alive and blessed by his friendship. Inspired by his example, as if guided by Ayri's magical stewardship and humbled by his confidence in me, that night on the beach I talk to Ayrton as I always do. His foresight made fulfilling my solemn promise and completing these Caribbean chronicles possible, my life's work honoring his memory.

As profound as my gratitude, equally indelible is Ayrton's imprint upon my life. Especially the way he died has changed me. Six months later, and I'm still having difficulty coming to grips with his death. Awake and asleep, there are moments when I feel his presence, sometimes fleetingly, other times forcefully, when it seems Ayri inhabits me. I miss my friend, responsible for all these experiences. Without Ayrton, none of the love and intrigue, these Caribbean adventures and his memoirs wouldn't have been possible. Without his foresight, I never would have travelled to Martinique nor met Catalina, whose gifts of love and her time truly saved my life.

None of this would have been possible without Ayri's prescience. Ayrton changed my life in so many ways beyond expression. With his friendship, and entrusting me with this assignment and the many resulting rich experiences, to say nothing of his ultimate sacrifice, saving my life. His death has imbued my life with deeper appreciation and understanding. My life is now different, tempered. Diminished yet, despite his tragic loss, strangely somehow fuller.

The time has come, though. After six months and a finished manuscript in hand, it's that time. It's time to say farewell to Martinique and *Hotel Madinina.* After four months of accommodations, *Madame* says, "At any time, your suite will always be waiting for you, *monsieur.*"

Q

The morning of my last night's stay, *Madame* assembles the entire hotel staff, including her three daughters whom she previously kept well away from the suspected 'boom-boom movie maker.' Each staff member courteously introduces them self by name and bids me farewell, and together we enjoy a final breakfast meal amidst much *bonhomie* and fond remembrances.

It's also my last night with Catalina. Where once there was grief, Catalina's washed away the past's pain and reanimated my senses. Life and love now fill me, making me whole, a better man, a better writer even. So much so, without her love, predicted by Ayri, I never could have written this, his ode.

At sunset's last light, the marina view of Fort de France's nightline twinkling on the horizon, that night the hotel kitchen lays out a sumptuous Creole feast under *Madame's* personal *aegis*. As on other intimate occasions, again the spacious balcony is center stage. At the dinner hour, we're seated at a candle-lit table setting, replete with white linen and floral arrangements, finest china, cutlery and crystal. With every attention to detail topped only by superb service, Catalina and I are treated to a Creole smorgasbord of *Sur La Mer's* choice gastronomy on offer. A spread prepared and personally served by *Madame* herself.

After the loving, evening gives way to the night. The night, though, advances only slowly towards dawn. I'm restless and unable to sleep. I know I must leave, but my heart is torn. So torn, I disengage from our slumber's embrace on the balcony bedding, get dressed, then quietly slip outdoors for one last walk along the beach.

There is a full blue August moon over Martinique. Beneath, where Atlantic and Caribe meet, the reflecting pool's rhythmic ebb and tide lap at my bare feet. Clear and star bright the night, gentle the trade wind's cool air, and rare the moment, with *O Amor Em Paz* playing in the background. Within this tropical matrix of the moon and the stars and the seas, between the music and memories of Ayri, of Martinique and Catalina, pure perfect is the moment. My mind at peace, my body in need of rest, I rejoin Catalina on our balcony bed. There, as if to music, I memorize her. A woman couldn't possibly be more exquisitely curved.

Satin sheets caress Baby Girl's cheeks and hollow of her thighs. Her breasts, rising and sinking with each breath, her areola and navel winking like dark eyes. Awake, her eyes couldn't be any deeper or any more intoxicating.

Her hair tossed, rosebuds her lips and mouth's template, her ears the shape of delicate sea shells. From her neck to her shoulders and slender arms. The shape of her cheek bones and small of her waist. From her hips, her thighs, to the tips of her toes. Her breasts, her hips, her thighs, her buttocks, and in between.

Cinnamon on satin, her body ripe, perfect in every dimension, her body calls my name with her every sleeping breath. Even Pygmalion daren't have altered as whole a beauty, fashioned in her own image. If created out of thin blue, what would I name her? How would I know her? By the colors she prefers? Her fragrance? The way she wears her hair? By the taste of her? I'm spellbound.

Four months of memories flood my senses. Four months of loving, laughing and sharing, my need for her so strong. The sounds she makes, the way she moves whenever she responds to my touch, to our thrusts. That febrile, she boils my blood and has infected my brain. I see and want only her.

I need to memorize and always remember every detail about her. All of this. The night's full blue August moon and star jewel tapestry enveloping us. The balcony still life, the banquet table's white linen tablecloth and floral arrangement. Empty champagne flutes and crumpled napkins, a spent *ganja* pipe. The way the piano fingers the melody, the saxophone's rippling orgasmic riffs.

I want to recall always every detail of every moment about everything. Relaxing at the beach. At the arts festival. Leaning over my shoulder and kissing me as I write. Every day, breakfast, lunch and dinner. Her expression when we couldn't hurry back fast enough to love each other to sleep in intimate trance embrace under the stars on our balcony. Everything.

There under the full moon, I adore her nude sleeping beauty, holding her in gentle caress. In her slumber, over and again kissing her hair and face, the nape of her neck, caressing her back, thighs, the round of her rump, whilst in my mind's ear the melody plays on and on.

Captivated by her spell, transfixed by the sight of her sweet slumber. Intoxicated by her sweet scent and taste, I continue memorizing her beauty's details and caressing her until she awakens, and indulge again, there on our beloved balcony. There, once we loved. There, *o amor em paz.*

Q

CHAPTER TWELVE

DEAD MAN'S SWITCH

"The conquest of the earth,
Which mostly means the taking
It away from those who have a
Different complexion or slightly
Flatter nose than ourselves,
Is not a pretty thing when you
Look into it too much."
Joseph Conrad

The morning of my departure, after inspecting my mail I rush to the hotel lobby in search of *Madame.*

"*Monsieur Q!* How many times have I told you? *Hotel Madinina* is a respectable establishment, not *Hotel Bamboo.* You can't just come into the lobby barefoot and wearing only a towel. What is it now? Is there something wrong with your bill?" *Madame* says.

"No, *Madame*, not the bill. This. You usually close nights. When did this arrive?" I say.

"*Oui. La lettre.* It was late last night, while you were out walking. He came into the marina in an orange rubber motorboat and demanded to see you. The one you were arguing with in the restaurant when I called the police. Was he angry! Those snake eyes of his. I didn't tell him you were walking on the beach. I told him it was too late and that I wasn't going to disturb you, but he insisted. I felt threatened, so, *Castor* and *Pollux...*" *Madame* says.

"You... sicced... the... dogs... on... him?" I say.

"*Mais naturellement. C'est pas problem.* Especially after your restaurant *contretemps* when you asked me to increase security. You well know, the two Dobermans guard the hall to your suite. Well, when you went for a walk *Cas et Pol* followed you downstairs. They are used to guarding the restaurant, boardwalk and pier. It was already late, and then he arrives.

"*Alors, toute suite* I recognized him. When I told him to leave, he keeps demanding to see you. Now understand, by now it's two o'clock in the morning. I must open for business at seven o'clock. My feet hurt. I'm tired. Naomi isn't happy. I also know you're walking the beach, just out of sight." She says.

"I assume he's armed again and I don't want him to see you. So, I said to him: 'The cameras are on. *Monsieur Q*, he ordered you to leave Martinique. I'm ordering you to leave my hotel.' He became angry.

"So, *Castor* and *Pollux* ran him off. He reached for his gun and would have shot them. *Mais Cas et Pol*, they caught him and bit him up and down his arms and legs. He was screaming. He'll need to see a doctor right away and get many stitches and rabies shots." *Madame* Madinina says.

"That's great!" I say. Then to her surprise, I hug her and kiss both cheeks. "*Merci!*"

"*Monsieur*! You are hugging, kissing me... in the lobby... wearing a towel. *Alors...*" *Madame* says as I embrace her.

At first, I assume my public physical contact has offended her. But *Madame* doesn't pull away. Instead, she says.

"Be careful of the feelings you stir in an older woman. It's been a long time since a man wearing only a towel took me in his arms and kissed me. I just felt something I thought I had forgotten. Be still my heart. I heard the two of you last night. Oh, the sounds of loving. It's music. Don't make me remember." She says fanning herself while separating herself.

"*De toute façon* (anyway), as he ran off, he shouted, 'Make sure he gets this.' Then he threw *la lettre* on the boardwalk and, with *Cas et Pol* biting him and chasing after him into the ocean, he ran for his life.

"*Et, monsieur Q.* When you checked in you paid three months in advance and now you are paying three months more even though you have been here for only four months. Are you sure? That's two months' gratuity? It's very generous. *Merci très beaucoup*. And know that, as you requested. Yes, I will look after her like she is my own daughter." *Madame* says.

Prior to my departure *Madame* and I took steps for Catalina's wellbeing. Once my brother downloaded my manuscript, after shopping it he managed to secure an advance from my longtime publisher, *Chitlin' Circuit Media*.

Between the advance and Ayrton's generosity, I'm able to set up accounts for her. *Madame* Madinina plans to retire and will hire Catalina as the hotel business manager and will also be living there. She'll also have a car and complete *University of the West Indies'* Martinique degree program.

My gratitude runs deep after everything she's done for me. Things she doesn't even know about. She saved my life in different ways but every bit as much as Ayri did. Her love healed my soul and the past's pain and allowed me to write again.

"You are a good man looking after her this way. We all await your speedy return to your new home. *À bientôt, monsieur.*" *Madame* says, then hands me the letter.

La lettre reads: "This isn't chess, this is checkers. You think long, you think wrong. My client wants his property back. No questions asked. The finder's fee is very generous. Remember: I know where she works. I know where she lives. What I don't know – yet – is where this one's birthmark is. Don't make me find out. You know what to do."

Canton long ago hoisted anchor and vanished and is nowhere in sight off southern Martinique. Considering my precautions, he was rightly afraid of the consequences to stick around. Gone for the past few weeks, probably meeting with the Sinister Prime Minister. But now this. Sneaking back into Martinique under cover of darkness and coming to my hotel. But why now? *Gulliver* really must be desperate. And with good reason. The flash drive's information against him and Geremi Quarrles is massive.

Even though the information is safe, I'm rightly worried about Catalina's safety. He's already threatened my parents and Catalina, and considering what he did to Didi and Ayri. And now this letter threatening Catalina.

If anything happens to anyone else – again - it will be my fault; again. Am I really that driven and riven by a story? That completely consumed to the point of putting Catalina, my parents, myself - everyone and everything - at risk over and again? Especially after what happened to the Mentis family, Clotilde, G-Mo and his family? Am I really that obsessive?

I keep asking myself that same question in different ways. The answer remains the same; yes.

En route to the airport, I grow more anxious. Worried that *Gulliver* will retaliate at the last moment when I least expect it. I even think he might have planted a bomb on the plane. After all, he's a hitman, a terrorist.

Once inside, I scan the terminal crowd, but there is no glimpse of him. Turns out, though, I have every reason to be suspicious.

Prior to boarding my flight, customs and security officials pull me out of line and escort me to a customs office. They lock me alone in a room, bare except for two chairs, a table, a locked file cabinet and a mirror on the wall, presumably a two-way mirror. Minutes later a customs official enters the room, locks the door, and then examines my passport.

"Why was I pulled out of line? Why are you detaining me? My plane is about to take off. What do you want?" I say.

"You didn't check in any luggage. Where's your luggage?" He says.

"I don't have any." I say.

"What do you mean? You're not carrying anything. Where are your belongings?" He says.

"I'm traveling light." I say.

"Your clothing? Your computers? Where are they? Are you concealing a weapon?" He says.

"Says who I'm walking with steel? Laptops? What laptops? Show me where? Look. I have a plane to catch. You need to call a supervisor." I say.

"A supervisor? Uh... Just a moment." The customs official leaves the room.

Seconds later and much to my surprise, the U.S. *Chargé d'affaires* enters the office and locks the door.

"Well, I'll be damned. So, you're the supervisor? What do you want? We need to get this over with. I have a plane to catch." I say.

"From the moment you arrived, red flags started flying all over the place, one after another. In any sport, you'd have been disqualified. Your passport told me you were trouble when I saw you had been in Amada during the *coup*. That's all I needed to know.

"That, and then there's your clandestine entry into St. Lucia from Amada without a customs stamp. Your immediate hospitalization for an unknown illness and probable surgery once you arrived in St. Lucia. Your sudden financial windfall upon arriving in Martinique.

"Oh, we contacted *Columbia*. You're a teacher; but not a 'folklore musicology research director.' They're none too happy with your misrepresentations using their name. Still, they stood by you. 'Yes; the journalist is affiliated,' they said.

"Buying up all the flash drives in Martinique. Your sudden mission of mercy to St. Lucia. Your *Message in a Bottle*. Agents of the so-called New Amada Republic chasing after the *Bottle's* sender. Using journalism credentials to aid and abet the escape of persons of interests. Using aliases. Posing as a foreign national. The likely misappropriation of proprietary information. You're radioactive." He rattles off a litany.

"Say what? What do you mean; 'misappropriation of 'proprietary' what? Radioactive? You need to slow down." I say.

Q

Only *Gulliver* knows about the flash drive and using a German alias. Given the *Chargé's* sudden involvement, *Gulliver's* activities in the region now take on different, larger, far more ominous dimensions.

"I knew it. Ever since I got here, I always had that feeling someone was watching or following me. Looks like I was right all along. It was you." I say.

"Let's skip the foreplay; why don't we?" The *Chargé d'dffaires'* says.

"Don't worry. You're not my type. Let's make this a quickie. What do you want?" I say.

"Your luggage? Where is your luggage?" He says.

"Like I said before; I'm traveling light. Why?" I say.

"I need to search your luggage. National security." He says.

"U.S. national security? Oh yeah? Then show me a search warrant." I say.

"We have reasons to believe you're concealing a firearm and that you misappropriated classified material." He says.

"Only because that's what you want to believe. I just went through a metal detector scan. And what's with the royal 'we?' Who 'we' be? The government? Are you, that is, the government, saying I have U.S. classified material? Is that what the government is saying; or you? Is the government accusing me of treason? Or are you calling me a traitor? You're trying to set me up. Show me warrant. You never answered my question. Exactly who 'we' be?" I say.

"I didn't say that. We think you're carrying contraband." He says.

"Who's we? You can't keep your story straight. That's a sure sign you're lying. First, it's misappropriated. Then it's classified. Next, it's a firearm. Now it's contraband. Which one is it? And you still haven't answered my question. Just who 'we' be? As near as I can see, it seems to me 'we' is Spañadan national security. 'We' is *Backwater* security. That's what 'we' smells like to me." I say.

"Where's the gun?" He says.

"What gun? Oh! *That* gun. You mean my *trophy*? Ask him how I got it. Brandishing a gun in public, that's not too smart. That gun's mine now. *My* trophy. And *my* gun's long gone. Did he tell you about *Castor* and *Pollux*? What? He didn't tell you? I wish I had seen that." I say.

"*Castor* and *Pollux*? Where's that gun? Where's your luggage, sir? All those flash drives?" He says.

"My gear? My gear's gone. It's in storage. My laptops, everything. Especially my trophy gun. That stuff's gone. Been gone." I say.

"What do you mean; in storage? Where's your stuff?" He says.

"I told you. It's in storage. It went out weeks ago. *Gulliver*, he didn't tell you? I told him how I got rid of what everyone's been looking for weeks ago. It's been gone. I mean, I'm not suicidal. You really thought, after everything I've been through, I'd show up with my gear at the airport? That's wishful thinking. I knew I'd be stopped. Why should I make your job easy and help you confiscate my belongings? That's why I had it shipped ahead in the first place. I mean, I may be stupid but I ain't dumb." I say.

"What do you mean; you 'had it shipped?' If you didn't ship it, who did?" He says.

"You follow me. You open my mail. You track my movements and internet browsing and report it to him. Hell-to-the-no, I didn't ship it myself. As a valued guest, my hotel shipped most of my belongings. The bank, as part of their customer courtesies for large account holders, shipped my other valuables as a gratuity. They were customs-declared prior to duty-free shipping and not subject to customs search. Including my computers and *my* gun. As an alumnus and affiliated *CJR* editor, I enjoy certain privileges. Among them, storage facility privileges. He didn't tell you? I wonder why? Or, maybe he just forgot. Just like he probably forgot to tell you that dead man's switch." I say.

"No; you didn't." He says.

"Oh yes; I did. Ask him. Ask him about *Castor* and *Pollux*."

"What do you mean? *Castor* and *Pollux*? Who are they?" He says.

"*Cas et Pol* for short. Although he probably doesn't know their names. One mean tag team. They messed him up good. You'll see. Well, that's the big picture. Now let me spell it out. I told *Gulliver* and I'm telling you the same thing; I don't have it. It's gone wiki-viral. Like it or lump it; it's gone.

"It's like that, and that's the way it is. It is what it is. It's bye-bye gone, and time to move on. So, for the last time, tell *Gulliver* to tell the Sinister Prime Minister; it's gone. I don't have it. Tell him, if he wants it, he can 'read all about it,' as they say, in the next editions of *Columbia Journalism Review*. They're publishing excerpts. Subscription only, however." Then I say.

Q

"Oh, and, ah, by the way. FYI: those Amadan drilling, patent and trademark applications. You know the ones I'm talking about; right?" I say, now taunting him.

"What about them?" He says.

"They were filed six months ago for all future rights, trademarks and licenses under an offshore corporation for Amada. With no objections filed to date, according to the attorney of record, they've been granted by now. From your expression, I see how you are overjoyed by the secure future prosperity for the people of Amada. It's a wrap." I say.

Plenty peeved, the *Chargé d'affaires* paces about, occasionally glancing at the mirror on the wall.

"You do work for the American people; don't you? It's the American people paying your salary; remember? Well, I'm an American citizen in trouble in another country, and you're supposed to be on my side. Or is it the Sinister Minister and whoever is on the other side of that two-way mirror you keep looking at the side you're on? You have every reason to be worried. Your name is among many names on that flash drive. I know the administration was involved in toppling Amada and reinstating Quarrles. Operations headquartered in Martinique. So? Who's next? Venezuela? Brazil? Stay tuned, another government is sure to fall, coming soon to another country or island near you. "I'm not surprised. I'm not surprised at all. It couldn't have happened without the administration's prior knowledge, approval and coordination. Your Monroe Doctrine in play." Then I go on to say.

"And just so we're clear; I don't have any classified material. Especially not U.S. classified material. No contraband, either. What you're referring to is criminal evidence of something that took place in another country. You have no jurisdiction. A copy of the flash drive already has been delivered to the *United Nations*, *Amnesty International*, *Columbia Jouralism Review,* and the *ICIJ*. Looks like game over. Anyway, my plane's about to leave. I have no luggage. Not having luggage isn't a crime. If I don't have luggage, how can I be carrying any contraband, classified material, or concealed weapons? That means I'm free to go now." I say.

Obviously, I'm being observed through the two-way mirror on the wall; no surprise there. They already opened and monitored my mail and tracked my computer searches. They followed me and would have searched my belongings, had I arrived with any. And they would have confiscated my laptop and the flash drive. Hell, they would have performed exploratory surgery on me, if I hadn't escaped. So, they're not above a two-way mirror and recording devices in the room.

The *Chargé* exits the room.

Time starts to gallop. I'm feeling increasingly anxious and start pacing, worried not just about missing my flight. Once that plane is airborne, Catalina will have no way of knowing I'm not onboard. No one will ever know I'm trapped in an airport security office in so-called 'international territory,' a black hole beyond jurisdiction.

Alone with a CIA agent who considers me radioactive; and behind the mirror lurks a murderer trying to kill me in no man's land, where anything can go down.

Through the door, I hear voices coming from the adjoining room. "It's too late. He told you he got rid of it. And why didn't you tell me about that dead man's switch?" The *Chargé d'affaires* says.

"He's lying. I know it. Don't believe him. He still has it. Strip search him." *Gulliver* says.

"Are you crazy?" The *Chargé* says.

"Don't you ever call me crazy without calling me horse. Do you understand me? *Crazy Horse* said strip search him. Treat him like a cartel mule. Give him a barium enema. I don't care. Never mind. I'll spread him all over that desk and do it myself. Get out of my way." *Gulliver* motions to enter the adjoining customs room where I'm being detained before the *Chargé d'affaires* blocks *Gulliver's* path.

"You're violating procedure. We can't touch him without a warrant from the Martinican police." The *Chargé* says.

"Get out of my way. I'm going to search him." *Gulliver* says.

"No, you won't. We don't have jurisdiction or standing to interrogate or search him. Martinique is part of France. France is in the EU. I won't spark a diplomatic incident, violating an American citizen's rights overseas. I'm not about to jeopardize my assignment. This place is paradise. Besides, without probable cause there isn't much I can do." He says.

"'Probable cause?' How's this for 'probable cause?' He probably has it. There's your probable cause. Plus, he writes in code. Nobody in their right mind is going to let something that valuable out of their sight for one second. He still has it. I know it. It's either on him or in him. What are you waiting for? Stop him. He can't get on that plane. The Prime Minister said..." *Gulliver* says.

"Look. We monitored his mail and internet searches when he started visiting your web site. He's had a tail on him once

Q

he cashed that check. But all he does is spend time at the
beach swimming and playing soccer and hanging out with his
girlfriend at night. He's not doing anything suspicious. We
can't trace one thing to him. We have nothing. There's no law
against writing - yet. He's not a spy. He's boring." The *Chargé
d'affaires* says.

"If it's not on him or in him, it's at the bank. I know it."
Gulliver says.

"What? We're supposed to break into the bank and search
every safe deposit box? Who knew he'd cultivate the bank
manager and use the bank to write? Hide his stuff and have it
shipped? Who knew he'd use the hotel to ship his stuff ahead
of his departure? That's rather smart. Very strategic thinking.
If nothing else, he's a survivor. You've got to hand him that.

"Besides, do you know how hard it is, finding something as
small as a flash drive? He could have gotten rid of something
that size a hundred ways to Sunday. If it's not on him, the
odds are you'll never find it. You'll just have to tell the Prime
Minister it's gone. Anyway, why didn't you tell me once you
found out he had shipped his stuff? Besides..." The *Chargé
d'affaires* says.

But Gulliver interrupts. "That's why I ordered exploratory
surgery. To see if he has a chip or implant and if he's walking
around with that thing inside him." *Gulliver* says.

"Exploratory surgery?" The *Chargé* says.

"Better you believe it. We scheduled it when we first
captured him in Amada, but he escaped. You can give the
order now, though." *Gulliver* says.

"What order?" The *Chargé* says.

"Exploratory surgery. It's not too late. He has a chip or an
implant. I know it. Just arrest him, and we'll see." *Gulliver*
says.

"I'm not rendering let alone authorizing exploratory surgery
on an American citizen based on your say-so 'chip implant'
theory.

No. Just like we're not breaking into the bank, looking for a
needle in a haystack. No. There are no signs of recent
surgery. No wounds, scars or suture marks. No." The *Chargé*
says.

"Then render him to Guantanamo. That's what they do
there." *Gulliver* says.

"You don't fully appreciate how the United States works.
It's like this. Things must *seem to appear* a certain way. They
don't have to be that way, or appear to be that way. No.
Things must *seem to appear* a certain way. It's all about

appearance and perception. They're everything. Appearance and perception. It's psychology 101. That's the key. They're crucial for the country to work the way it does. We're fortunate because our system has been in place now for so long, certain things have become engrained." The *Chargé* continues.

"Take the media. For the most part, the media is pretty much under control. Meaning that the media control themselves. Or, better said, the media know what to do and how far not to go. That's because journalism no longer is a trust. It's become a business. A business with all kinds of legislation and regulatory matters pending before Congress. They have too much to lose. Tax regulations. Interview guests, programming. Political campaign advertising revenue and other funding sources." He then says.

"So, media go along to get along. It's the American way and cardinal rule of business and political life. You've got to pay to play. It's in everyone's best interests and mutually advantageous. We don't have to set any parameters. They know what to do and when to fall in line. Entertainment, sports, celebrity gossip. Game shows. Reality TV. Self-censorship. That's what's important; not journalism. Anything but. Look it. The media never have been fair or free. They have their own agenda and only serve their own and their owners' business and social interests. The media, they only have to *seem to appear* to be objective while talking their high horse sanctimony. It's all about appearance and perception. If the media don't *seem to appear* to be fair, even when they aren't, then people will begin questioning the system." He says.

"We can't have that, people questioning things. Next, they'd start thinking for themselves. That's not good. People must continue trusting appearances, and the media must continue entertaining people and keep them believing that things *seem to appear* to be what they aren't. Creating appearances and managing perception until they become self-propagating and make people stop questioning things. That's the American way." The *Chargé* elaborates.

"And just like the media must *seem to appear* fair, then government must *seem to appear* to accept the fact that a story occasionally gets out. That way, when something goes wrong, when someone goes rouge with information, like Snowden, Assange, like Manning. Like now. Then government must *seem to appear* to suck it up and make things *seem to appear* the way things aren't." Then he goes on to say.

"You yourself know; there's far worse stuff out there we've been doing that must never see the light of day. Government can't catch everyone. This is one of those situations. The system must *seem to appear* to be democratic. This way, people are reassured that the government doesn't always win. That way, American democracy *seems to appear* to be fair. This way, government lives to fight another day. What's important is that government learns from it so it never happens again by publicly making an example of whistleblowers to deter future ones. While behind the scenes, we try to catch and punish the bastards, like we did to Assange and with Manning." He adds.

"There must be consequences and deterrence for going off the reservation. It's simple. Things don't have to be one way or the other. Things should only *seem to appear* a certain way. Appearance and perception. Keeping people entertained and lulled into not thinking and trusting government. Political stability. How? By means of subliminal manipulation and social thought control. That's how." He continues.

"Look, it's all over. Let it go. It's the one that got away. The information's already offshore. Once it's no longer local, once it's wiki-viral, there's nothing we can do. It's too late. Spy game's over. Another thing he mentioned; those patent and drilling applications, they were filed. No objections were registered because we didn't know. Well, you know what that means? They've been granted." Says the *Chargé*.

"What?!" Gulliver says.

"Not only that. He also said that excerpts of the flash drive are about to be published in *Columbia Journalism Review. CJR?* That's not blowback; that's fallout. There'll be payback, bigtime. And after all that exposure and fallout, now you're saying we should render him to Gitmo and perform exploratory surgery – on an American citizen - looking for some chip or implant? I don't think so. That'd be seriously bad appearance and perception. That would *seem to appear* to make us look bad; really bad. We don't need that." He continues.

"Look, I don't like him either. You're probably right. He's been a pain since Day One. But the USA doesn't that kind of bad PR, bad optics. Bad appearance and perception. Unless, that is, he were a Muslim. Then we could say he's an Islamist and render him to Gitmo. That's different, though." The *Chargé* says.

"No, that's brilliant. There's your appearance and perception. Just say he's *jihadi.* He looked like one with that beard and those dreads. There's your appearance. Say he's a sleeper cell. That's the perception. He *seems to appear* to be a terrorist. That's enough to render-send him to Gitmo. We'll never see him again. That's perfect. Good idea." *Gulliver* says.

"Leave it alone. Just let it go." The *Chargé d'affaires* says.

"Why are you shaking your head? This is all your fault. He's a journalist. He wasn't even supposed to be in Amada to begin with. That's why we put that naval blockade and quarantine, that news blackout in place. That's why we timed the Amada and Spañada operations so closely together. All the logistics were in place. That embargo was your only job, your only responsibility. That's what he pays you for. All of this could have been avoided. It still can be. All you'd have to do is give the order for an MRI. But, of course, you won't. Just like you won't say he's a sleeper cell *jihadi* and render him to Gitmo. But you and that 'appearance and perception' nonsense. This is all your fault. Whatever you say has no credibility. Now you listen to me. Then give him this." *Gulliver* says.

A few minutes later, the *Chargé* reenters the room. "This is off the record." He says.

"I doubt you want me on or off the record. On the record, I'm reporting you to the State Department if I miss my flight. I'm sure there are some ethics canons prohibiting fraternization with criminals. Off the record, I'll expose you in print. So, keep it short. I'm not going to miss my flight. What's the deal?" I say.

"This is for you." The *Chargé d'affaires* says.

"What? You mean like another *Message in a Bottle*? Just tell me what it says. I know you already know. Just read it to me. "Or, since you like reading other people's mail give me the condensed version." I say.

The *Chargé* hands me an envelope.

"What's this?" I say.

"It's for you. You should read it." He says.

A note is attached: 'Best final offer.' Enclosed is a blank signed check. The note concludes, 'Fill in the amount.'

"I don't have it and I wouldn't sell it to him if I did. I'll keep this check and the videos of him threatening me and I'll keep both your identities secret in return for the safety of me and mine. And tell him that, if anything happens to me or mine, I'll trip that switch from the grave." I say.

"You really did set up a switch; didn't you? Those flash drives; right?" The *Chargé d'affaires* says.

"Not just the flash drives. Ask your friend. He didn't tell you what else? I told him. He knows exactly what I have. Then

Q

you can ask him about *Castor* and *Pollux* at the hotel. Must be something else he forgot to tell you. Sounds like the two of you don't seem to work well together. You've got communications issues. Maybe it's a trust or turf battle going on? But that's none of my business." I say.

"Whatever you do; just don't trip those switches." He says.

"Not as long as I'm alive. The *ICIJ* and other media organizations already have copies of everything. If I don't check in with them. If anything should 'happen' to me. If dude comes close to me or looks at me side-eyed. If I even think he's even thinking about me. If I miss my plane. So, help me. I'll put you on blast long and urban loud. Social media will blow up about the Sinister Prime Minister's activities in Amada and the government's role. Imagine the hashtags.

"That's why it's in everyone's continued best interest, particularly mine, that I stay happy and healthy, and nothing 'happens' to me. Now, call the tower and hold my flight. Don't make me trip that switch. You get me on that plane. I'm serious." I say.

The *Chargé* exits, followed by a scream and arguing coming from the adjacent room.

"You're out of control. Your orders are clear. You are to report to me before doing anything. What were you doing, going rouge at his hotel? Why didn't you tell me about that switch? I'd have called time on this operation a long time ago. This mission was doomed once those applications were filed.

"And those two agents, codenames *Castor* and *Pollux*? Who are they? Man, what happened to you? Yikes! You're bleeding out all over the place. You need to go to the hospital." The CIA agent says.

"I'm not going to any hospital. I'm going where he's going; New York City. I'm taking the war to his door. And you can't stop me." *Gulliver* says.

"Hang on! You didn't answer my question. *Castor* and *Pollux*? Who are they? What's their branch? Are they military, political or corporate?" The *Chargé* says as *Comandante* leaves the room and slams the door.

The original airport custom officials reenter and restore my belongs and paper and ticket, and I'm finally released with barely time to catch my flight.

Once back in Harlem, events unfold rapidly. *CJR* analyzes portions of the flash drive's data and serializes excerpts of my forthcoming book to critical praise.

Within months, *exposé* chapters are 'leaked' online detailing events in Amada. Life on the Row, Ayri's death. The role of the *Guiding Star* and events in Spañada. *Backwater's* involvement and Geremi Quarrles' regional ambitions.

Babylon, Babylon is published, raising questions about the activities of the energy companies, airline and hospitality industries, particularly casino interests. That, and what role U.S. and other intelligence agencies played in Amada's *coup* and reinstatement of the Sinister Prime Minister.

The hydrocarbon energy sectors come under Congressional oversight and Committee scrutiny. Foreign policy questions are raised, particularly regarding energy policies, corporate use of so-called 'security consultants' and 'contractors' and 'irregular militia forces,' euphemisms for corporate private armies. As well as previously unknown corrupt dealings of the airline, hospitality and hydrocarbon industries and their interests.

Congressional committees launch investigations into intelligence activities and subpoena my testimony concerning my acquisition of the *Smoking Gun* and knowledge of its content. I recount my Amadan experiences with *Guiding Star* and Geremi Quarrles' regional role in recent events, with testimony broadcast live on *C-Span* and *NPR*.

My life changes in ways beyond belief. *Babylon, Babylon* goes on to become critically acclaimed and a commercially successful bestseller with multiple upsides.

As Ayri had hoped, *Babylon, Babylon* turns into a documentary. Also, the book's movie rights are optioned, and I begin working on its screenplay adaptation.

Also, thanks to *Babylon, Babylon*, *Homeboy* escapes being remaindered and is in its third print run and enjoying robust sales, and has been optioned as well. Together these projects make me a financially independent working writer able to choose assignments. No longer loud and proud *Harlem High*, now I teach creative writing at *NYU*. By now, Catalina has visited me on several occasions. Life's good.

But all that's about to change.

War's about to break out at *my* door.

CHAPTER THIRTEEN

ABOVE ELYSIAN SPHERES

"More light!"
His Last Words,
Johann Wolfgang von Goethe

No matter my new prosperity or the passage of time, I continue experiencing post-traumatic stress flashback attacks, although less severe and less frequently.

Not much later, one evening after teaching class I can't stop ruminating about the past. Melancholy soon morphs into depression that gets a firm grip on me. This night is different, though. Anxious, angry, agitated for no good reason, so severe I seek refuge in the comforts of old. My father's piano recordings playing solace in the background, a summer night's breeze fans the balcony as I retreat to my balcony rocking chair.

There are still so many unanswered questions. Not knowing what happened to Ayri, Didi, and the rest of the Mentis family. What about G-Mo? I miss Catalina. For those and other reasons, I've been unable to make peace fully with the past or find closure, let alone move on.

But it's more than that. It's writing itself. It nearly cost me my life. It's all the publishing and marketing demands. Having to be in different places at the same time. Teaching. All the downsides of being a successful writer.

I'm burned out, fried and done. I can't write anymore. It's not that I can't write. I don't want to write anymore. It's not writer's block, or the ability and desire to write; I have that. This is something else. I've lost perspective and life's balance.

This and more weighs on my mind that night. Flooding memories begin their familiar hauntings, and soon I'm having another PTSD attack. I begin hyperventilating. My blood's roiling, my pulse racing. I'm febrile, fitful, perspiring.

This time's different, though. This evening I'm paralytic, my mobility constricted as if weighted by some gravitational force.

Light of being, dizzy and disoriented, My thoughts are clear, still, as if anesthetized, my body won't respond. I feel myself drifting in and out of twilight consciousness, yet at the same time hyper alert. But without drink or drugs and wide awake, how can this be? Lucid yet outside of myself, free floating in an altered state but unable to ambulate? How?

In this state of other-mind, I hear an odd noise. A sound like, but much stronger than the winds, as if like the heaven's movements, or its spheres being flung wide, roaring open.

From my rocking chair, the balcony view transforms into an incomparable vista view of vivid visions, visitations, and spirit conversations unfurl before me in the theater of my mind.

"I've always loved your father's music. I keep telling you, the two of us, we're so much alike. More than you know. Both of us, we are shaped by our fathers, as were they by the spirits of old." He says.

I can't believe my ears. That baritone and thick Caribbean/Latin accent. His pronunciation of my name. It's him. *Mi hermano!*

"Ayri?" I gasp.

"Si. Soy yo!"

"What the...? Ayri? Where are you?" I say.

"Que pasa, Q? Realmente soy yo. Ahora si!" (What's up? It's really me. That's right!)

"I can hear you but I don't see you. Where are you?" I say. Gradually, an outline or apparition, bathed in a corona, takes on blurry shape.

"I'm right here, Q. Close your eyes. Open your mind. Look closely. See?" Ayri says. Verily, distorted nonetheless fully recognizable, cloaked in black.

In my mind's eye, I watch us embrace, and as he then drapes his cloak around me, and then says, "Don't look down."

Were it not so, literally then we levitate in an out-of-body, trance-like suspended animation experience. From above and beyond I behold the past and future events being displayed on scores of collapsing and expanding polygonal, paginating liquid windows and panels, mirrors and screens.

Upon each of them, wondrously questions and answers simultaneously suggest themselves as cubist images and hieroglyphic, symbols and equations. Sanskrit fragments, and other ancient language particles. Runes, Latin and Greek quotations. Expanding trees of knowledge and collapsing collages of ideas revolve double helix-like, that intuit insight and understanding at the speed of thought.

Above Elysian Spheres in telepathic communion with Ayrton's ghost, the many startling unknowns about the past finally begin unpacking themselves in a series of preternatural revelations.

"First off, let me say that I'm aware that, at that time, you were under the false impression that I'm dead. I know this, because Guillermo, he told me so. But as you can see..." Ayri says.

"G-Mo?" I say.

"*Si, Q*. Guillermo. Somehow, as big as Brazil is, he found us. By then he was a nervous wreck. Imagine his surprise around a year ago, when he saw me again. I swear, he passed out! Fainted. Dropped to the floor like a pile of bricks! Bam! Just like that. He's doing better now. Presently he's working for our family as a kind of *factotum*. We have come to rely on him and can't imagine being without him again. 'Loyal to the end.' He told me everything. About hearing shots ringing out and how he never would have escaped without you. You took tithing to another level. Nice touch on your part. Many thanks, *mi hermano*." He continues.

"At any rate, *Q*, maybe two weeks after you escaped, late one night/early morning, *Guiding Star* came for me. The next thing I know I'm in the Room of Doom. There in the middle of the room, also shackled - my parents and sisters. You can't imagine how that felt. I hadn't seen them in weeks, only to see them like that? Hogtied? Gagged? My mother even? Thinking about it; it still hurts. Soon I noticed someone lurking in wait in the wings with a gun aimed at my family." Ayrton continues.

"It was him, the one we talked about the last time. The big, blond, blue-eyed *gringo* with dilated pupils. Very scary looking, like he had never tasted love or the milk of human kindness. The one who interrogated you - *Comandante*. There. See for yourself. Remember?" Ayri says, pointing below.

In zero gravity's realm, Elysian Spheres' panorama overwhelms the senses beyond comprehension and natural description. Time and space and fields of depths appear bent, blended and blurred, as if some unifying dimension, were overarching and governing other dimensions, in play.

Colors and thoughts, light and darkness, motion and ambient background, they appear suffused in broad curved strokes. A hallucinogenic, kaleidoscopic meld unfolding in slow motion, as if not governed by the laws of nature, motion or reason. Descriptive but beyond description, beyond credulity or comprehension. Ayri then continues.

"I'm helpless, handcuffed, shackled. My family, shackled. At this point, I'm only worried for them. *Comandante*, that's what they called him. But to me, with that gun aimed at my family like that, he really was *el diablo*! And that's not the only reason why I called him that. I'm already gagged. Next thing I know, *el loco diablo* gets right into my face, grabs my nose and kept twisting and turning it with all his might. Harder and harder, until I heard it popped." Ayri says.

"He did what?" I say.

"*Malparido!* He broke my nose. I still can't believe that *perro* did that to me. It bothers me to this day. I'm gagged, I couldn't breathe. My nose, it wouldn't stop bleeding. Now I'm gagged, I'm hemorrhaging and choking on my own blood, but he wouldn't let go and just kept on twisting it. Twisting it with torque, turning his shoulder into it. My lungs were filling, and I was slowly choking to death. My legs started giving out from under me. I felt myself passing out." He says.

Free floating along the time/space continuum as past events are displayed on liquid windows, by now, no longer do I question reality or my sanity, nor any longer do I intuit his being as phantom or ghost. Instead, I'm at ease in conversation with what is Ayri's hologram silhouette.

"He knew exactly when to let go, just when my lungs were about to burst, then I collapsed to the floor. Then he removed my gag, the handcuffs and leg shackles, and everyone else's too.

"I lay gasping and purging, heaving and seizing, still hemorrhaging. Eventually I crawl away from him towards a corner and brace myself against the wall. That's when I noticed his shirt. He was wearing your shirt. The one with all the cool pockets, buttons and zippers, buckles. You wore it when you first arrived. He really stole that shirt from you? I always liked that shirt." He says.

"Me too. He was constantly wearing it in Martinique. That or my jacket every time I saw him." I say.

"You saw him in Martinique?" Ayri says.

"Oh, yeah. Steady 'round the clock. I peeped him way before he recognized or remembered me. I had to go deep *incognegro* on him. When he found out, things got ugly, more than once. I recorded him threatening to kill me and admitting that he shot you. I took his gun as a trophy for the stuff he took from me. I swear, it felt like you were there." I say.

"When *Mami* cried out I started crawling in her direction. That's when he put his foot into my back, like I was an insect, and stepped on me. Then he leaned over, motions towards my mother, and he says. 'So, help me, I'll give her a heart attack making her watch me kill you here on the floor.'

"Then he stepped hard into my back and said, 'And I'll shoot the first one of you who tries to help you. You know what I want. Where is it? Don't make me do it. Don't force my hand.'" He said.

"That's when *Papi* spoke up. '"We are non-combatants and have diplomatic privileges.'" Ayri says.

"'Consider them revoked.'" *Comandante* said and then cocked and aimed the weapon at *Papi*."

"'Not by might of right; only by right of might. Because you have a gun. Otherwise...'" Dr. Mentis said.

"'This isn't a gun; this is the Peace Keeper. This is a new day. There's a new peace, a new order, in Amada now. *Novi Orbis.* Resist *Novi Orbis,* and you'll rest in peace.

Now which one of you will it be? You're a doctor. Your son will bleed to death. I'll induce your wife's heart attack making her watch him die, and there's nothing anyone can do about it. You know what I want, and what I'll do to get it. I don't want to but I will. So don't make me. Now, where is it?'" *Comandante* said.

"That's when I said, 'You can forget about the dossier. It's gone. It's out of the country. You'll never find it.' You'll never guess what that *El Loco* did next *Q,* ever. Then he says, 'I will give you a final moment together to say goodbyes. But first, let us pray. Sinners all, let us repent our ways.' Imagine. He prays before he kills? What's up with that?" Ayri says.

"You'll never believe this. He was supposed to become a priest but he turned against God. From aspirant seminarian to fallen angel, with a skill to kill just for a thrill. A sociopath. That's him." I say.

"Then *Comandante* says, 'Time's up. Line up against the wall. I'm sure you know the words. Repeat after me.'" *Gulliver* said.

"Repeat what?" I say.

"*Q,* he started speaking Latin." Ayri says.

"Latin?" I say.

"It was pure surreal. The man was insane. Imagine; he got up, assumed the posture of a priest saying Mass, then strode the cell reciting *Pater Noster* – The Lord's Prayer - in Latin." Ayri says.

> "'*Pater Noster, qui est in caelis,*
> *Sanctificetur Nomen Tuum.*
> *Adveniat Regnuum Tuum.*

Fiat Voluntas Tua,
Sicut in caelo et in terra..."'

"Believe me when I tell you; I prayed out loud, too! Very slowly, I was praying. Then, when he got to the passage:" Ayri says.

"'Give us this day our daily bread,
And forgive those who trespass
"'Against us, as we forgive our debtors.
And lead us not into temptation,
But deliver us from evil...'"

"That's when *Papi* stepped forward." Ayri says.

"'No longer can I stand by and watch in silence. As a physician, as a husband, I took oaths. First, 'do no harm.' To treat injuries and save lives. I have stood by and watched you nearly kill our only son. The other oath, 'til death do us part.'

"As a doctor and diplomat. As a father and as a husband, I say; enough. Enough is enough. I'm an old man, I can't stop you. But if death be for one of us, then death do part all of us. So say I, for better or worse, for all of us.'" Said Dr. Mentis.

"'On your knees, old man! Do it. Fast.'" *Comandante* said.

"'Neither my knees nor my conscience will permit me to bend. My only weapons are my stand and my voice. But you, you can bend. So, ask yourself; why don't you stand down?'" Dr. Mentis said.

"'Once you tell me where it is. Our sources say it's in Brazil.'" He said.

"'Your 'sources?' You mean Geremi Quarrles and *Guiding Star.* That's your 'source.' That's who you mean.'" Ayri said.

"'Tell him to shut up, or I'll do it... for good.'" *Gulliver* said.

"'Ayrton...'" *Señora* Mentis said.

"'Now, where is it?'" *Comandante* said.

"'I will tell you. But first, no more harm. In return, we leave Amada together - and alive - the whole family. Give us your word, and let us put the present where it belongs – in the past, behind us. Instead, let us look ahead to the time left to us. Your word.'" Dr. Mentis said.

"'You've got guts. You're a fighter, old man. You've faced death before; I can tell. I admire courage in a man; unlike your son.'" *Comandante* said.

"'It's true, I have faced death many times before, as a physician. But not your kind of death. I don't have that kind of courage. You need courage to do what you do. Risking limb and life, full time and all the time, for what; money. Unlike you, my love's labor is free. I work only for love. Healing, public service. Love of family - even my hot-headed one.

"You have already hurt him and us enough. Enough bloodshed. Enough violence. No more death. At one point, it must stop. Let the two be the ones to stop it, here and now. You know you can't continue like this. At one point, everyone and everything must stop. Let this be the time and place when the two of us say: enough is enough. Your word. We are free to go. All of us.'" Dr. Mentis said.

"'You have my word. Now, where is it?'" Said the terrorist.

"'The information you're after went out one month ago with the last Amadan diplomatic pouch.'" Dr. Mentis said.

"'Destination?'" *Comandante* said.

"'Martinique.'" Dr. Mentis said.

"'Who's the recipient?'" *Comandante* said.

That was when Ayrton objected but Dr. Mentis overruled him. "'*Q* can take care of himself, son. My responsibility is to us.'" Dr. Mentis said.

"'*Q*? That's that spy. The one with that codename and fake American passport who got away. What's he doing with it? Why him? What branch is he? Military, corporate or political espionage?'" *Comandante* said.

"'No. His papers aren't fake. It's not a codename. He's not a spy. He's an American journalist from Harlem. 'Q' is his byline and pen name. He's is a life-long friend. He's practically family. By now, he's in New York and has released it to the *ICIJ* and his publisher, *Chitlin' Circuit Media*, and other press oulets.'" Dr. Mentis said.

"'Geremi Quarrles, he's done and dusted.'" Ayri said.

"Back then we thought you'd already left Martinique and had returned to New York City. We never thought you'd have stayed behind. Inadvertently, we sent him on your trail. I'm sorry we put you in danger; again. From the looks of things, though, Martinique worked out well for you." Ayri says.

Once *Comandante* knew the flash drive was gone, he changed his mind. "'That's too bad; for you. No flash drive, no deal. Nothing personal. But once the facts changed, my focus changed. And the fact is, you're no longer important to me. You may still leave though, under certain conditions. My priority now is finding this *Q*.'" Ayrton says, motioning to a panel depicting events.

Then *Gulliver* turned his attention to Ayri. "'And you. Mr. Under-Secretary. Proponent of 'new paradigms of scale' and 'regional determinism.' Ed-op contributor, you call for 'prudent regional resource husbandry' and advocate 'moral versus casino economics.' You denounce bank fees as being 'parasitical usufruct living off others.' You accuse international finance of practicing 'debt slavery.' You rail against 'transnational strangulation.' You advocate the 'abolition of compound interest.' Your *Mensa* blurb is, 'Interest is evil.' The press, they love you. '*Mr. Lucky*,' 'Caribbean *Dauphin*.' 'Statesman ascending.' 'The people's economist.' He continues.

"'Rarely has one person managed to inflict more harm and financial loss to corporations and countries. All but singlehandedly, you interfered and succeeded in disrupting the flow of commerce and fulfillment of contracts, future transactions and billing cycles. One man; you. And for that, you're going to pay dearly. The damage you've done. The costs are great. Greater even than you warned less than a year ago." He goes on.

"'The fate of the region is up for grabs.' That's what you proclaimed from the well of the Dial when you opposed foreign and corporate drilling and refining rights and hospitality industry privileges. Remember? At the time, you cautioned that 'the archipelago's resources are being expropriated by corporatism wearing happy faces. But beneath those emoji,' you warned, 'corporatism is fast turning the archipelago into a tropical theme park.' Those are your words. What we didn't anticipate was that you would discover so quickly that the fate of the region had already been decided. You must have had well-placed source in Spañada. Another thing we did not foresee was that Amada would respond so decisively by limiting private ownership to forty-eight percent." He continues.

"'Or, that at a regional summit you personally persuaded seven other neighboring islands to follow suit. The *Antilles Eight*. Your manifesto: 'Regional economic steering.' 'Common currency and resource utilization coordination.' 'Limited development and targeted investment.' 'Manageable growth.' The so-called 'National Wellbeing Index.' 'Solar and wind energy harvesting.' 'Ending all hydrocarbon production by 2025.' 'The *Antilles Eight*,' you call yourselves. The result is this regional contagion of your toxic ideas. The *Antilles Eight*. You declared war on everything that had been put in place. All the planning and investment in place. The *Antilles Eight*. You declared war on nothing less than the continued production and unimpeded flow of life's most valuable commodity. Energy, its production and supply, pricing and distribution, and the workings of power that come with and flow from energy's benefits. Because of you and the *Antilles Eight*, revenues and growth are flat, as are profits and dividends. At best, growth rates are marginal. Not to mention loss of investor confidence, increased market volatility, negative forecasts.' 'Why?" He then continues.

"'Because of one man. One man is responsible for so much havoc. You. You declared war. You want war? Guess what? You just brought war to the '*Antilles Eight's*' door. Who do you think you are? Do you really think you can change the immutable order of things where others before you have failed and will fail in the future? Don't you know that, since time immemorial, power inherently insulates itself to protect and preserve itself against challenges and usurpation?'" He goes on to say.

"'We, *Novi Orbis*, we stand sentry against those challenges and usurpation and will continue doing so. We are legion. Who do you think will fill the void if corporatism vanished? What infrastructure would you use? Do you realize how long it takes to put production and distribution and supply chain systems into place? That, Mr. Under-Secretary, is the natural, immutable order of things. Don't you know this by now? Or are you really that conceited you just don't care about the consequences of your actions? Well, *Mr. Lucky,* you just ran out of chips. Life's about to teach you some choice lessons.'" *Gulliver* said.

Ayrton's replied. "'What you're talking about is privatizing sovereign national wealth. In effect, expropriation financed by drastic austerity measures. The people are being shorn of their assets and then charged exorbitant interest payments and fees. The debt service becomes an eternal yoke. It's debt slavery, a racket and crime by any other name, including *Novi Orbis*.' 'Getting rich off interest and banks fees, stealing the resources and labor of others, it's predatory economics. A parasitical, usurious relationship, constituting unjust enrichment.'" Ayri continued.

"'Robber baron cartels will never dictate our planning or determine our resource production goals or price points. We'll never sell our resources to the lowest bidder. We will never produce beyond our capacity to absorb. 'Thrice our needs.' That's our production creed, and we will exercise prudent husbandry. Our wealth will last. Amada will never become another devil's playground, like *Emperor Jones'* Spañada.'

"'Thanks to technology, social media platforms, data transfer at the speed of thought, word is spreading. These communications technologies in the hands of savvy people, they're transforming the world and spreading the word. And that word is freedom. And that word is spreading fast the world over.'" Ayri went on.

"'That's the real new world order. It used to take six months for news to travel around the world. That's the yesteryear you and your old '*Novi Orbis*' still inhabit. Now it's what? Six seconds? Six seconds. That's all it takes in real time. Communication. That's the new, real-time world order. A world order populated by folks fluent in every communications platform. They, we, outnumber you, and there's nothing you can do. You can't stop progress. You can't prevent change nor stop people from thinking for themselves. You can complain and try preventing it. But you can't kill an idea nor stop it from spreading. You can't stop people from wanting to be free. You can't stop time, not even for six seconds. *Q* owns those six seconds. And by now, he's reached safety and is writing the record.'" Then Ayrton said,

"'Go ahead. Laugh all you want about Amada's National Wellbeing Index. Indeed, Amada encourages people to retire at age fifty. For the time being, Amadans pay no income tax. Health, and education is free. Yes, foreign ownership of our natural resources will remain restricted.' In Amada, the people, not *los gatos gordos* (the fat cats), will benefit. Amadans are not hamsters on treadmills producing wealth for others. We will not live beyond our means or enter debt slavery. Our best and brightest, young and old alike, will find happiness in Amada.'" Ayri continued.

"'At life's end, reflection is never about material wealth. Personal happiness as defined by health, loving and being loved, that's all people want. That's the full tally of personal wealth and true value of life. That's Amada's National Wellbeing Index.'" Ayri said, as these and fluid scenes continue unfurling with clarity before my mind's eye, as Ayri continues recalling his experiences.

"'Call me what you want. Kill me. Kill all of us. Kill the dreamer but you can't kill the dream. People live and die for life's dreams. People all over are itching to pick up the baton and keep alive the fight for freedom. That's what people the world over want, and will do anything for; freedom. For many, freedom has become a social religion. It's the song of time, ballad and poem, told over and again in prose and rhyme. Once people lose that dream, when life no longer has value, and instead becomes a living death. When the fear of living is greater than the fear of death itself, then people with nothing to lose will do anything. So, beware and don't be surprised when, as you just said, others decide to bring the wars to *your* shores one day.'" Ayri said.

"'Mr. Under-Secretary. As, no doubt, you may be able to tell, you're in no position to hold forth. You see, that's the thing about you. Your tone, your smug, condescending self-superiority. I don't like you. Who do you think you are?'" He said.

"'I'll tell you who I'm not. I'm not some supplicant or sellout, another *Emperor Jones.* I don't crave power or wealth nor curry favor. Amada is my country. These are my people. These are our seas and soil and everything beneath and above them. It's all one love. And that's why I won't put my family through anymore of this. I'll leave. You agreed we could. But you, too, must leave my country.'" Ayrton said.

"'I said you could leave together, alive, and you still may. But you may never return from exile, ever. First, you must renounce your right of return. Never return, ever.'" *Comandante* said.

"'Yeah, *If Six Was Nine.*'" Ayri said.

"'What did you just say?'" He said.

"'I said, *If Six Was Nine.* Jimi Hendrix; never mind. Who are you? A foreigner telling me not to return to my country? Like Jimi said, *If Six Was Nine.*'" Ayri said.

"'You and your snarkies. See? That's what I mean. Didn't I just tell you? I don't like your attitude. Telling me what you think isn't necessary. It only makes me want to teach a lesson. A life's lesson. One you'll remember with every step you'll ever take. Get ready. Here comes the pain.'" He said.

"Q, that's when he gave me the gun and he shot me! He shot me, twice! Once in each foot! My feet! Such pain, I passed out. That's what Guillermo heard. From then on, I don't remember anything, only what my family tells me. They say he sent for a body bag, and then personally bagged my unconscious body." Ayrton further explains.

"Next, he ordered *Guiding Star* to escort us to a waiting ship and sent us into exile to the mainland, Brazil. Once at sea, the pain became unbearable. *Papi* told me to soak my feet in the ocean but I could only do it for so long because my feet were still bleeding, and the blood kept attracting sharks. The whole time *Papi* kept repeating, 'Salt, salt cures. Salt, salt cures. Salt cures.'" Ayri says.

Ayri's injuries were severe. Time wasn't on his side. Hadn't his father been a physician, Ayrton probably would have died at sea. The family persuaded the skipper to detour to nearby Maracaibo, Venezuela, where Ayri was admitted to hospital for emergent medical treatment. It was touch-and-go there for a while. My feet had become infected. All the bones in my feet were shattered. I spent weeks in the hospital receiving extensive treatment. But no matter all the care, my feet just wouldn't heal properly. The doctors, everyone was worried that gangrene had set in and spread. You know what that means. Amputation. The thought alone hurts. It got so bad I had to be transferred from Maracaibo to a hospital in Caracas." Ayrton recalls.

"Well, one day, Didi, she showed up at the hospital. Somehow - don't ask me how - but somehow, somewhere in all of Caracas - Didi found a root doctor - a shaman. He told the doctors and nurses to get out of the room, then performed ceremonial incantations and wrapped my feet in herbal leaf packs and fanned incense. Of course, the hospital staff was not amused by his shamanic antics. That's how desperate things were, though." Ayri says.

"By the way. Didi; how is she?" I say.

"Not good, not good at all. She's not herself anymore, ever since the two of you were arrested. We were separated. Something happened to her. She's become depressed. She won't talk. She keeps asking for you. You'll see. Look over there. Anyway, my prognosis was grim. The doctors' recommendations were unanimous. Amputation of my feet now, or they would have to amputate my legs below the knees, if not both legs above the knee in the future." He goes on.

"You know, *Papi's* truly an amazing man. Throughout, even after the boat trip, he kept mumbling to himself. Like he was talking to some invisible person. He kept saying, 'Salt, salt cures. Salt, salt cures...' Well, one day he suddenly signed me out of hospital, packed us up, and rushed us to the ocean. He strapped me in a wheelchair and like a madman he plunged us waist high in the ocean. He kept me there for hours. We'd leave, treat my feet, then eight hours later we did the same thing again." He recalls.

"Three times daily for weeks, we did this. We would sit in the ocean and just talk. We talked about everything. Family, our lives, the future. Politics, history, sports. We'd sit and talked for hours. This wasn't just father and son talking. This was something else. This was beyond friendship or kinship. This was seeing someone I'd known all my life as if for the first time. Those moments in the ocean were Pentecostal. A revelation. And this, *mi hermano,* will be one of our new editorial projects." Ayri says.

"One of what? What did you just say? I hope I didn't hear what I think you said. Please tell me that's not what you said or what I think I heard you say." I say.

"Oh, yes. You heard it because I just said it, *Q*. And I already have a title: *Conversations with Rodrigo.* Forget about the other project, *Cultural Wasteland.* And just wait until I tell you about the other project ideas. Being back in Harlem City! Just like old times. The sights, the memories. It's like I never left. I'm starving. I'll explain everything over dinner at *Red Rooster,* my new favorite place. This time you pay, though, rich writer, you. I'm close by." Ayri says, adding.

"You know how I get. That's why you must stop me from interrupting myself so I can finish telling you about the agony of my feet. In the beginning, they were black, swollen, tender. Edema and pain so severe, I couldn't stand. Bandages, socks, caused unbearable pain. Until ocean therapy. *Q,* believe me when *Papi* says, 'salt cures.'

"At first, I didn't notice any improvement. But eventually my feet, they stopped throbbing and soon the swelling subsided, and gradually the pain began easing. I couldn't wait to get back in the ocean. After a few weeks, the discoloration of my feet gradually went from black to purple. From blue to greenish to yellow, now back to my brown skin. The swelling, the infection and puss subsided. The circulation in my feet increased. I began developing new dermis. It was a miracle.

"There also was some humor, much irony, in the whole situation. As you know, *Papi* is an osteopath. Because events in Amada were all over the news in the Basin and in South America, my treatment was *gratis* as a professional courtesy to *Papi.*

"Well, when we returned to the hospital for my checkup and new antibiotics and other prescriptions, the doctors thought we had returned to schedule amputation surgery. They had already sharpened their scalpels and informed us that the best orthopedic surgeons in South America were on standby and that 'post amputation psychiatric and physical rehabilitation and prosthesis consults were pending.' They even wanted to do a long-term recovery case study. They thought they knew best. And we are most grateful for their care and planning. So, imagine their surprise when they saw my feet. You should have seen those proud Castilian doctors, South America's elite, descendants of the *conquistadores,* being bested by a descendent of slaves. An osteopath, with two words: 'salt cures.' "Four months after arriving in

Venezuela we made our way by land to Brazil and temporarily settled in Pernambuco.

Between my hospitalizations, recovery, and on that boat, I had lot of time to think. Especially about all the things I did wrong. I knew then and I know now that I never should have involved you. When I think about the time I saw you in prison. Seeing you like that. Your injuries, your anger at me, at Amada. You thinking I had set you up, that I stabbed you in the back. I'm so sorry this happened to you as my guest under my protection in my country." Ayri says.

Above Elysian Spheres, across and along the continuum's rainbow color crest, weightlessness and sheer lightness of being suffuse my spirit, as I behold scenes of the past's timeline sequence playing themselves out, in reverse order unfolding before me on fluid, polygonal screens and tiles.

"Glad to see you've recovered from your injuries faster than I have. After he shot me, I fell and cracked my skull and fractured my cheek and face in different places. For a long time, I wore sunglasses and a baseball cap. I have sinusitis, a constant post nasal drip. My eyes tear and seep, my vision in my left eye is blurred. I have metal plates in my feet and skull. I keep setting off the airport security alarm must X-ray me first. I can't use a cell phone. I even disrupt wifi hotspots. For a while I was partially disabled. I still need to walk using a cane. I have something called Spaulding's Disease. It's a nerve disorder. The nerve endings, they droop. They describe my condition as being like hypothermia or neuropathy - dead nerves. But shaman and Castilian quacks assure me that I will eventually regain sensation and that my feet will heal. Who knows? I'm realistic about my base line functioning. Certain things, like running, I know I'll never be able to do again. But then again, with hope who know? After all, didn't a wise man once say, 'salt cures?'" He says.

Ayri then goes on to explain how devastating the ordeal was to his parents. "I saw them age before my eyes. I felt responsible. We had no money for necessities, let alone surgery or travel. Although treatment for my feet was as a professional courtesy, the plastic surgery I needed wasn't.

"It was very difficult seeing *Papi* that way. He is such a proud man who came so far in life, only for us to be reduced to refugees, living in the poverty he tried all his life to escape. He was always used to taking care of us, especially my mother. He felt he let us down, which we kept on denying." Ayri says.

Once he entered politics Dr. Mentis stopped practicing medicine. Thirty years later, and his skill set had eroded. Fortunately, though, having studied in Brazil and due to his diplomatic career, Dr. Mentis still developed valuable contacts. Among them, a medical school class mate and medical textbook publisher in Sao Paulo who hired Dr. Mentis as a text translator/editor on the strength of his background and language skills; and with good results. The task sharpened his medical knowledge.

"So much so, *Papi* recently passed the board exams and is practicing family medicine again in Brazil. His determination, his concentration... I'm very proud of him. He's an inspiring example I will never equal. Every day I strive to make him proud of me." Says Ayri.

Rightly concerned about being detected by *Guiding Star,* for safety reasons the family split up temporarily. The parents moved with Re-Re and Didi to Sao Paulo. Ayri remained in Pernambuco for continuing therapy, and because it was closer to Amada.

A fascinating backstory which recently occurred involving *Donna* Dolores. "My mother's family, the Villareals. Well, how can I say this modestly? Well, they enjoyed substantial holdings. When my grandfather, Alejo Villareal, God rest his soul, died many years ago when I was a teenager, my mother together with her two brothers each inherited one third of the estate. My father always was the breadwinner and always provided for us, so that over time she completely forgot about her inheritance. It was only when one of her brothers, who recently died, willed part of his estate to *Mami* that the probate attorneys pointed out that the inheritance's interest had accumulated without dividend disbursement for over thirty years." He then says.

"*Q,* as an economist I've advocated all my life against compound interest. That is, until it became personal. Let me tell you; the money and interest have turned into a veritable fortune many times larger than the sizeable principal, far surpassing my grandfather's original holdings and her brother's current combined holdings. Thirty years of compound interest. We're talking about many double-digit millions. *Hermano,* literally life-altering wealth. Many lives, including Guillermo and his family. It's afforded me the best treatments. My face has been reset and filled. I almost look like myself again. I'm back in the ocean again. 'Salt cures.' I still have some trouble walking, although I'm much better." Ayri goes on.

"It's hard to believe I'd ever change my mind about the evils of compound interest. But don't let the smooth taste fool you. Compound interest and finance capitalism are gouging the public. The profits are shared among the select few instead of the greater good. In our case, it was equity, dividend and interest that did much great good. It's enabled our new lives in South America. Clotilde, G-Mo and family is still with us. Sometimes I think if they had to choose, my family would have left me behind and given her my place on the boat." Ayri says.

Eventually *Donna* Dolores opened a kindergarten and literacy program in Sao Paulo. But the family more than has their hands full with Re-Re.

"Of us all, Guillermo's family included, Re-Re's having the hardest time. She has dropped out of university and has become very defiant, always angry. She listens to nothing but that brain-dead, attention-deficit disorder, anti-social rap-hop all day long. These negative influences complicate matters.

"She's become very problematic. My parents took her to a psychiatrist, where she is currently under treatment for something called 'adjustment reaction disorder with mixed depressive features. Rule out psychosis.' All that's a fancy name for spoiled brat. That's her real diagnosis. I remember how my parents, all of us used to spoil her, pampering her and catering to her every whim. She got away with everything because she was the youngest. Now look at the monster we created. And Didi's not helping. No matter what Re-Re does, Didi defends her. She's overly protective of her. So, that's weighing on Didi too. She's become very quiet. She won't talk about what's bothering her. She has become withdrawn." Ayri says.

"What do you mean?" I say.

"Sometimes she becomes very angry and starts lashing out, then suddenly breaks down crying. At first, I thought she was homesick, like the rest of us. But this is something very else. She used to be your typical, hot blooded, '*Ay!*' Caribe. You'd say, S-A-L, she'd say, S-A. Full of life, you know. But not anymore. I don't know what, but something took her joy. Something took her away. She's become very introspective. She's no longer S-A-L-S-A. She's *morosa*." He goes on to say.

"You know, *Q*, there is a saying: 'In times of war, beauty is a curse.' In jail, we were all separated, other than *Mami* and Re-Re, who remained together. So, we don't know. But I thinksomething happened to Didi once we were separated." Ayri says.

Q

"What are you saying?" I say.

"I don't know. She won't say; and I won't ask. I don't have to ask to know that something happened to her. Deep down I know. And deep down, I don't need to know. That something's not right. I feel it." Ayrton continues.

"Then suddenly, one day she just up and leaves Sao Paulo for Rio, literally within a week. It gets weird. She's become this professional student. She recently switched studies from architecture to journalism and literature." He says, then turns facetious.

"Now she's started wearing these school boy tortoise shell eye glasses; just like you. Says she wants to be a 'jazz writer.' Novelist and journalist. Sound familiar? Now she listens to this morbid classical music. Stuff, like Mahler and Rachmaninoff. Copeland, Orff's *Carmina Burana*. That, and your father's recordings. Catch my drift? If it's not that, it's jazz. Charlie Rouse, Horace Parlan. Shirley Scott, Tina Brooks. Ike Quebec, Grant Green. Junior Mance, Oliver Nelson. Jazz, instead of her culture. Our Caribbean Latin music. Completely out of character. *Ay!*

"It's not good, Q. Now, she's studying philosophy. Esoteric stuff like Kant, Hegel, Schopenhauer. Nietzsche, Wittgenstein, and the Enzensberger brothers, whoever they are. The only thing Didi isn't doing - yet - is speaking German. I mean, Kant and his categorical imperative, that's heavy enough. But Hegel and Schopenhauer, that's narcoleptic stuff. And well, Wittgenstein is so dense with thought it's impossible to know what it means. Nietzsche's cool, though. He makes sense. He understood the man of action, like I am. But the Enzensberger brothers? I mean, come on! What's the point? Point/counterpoint? It takes more than one of them to express a single thought? As an economist, I assure you; one or both of those brothers is underperforming. That's not very German." Ayrton says.

"Seriously though, Q. She speaks highly and often of you. We all do. She was very worried when we lost contact after you saw Guillermo in St. Lucia. We thought you had left Martinique right away. We didn't know you stayed. On the way to Venezuela, on and on Didi went about you, swooning rhapsodic at the mere mention of your name. How heroic and strong you were that day on the beach when the two of you were captured. How *Guiding Star* all but needed Kryptonite to subdue you. How you 'valiantly fought in protection of her honor.'

"Yeah, right. A real superhero you are. What? 'Have no fear, *Writerman* is here.' What's *Writerman* going to do; explain stuff? Wow! I'm scared. 'Have you heard from him?' 'Why haven't you heard from him?' 'Where is he?' 'Why don't you know where he is? 'Is he okay?' 'You just said you don't know where he is; so how can you say he's okay?' 'When's he coming back?' 'When's his birthday again?' Or, my other favorites, 'He's so gentle.' 'I need to talk to him.' 'He understands me.' And, 'is he involved with anyone now?'" Ayri becomes angry. See?" He becomes agitated.

"There you go again with that blank, zoned out, Zen stare when you don't say a word. It drives me crazy. Don't pretend you don't know what I'm talking about. Answer me, *Q.*" Ayri says, then turns agitated.

"Answer you? Answer you what? You didn't ask me anything." I say.

"What? You think I'm *stupido*? That by now I don't know? That I didn't know back then? Before Amada? In Harlem City? When we were in school? *Si*. I know everything. No? Really? Okay. You're so busted. I walked in on you two one day when she and I were roommates when we were in school. The music was on, you didn't hear me. There you are, the two of you in bed. You're on top of her. And then, what do you do? You roll to your side and onto your back and, with one move, now she's on top of you. Her eyes bulge and she's going buck wild all over you. If I didn't know her, I wouldn't recognize her. I had to leave my own apartment because you were flipping Didi. *Ay*! You'd better wipe that *stupido* grin off your face. You turned her into this 'can't-stop-won't-stop' she-beast. Looks like you more than had your hands full. I never knew Didi had a birthmark? Ayri goes on.

"From the beginning, I always knew you two were going at it like minks back then. And don't think I didn't. I should drop you right here. Tell me why shouldn't I drop you? What kind of friend are you? How can you be *mi hermano* after you turned my sister out?" Ayri says.

"Because she not my sister; that's why. She was afraid you'd go all big brother *machismo*; so was I. Just like I'm afraid you'll drop me now. Yo, man, don't drop me, bro. I can't even see that far down." I say.

"I told you not to look down. And don't try brother-in-lawing me. You two had every reason to be worried." Ayri said, adding.

"I'm glad it was you, though. Lucky dog, you. My sister's a beautiful woman, and you treated her well. I thank you for

Q

that. But you're about to have a problem, a real big problem. Actually, two big problems. Or, depending on your multiplier, four problems. You always were a sucker for women with curves and *tatas*." Ayri points at one of the tiles.

"Well, look over here. Here they come." Ayri says, pointing to a future screen scene. Two women with suitcases, Didi and Catalina, curves and *tatas* galore, arriving within minutes of another at my door. Trouble's on the horizon and about to go down; again.

"She loves you, Q. Ever since Harlem. And now again, when you came to Amada. I told you; Clotilde told me everything. About Didi showing up at night, sex on the beach and you flipping each other. Oh, I know all about your smooth signature moves, especially from up on high here, and I'm sick of it." He goes on, saying.

"Plus, Didi isn't the only one. Years ago, I never should have introduced you to the family. Re-Re says you're 'to die for.' Actors, musicians? Writers, painters and dancers? Artists - what do they know? *Mami* finds you 'the brooding, romantic type.' A 'romantic' German? Now that's an oxymoron, if ever there was one. According to *Mami*, you're 'quite the *caballero.*' She watched you 'intently' when you visited us. Says you're 'so well-mannered and so properly reared' by your parents. What was it she said? 'The kind of man who'd be an excellent addition to have in the family.' 'Excellent son-in-law material!' That alone tells me Didi confided in our mother. Bet you; Didi forgot to tell *Mami* you taught her how to flip, and your other smooth signature moves. I assure you though, *Donna* Dolores will be the opposite of amused once I tell her.. Ayrton interrupts himself.

"I'm sorry. Did I say, 'once I tell her?' Is that what I just said? No, I didn't. I did? What was I thinking? That was just - you know; a flip. There I go again. I mean parapraxis, a slip of the tongue. Nothing Freudian though, I assure you. What I meant to say was *if* ever *Mami* were to find out. You know; like lipstick writing on the bathroom mirror? Maybe a distorted voice recording? An anonymous note? Like a *Message in a Bottle*. That kind of thing. Pure happenstance, actuarially and metaphorically speaking, of course. You know.

"Now, all of them compare me to you. And *Papi?* He's the worst. On and on he goes. How you're 'a man of few but well-chosen words.' About your 'fund of knowledge,' your 'bright future.' Your 'firm handshake while looking a person straight in the eye, and what that says about a man.' How 'rare is the listener who commands the conversation.' How 'Q has this

edge.' How I should 'be more like *Q.*' Be more like *Q?*' I think
not. There's one thing sure and two things certain: *Papi* will
kill you once he finds out you've been grooming his daughter;
if *Mami* doesn't kill you first. There I go again, speaking in
subjunctive mood. But English isn't my mother tongue.
Meaning, sometimes things get lost in translation. But only
when I want things to. After all, I am a diplomat." Ayrton
continues.

"Seriously though, I thought about returning to the States
but, as much as I love Harlem City, but I'm Caribbean. Brazil's
more comfortable, familiar. The music, the food, the culture,
the vibe. Brazil's just fit better. It's the next best thing to
Amada. Besides, I don't want to be too far from the family,
and with Re-Re wilding out, straight-up hip-hop crazy, and
Didi's depression. Plus, I'm only three hours away from
Amada by plane. As good as life is in Brazil though, we're still
homesick beyond words. I ache. What makes it worse is the
way we were forced to leave. I'm still involved with the
resistance movement in Salamar. Our ranks are growing, and
soon I will resume my rightful place among my people." Ayri
says.

"If you're involved, I'm sure success is certain. Funny, how
the circle closes. The last time we saw each other in prison I
remember begging you to work from afar with the
underground movement; and now you are." I say.

"From near and far, separate and together, we both did our
part. Thanks to you, the world now knows about events in
Amada. The role of *Guiding Star,* about Geremi Quarrles and
their nefarious connections with the cartels. In behalf of my
country - thank you, *mi hermano.*" Ayri says.

"Help me understand something, Ayri. How did the flash
drive originally come into your possession? And why is there
bad blood between Amada and Spañada?" I say.

"Ah, Spañada. Enmity between Spañada and Amada, it's
ancient and rooted in everything; mostly colonial non sense.
We speak Portuguese/Spanish, they speak English. Silly tariff
disputes. Cricket and soccer competitions. Fishing rights
disputes. Bragging rights. Amada is prosperous, Spañada has
always been poor. Much like the Dominican Republic and Haiti,
even though we don't share territory and we're not racist
towards Spañadans, the way the Dominicans discriminate
against the black Haitians." Ayrton recalls.

"And then, when Geremi Quarrles came to power, *Papi*
used to speak out and regularly warned against his
dictatorship at regional summit conferences and at the *United*

Q

Nations. Democrat versus autocrat. It was *Papi.* He coined the phrase, 'Sinister Prime Minister.' Ever since, it's been personal. Geremi Quarrles has been the pawn of the energy, travel and hospitality globalization efforts for some time. Once Quarrles found out about Amada's oil he hired *Backwater.* They chartered *Guiding Star,* mostly made up of old *Mongoose Squad* confederates, which in turn spawned *Comandante.* Obviously, a man like Geremi Quarrles has many enemies, more at home than abroad. The flash drive was smuggled to us through backdoor channels. Something called a *Message in a Bottle.* You may have heard the expression before. The rest, you know. After all, you survived to write about it. That, and with a little help from axis." Ayri says.

"What's with this 'axis' I keep hearing about?" I say.

"It's the network of the spirits and saints helping wayfarers transition the dimensions' continuum." Ayri says.

"Say what!?"

The axis. The axis knows. *Ay!* It's everywhere. With the passage of time, you will know." Ayri, cryptic, says, adding.

"Well done. Done well, indeed, Q. *Babylon, Babylon* is a monster. *Jibaro*'s in its third print. Back-to-back best sellers. Documentary. Movie rights, screenplay options for both books. *NYU* instructor. Harlem City high rise apartment office overlooking Central Park with a view of Manhattan better than anywhere in New York, with wrap around balcony, hammock with mosquito net, rattan patio furniture and rocking chair, outdoor grill. Feels Caribbean, like I've seen it before. The only thing missing is the ocean view. Choice furnishings collected during your travels, very eclectic. *Shou Sugi Ban* platform bed. Buddha shrine, glass top drawing board computer desk with, double computer screens. Bent wood rocking chair, pool table. Chess board, pinball machines. Donald Trump dart board. Framed music album covers art work. A framed nickel-plated .38 caliber Glock. So, this is how a jazz writer lives, when 'the story is the star.' Well done. Done well, indeed." Ayri says.

"That's true. Thanks, *Mr. Lucky.*" I say.

"I'm happy for you. *Q.*" Ayri says.

"I'm just glad I'm still in the land of the living. *Babylon, Babylon,* it's really your story. Your family's, your country's story. Mine's just the hand that wrote it, and I'm honored having done so." I say.

"In seeing the information to safety, you risked life and limb. Not only that. You made sense out of complicated material and wrote a bestseller. Because of you that the world now knows about Amada. Your hard-earned success is well deserved." Ayri says.

"And you deserve your country back." I say

"That's the only thing I want; I want to go home. No one can give me that. Only we, the Amadan people, can make that happen, and no one else. And we will." Ayri says.

"Listening to your dad's music, I realize how fortunate you are, growing up around that kind of talent and being etched by an environment of beauty. Star-kissed. The arts, writing, they're your destiny, just like public service is mine. Your parents, and especially you father as an artist, they must be proud. I know I am. Proud that you're my friend and proud of the writer you are. What's the saying? 'The artist, not finding a sphere, invents one?'" Ayri goes on.

"That's what you did. You found a way to tell our story. And now, here we are; again. The two of us, the journalist and the politician. Coincidence? I don't think so." Ayri continues.

"Remember those commentary and corrections sessions at the beach villa, editing the previous day's work? We were a good team. Watching you, learning how writers and journalists work. Your attention to detail and dedication to craft. I appreciate witnessing your talent on display. I miss those days, and your smart company." Ayri says.

"Ditto, *mi hermano*." I say.

"The journalist and the politician. It must be fate. Think about it. How else? Who else could have gotten the story out and written it; if not you? No one. You're the only one, *Q*. Only you. I'm proud of what the two of us accomplished together. That's why I'm here, *Q*. I've come to thank you. I know how vexed you are. But don't be. We were a good team." He says.

"Best-ever; and still are." I say.

"Speaking of which; I haven't even told you the best." Ayri says.

"Meaning?" I say.

"Meaning that thanks to *Babylon, Babylon,* not only heightened SEC scrutiny of hydrocarbon, travel and hospitality activities and Congressional oversight of 'security contractor mischief' in the archipelago."

"Thanks to you - and to *Babylon, Babylon* - in my country, too, in Amada, much has changed." Ayri says.

"What do you mean?" I say.

"Meaning that thanks to you... Your brother filed the application on time. Better than we ever could have hoped for, once those patents were granted our drilling proposals were approved. As a result, an injunction was finally granted. Thanks to you..." Ayri says.

"Thanks to *us*..." I interrupt.

"Thanks to *us*, all foreign oil drilling operations have been ordered to stop. Thanks to *us*, all paramilitary mercenary forces have been ordered to leave Amada. That means *Guiding Star* is no longer in power. The *United Nations* will be sending peacekeepers to check Geremi Quarrles' mischief. Thanks to *us*." Ayrton says.

"Are you serious? When did all this happen?" I say.

"Not yet; tomorrow, at the *United Nations*. That why I'm back in town. Thanks to *us*, as of tomorrow, the Sinister Prime Minister is gone. Thanks to *us*, *Comandante* is long and far gone. I'm on my way to you now. Tonight, we celebrate! *Ay!*" Ayri says.

"A just ending. Without you, without your father and family. Without Amada there's no story. The book wrote itself; you said it would. It's your story. I'm grateful to have been its *amanuensis.*" I say.

"I also came to say that, thanks to *you*... No... Thanks to *you*, Q... we're going home." Ayri says.

"You mean, like home? Amada?"

"*Si*, Q. We're going back home, after the U.N. assembly. To Amada. New elections will be scheduled next year. When they are... When the family resumes our rightful place, that day we want you to return to Amada and write about the restoration of our democracy and reconstruction of my country. That's another reason I'm here. There still is much for us to do." Ayri says.

"Oh, I don't know about all that. First *Cultural Wasteland*, then *Conversations with Rodrigo.*' And now this? We just came off that road. Remember? I'm still a little raw from the last go around." I say.

"I know what you're thinking. Amada - once is too much. Amada - banana republic. No more the politician and the journalist. But you see, the thing is... Our parliament, the Dial... They have appointed my father... He will be... Prime Minister." Ayri went on.

"Meaning, things will be different this time. Unfortunately, this time there won't be any perks, though. No villa, no jeep. We must first rebuild our country. But it'll be like old times. We'll be working together again. Think about it. The journalist and the politician, working together again. Together, we wrote history." Next he says.

"So, who says the journalist and the politician, together we can't help write and shape the future? These are dangerous times, *Q*. Since the beginning, human nature wars with itself. It's eons later, and charlatans and dilettantes, madmen and generals. Passion and prejudice, they still rule." Ayri then recalls.

"In your anger, the ugly American in you said many things that day in jail. 'Amada, Third World Banana Republic.' 'Amada, Hell on Earth.' Those words hurt. You sounded so American. So dismissive, so judgmental of a small country's national pride and problems. But, then again, you almost died, so I understand. Well, I have opinions about *your* country. I know America well. I loved living in Harlem. In terms of technology, fashion, music, America is unrivalled. It's the America the world has always admires. Planet America, or Brand America. Lately though, we, the world, we watch, wonder, and worry." Ayrton explains.

"America's changing. Everything does. But I fear for your country, and the planet. America, the whole world, is dividend as never before. The world has more weapons to destroy the planet. Time has become so compressed, one wrong decision, one false move can bring about the unthinkable. It's scary. Particularly because of what we are witnessing in your country. The other America. The ugly America." Ayri goes on to say.

"Since its founding, hatred and violence gave birth to the United States and are central to understanding your country. It's like some virus or vaccine injected into the American body politic. Increasingly, we are seeing that many Americans dislike each other. The rhetoric is disturbing, people talking past each other, and even refusing to listen to and instead blaming each other for the country's problems, and the country's gun fetish only makes things worse." Ayri then says.

"In America, there are more guns than there are people. Guns have more rights than people have protection from guns. In your country, it's easier to get a gun than baby formula. What's wrong with that picture?

At home and abroad, America has become this circular firing squad, a shooting gallery. Not even children in schools and worshipers in churches are safe. Americans kill each other in numbers resembling mass war casualties in any other country. At perpetual war, abroad and with itself." Ayri continues.

"U.S. politics has become a reality TV show, everyone looking for a snarky sound bite. Government offices and candidates are for sale, elections bought. The candidate with the most money mostly wins. Money rules every aspect of American life. Americans are being played and pitted against another and don't even know it. Brainwashed by billionaire candidates, claiming to identify with working-class problems by stoking fear and divisions. By any measure, the fix is in. The system has been gerrymandered and rigged at direct odds with democracy and the greater good, and resembles a criminal enterprise by any other name." Ayri says.

"The world is watch things falling apart in the United States, a country divorced from reality and has left the world wondering if it will survive as we know it. The country trapped in a parallel, virtual reality, its civic consciousness in a state of collective cognitive dissonance, induced by an endless feedback loop of self-worship and fear mongering. America has entered the looking glass. Unable to tell fake from fact, or right from wrong. Shadow from act, appearance and perception. It's kabuki theater. In a country allergic to criticism, indifferent to how others see it, ignorance is trump. Power is religion, and money is salvation. Television serves as altar. Sermon and hymn alike preach the gospel of plenty. A house of mirrors, its distorted images presented as reality, set to a celestial choir proclaiming the Good Life everlasting.

"Life is short and talk is cheap; that's all I know. By their deeds you will know them, says the Good Book. All the subliminal appearance and perception manipulation, all its military muscle, can't hide certain truth about the dark side of your country's history of genocide, slavery and racism. That the United States it's everything it says isn't, and nothing it says it is. Looking in from the outside, something in the milk isn't clean. Your country is crazy.

"The world is at a tipping point. The planet and humanity are imperiled as never before. In that sense, the United States is really nothing less than a metaphor and microcosm of the world. If America doesn't work, the world can't work.

"It's time, that moment of truth. Time to muster courage. Time to wake up, and step up. Time to save ourselves from ourselves and our past. Time to rescue the future from the present for posterity's sake. The stakes couldn't be greater. Freedom, democracy, our very survival. It's that, or *Novi Orbis*. This isn't a screed, more a plea, *un cri de cœur* from the world to the United States. The world, we cheering you on, so keep heart. Fear no evil. Remember, this is still *our* world. Together, anything's possible." Ayri says.

"*Ay!* And Amen to that." Say I.

Above Elysian Spheres, scenes from childhood on are displayed in my Book of Life. Ayrton's death, Didi's plight, my near-death experiences and survival, Catalina's love. Rites of passage, rebirth and salvation experiences. Separately and together, they've marked me a changed man, more introspective, matured and wizened beyond my years. My appreciation for life, my understanding of human nature deeper, as if seeing life and myself for the first time with new eyes and finally at peace with the past.

But everything can't be destiny. Is love destiny?

"It's that time, *Q*." Ayrton says.

"What time is that?"

"Time's come. Time to warn you, *Q*. I know you love *Martiniquaise* woman. She loves you too." Ayri says.

"She saved my life in more ways than I can count or thank her. She healed me and taught me how to feel and love again. "She made writing *Babylon, Babylon* possible. Without her... You know; you made it happen." I say.

"Do you love her?" He says.

"That's what I just said; yes. You said so too." I say.

"I know. Still, you must let her go. I'm sorry, *Q*." He says.

"What do you mean? Why do I must?" I say.

"We need you; the family. It's Didi. She's in a dark place and very depressed, seriously so. We're afraid she might even try to...

"Didi loves you, *Q*. Ever since New York, and again when you came to Amada. I told you; the family knows how she feels, and how you feel about her. I know you adore her. It's mutual. Everyone knows. It shows. You two glow when you're together. There's trust. It's all that flipping. That's why I'm asking you this. We think it best that she should move back to the States. She's going back to New York. She loves Harlem City. And since you live here... I'm hoping... We're hoping. She doesn't know anyone here. Plus, you two have history. Maybe you can support her through this? Be there for her and keep an eye on her for us. You two are fond of each other. She feels safe with you. Maybe being there for her will help her through this? She trusts you, *Q*. We trust you. Without you, I'm not so sure. I'm serious." Ayri says.

"No worries. I'm honored you trust me. She's safe with me. I'll take care of her. I promise; with my life." I harken my prior pledge to protect Didi.

"*Muchas Gracias, mi hermano*. Well, I guess that really makes us brothers-in-law after all. And don't you worry about any imminent torment at your doors and in your bed. Didi, she knows all those cures. The potions and antidotes and their application to ward off those revenge and break up spells." Ayri says.

"'Revenge and break-up spells'? 'Potions?' 'Antidotes?' 'Curses and cures?' 'Imminent torment at my doors and in my *bed*?' What are you talking about?" I say.

"Oh nothing. Just... You know..." He says.

"No, I don't know. What are you talking about?"

"You and Didi will become targets of evil. *Martiniquaise's* revenge and break up spells. Your pictures framed in chicken feathers and surrounded by thirteen candles and draped in black and red satin cloths. Buttons, stones, beeswax and thyme. *Voodun* dolls with many pins in them. Knife and shovel pointed at demons of torment hidden in trusted household items. Bottled water and vinegar, yam root mixed with cinnamon. Lemongrass and milk, goat and human hair, fingernail clippings and entrails. Purification rituals, *Macumba* curse instructions and witchcraft idolatry." Ayri goes on to say.

"But no worries, *Q*. No worries at all. This is *our* Caribbean culture. I promise, Didi, she knows the antidotes and what to do once *Martiniquaise* Creole woman goes ham guerilla *voodun* crazy seeking revenge on you and Didi. What, you don't believe me? No? Okay. On that screen showing the past over there; look. No, look over there. There, see what your 'Baby Girl' will do? Look. See sweet loving 'Baby Girl' cutting your hair and beard when she gave you a mani/pedi on the balcony? That's right. See what else she did? She sneaky. She hid your hair and nails. Now she has your DNA, your soul. Oh, look what she did to you. You look like you're twelve years old. "Now, look there. She will steal your socks. *Mi hermano. Q*, you must know what you're working with. Haven't you felt different somehow? When she prepares food, she laces it with roots and potions that make you strong like bull. See?" He says.

"I don't need any roots or potions. I'm naturally virile and already strong like bull. I know how to love a woman to sleep." I say.

"Full of bull! That's what you are. Now look at that future panel there; see? See what she'll do when she finds out about Didi. See what she will do, your 'sweet loving Baby Girl?' Well, as you can tell, your 'Baby Girl' here is going to fashion an effigy with a picture of you, framed in chicken feathers, and stick pins in it. She'll cut your soiled socks into pieces and using your hair and nails, along with chicken hatch straw and dried potato peelings as kindling and burn your effigy on that mini-altar. Next, she will cover her door and her bed frame with a root and blood mixture to ward off negative energy. Then she'll prepare dangerous hallucinogens droplets carefully blended with aromas of rosemary and thyme, cinnamon and anise which she'll apply to a pillow case she is going to prepare especially for you. Then she'll incant and invoke sermons of harm, possession and revenge spells." Next he says.

"Classic *voodun.* She knows exactly what she's doing. From the looks of it... she may even be... *Ay, caramba*, Q. O, Q! Mi patrons. O! Orishas all! For your sake, may it not be true. You have no idea what you did. None." Ayri is aghast.

"What did I do?" I say.

"You have no idea. You really don't; do you? You never noticed anything strange going on when you were with her? No, I can tell; you're curelessly in love. That's how good she is." Ayri says.

"What are talking about?" I say.

"Your sweet loving 'Baby Girl?' How can I put this? Okay; think Hendrix." He says.

"Here you go again with Jimi. Every time there's something you can't explain, it's Hendrix. What's Jimi Hendrix got to do with any of this?" I say.

"That song? What's that Hendrix song, *Q*?" Ayri says.

"Just don't start playing air guitar, Ayri. You look stupid whenever you do Hendrix at *Monterey*." I say.

"What's that Hendrix song? V*oodoo Chile?* That's it. *Voodoo Chile.* She's Priestess. That's bad enough. But for you, that's the least of it. *Q!* You didn't just flip a priestess. She's High Priestess! Do you know what that means? You're in a world of big hurt and *voodun* trouble. It's High Priestess you must scorn. *Heyo!* Why? Because you violated the man-code, *mi hermano*." Ayri says.

"'Priestess?' 'High Priestess?' The 'man-code?' What are you talking about? What article of the so-called 'man-code' did I violate?" I say.

"Remember we talked about axis? *Martiniquaise*, she's a medium. A spirit guide conduit helping wayfarers safely transition the dimensions' continuum. *Comprende?*

"And what's with you accumulating all these man-code violations? Every time you go *cherchez la femme*, you permit these false expectations. Yes, she loves you, you can see. Look, she's crying. She's afraid she will lose you. You, and her

Green Card status. She loves you, true. But 'Baby Girl?' She loves a Green Card too. No *Q*, no Green Card." Ayri says.

"Look, over there. The whole family, they will want Green Cards too. And why? Because you allowed runaway expectations. That's another clear violation of the man-code. That's why. You know how women are. They hear things men never said, then say men said so, because that's what women want to hear. That's why you must be firm and tamp expectations. Especially with Didi. Trust me, *Q*. I know my sister." He goes on.

"See *Martiniquaise* getting angry? Look what your 'Baby Girl' is about to do. After seeing you with Didi, she will chase Didi down the street. You'll have two Creole women fighting over you. See? Didi won't back down, though. It looks like fighting will lift Didi's depression. "*Mi hermano*, I know women, and she's one very angry bird. Get ready. Now *you're* about to get flipped. See how she will go upside your head? Oh, that's going to hurt. Now look what she'll do when she returns to the hotel. She is bitter. Oh, no! She's about to cut off your effigy's hands and feet, your arms and legs! Oh, her vivisection will be worse than exploratory surgery. Watch out! She's about to go straight for your manhood and is going to castrate you. No more, strong like bull for you. Oh, that's it. Curtains on that scene." He says, adding.

"You'd better be very careful. Trust me, *Q*. It's best this way. At least now, you know. This way, you know the truth and won't be blindsided. "And remember; whatever you do, *Q*. Don't let your head hit that pillow case and fall asleep around your sweeting loving 'Baby Girl.' You'll wake up a zombie. And I've been meaning to tell you, *mi hermano*. That name; 'Baby Girl?' Beware. She's anything but. She is cunning. You will see.

"And thank you again, *Q*, for looking after Didi. She really needs your help. The family does. She says she feels safe in Harlem City; and with you. I told you; I know. You two nearly got married. I've known all along. But you wanted to become a writer. Even back then, you did it. Man-code violation. Red card!" Ayri says.

"I'm getting just about more than damned sick and tired of your chucking 'man-code.'" I say.

"That's because, again, you allowed false expectation. Honestly *Q*. That's why I didn't contact you all these years. Didi told me everything. Your decision that you loved writing more than you loved her. True, those are her words. But you hurt her. No, you wounded her. You hurt me when you did that. I... I'm her brother. As close as the two of us were, I had to cut you loose. It was that, beat you up, or kill you. And since I enjoy diplomatic immunity, I'd have been acquitted. She's my sister. You broke her heart. You hurt me when you did that to her. I had to cut ties with you." He says.

"I know; but I couldn't lie to her. She deserved better and more than I could give her then. When I was freelancing, there were times when I was barely able to support myself. She wanted a family. Back then she said, 'Teach. Write in your spare time. We'll have health insurance.' And that's exactly what I ended up doing. If that ain't karma." I say.

"Except that, between then and now, Didi got married. You didn't know; I know. But she didn't want you to know. I had to respect that. She never should have married. Then a year later, when you dropped *Homeboy,* all of us went, 'Wow! Excuse me. Now I get it.'

"Poor Didi was heart-broken. She felt she underestimated you, your talent. That she abandoned you and that she had been selfish. But it was your dedication: 'To DVM. This labor's lost love's high price.' And then, when she saw you on *Oprah,* and you wouldn't talk about the dedication because it was too personal, she was devastated. She says she should have stayed with you and supported your writing career, and instead getting married was the biggest mistake of her life. A week later she filed for divorce.

"Once she knew you were coming to Amada she worried about how you would react. That you might be angry she left you. That you no longer care or couldn't forgive her. That's why she wanted to talk to you '*entre nous.*' But you were most gracious. You just said was, 'Time becomes you... We'll work things out...' And you left it at that. Like nothing ever happened. That's when I understood. It's between A and B. I had to C myself out of it. She's the one, *Q*; it wasn't me. It was Didi all along. Didi pushed *Papi* into writing his memoirs. *Ay!* She was relentless. She sent me to New York for the two of us to make peace and to offer you the writing assignment. And that's why I'm here now. For Didi's sake. She trusts you, *Q*. We all do. All I want – all we want – is Didi back. I just want my sister back. Take care of her for us. You're a part of the family now. You always have been. First, *mi hermano.* Now, I guess we're really brothers-in-law. What a scary thought. Even scarier, fully formed *Q* clones. Babies with glasses and beards speaking German running around under foot. Warning signs should be posted, '*Vorsicht! Q Kinder unterwegs.*'" Ayrton says.

"Thanks, Ayri; I think?" I say.

"Want to know my favorite part of the book?" He says.

"I'm afraid to ask." I say.

"Never that. If anything, you should be very proud. No, it's the way you ended *Babylon, Babylon.* with the words of our national anthem:

'Now the evening star is fading
Dawn is drawing to a close. If
Our hearts are heavy laden, full
Of sorrows, full of woes, this do know.'
Oh, Amada! Amada *mia*! Guiding
Star to all, if on land or sea we
Wander, we will ever heed thy call.'
Amada, Amada, country dear,
May joy be yours throughout
The years. Thou art our inspiration,
Thou art our guide so fair. Thou alone
Art consolation when our hearts despair.
Hark! The bells are sweetly ringing,
Night has come and we must part.
But to us a strand is clinging
It can never leave our hearts.'
"'Amada! Amada! Home of soldiers
Brave, we shall ever cherish and love
Thee, ever for thy spirit crave!
Amada! Amada! Ere the sun doth
Rise, may light be yours. May all
Ours be sweet peace! Amada!'

"Again, *Q*, thank you for your choice of words. That's why *Babylon, Babylon* is so *en fuego*, and why *Jibaro* is so powerful. You've developed your own voice. A writer known only by your pen name and byline. A cipher; '*Q*.' Your tagline: 'The story's the star.' Your creed: 'Writing's fighting.' Jazz writer. You keep writing, keep fighting, *mi hermano*. Keep making it 'do what it do,' *Q*. Destiny awaits. Yours will be great. Time has come to release you, though. Don't look down. Don't worry, I won't drop you. But you must return." Ayri says.

"*A donde vas*? (Where'd you go?)" I say.

Suddenly his apparition reappears, holding something miniature in his hand. "'Well done, *Q*. Good and faithful friend, you.'" He says.

"'...Loyal to the end.'" I conclude the saying.

"Here's another trophy you've more than earned. For six seconds never better spent. Let alone never having to trip that dead man's switch. Here. Catch!" He says.

His black caped corona morphs into a black bird, drops the original flash drive, the *Smoking Gun*, in my hand, then transmogrifies yet again, this time into chimera *Gestalt* that dissolves into the night's ether.

"I just pulled up. I'm outside. Right across the street in Central Park. Meet me downstairs. *Rapido! Red Rooster!* I'm hungry. Let's eat!" He says.

How long did I dwell above Elysian Spheres, alert yet in such altered states? Minutes, hours? I don't know. Then, just as abruptly, as if hypnosis, the spell lifts. My surroundings, I'm still seated in my balcony rocking chair, my father's piano music still playing solace in the background. My recall, its clarity and immediacy of events, vivid. Most miraculously, I'm holding the *Smoking Gun* again.

Next, I hear him say: "*Laissez les bon temps rouler, Q! Ay!*"

On my way downstairs, I hear noises coming from the busy streets below. Tires skidding, screeching followed by the sound of a traffic accident. A car collision. Multiple dull impact thuds. Shattering glass. Pedestrians screaming. More tire screeching. Then there's another car crash. I rush outside.

"Man, dat be like just all messed up. Dude ain't had no bizness drivin' without no lights and ain't even blow his horn. Tryin' to jump a red light and hit dat old man like road kill. For what? A red light. Dat ain't make no sense." One bystander says.

"Man, you can't be jaywalkin' up in Harlem. Not with the way they be drivin all up around here. O.G. should be knowin' better." Another bystander says.

"Yo bruh, it ain't go down like that at all. I seened it. Sumpin' real tricky done just jumped off. Yo! Things ain't what they seem. I seened it. I'm tellin' y'all. Sumpin' real tricky done gone down. I done seened it all." Someone else says, as sounds of police and ambulance sirens grow louder.

"That don't make no never mind. Pedestrians should always be havin' the right of way. Specially ole head with a cane. You respect the elderly; period. People who be drivin' all crazy like dat ain't got no insurance to begin with, for real for real. I ain't tryin' to hear that. People wit insurance don't be drivin like dat 'cause they don't want they premiumses be blowin' all up. I know, 'cause my cousin, he be havin' good insurance. Homeowners, too." Another bystander says.

Q

On the scene, I find Ayrton, crippled and seriously injured in the middle of the street surrounded by a growing crowd.

"Let me through." I say, pushing myself through the crowd. Someone says, "You know ole head?"

With faint respiration and, at best, only minutes of life left, there lies Ayri's maimed body collapsed into a shapeless heap.

"Step off. Stop calling him 'O.G.' and 'ole head.' Ayri?" I say pushing my way to his side.

"My bad. No disrespect intended, my brotha. But dang. Dude sure be lookin' all ole to me. How you be knowin' him? How ole he be and whatnot?" He says.

"Yo, man. Why don't you go look for a job and whatnot?" I say, kneeling at Ayri's side.

"Youse ain't gotta go gets all inter-personal and whatnot. All's I's axed is a question. But hey, it is what it is, and it ain't that important to me. I'm out." He says.

"*Q?*" Ayri says.

"I'm right here. I got you, *mi hermano*. I got you." I say, cradling his head and shoulders.

"Being back in Harlem City... I was so close. All along the cab ride, I'm remembering and rehearsing all the things I was going to tell you that happened since we last saw each other. I'm talking to myself talking to you. I looked and... I didn't see anything. I looked..., *Q*...I always look ever since after what happened... Then, out of nowhere... A car... No headlights... I'm in the middle of the street... I'm trapped... I can't get out the way. Why didn't he stop? He had to see me but he didn't stop..."

"The next thing I see is you. I'm cold, *Q*. I'm so cold... Listen... Do you hear it? The train... Listen, *Q*... The train..." The sound of approaching sirens swells, as does the crowd.

Pedestrians offer clothing articles to keep Ayri warm. By rights, I shouldn't even be alive. He saved my life. And now, shivering he's dying in my arms. By then, the paramedics arrive on the scene. But it's too late.

"How did you do that? I dreamt of you. I saw you. We talked. We went places. We did things, time surfing. It was when we... It had to have been when... when you were thinking about me and talking to me on your way here. It had to be. And when I woke up, I found myself holding the *Smoking Gun*. How did I end up with it? How did you do that?" I say.

"I was holding it... but... when I got hit... I let it go. It flew in the air. The rest, that's the miracle. *Shango*, *Obatala*. The spirits and saints of old... They know... The axis knows." Ayri says.

"Say what?" I say.

Struggling for his last breaths, with one last adrenaline surge Ayri sits upright.

"In life... in life we dream of miracles, and sometimes dreams come true, ... and miracles happen. Look closely. You will see that... in life as in dreams... miracles happen all the time.... Just close your eyes... Open your mind... Follow the way of the light... Lock in, and you'll see... They're one and the same. Life is a miracle, wrapped in a dream. It's all one love.

"Look, Q. The lights! I'm outside of myself, free floating... levitating...A bird's eye view! Look! Wow! I see in dimensions. I see e-v-e-r-y-t-h-i-n-g! I'm flying. I see you in hologram. See? You did it too. Why'd you get to do it first?"

Fading fast, his head propped against my chest, glassy-eyed he looks up at me. Squeezing my hands, his last words are: "Write, Q. Fight... Follow the way of the light. And... tell them... I said so..." He takes and holds his last breath, seizes and, slumping into my heavy heart's arms, Ayrton expires.

Paramedics place Ayri's remains in the ambulance then provide me with directions to the coroner's office before departing.

Night envelopes me as I stand there long after he's gone. Numb and far from able to begin processing events that will take a lifetime never to understand.

Three times wrong. Twice, I falsely believed Ayri had died. First, shortly after my escape from Amada, when I thought that Ayri had beheld the face of God above the firing squad. Then, based on Guillermo's account, that Ayri had died at *Comandante's* hands. Turns out, *Comandante* told the truth all along. He didn't kill Ayri. He gave him the gun and he shot him; but he didn't kill Ayri. He told me, but I didn't believe him. That makes me three times wrong.

If only I had found out sooner that he was alive. Everything would be different and never have played out this way. After a *coup d'état* and exile, abuse and imprisonment. His injuries and surgeries, near amputations and permanent disabilities.

After all these misadventures, only for such a rare person to die such a random way. An arbitrary event, an actuarial variable. A statistic. A tragic accident played out at my doorstep. So near yet too far, when not moments earlier in mind-meld together we had been soaring above Elysian Spheres, only to be plunged into unplumbed despair. Nothing is crueler.

Q

He knew his time was up. He said as much quoting his favorite artist, Jimi, when Ayrton heard his *Train's A-Comin*. Strangely, no matter his many injuries he never shone more brightly. Now transcendent, Ayri wasn't merely a diplomat and born patriot. In the words of Bob Marley, his was 'one love,' and he that love's loyal servant.

Where will I find the strength to tell the Mentis family the tragic news? That the light of our lives is gone, lost in such a sudden, senseless manner? I fear the shock this will have on his elderly parents. With Re-Re already on the cusp, this may push her completely to the dark side of hip-hop/rap madness. Didi's already fragile, and this may undo her, as it's undoing me on the scene. It's gut check time all around.

My feelings for Didi run deep; they always have. I can't think of another woman as prepossessing as Didi; not even Catalina. Woman just got me. She always did. Didi and I go back. Back to student orientation, when we three first met. Didi and I have history. In fact, she gave me the idea to write my first novel, *Homeboy*. It's dedicated to her.

The truth is, we nearly married. And then once I arrived in Amada we 'secretly' resumed our relationship. Although we suspected that Ayri knew - and he did - he never let on. But Ayri knew, he knew the whole time. He knew then, many years ago, in Harlem. And he knew recently, in Amada.

He always knew. He also knew he would never have to invoke 'diplomatic immunity' with me. He knew the depth of our feelings for one another. The trust and intimacy. Our comfort level and existing bond. That tie of time that will only deepen after what happened to Ayrton.

According to him, she already needs me and after his death she's going need me to help her grieve and heal the same way Catalina's love once helped save my life. Only more so this time. Just like I'm going to need Didi to survive Ayri's death. Both of us were wounded at the same time by a common experience. Shared post-traumatic stress, we're going to need each other now more than ever. Or will we be a constant reminder to each other of the kind of pain that won't go away? Condemned to a grief and depression that never heals? How can anyone ever recover from something this devastating? It's impossible. Nothing will ever be the same.

Sobering, my sense of responsibility for the Mentis family, for all of them, as if they were my family. And in many ways, that's what they've become.

Had Ayrton made it across that street and survived those few steps too far, I'd probably never have experienced Elysian

Spheres' polygonal panorama and kaleidoscopic vistas revelations along the time and space continuum. I'd never have peered into the past nor ever peeped what the future holds.

It had to have been telepathy or spirit migration, second sight or psychic encounter. Some premonition phenomenon and harbinger of Ayri's sudden death. Without teleportation, I'd never have learned the whole story. That's why, my mind although lucid, I felt paralyzed. There is nothing I could have done. Nothing, except behold. Otherwise, everything about Amada, about Ayri and the Mentis family. Those on the ground, real lifetime events in Amada. The truth would have been suppressed and history rewritten, the Mentis family's sacrifices erased; except for these Elysian revelations. There can be no other explanation. Particularly the mysterious way the *Smoking Gun* kept coming into my possession. But even telekinesis doesn't explain how I it ended up with it this time around.

This much I do know, though; I must move immediately; tonight. Having to exit and enter my building another day, steps away from where Ayri died? I can't do it. I Can't sleep here another night. I'll have to rent a hotel room.

About to enter my apartment building for the last time and collect my identification before heading to the coroner's office and finalize arrangements for the disposition of Ayrton's remains, when from adjacent Central Park I hear a voice whispering with such urgency I can't ignore it.

"Mister. Mr. Man. Mr. Man!" I feel lured to the voice coming from the dark bushes.

"Psst! Mister. Mr. Man. Mr. Man. Yes. You, Mr. Man!"

"Me?" I say.

"Yes! You. Mr. Man. Him? Him there ye friend?" A woman says with a thick Caribbean accent.

"True that. And a man greater there'll never be." Say I.

"That wat just happened here? Dat no accident. Ye friend, him was targeted." She says.

"What are you talking about? What do you mean; 'targeted?'" I say.

"Me sit here waitin' for tha bus e'ery night. Here on tha bench, under dem here trees next to tha bushes on me way come home from work. Here where me stand now. Me skin so dark as tha night, dem no see me." She says.

"What are you talking about? Who is 'dem?'" I say.

"Dem who's parked here unda tha tree in front of me. Dem car lights was off, but tha motor keep runnin'. Like dem was waitin' for someone. When ye friend, him get out tha taxi, dem in tha car..."

"You keep saying, 'dem' in the car? How many of 'dem' were in the car? Who?" I say.

"Dem's two. One man black, one white. Tha black man, him dress very strange; even for Harlem. White dinner jacket. White shirt, black bow tie. White cummerbund, black tuxedo trousers. Cowboy boots, big cowboy hat. Him wore sunglasses at night.

"Him look a lot like dat Caribbean dictator, Geremi Quarrles. Him drivin'. Tha other man, him big white man wit blonde hair and crazy looking eyes. Him sat up front. When ye friend him get out of tha taxi, tha driver never turn on his lights and instead him step full on tha gas and den run down ye friend. Me seened it all. Dat murder." She says.

It gets worse.

"Den dem get out and search ye friend pockets lookin for someting. Den tha blonde one him point to ye buildin'. Dem evil. Pure evil." She says.

"How do you know where I live?" I say.

"Me just see ye come from tha building. Me wait here e'ery night for tha bus. Me recognize ye from the *Oprah Show*. Ye tha writer man." She says.

"But what about the car that crashed?" I say.

"Dat not tha car dat hit ye friend. Dat tha car tryin' to avoid hittin' ye friend after him already been hit. It lose control and crash, den tha first car drive away and make it look like second car who hit ye friend. Dat no ordinary hit and run. Dat murder. Dem killer." She says.

"Is there anything else you can think of you haven't told me?" I say.

"Me know what dem lookin' for." She says.

"How do you know?" I say.

"Because ye friend, when him got hit, him let it go. Den it flew in me direction in tha dark. Dat when me catch it." She says.

"You caught what?" I say.

"Ye know. It's you who caught it after me did." She says.

"But how did it get to me?" I say.

"A bird flew by. A black bird. Black like me. It took it from me hand. Tha rest, me no know. Axe *Shango*. Axe *Obatala*. Dem who know." She says.

"What's that mean?" I say.

"Tha axis, dem know. Dem tha network of ye saints and spirits of old. Dem transition wayfarers through tha dimensions' continuum. Tha *Orishas,* dem tha ones. Dem safeguard ye escape jail. Dem tha ones lead ye to priestess. She heal ye, teach ye to love, to write again. Dem's who save ye friend's legs' amputation. Tha axis, dem's who gift ye knowledge. Two times now, dem done gift ye information. Just like now. Dem gift ye understandin' of what otherwise ye would never know. Dem tha ones. Tha network of our fathers and their fathers' fathers' spirits and saints. Tha *Orishas.* Tha axis know." She continues.

"And now, now dat ye know all dees little tings, dat dey make one big ting, one love. Now dat ye have e'eryting ye ever wanted. Wat tha matter wit ye? Lose ye way and be singin' tha blues all day. Why ye no longer write? To know if ye happy, to find tha road to happiness again, axe yeself; wat ye want? Simple question. Not so simple tha answer, which must never be more complicated then life. Life, in turn, is simple. Do good. Love ye family and friends. Help others. Know and be honest with yeself and others. Life couldn't be simpler. Do good. Dat's it. It is tha way of tha light and only true road to happiness. Otherwise ye will never find joy and remain a prisoner and victim of ye own makin'. So, choose wisely." Then she says.

"And writer man? Best ye beware. For wayfarer, ye troubles, dem troubles will follow ye, just as surely as ye will choose to scorn Priestess. Ye will know. Soon." Invoking *Santeria* deities, this speaker of sooth, seer of saints and spirits omens, her silhouette recedes into the indistinguishable blue-black night, then melds into Harlem City's nocturne.

Numbed by events, from Elysian Spheres' pure joy to this searing despair in the briefest span. After everything I've experienced, and now this; Sibyl's oracle.

My doorstep now an active crime scene, I return home for one last time and again retreat to my balcony rocking chair and sit there, my father's piano recordings playing the background. Conflicted in baffled recall of the mystery and reeling from the blowback of it all, rocking and remembering and wondering.

The real cartels, the hydrocarbon, the travel and hospitality corporations. *Backwater.* The Sinister Prime Minister and *Comandante,* they are in Harlem now and will stop at nothing, not even 'targeted' assassination. I'm in grave danger again. This time though, the war is at *my* door. What will I do? I must move - tonight. The realtor will have to pack my belongings. I have no choice. Once more, I'm being forced to go … *incognegro.*

Q

Other decisions loom. Both Didi and Catalina are due in
New York soon - at the same time - as forecast above Elysian
Spheres. What will I do?

My decisions involving Catalina are especially troubling.
Yes, I love her very much. But I know Didi better, longer. I
love her differently, deeper. Yes, more than I love Catalina.
Didi and I nearly married. Back then, I chose writing. This
time it's different, though. Didi will need me more than ever.
Not just now; but in the future. No one could need me as
much, more, nor for a better reason. More than any Green
Card. And I will need Didi more than I've ever needed
anyone; even more than I needed Catalina in Martinique.

No less disturbing my panoptic view of Catalina's past and
future behaviors. Lacing my food and drink with potions and
casting spells to make me 'strong like bull?' Secreting my
DNA, my hair and nail clippings? Fashioning an effigy with my
likeness as her *voodun* pin cushion? Dismembering, even
castrating and burning my effigy at the stakes? Assaulting
me, then going after Didi before Didi drops her to the ground?
A poisoned, zombie pillowcase my head must never touch? I'd
never have suspected her of having such a dark heart.

The Creole in her is more dangerous than I ever could have
imagined. Baby Girl ain't just a sorceress. Baby Girl's *Orisha!*
Now that's some sure enough supernatural stuff.

All this, but for Elysian's Sphere's magic tiles and screens,
this and more I'd never have discovered. What would have
happened then? Knowing what I know, I'd have to sleep
with eyes wide open. No telling what *Orisha* would do,
should my head ever hit that poisoned pillowcase and the
Creole in her gets out;' again. She's already spiked my
food. And after everything she did to that *voodun* doll? Ayri
warned me. *Voodoo Chile's* got a mean streak. 'I done
seened it all.'

Here I am then, in love with two beautiful Caribbean
Creoles. One's depressed, the other's a volcanic sorceress,
Orisha. That, and death squads hot on my trail in Harlem. Pick
a poison. This can't end well.

Recent experiences tell a cautionary tale about our dark
side. Its moral is grim. We've become a danger to ourselves,
to our planet, to our very survival. We haven't just lost our
way. Way more than our way, along the way we've lost our
minds too. The question then becomes; what are *we* going to
do?

To and fro rocking, listening, remembering and pondering
in the dark. Back and forth, steady rocking. Reliving events,

ruminating from dusk 'til dawn. After all that to and fro rocking, remembering and ruminating about things gone wrong. Listening and thinking until morning's dawn. Wondering, worrying, pondering this, that, and a third. That, although deep down I long know the answer.

Chances go around, and mine are slim to nil at best. The truth is, I never had a choice. *Haiku* in design, my destiny writ large was outlined in simple broad strokes above Elysian Spheres. I've been a player all my life, and once more I'm being called upon to play my part, the fight mine now to carry on. For him and his. For me, for mine, and for others. Mine to carry on the only way I know. More than ever, writing is fighting.

It's time, that moment of truth and courage against which we're measured. True, charlatans and dilettantes, madmen and generals. Yes, clowns to the left, jokers on the right, they still rule. The stakes couldn't be greater. All is far from lost, though. The rewards far outweigh every risk. The choice is clear. This is still *our* world. Love makes bold. Fear no evil. Together, anything's possible.

Mi hermano was right. Said Ayrton Villareal Mentis:

'... In life we dream of miracles, and sometimes dreams really do come true. Look closely, though, and you'll see that, in life as in dreams, miracles happen all the time. Just open your mind, follow the way of the light. Lock in, and you will see they're one and the same. Life is a miracle, wrapped in a dream. It's all one love.'

Nothing truer has ever been said.

And that's the way I remember him.

Ay!

THE END

Magister Ludi
8.25.2022@03:17

www.ingramcontent.com/pod-product-compliance
Lightning Source LLC
Chambersburg PA
CBHW031058020726
47495CB00007B/1941